RAVELER

L.H. LEONARD

Each Voice Publishing

Copyright

RAVELER

Chapter 1

Sea Crypt

Amryn set out alone, with no breath but her own for company. Her solitary task demanded she go unaccompanied, spiriting the dead away, as she had since her fifteenth year.

Crystal moonlight fell from a cloudless sky and splintered over the Endless Ocean. Restless waves swelled, rising to feed on the shards. The sea was a creature born of the night, an ancient and living water, breathing with the tides. Not god. Not mortal. Yet as enduring as the stars.

Amryn tugged on the tiller and tacked along the rocky shoreline. A mischievous wave rocked her dhow and sent the canvas-swaddled body on its deck rolling to bump the gilded railing. Amryn muttered a curse and steadied her grip. Handling the craft alone was a challenge, but the dead made a useless crew.

As the cliffs loomed closer, she squinted to sharpen the shadowy shapes lurking in the weathered rocks. Skirting the Janlin jungle north of Ealim, the dark stretch of coastline was unremarkable, and the rocks indistinguishable, one from the next. Bored captains and busy sailors might sail past the turtle's head rock a thousand times without taking notice.

But not Amryn.

The Endless Ocean was never silent, yet it softened its voice at night. Above the rush of wind and chatter of the surf, an eerie whistle reached her keen ears. The flute song of the odd rock she sought hummed in the darkness as the wind skimmed the hole atop its turtle-shaped head just so. She guided the dhow near enough to anchor—and then a bit nearer.

Hastened by the overloud splash of the anchor and the metallic gurgle of chain slithering into the sea, Amryn unbuckled her sandals and shed her clothes. The salty breeze tugged at her undershift as she tied on a silk sash and fastened a candlewand beside the well-honed jambiya at her hip.

"Sooner started, sooner done," she muttered as she knotted the tether around her waist. The dead were no help in seeing themselves settled, either.

Pulley and winch cast creaks over the moonlit waves, but no one was around to hear their complaints. Of that, she'd made certain. And she was practiced and quick at hoisting a body overboard. Soon, the cocooned corpse bobbed in the dark water, buoyed by air bladders secured within the folds. Waves licked the shroud, tasting the unexpected delicacy with hungry curiosity.

"Sorry to disappoint," she said. "But you tend to spit the bones back ashore. I can't have that, can I?"

Amryn jumped into water still warmed by the day, and salt stung her eyes. She would never grow accustomed to the sting, no matter how many years she spent in Ealim. Sucking in the deepest breath her chest would hold, she ducked beneath the surface and swam for the base of the turtle's head rock. Diving deeper, her strong limbs propelling her down, she swam until the tether grew taut around her waist. She gave the rope a commanding tug, and the bobbing cocoon dipped beneath the surf to follow her.

As she groped her way into darker waters, her bare hands met familiar stone. She skimmed her fingers over barnacled rocks, found the toothy rim, and pulled herself through the underwater maw. The need to breathe tickled her throat, not in urgency, but as a teacher might tap an exam clock. She tugged the rope and hauled the swaddled body through the maw after her. Halfway through, the body stopped and refused to budge.

She swam back and unsheathed her blade. Running her hands over canvas and ropes, she found nothing snagged. A hurried second pass found the same, and the tickle in her throat began to burn in earnest.

Fear kills. Reason survives.

She wedged her arm past the stubborn shroud and reached beyond the maw, feeling her way over the rough surfaces beyond her sight, until her fingers found a torn edge of canvas hooked in the barnacles. One clean slice of her jambiya cut it free. She braced her feet against the rocks and maneuvered the bundle through.

Amryn spun in the dark and kicked hard, grasping handholds to hurry her way through the passage. In the distance, a faint ring of light appeared the darkness. Her pulse thundered in her ears, and her lungs burned with urgency. Another delay, and she'd have to cut the tether, or the sea would claim both her and the dead she had denied it.

Closer now, the faint light shone like a beacon. The sight of her sanctuary refueled a reserve she'd almost depleted. No longer mindful of the tether, Amryn swam hard and burst to the surface, gasping for breath, coughing, and sucking in sweet, salty, precious air. The cocoon bobbed up beside her inside the hollow sea cave.

"Ha!" she said, slapping the water. "You see? I told you. Reason survives."

Amryn swam for the cave walls, ready to be done and gone. She climbed knobby rocks and pulled herself onto the nearest ledge. Seawater dripped in rivulets off her skin, and her lips curled at the salty taste. She rubbed the sting from her eyes and sat dangling her feet in the water. The tide was coming in. That would help get this one settled sooner. Overhead, the moon peered down through a near-perfect circle—the whistle hole in the turtle's head—and the beacon that had guided her through the dark.

Discovering the hidden sea cave had come by pure happenstance. Not long after her mother left Naré to assume Firstwife oversight of the Gyakari's interests in Ealim, Amryn had set about learning to handle a dhow on a restless sea instead of the fat, slow rivers she knew. Not that she had anywhere in particular to go, but an excuse to be beyond the scrutiny of the emperor's court was a good one. Even in Ealim, a summer palace far from the power-grubbing snakes of Naré, censuring eyes followed Resa's only daughter.

Wrestling sails and tiller on her own were second nature to a young girl who liked to be elsewhere, and Amryn had mastered her skills sailing the placid River Ketet in Naré. The Endless Ocean proved a wilder beast and mocked her attempts to navigate its waters. Humbled by frustration, she swallowed her pride and asked her elder blood-brother Nefi to explain how she was to keep the infernal waves from washing her ashore or toppling her sail into the surf. Crown Prince Nefekari was an accomplished mariner, having traveled the known world, vanquishing every scurrilous pirate he'd faced and any enemy who'd dared challenge the Ari war fleet. Nefi had laughed and taken her out on the dhow that same day. For reasons she was reticent to question, Nefi had always treated her as a curiosity to be studied rather than keeping the wary distance most of the family gave Resa and her daughter.

After declaring her a competent sailor, Nefi asked her to courier a message to one of his captains patrolling the coast north of Ealim. She jumped at the chance to be of use and delivered the message in good time, then made no hurry of the return jaunt, buoyed by her success and a flush of independence.

On that warm, sun-drenched day, an enormous white pelican streaked from the sky and pierced the waves like an arrow, disappearing a mere arm's breadth off her bow. She had never seen so large a pelican and scrambled over to watch it chase its prey. With a flash of white to starboard, it vanished into the azure depths. She scanned the surf, watching for the pelican to burst from the sea with its catch. Instead, the great bird burst from the rocky cliff and perched on an outcrop to savor its meal—an outcrop shaped like a turtle's head.

By following the pelican's path, Amryn found the sea cave. She didn't believe in fate or gods. Reason and science explained everything she'd ever found needed explaining. Happenstance and a healthy dose of curiosity were enough to lead her to the rock hollowed by sea and wind, its belly rimmed with tiered ledges like barnacled ribs, and its only access a submersed passage or a whistle hole too obscured for anyone to find from above.

Amryn had since put happenstance to use. Though the Fang left some targets to be found as messages, others simply needed to vanish. The turtle's head cave made a useful crypt for those whose last encounter with Resa had left them dead.

Amryn pulled the candlewand from her sash, saved for when she needed it most, and twisted it to break the wafer inside. Yellow and blue solutions swirled together in glowing exuberance, and pale green light swept the cave. Shadows sprang up to dance, and the skeletons seated on the ledges... did not.

Eight sets of bones, she reflexively recounted. Eight not meant to be found. Skulls. Ribs. Bones scavenged clean by birds and crabs. Bleached by sunlight and salt spray. Resting to the songs of sea birds

4

and the whistle of the wind. Not rotting in river muck or churning in a crocodile belly.

The dead never knew the difference, but she did.

Amryn chose a spot on an upper ledge. She made quick work of the hoisting, settling, and securing with pulley and rope. One last task, the unveiling, was always the hardest. Slice open the cocoon and look into the face of whomever her mother had killed this time.

She hesitated with her blade poised over the canvas. Would this be a face she knew? If she relented to her mother's chiding and did the killing instead of the hiding, would she have the cold resolve of an assassin? Was she a fool for refusing to test the ice in her blood?

Canvas splayed beneath her blade, and a head lolled to the side. Death gives skin a bluish tinge and fades the color of life. Even so, the markings on his skin stood out in contrast. The telltale stripes of his kind curled around his neck. And the face... young... far too young.

"Killed for cause, not sport, then," Amryn said with a sigh.

"One and the same," a low voice answered. "For a cursed N'si."

Amryn skittered around and pressed her back to the rocks, searching the shadows beyond the candlewand's glow. Ghosts in the crypt? What an irrational notion. No, someone had found her hiding place.

A movement in the darkness, opposite her across the hollow crypt, confirmed the improbable. Someone was there, watching her. Amryn glanced down at the candlewand. She could dive back into the water, douse the light, and throw the cave into darkness. To her advantage.

"Don't bother. My night eyes are sharper than yours."

A man leapt from above and landed on a ledge within view. Surefooted and shadowed, he rose like a tiger from a crouch. Beyond the reach of a swiftly thrown blade? Beneath her feet, black water swirled between them. Her escape, if she chose not to fight. Her fingers curled around her jambiya.

The man moved closer, stepping over a skeleton's legs and into the candlewand's glow. He was black-haired and beardless, with coppery skin burnished by the sun and teeth of pearly white. When he folded his arms across his chest and lifted his chin to the light, Amryn caught her breath. He was no man.

5

N'si markings covered his neck in graceful arcs and swirls, and the patterns held the portent of runes. Like none she had ever seen, the unique, tiger-like stripes every N'si was born with continued down his bare arms. Eyes of iridescent amber stared back at her across the crypt, assessing her in turn. He was older than she, though not by much. It was hard to tell with his kind.

"How many were like me?" His arm swept the crypt.

She owed him no answer, but weighed her options. The candlewand was growing dimmer. She gauged the time she had left.

"This one is the first," she said.

"I admit, that surprises me." He arched a brow. "Why would you lie about something of so little relevance?"

"Believe what you wish," she said. "The bones won't dispute me."

"Convenient, isn't it?" He prowled the ledge, edging closer. "Tell me. When the flesh is gone, are N'si bones different from the rest?"

Amryn stepped back, and he slowed his advance, though only by choice. She could outmaneuver a man, but a full-blooded N'si might be her match. How did he get in here? His hair and clothes were dry. She glanced down at her undershift... her *wet* undershift. Damn.

When she looked up, he wore a bemused smirk.

"Leave me to offer the death rites as his kin would, and I will be gone. You will not see me again. The crypt and its secrets will remain yours alone."

"I can't leave them here. If you found this place, then anyone—"

"I am not anyone."

Killing him would ensure that was true. Could she? Resa would, without hesitation, and she would expect no less of her daughter. But Amryn was not her mother. And she would never be. If she had doubted that before, tonight cemented her resolve.

"Do not make me regret letting you live," she said. "I've trained in ways to remedy such a mistake since I was old enough to tie my own sandals."

"No doubt you have," he said. "Let us be glad neither of us had to make that choice tonight."

Amryn stifled an empty retort. Bluster had never come readily to her, and the attempt felt petty now. Having decided to spill no blood, she sheathed her jambiya and gathered the canvas and air bladders for the next use. Without a word, she strapped the bundle to her back and dove from the ledge. When she surfaced in the water below, the candlewand had gone dark. A waft of chilled air brushed her neck. The N'si stood silhouetted in the moonlight.

"Tell Resa our people belong in this world," he said. "Yuji holds her to her promise."

Chapter 2

Relic

The next day, Amryn walked through the busy marketplace with her eyes focused on the bricks and her mind elsewhere. After returning to the palace in the darkest hour before dawn, she had found the expansive apartment Resa claimed by right of Firstwife empty. Discovering her mother gone would have been of no concern if they were still in Naré. On the night of a kill, Resa shared the Gyakari's bed. It was on such a night Amryn was conceived. But they were not in Naré, the Gyakari was not in Ealim, and Resa had not returned by morning.

"Watch your head, girl. Are you sleepwalking?" Amryn glanced up and nearly cracked her forehead on the hot brass of a low-hanging censer.

"Stealth of a tiger." Ottah chuckled and shook his head. "You stayed up all night reading again, didn't you?"

"Maybe." Amryn smiled. "How else am I to stay ahead of you?"

"To catch me, you mean. Never happen. But I do admire your persistence."

Ottah's rumbling laughter lightened her mood. Her mother would be laughing, too. Resa Nisari, the deadliest blade in the Fang, acting Regent of Ealim, and a favored wife of Grand Musa of the Ari Empire, did not need her daughter fretting over her whereabouts.

Ealim's bazaar skirted an arc along the fortress walls lining the harbor. Though half the size of the grand marketplace in Naré, the sandstone-bricked aisles were predictably crowded by midday. Bright awnings and shadesails draped merchants' stalls in myriad shades of blues, reds, yellows, and greens.

"Spices, spices, cinnamon sweet," a young man sang out, his skin pale as the sand and a beard sparser than the strings on his lute. "Savory curry and peppery heat."

Amryn rolled her eyes. A foreigner, thinking he could sell spices in Wodi. While she held the man no ill will, she questioned his soundness of mind.

Nefekari said the sensory-delighting bazaars found in every city on the continent of Wodi had no equal anywhere in the world. Like most of what Nefi said when entertaining the family with tales of his adventures, Amryn considered his claim a theory to be confirmed rather than irrefutable truth. Still, familiar as it was to her, walking the market was a festival for the eyes, ears, and nose.

The thrum of a chalice drum, jingle of a tambourine, and lament of a flute transformed the chatter of bargains struck, shouts of merchants hawking wares, and bickering of gulls over the harbor into the chorus of life. Wind chimes on awnings and silver bells on anklets joined in accompaniment. Geese squawked, donkeys brayed, and a fox-faced dog roused from sunning itself to bark at a tabby cat prowling the stalls, purring for another, always plentiful, handout.

The mesmerizing aromas of coffee, jasmine tea, scented oils, incense, and crafted leather blended in the sea breeze blowing off the Endless Ocean. Smoke from roasting kababs, steam rising from simmering fish stews, and the savory scent of kofta sizzling on the grill made her mouth water.

Keenest of all, though, was the sense of belonging. There was a bone-deep bond to desert, jungle, river, and sea every Wodian shared. Even those whose veins pulsed with the mercurial blood of the N'si.

"Crab pie or kabab?" she asked Ottah. The answer never varied, but even habits merited affirming.

"Crab," he said. "Three. Jasmine or ginger?"

Amryn cocked her head, dissatisfied with predictable choices.

"Mint."

"Mint? You never want mint."

"Today, I do," she said. "I'm feeling rebellious. And a pastry. Caramel."

"Rebel? You're a downright anarchist."

Ottah grinned and left her at the food stall, embarking on his customary task in their efficient, parallel procurement effort. Amryn was in no danger, left unaccompanied in the bazaar. No pickpocket would dare approach someone marked by the golden lion of House Ari. Death came soon, and seldom painlessly, to those who did.

Ottah departed, towering over the crowd. Dressed all in white, his oversized frame ladened with satchels and pouches, each filled with tinkerer's tools and gadgets, he parted the crowd like a giant, windblown sand dune. Most people assumed he was yet another bulwark of dull-witted brawn, but his mind was sharper than any sculpted warrior in the Gyakari's service. Ottah had a good head on his shoulders, and a scholar's heart beat inside his sturdy chest.

They met from their errands in the Seeker's Garden, a hectare of flowers and trees around a palm-lined reflecting pool. Designed to inspire acolytes of the Unraveling and nestled at the foot of the mountain they served, the garden overlooked the city that sustained their mission and honored those who traveled here to unravel its mysteries.

In the early years after the Chalyn War, the newly liberated Tokju had been a destination for inquisitive travelers. The city perched on the edge of the world was a curiosity. Things ended up here—pink marble from Erusa, sculpture from Tallu, and swords from Rhynn. Tokju was where people and their things went to disappear.

But then, the Gyakari laid claim to the city and renamed it Ealim. What came to Ealim these days was more than mere curiosity. The brightest minds and most esteemed scholars worldwide migrated to Ealim to join the Unraveling and decipher ancient mysteries from the font of Watcher knowledge. And, of course, the merchants and artisans vying for their coin soon followed.

Viewed from the Seeker's Garden, Ealim looked like a city undecided about what it wanted to be. In the seven years since the Chalyn War, the city that had once been Tokju, last bastion of the reclusive and mercurial N'si, had transformed into Ealim, the newly founded bastion of Ari science and reason. Unsurprisingly, not all were enthusiastic about its transition. Some argued the Gyakari should wall off the Watchers' Den, seal its dark science away, and forge ahead untainted by failed Cycles of the past.

But doing so meant abandoning a treasure trove of knowledge, discarding accomplishments of those who had lived and died over eons of meaningless Cycles, pawns struggling to survive the whims of the Watchers. And it would dishonor those who had suffered under the callous disregard of Kitsune, the metalmind that had conquered the Watchers and turned this world into its playground. Never more. Sifting through the ruins and gleaning the remnants of science for the sake of science, the Gyakari had declared, was the only logical path.

And so, sandstone minarets and gilded domes began replacing the swallowtail roofs and bamboo pagodas of the N'si city. With each passing year, Ealim looked less like Tokju and more like Naré. Because the future belongs to the victor. What little remained of the dragon city seemed fragile by comparison, temporal bits of myth and shadow, fading memories on butterfly wings of red, green, and gold.

Ari permanence had taken hold, with solid structures built to withstand the vagaries of time. Water gardens laced the walled garden courtyard. Mosaic arcades connected communal rooms beneath soaring, ribbed vaulting and filigree stucco work. Honeycomb labyrinths and mathematically complex, intricate geometrics repeated the infinity patterns that extended beyond the material world. Such was the pragmatic grandeur of Ari construction.

Above the city, stonecutters had scaled the mountainside, chiseling away at the gargoyle's face. Gone was the grotesque mouth from which the blood of sacrifices had once flowed. Instead, they transformed Kitsune's snarl into bands of glyphs—constellations, elements, mathematics, and geography recorded in every known script. The glyphs represented the treasure buried beneath the mountain. It seemed fitting knowledge now adorned the mountain rather than the face of a failed god.

"Not here. Up by the orange tree," said Ottah. "I have something to show you."

With anyone else, she'd be wary of going off alone. Resa had enemies. But this was Ottah. When they were children, he had appointed himself her defender. Sure, Amryn was peculiar and tended to attract trouble, but she shared his obsession with learning how the world worked. Ottah would show up out of nowhere, swat a bully away with his big arm, and haul Amryn off to talk about his newest theory.

They settled in the shade of the orange tree. Weeks had passed since he'd last left his fellow acolytes in the Watchers' Den long enough to sit and talk. She launched into the inquisition.

"The skimmer," she said. "Did you try replacing the wiring, as I said?"

"Haven't had the chance to try." Ottah swiped an olive from her basket. "Master Oxnarfon told us to leave the skimmers be, for now. He set us to work duplicating that contraption he found in the archives. Remember? I showed you the schematic."

"Yes, that oddity he called a bicycle." Amryn made a face. "Why anyone thinks pedals and gears are more useful than getting a skimmer working again is beyond me."

"An exercise for the mind is never a waste." Ottah shrugged. "There's so much down there, Amryn. More than we can tap in a hundred lifetimes. The wonders of every Cycle that ever was."

"Yet they ration it out to us," said Amryn. "Chalyns feast until they have their fill, and they feed us with a spoon."

"Chalyns have seen Cycles rise and fall. The rise is beautiful, but the fall is not. Apocalypses. Pandemics. Air we can't breathe and water we can't drink in a world we depleted." Ottah grew quiet. He disliked talking about the dark times he'd seen, even filtered as that view was. "This Cycle must endure, Amryn. Everything depends on us not messing up this time. No one is left to clean up after us."

Amryn sipped her tea rather than press the point. Maybe Ottah was right, and the slow, painstaking crawl through the Watchers' Den was the prudent approach to delving into mysteries from a tumultuous past. Or perhaps the Chalyns hoarded the prime secrets for themselves, metering out crumbs of knowledge as they saw fit, ladling truth into our bowls to keep mere mortals in our places.

Amryn knew she was being irrational. Suspicion sprouted in bitter soil. It was for the best, she supposed, not being allowed to join the acolytes of the Unraveling. She would have broken every rule from the start. Conformity had never held her back from the sheer joy of knowing. The Unraveling should be free to explore the Watcher's knowledge unrestrained and trust reason to prevail.

"Besides, bicycles will revolutionize how we get about in the cities," said Ottah. "Faster than a donkey and no mouth to feed."

"You? Begrudge a mouth being fed?" Amryn laughed.

As usual, Ottah had devoured three crab pies in the time it took Amryn to finish a kebab. He brushed off his big hands. She'd always found it incongruous how those hands could be so adept at the delicate work of science. Focusing a microscope or dissembling and reassembling a gadget. It was the reason he always wore white. Easier to find tiny parts his big hands dropped.

Ottah tugged a drawstring on one of the many pouches hung from his shoulders. He upended the pouch, and an assortment of gears, switches, black glass, and wires tumbled to his lap.

"Here. I brought you something." Ottah picked up the black glass. "Against every oath I swore, and because I'm a complete idiot, I snuck this from the Hall of Relics for you."

Amryn's hand went straight for the relic, and Ottah lifted it just out of reach.

"You will let no one catch you with this," he said. "And you will stop asking questions you know I'm not allowed to answer. Promise?"

Amryn sprang to her feet and snagged it from his fingers. Ottah leaned back and laughed as she held up the trinket, examining the featureless black glass from all sides. Cool to the touch and rather unimpressive, the slim tablet was no bigger than her hand.

"What does it do?" she asked.

"Nothing."

"How underwhelming."

"Nothing *yet*," he said. "That's yours to figure out. Get it to do whatever it does. Prove you should be down there with us."

Amryn swallowed the ache rising in her throat. Dear, sweet Ottah. He knew how badly she wanted to take the Unraveler's oath. She would even try to obey it. But her value to the empire was as Resa's daughter, a Fang assassin raised in the sect Resa founded, and trained by Resa herself since the day she'd been old enough to lift a blade. Amryn excelled at feats others in the sect struggled to master. She could move with stealth, pick a lock, contort herself inside an urn, slow her breathing, and hide in wait for hours. She could scale a wall, leap from a rooftop, and vanish into the night. Exercise hardened her muscles, and running stretched her endurance. She was proficient with blade, dart, strangle-wire, and poison.

And she had yet to take a life. Given a choice, she never would.

All it would take was one word from the Gyakari, and she could devote herself to the Unraveling instead. But her father never intervened on his children's behalf. Numerous as they were, he would have had time to do little else. He expected each of them to determine their own destiny and left any intervening to their mothers. Resa had decided Amryn's destiny was to follow in her footsteps.

It was a reasonable expectation, considering Amryn was the only child of the only N'si among all the Gyakari's wives. N'si had few options these days. Those not killed in the Chalyn War for their poor choice of allegiance had scattered. Some fled north to Rhynn, to the province held by the Firstborn nenes. Some headed for Tallu to plead for sanctuary with their reclusive nene kin, the Nunyaehi. Some were said to lurk in the green depths of the Janlin jungle or haunt the Brong Desert like sand demons. Few N'si, those wise enough to have sided with the Gyakari in the war, held positions of respectability within the Ari court. Resa and her Fang were foremost among those. Others were merchants or sailors in Nefekari's war fleet. All had affirmed their oaths of loyalty to House Ari. But, as everyone knows, the oath of an N'si is a fluid thing.

"We both know proving myself isn't the problem," said Amryn. "Even if I convinced my mother to let me apply as an acolyte, there are those who would see me denied for spite."

"That, I cannot change," said Ottah. "But the word of a Chalyn would. They value potential over patronage."

"Are they still so involved in the Unraveling?" said Amryn. "I thought they'd gleaned the gems and left the more tedious archeology to mere mortals."

"You don't like them, I know." Ottah frowned. "Chalyns rid us of Kitsune. If they hadn't, the monster would still be guarding the den, and we'd have no access to Watcher knowledge at all. Yes, Chalyns care about the work of the Unraveling. Occasionally, one will chime in with clues, offer guidance. They may not be our fellows, but they are our..."

"Watchers?" said Amryn. "We traded one set of eyes for another."

"It's not like that."

"So, you can sit down with a Chalyn and chat about your theories?"

"Of course not."

"How presumptuous, expecting to converse with a demigod."

Ottah gave her that stare. She was crossing the line, that very wide line he granted no one but her. Amryn looked away. Ottah mattered more than any remote demigod.

"Pay me no mind," she said, taking his hand. "It's envy talking. Thank you for risking it, bringing me the relic."

"Amryn, I wish you—"

"So do I."

Chapter 3

Escape

Night fell, and Amryn took dinner alone in her room. Resa had yet to return. Perhaps she'd been summoned to Naré to dispatch a troublesome upstart. Or she could be leading a party into the Janlin to eliminate a rogue N'si. Or she maybe was alone in the desert, perfecting some new striking form to enhance the deadliness of the Fang. She might be anywhere. But Resa was in absolute control of her circumstances, whatever those might be.

Amryn pushed any contrary notions aside.

Years ago, both sides had agreed to an exchange in yet another attempt to bring the reclusive N'si houses into the Ari empire. The Ari fleet would extend their patrol of the eastern coast to Tokju and lend aid to N'si merchant ships accosted by pirates in those waters. In return, Tokju would send one of their own to Naré to join the elite palace guard and train them in khanti, the renowned N'si fighting art which honed dexterity to lethal precision. The young N'si they sent was Resa, and the earnest young Prince Gya was among the elite fighters she trained. Love was not part of the bargain, but the heart makes bargains of its own. After rising to claim the empire with Resa by his side, and with no one daring to tell him he could not, he made his N'si lover one of his wives. In the decades since, Resa had survived, even thrived, in a family that still whispered about the outsider, a barely human nene, and worst of all, a wily N'si.

Worrying over Resa was like worrying the sun wouldn't rise.

After dinner, Amryn wandered to the courtyard, lit a lantern, and settled on a cushion beside the pool. She curled her feet under her and took the relic from her pocket. The lantern's light glinted off the black glass. She turned the slim tablet in her hands, searching for any anomaly on its smooth surfaces. Was that a faint line? A seam, perhaps? Or just a scratch in the glass?

She laid the relic on the tile and bent over it, staring into its enigmatic face. Dead, like the bodies hidden in the crypt. Maybe heat would awaken it. She brought the relic to her lips and blew out a breath. Warmth fogged the black glass for a moment, then vanished. Did she imagine a fleeting image? A flicker inside the glass?

Maybe it wasn't heat or light. Could it be sensitive to touch? She tried tapping the glass, swiping her thumb over its face. Nothing. She flipped the tablet over and tried again. A tap drew no response. A series of taps. A curlicue with her fingertip. Nothing. She frowned at the dead relic.

"Prove you belong in the Unraveling, huh? I guess this proves I don't."

Footsteps interrupted her, and she slipped the relic back into her pocket. The gate swung open, and a guard entered the courtyard, followed by another. Their breastplates bore the golden lion of House Ari. Strange of them to intrude unannounced, especially on Resa's domain. Unless...

Amryn rose and felt for her blade as more guards fanned out behind them.

Habibah walked into the courtyard, her face a mask of ice and her kohl-rimmed eyes glinting with malice. What was she doing in Ealim? Favored sister of the Gyakari, Habibah was pampered, petulant, and vindictive. She was the eldest of his siblings, and in their own father's waning years, Habibah had supported Gya's campaign for the throne over his brothers. Together, they had wrested control of the Ari dynasty from their rivals. Such was the law of succession in House Ari, passed not by birth order but won by survival and cunning.

Habibah hated Resa. She had always hated Resa. And by extension, she hated Amryn. Yet, for all her vitriol, easily deflected by Resa's wiles, she had been little more than an irritant over the years.

But the Chalyn War had hardened her. Habibah's only daughter, Salihah, had defied the family and goaded the stupidest of her kin into challenging the Gyakari. Salihah died for her misplaced ambition, alongside Ari traitors and N'si malcontents who had joined her on the losing side in the war. Bitter with grief, dangerous as a wounded animal, Habibah wrapped her pain in anger and lashed out in vengeance. Her precious Salihah was dead, and she cast blame everywhere but where it belonged. She blamed all N'si.

"Resa betrayed her vow," Habibah said icily. "She abandoned Ari for her wretched kind. Traitors to the empire pay. Always."

Amryn scanned the guards' faces. Some she recognized. Not one dared meet her eyes.

"Mother betrayed no one."

Habibah raised her fist and uncurled her fingers. An amulet fell to the ground. A jade cobra on a silver chain. Resa's amulet.

"Resa deluded my brother," said Habibah. "But I am watching his back, as always. He will hear the truth from me. His beloved Resa has deserted the Fang. She fled into the jungle and is conspiring against him, gathering N'si to rise against the empire."

Amryn stared at the amulet lying on the tile. No, Resa would not leave Ealim willingly. But if Habibah had taken the symbol of Fang authority from around her neck, that meant Resa was dead. Otherwise, Habibah would not dare spread such blatant lies.

No, that could not be. Resa was invincible. No one could kill her. Especially no one as weak as Habibah. The thought was... too improbable. Until she saw her mother's body, Amryn refused to believe it was not another of Habibah's petty tricks.

"You're lying."

"Ah, a clever little demon." Habibah smiled. "My brother should have offered you to the Rhynn prince instead of my Salihah. We would have one less conniving N'si tainting Ari soil."

Grief had made Habibah stupid, as well. Amryn's skills made her too valuable to send away. Despite her ambition, Salihah would have been of little use to the empire other than breeding a pack of future Ari allies in Rhynn. Instead, she had refused to wed as the Gyakari commanded, incited a doomed rebellion, and died for her stupidity.

"The Gyakari is no fool," said Amryn. "He knows Mother would never leave me behind."

"No, she would not," said Habibah. "How unfortunate for you."

The guard captain drew his sword, still not meeting her eye. His guilt was warning enough. They had come to kill her. Amryn backed away with a deliberate wobble and swung her thick braid over her shoulder.

"I will weep when I tell my brother how I discovered your mother's treachery," Habibah smirked. "And I will sob over how you conspired with her."

"He will never believe you," said Amryn. "Not after all Resa has done in his name. The secrets of a lifetime bind them."

Habibah drew an envelope from her pocket. She waved it before Amryn.

"Your confession," she said. "You wrote it tonight, before you fled the city. Wracked by guilt. You beg your father's mercy, but you must honor your mother's command."

The woman was insane, but she had plotted her ridiculous scheme in painstaking detail. And if Habibah stood here tonight, daring to threaten Amryn in Resa's own home, then...

"Where is my mother?"

Habibah smiled. Malice and madness danced in her eyes.

Amryn didn't wait for an answer. She plucked out the Fang quill blade hidden in her braid. Her aim was sharp, but her heart was hesitant. Habibah screamed when the blade pierced her thigh instead of her throat, and Amryn sprang for the pool.

An arrow sliced the water, scraping her arm. More arrows rained down around her as she swam to escape, outpacing the guards running alongside the pool. She had no doubt they would kill her. After hearing Habibah announce her scheme so boldly, they were as guilty as she was. But Habibah's screeching and the guards' guilt at betraying a daughter of the house they were sworn to protect gave Amryn a slim chance.

A moment's delay. A second's hesitation.

When she burst from the pool, their hesitation was all she needed to scramble for the window. She kicked open the lattice and jumped.

#　#　#

Amryn ducked into an alley and pressed her back to the wall, counting her breaths until the guard ran past. Another one she'd evaded. She closed her eyes and listened as their footfalls scraped the sandstone bricks, but they didn't call out to one another. They knew what they were doing was wrong, and they'd be executed if their treachery was discovered.

Vanish, her mother's voice urged her. *Become the night.*

Amryn looked up at the stars. Pinpoints of light in the endless black night. Her escape.

She turned and gripped the doorframe. Silently, she scaled the wall, as her mother taught her—a sand lizard flitting through the shadows. Lying flat on the roof, she watched Habibah's guards searching the vacant streets below, retracing their path. They would not soon give up.

Slinking from rooftop to rooftop, Amryn made her way toward the harbor. She scanned the empty bazaar below for movement, leapt over shuttered stalls and furled awnings, and landed atop the fortress wall. As she crouched in the darkness, the slow creaking of ships quarreled with the chittering wind and lapping waves. Amryn raised on her toes and peered down a cannon port, searching the rows of vessels moored below the walls. Some ships were familiar, but none with captains she knew well enough to trust with her life.

A thick mist hung over the harbor, full of light and muffled voices. A pair of Ealim harbor guards patrolled the boardwalk. Setting out in her own dhow would be a gamble of their loyalty with Habibah's guards still after her. Beyond the wharf, the Endless Ocean watched and waited, a mildly curious beast unmoved by her predicament.

Fear kills. Reason survives.

She couldn't go back to the royal compound. Not with Resa unaccounted for and without her protection keeping the wolves at bay. Not without knowing how far Habibah's scheme extended or who she could trust. Reaching out to the Fang for help was not an option. Only her mother knew the other assassins' names. Of the few other Fang agents Amryn had trained with, she might recognize only their eyes, as veils and masks always obscured their faces.

Time. She needed time. Nefi was at sea. Ottah was... she refused to draw him into Habibah's madness. Soon enough, Resa would reappear. Of course, she would. Resa would stalk into the palace and expose Habibah's treachery. The Gyakari would see his sister for the vengeful creature she had become. Until then, Amryn's only reasonable choice was to remain hidden. To vanish like the dead.

Settled on her decision, she started the stealthy climb down the fortress wall, blending into the shadows beyond the reach of lanterns lighting the stairways down to the wharf. When her feet touched the planks of the boardwalk, she crept to the edge, slipped under the rail, and shimmied down the nearest piling. Then, sinking into the comforting obscurity of the dark sea, she swam underneath the pier, from berth to berth, considering the moored ships.

Banners bearing the Ari lion, she bypassed. One of those ships had brought Habibah and her vengeance to Ealim. The fishing trawler seemed a safe choice, but the thought of hiding amidst its smells made her queasy. The dhow in the next berth might be one of Nefekari's couriers, perhaps with a crew she could trust. But if not, the ship was too small to chance finding a hiding spot.

Amryn swam to the last berth and stopped, treading water before a handsome three-masted schooner. The ship was sleek and well-outfitted, with Tallu rigging and a black locust hull, and like none she'd noticed docked in Ealim. Whoever captained this beauty hailed from far beyond Wodi.

Amryn smiled. The dinghy nestled against its stern offered a tempting hiding spot.

"Reason survives."

Chapter 4

Destiny

Hobi strode down the wharf, intent on reaching his ship and fighting the instinct to break into a sprint. A gait of haste, not purpose, could draw the curiosity of a patrolling guard.

Although the flowing Ari robes and headscarf he had taken to wearing since the war covered his markings, nothing hid his distinctive eyes. Someone might recall passing the N'si in a hurry, remember seeing a thief on the run.

The *Seeker* was within hailing distance and readied for a quick departure. Beyond her, backlit by a fiery orange sunrise, a blanket of purple-bellied clouds skulked along the horizon. With a fleeting smile, Hobi thanked his uncanny good luck for the change in weather. Whatever its source, his luck seldom abandoned him.

No time was the right time for the voyage he planned. In early summer, the prevailing winds of the Barrens Monsoon season shifted, and for a few short weeks, sailing into the Endless Ocean was not a futile battle against the headwinds. Even so, a ship venturing too far into the eternal expanse of water did not return. No man willingly tested the limits.

But he was no man.

Hobi took the gangplank in long strides. Cora and Rafael met him on deck. His brusque approach needed no explanation.

"You are alive," Rafael noted. "And mostly unscathed, yes?"

"Disappointed?" said Hobi.

"We were about to roll dice for your ship," said Rafael.

"Roll dice? Ye insult the *Seeker*." Cora drew her sword. "Duel me for her, pretty boy."

Cora was a big woman with sea-green eyes and sun-streaked braids. She was never without her wide-brimmed hat with a trio of long hawk feathers sewn into its band. Like a stout oak some whimsical god had coaxed from the sea, Cora belonged under the sun. A Rhynn from the seafaring Clan Dunbar, she fled Rhynn years ago when the Prophet was hunting mindgifted and burning empaths for sorcery. She took to the sea and never looked back.

"Entertaining as it would be to see Cora run you through," said Hobi, "perhaps it should wait until my demise."

"May it be long in coming, Captain." Rafael brushed aside the blade poking his chest.

Rafael d'Ortega had the polish and swagger of the typical useless Laradian aristocrat. Smaller than average in stature, he thrived on being underestimated. He had served the Orthodoxy before the Chalyn War as one of the clandestine enforcers answering to His Supreme Holiness alone. On command, kings fell, fortunes turned, and the misguided saw the folly of straying from their faith. Rafael gained valuable skills while improvising his way into and out of whatever the mission demanded. He was adept at fixing things—nets, rigging, waterwheels, harpoons—and crafting precisely the gadget any situation required. And, of course, no cell on earth could hold him.

"Well, did you get the prize?" Rafael asked him.

"He's here, isn't he?" Cora sheathed her sword. "How long 'til they catch up to us, Captain?"

"An hour." Hobi shrugged. "Probably less."

"Make ready," Cora shouted to the crew. "Look lively, or I'll leave ye to the Fang. They'll be itchin' for a fight after the captain bested them."

Talk ceased, and the desire to continue living took precedence. The crew set to their tasks without question. Each had made their choice when Hobi stepped back onto the ship. They weighed the risk as they always did. And they cast their lots with his.

They were a misfit bunch of antiquity purveyors, archeologists, adventurers, and opportunists. Each embraced the risks and rewards for their own reasons. Relic hunters were generally not known for their longevity. Yet the crew of the *Seeker* had a knack for resilience, despite prowling sunken wrecks and uninhabitable islands. In their few short years together, they had been chased, scammed, pirated, stuck adrift, eel-stung, shark-bitten, and nearly drowned—more than a few times. Yet, a string of successful expeditions soon began drawing attention and an abundance of eager investors.

Hobi set to work beside his crew. The wind picked up, blowing hot and dense off the jungle, blanketing Ealim in its steamy breath. The sea smelled closer and heavier in the harbor—salt, sulfur, brine, and creatures that fed at its shores. And aboard the *Seeker*, the flurry of activity belied the efficiency in their routines of muscle and sweat.

Thunder beat a distant bass drum, and the first raindrops fell. Hobi hurried to the stern. The windlass was already humming, its chorus of ratchets and sprockets fine-tuned by Rafael's expert hands. Weighing anchors on the *Seeker* took a mere three men—or one Khaldun.

"Aweigh," the giant Wodian's voice rumbled across the decks. Sails snapped taut, and the *Seeker* lurched for the sea like a long-lost lover.

Khaldun noticed him and turned. The dark eyes beneath his heavy brows were calm, for a hulking menace, and conveyed the only question that mattered to either of them. Hobi trusted Khaldun as much as he trusted any man.

"Whatever Yuji knew, is ours," he said. "Give me tonight alone with... my father's memory. Tomorrow, come, and we will talk about what I've found."

Khaldun nodded and returned to his work, never parting with a word he didn't find necessary. A study in contradictions, the man was built like a bear, unrivaled in height, breadth, or brawn. Yet he was equally quick-minded, well-educated, and slow to anger. Yes, Khaldun excelled at a great many things. Interacting with people was not one of them.

When Hobi had first met him, they were sailing for Prince Nefekari, reestablishing the Ari Empire's territorial waters after the war, and learning the mariner's arts in one of the finest fleets in the world. The other crew kept them both at arm's length, Hobi for being N'si and Khaldun for his shyness. They often found themselves with little company but one another. Neither offered much about their past, and neither asked. After serving their years in the Ari fleet, they had parted ways, pursuing different paths to the same obsession.

When Hobi bought his own ship and was equipping her for his first expedition, Khaldun showed up one day and took a berth. Never one to question luck, Hobi accepted the man's unspoken application to join the crew. Khaldun became the *Seeker's* navigator, and no one was better suited to the task. With his massive, ink-stained hands and the tiny, gold-rimmed spectacles that seemed almost comical on such a big face, Khaldun had become an extraordinary cartographer and was one of the few whose Endless Ocean expertise rivaled Hobi's own.

"Underway and catchin' good wind, Captain," Cora called up to him. "She'll clear the harbor in another wink."

As a soft rain fell on his face, Hobi raised a spyglass to the city shrinking behind them. A band of black-clad figures came rushing down the steps, spilling onto the wharf. The Fang had come for him. Too late.

"You disappointed him, Resa," he said. "I will not."

# # #

Hobi retreated to his cabin, exhaustion closing in after too many days spent on constant alert, first pursuing, then being pursued. He would have to give in to sleep soon, but not yet.

Goblin leapt from a shelf to his shoulder, scolding him in that odd, rattling purr of hers. He had discovered the little orange cat on board when he purchased the ship, and she had summarily decreed Hobi belonged to her. Fierce for her size, she made an unlikely guardian, but he took what he could get.

"No worse for the wear, my lady," he assured her. "Where is our Demon hiding? Did you keep him fed while I was away?"

Demon could fend for himself and would reappear when he was in the mood for a warm, dry nest. The fat, lizard-like creature, a stowaway from one of the *Seeker's* island expeditions, was likely in the galley with Cook, pretending to be finicky and feigning interest in the old pirate's tales.

Hobi unwound his wet headscarf and changed into a dry shirt and trousers. Without the distraction of running for his life, a single thought was enough to light the lantern. As a honeyed glow warmed the cabin, he stood staring at the pack tossed on his desk. Stolen from him and stolen back. Inside it lay everything or nothing. Truth or fanciful lies. Or evidence of his father's madness.

Hobi had to know. The call of the Endless Ocean had grown too strong, and it would never release its hold until he followed where it beckoned. If only he knew whether following that call would him into madness, too.

He sat at the desk and pulled the braided silver chain from around his neck. Lantern light danced in the diamond-like prism he held in his palm. The colorless jewel was the size of his little finger, a five-faced bar cut from a rare gemstone he had yet to identify. Beautiful in its simplicity. Almost utilitarian in form. Yet, the colors and patterns shifting inside it were never the same. From the moment Hobi took the pendant from his dead father's chest, still slick with blood, it had bound him to its purpose. Whatever that was.

"Would've been helpful if you'd told me, Yuji."

Perhaps he had. Hobi opened the pack and slid out an oilcloth-wrapped bundle. Hesitating, he unwrapped the leatherbound journal inside. Handsomely crafted and well preserved for its age, with brass corners and gold-leaf edged pages, the journal was just as Hobi remembered. Though it had always been open then, lying on the writing table in Yuji's library.

More priceless than any relic Hobi had yet recovered.

He opened the journal and flipped the pages, tentatively at first, then more intently as the night wore on. Sketches, maps, and descriptions so vivid he felt as if he were living the elusive myth. What if it *were* real?

Hobi was not the only one who had recognized what this myth might mean to his kind—to every nene—but especially to N'si running out of time. Resa had denied him his destiny for too long. Now, if only he could figure out where it led.

Chapter 5

At Sea

Amryn winced from the cramp in her neck. She must have fallen asleep in her chair again. Though a trained Fang could sleep anywhere, that didn't make the waking part any easier. She stretched out stiff muscles, shaking off a groggy fog, and tried to get her bearings in the dark. Her elbow cracked against something hard. Her backside was soaking wet.

Then the recollections came rushing back. Habibah with her mother's amulet. Jumping from the window. Running for her life. Hiding on a ship.

The dinghy. She'd slept in a dinghy.

Amryn tasted the telltale bitterness of laudanum and fought a wave of nausea. Last night's dinner must have been tainted, and if she had eaten with her usual appetite, she would be Habibah's prisoner or worse. She drew controlled, counted breaths and centered her awareness as Fang training taught. A parched throat and aching head did little to help her concentration.

"Curse you and your spawn," she muttered. "Wretched old shrew."

How dare Habibah harm—

No. That was a lie. Resa was alive. Of course, she was alive. And in a righteous rage, no doubt. Out searching for Amryn at this very moment.

Amryn sighed and leaned her head against the hull. She'd never developed the patience for focus rituals, anyway. It didn't take a centered awareness to notice it was raining outside her hiding spot. Habibah's brutes had probably given up the chase by now. A quick peek from under the canvas should tell her whether leaving was safe.

She would find her mother, and they would deal with Habibah together.

She curled on her knees and lifted an edge of the canvas. Water rolled down and splashed her in the face. She detested Habibah even more, then. Wiping her eyes, she peered out again.

The wharf was gone. The entire city was gone. She was at sea, on a ship full of strangers, or worse, pirates. Damn it all. Leaving Ealim had not been her intent. She sank back against the hull. Maybe she would try that controlled breathing again, after all.

Fear kills. Reason survives.

Reason said a ship as handsome as this would be a passenger cruiser or perhaps a trader of high-end delicacies. Either would make frequent stops along the coast. She need only stay hidden until the next port, until the ship reached a town where Habibah and her brutes were not. She could find the Ari chieftain there and send word to Nefi or the Gyakari. Yes, that seemed a rational plan. Reason approved.

But how long until they reached the next port? Hours? A few days at most? Her stomach rumbled, and she felt for the pouch on her sash. Yes, it was still there. Most of the caramel pastry Ottah bought for her yesterday would be there, too. Soggy, perhaps, but edible. And it was still raining. She could cup the canvas and drink rainwater. Quite pleased with her cleverness, she patted the jambiya sheathed on her hip and smiled at her brief bout of fear.

"Pirates, beware," she whispered. "Your shadows have Fangs."

#   #   #

Amryn had always dreaded the focus rituals. Day after day of sitting still, doing nothing. Left her alone with her thoughts. Not the best company.

Another morning dawned behind the clouds, and the rain continued, soft but steady. The hours dragged by with torturous slowness, her solitude broken only by the occasional gull's cry or the muffled voices of the ship's crew. Worse, a bout of fever and sniffles had skulked in to torment her. It was infuriatingly tricky to cough in silence.

Amryn squirmed again, never quite finding a position that didn't involve being poked or scratched by something unseen. Canvas-wrapped dinghies had to be the most uncomfortable hiding spots on earth. Amryn made a note never to mention that to Resa, lest she find a way to incorporate dinghies into Fang training. Shifting to her side, she noticed yet another nuisance prodding her thigh. Reaching to push the irritant away, she realized it was the relic Ottah had given her.

She must have slipped it into her pocket when Habibah came barging in on her. She pulled out the odd artifact and wiped its sleek, onyx face. Ancient as it was, being drenched in seawater surely had done it no good. Still, it was a curiosity to occupy her time.

Amryn examined the thin, wafer-like relic anew. Cool to the touch, despite the suffocating heat of the day, it seemed solid, with no seams to pry apart, no fasteners to unfasten. She held the relic in a sliver of muted daylight. Not one scratch on its glassy surface, even after the uncounted centuries it had survived. Harder than glass or onyx, then. And opaque. A black diamond? Whatever it was made of, she had never seen the like.

She tried to remember what had coaxed a fleeting glimmer from it the first night. Was it the warmth of her breath? A sequence of finger taps?

"How can I coax you to talk to me, old one?"

Amryn drew her jambiya and notched a pattern in the hull. She tried the same pattern on the relic. Nothing. She notched another pattern and tried again.

#   #   #

For the next several days, Hobi spent every spare moment reading and rereading his father's journal. He tried to separate potential facts from intentionally interspersed fiction. There was abundant misdirection on every page, meant to keep the journal's secrets safe. For years, these pages had hidden the truth from anyone who did not know Yuji as well as Hobi had. Finally, when satisfied he had weeded out most of the tangents, ambiguities, and outright lies, he left Khaldun to make sense of what remained.

Now, standing over his desk, Hobi decided he had perhaps been too hasty. He frowned down at Khaldun's freshly penned map.

"But we've crossed those waters before," he said.

"Yes," said Khaldun.

"There's nothing there."

"Nothing we encountered."

Hobi rubbed his neck. He'd never known Khaldun to be wrong about... well, about anything. Though the man could hardly be wrong if he never stated an opinion in the first place.

"Recheck your calculations. You must have misinterpreted the results."

Khaldun stared at him as if he'd just uttered a blasphemy.

"Math does not form opinions, Captain. It states facts."

Hobi sank to his chair and buried his face in his hands. That was it, then—a flawlessly executed case of the renowned N'si mischief. Yuji had tricked him into chasing an empty myth. There was no ancient homeland, no pristine sanctuary waiting for what remained of his kind.

"Did you find my hope amusing, Father?" Hobi said bitterly.

Khaldun's big feet appeared by the chair. Apparently, the man had something to say. It was a rare enough occurrence, so Hobi sighed and looked up at him.

"Well?"

"How do you not know this about yourself?" Khaldun frowned.

"That I am as gullible as I am naïve?"

"That you are incapable of being deceived."

Hobi grunted. "Obviously not."

Khaldun sat cross-legged on the floor, bringing them more or less to eye level. And the look in those eyes was surprising. The man genuinely seemed concerned.

"No one can deceive you," said Khaldun. "I have seen this, time and again. I learned to rely on it as a fundamental law of the universe. If you believe something, I consider it proven."

"We N'si have a rather fluid interpretation of truth," said Hobi. "Recognizing its subtleties is a survival skill we learn young."

"I have known other N'si. I trusted none of them."

Hobi looked away. He had never been trusted. He never expected to be. No N'si would.

"Your father did not lie to you, Hobi. He couldn't."

Hobi realized the man could be right. In fact, he knew it as surely as he knew the sun would rise and set. Even as he tried to summon doubt, the doubt felt hollow.

"Maurya is out there," Hobi said, his confidence returning. "And we will find it."

"Yes, my friend. We will."

Khaldun got up, which meant he was done talking, probably for weeks to come, considering all he'd said in the past hour. There had to be some quota his mind rationed out, and Hobi had tapped every reserve today.

#   #   #

Amryn obsessed over the relic and fought her lingering fever for days of misery on end. The dinghy's hull was now covered in knife marks chronicling her experiments.

One morning, after she had traced one of a hundred random patterns, a faint blue light pulsed in a corner of the relic's face. Like a tiny eye opening and winking shut. She'd held her breath, mesmerized. A few heartbeats later, the eye winked again. And then, nothing. Hurriedly repeating the same pattern, she got the same response. And nothing more.

Mercifully, both the fever and the rain had stopped at some point. Thirst had soon replaced them tenfold. Amryn collected dew from the canvas, but it was never enough. The last crumb of pastry was long gone, and she had chewed the leather off her sandals.

She was no longer thinking clearly.

Reason might have told her to jump from the ship and swim to shore. It couldn't be that far, and she was a strong swimmer. Rather, she *had* been strong when she first crawled into this canvas-shrouded nightmare.

One night—not long ago she thought, though she was no longer sure—the clouds had cleared, and the moon shone bright. On that night, the relic had shone bright, too. Though how an opaque chunk of obstinance could shine, she couldn't say. Maybe her entire memory of the night was a hallucination. Hunger could do that to a person, she recalled.

But from that night on, the relic yearned. It wanted to go home. Amryn found this disconcerting, of course. At times, she would cast the relic away. She was certain she had watched it fall into the sea more than once. Yet, each time, she would wake and find it in her hand.

It always returned.

Reason also might have told her to call out for help. Climb out of her prison. Take her chances with the crew of strangers. She no longer cared whether they were pirates or a flock of pelicans. Nothing could be worse than staying where she was, trapped in a dinghy with a yearning relic.

Amryn reached to tear back the canvas, and the relic shocked her, painfully. She tried to drop it, but her fingers closed around it of their own accord. Colors swirled before her eyes, senselessly spinning, and shredding to grey, until an ancient black hand rose to claim her.

Some time later, the chaos of colors faded, and Amryn sensed a strange weight on her chest. Heavy enough it made breathing an effort. It occurred to her that she may have passed out. It was no longer night. If she were dead, she wouldn't have noticed that, would she? The dead were generally not observant about such matters. Determined to prove her point, she opened her eyes.

A scaly blue demon crouched on her chest, staring down with fiery red eyes.

Chapter 6

Stowaway

Hobi left Khaldun to do what navigators did and climbed to the deck. Midstride, he stopped and held his hand to his chest. That was odd. The prism was growing uncomfortably warm against his skin. Goblin growled on his shoulder, hissing at some unseen menace.

Suddenly, a bloodcurdling scream split the air. Goblin leapt down and darted across the deck as if she had a pack of gwynwulves on her tail. The cat jumped over the railing, and Hobi ran to look overboard.

The dinghy. Goblin was on the dinghy. With her claws dug into the canvas, her back arched, and every hair standing on end. And the dinghy was screaming.

Hobi vaulted down and flung back the canvas with a rush of dread. He stopped and stared. A woman was lying in the hull. Demon was on to her chest, his spiked tail whipping wildly, and doing his best not to get pummeled by flailing fists.

"Stop your screaming, woman! You're scaring him."

Hobi pried Demon off her and lifted the startled old lizard up to Cora's waiting arms. Goblin sprang to his shoulder, hissing at the stranger writhing at his feet.

"Oh, be still. You aren't hurt," said Hobi.

The woman went quiet, though her chest heaved with each labored breath. When she stilled enough, he got a good look at her. Dirty and thin as a street urchin, she was in a bad way. How long had she been hiding there? At least since he left Ealim. She must be running from someone or something. He could hardly fault her for that, as he'd done enough running himself. But she had picked the wrong ship for her escape.

He knelt for a closer look and stopped at the smell. If the woman sensed him, she gave no sign. There'd been a time in his life when he would've rolled her over the side and been done with the inconvenience—granted her a small mercy before his brothers could do far worse. Those were the lost years he tried to forget, numbed and wasted years spent running with his brothers and running from himself.

Hobi glanced down at the water. No, that wasn't who he was now, and maybe it never had been. He gathered the woman in his arms to carry her up to the deck. Tangled ringlets of black hair swept back from her face as she stirred in his arms.

"You." Hobi tensed. "What are you doing on my ship?"

"Hating every moment of it," she muttered. Then she looked up at him, and her bloodshot eyes widened. "The crypt. Y-you…"

The unwelcomed recognition was mutual. Resa's daughter fought to get free of him, squirming and kicking in his grasp. He shifted her under his arm like a sack of grain and climbed to the railing.

"Take her and bind her," he told Cora. "Rafael, I want a pistol leveled at her head."

"Gracia, Captain. The poor girl can barely stand," said Rafael. "Perhaps you—"

"She's a Fang."

Pistols clicked, and swords flashed. The crew circled the menace with newfound wariness. To squash any lingering shreds of sympathy, Hobi offered an introduction.

"*Seeker*, I introduce our captive. Amryn Nisari."

Murmurs erupted at the name. The smarter among them took cautious steps back.

"Yes, I said *Nisari*. Resa's own daughter."

Amryn lifted her chin defiantly, but her wobbly knees somewhat spoiled the effect. She appeared weak, but it might be a ruse.

No one can deceive you.

Hobi wasn't giving her the chance, not after he'd come this far.

"Cora, search her."

Amryn didn't resist when Cora confiscated her dagger. It was a beautifully crafted jambiya, the curved blade unique to House Ari. He remembered seeing the dagger when he startled her that night in the sea crypt. To this day, he wondered what had possessed him to step out of the shadows and let her see his face.

"Nothing but the blade on her, Captain," said Cora. "Hold on there. What's that in yer hand, Fang?"

Amryn held out her palm. She turned over a thin onyx trinket and held it up for inspection. Its featureless surface glinted like polished crystal. Hobi caught a fleeting sense of... yearning?

"My meditation stone," said Amryn. "Take it if you must."

"Keep it," Hobi said, though uncertain why he wanted it to stay with her. "If it calms you."

Amryn lowered her eyes and tucked the odd stone into her pocket. The prism beneath his shirt heated again, nearly scalding his skin this time.

"Lock her up."

Chapter 7

Captive

Amryn hugged her knees to her chest, alone in the tiny cabin they had made her cell. She considered her short list of options—try to escape or bide her time and learn what manner of misdeeds these outlaws were out to commit.

She had, thus far, succeeded in not dying and considered it an accomplishment she would like to continue. However, given that her captors had yet to torture or ravage her, killing her was beginning to seem less likely. Quite the opposite. They had fed her, allowed her to bathe, and even asked if she had slept well. Granted, Amryn had never been jailed before, but it seemed these people were not experienced at keeping prisoners.

That was it, she decided. They considered it a lucky boon, finding her stowed away on their ship. Obviously, they had decided to hold her for ransom.

A key rattled the lock, followed by a knock on the door. What sort of outlaws knocked?

"Come in," she said, having learned the knocking would continue until she did.

It was the Laradian this time. An elegant little fellow with gold rings in his ears and mischief in his eyes, he was the only one of the crew who occasionally deigned to answer her questions. He came in carrying a pitcher of water and poured it into the washbasin. Apparently, they valued regular bathing, even at sea.

"You are generous with your supply of water," she said. "The ship must be heading for port soon."

"Do not worry your pretty head, M'sita Nisari. The *Seeker* never runs out of fresh water."

An odd claim, but likely irrelevant.

"*Seeker*... How did she get her name?"

"Ah, do you not know? She carries the greatest seekers of all time," he said with a bow. "We seek that which is lost. Antiquities, artifacts, treasures of the past."

Amryn frowned. These outlaws were archeologists? Historians? Surely not.

"Bene fortune, m'sita. Behave as befits a lady of your station, and you may yet live to tell your grandchildren you were aboard the *Seeker's* greatest expedition."

He winked and left her alone.

\# \# \#

Days passed in the relative comfort of her cell, which, though small, was a considerable improvement over the dinghy. But Amryn had never been allowed to sit idle, and boredom soon made her restless. At least the effort she'd expended in not dying had kept her occupied before. Now, she spent hours watching dust specks dance in a beam of light.

The porthole was her only connection to the world outside the cabin. The direction of the sunrise should have affirmed the ship was sailing up the coast. Most ships leaving Ealim sailed north. Some headed south, supplying miners in the desolate mountains of southernmost Wodi or the soldiers in the outposts that guarded the mines. Only fishing ships sailed east into the Endless Ocean, though never so far as the *Seeker* seemed to be venturing.

She might have considered it interesting, accompanying an expedition of historians, hunting for ancient treasures, and exploring where no one had ever explored. But there was nothing out here but water for as far as she could see. Boring, predictable, endless water.

"Torture," she shouted. "You do realize boring someone to death qualifies as torture!"

Amryn got up and paced. That took all of a minute, since she could cross the entire cabin in one stride. She stopped and pounded on the door again.

"A book, at least. One book. Surely you people can read."

She may as well be talking to the washbasin. Her eyes darted to the shelf above her bunk. No, she was not touching that cursed relic again. It could sneak back into her hand every night if it wanted. She would set it back on its shelf every morning. She was not falling under its spell again.

"Spells," she snorted. "Listen to yourself. Going on about spells and curses. A scientist does not attribute the results of her experiments to magic."

Her eyes wandered back to the shelf. The relic tugged at her, relentless in its yearning. Though she felt like an utter fool, she feared what she may have awakened.

# # #

The N'si eventually visited her. He sat, staring at her for a long while, holding so still he scarcely seemed to breathe. Amryn read nothing in the amber eyes she remembered from the sea crypt, shining in the dark beyond the candlewand's glow. There was something ethereal about him. Unnatural and shadowy. As if he belonged where reason did not reign.

Captain, they called him. Never by his name. Yet, he knew hers. He leaned back in his chair and folded his arms.

"Resa sent you to kill me."

"Did you give her a reason to?" she said.

"She thinks so."

"Then I am the last person she would send."

A flicker of uncertainty, perhaps? A predator less sure of his prey. No, not a predator. A judge. He was weighing her every reaction on some mystical scale of truth only he could decipher.

"The Gyakari's sister, Habibah, came to our home unannounced," said Amryn. "I was there alone. She said Resa had betrayed Ari and abandoned us to lead a band of N'si rebels. She threw down my mother's Fang amulet as proof. When I threatened to challenge her lies to the Gyakari, she ordered her guards to kill me. I ran, and they chased me through the city to the harbor. I needed somewhere to hide until daylight, so I climbed into the dinghy. When I woke, you had sailed."

Once she started talking, she couldn't seem to stop. She felt compelled to make the impassive nene acknowledge that Habibah's deviousness, which she had barely escaped, was the only reason she had ended up on his damned ship.

"Had I known this was your ship, I would have chosen another—any other. No one sent me to kill you. I haven't seen my mother since... well, since before I met you in the crypt. What were you doing in the crypt?"

"My ship, my questions."

Amryn hesitated. "I don't know my mother is even alive. Habibah said she—"

"Resa lives."

"How can you know?"

"Because while you were escaping your aunt, I was eluding your mother. Resa chased me all the way to the harbor. I assure you, she is alive and quite put out with me."

"Why?" Amryn tried again.

He arched a brow, but refused her question. She decided to try one last confession to gain his trust. One only her mother knew.

"Despite your assumptions, I have never taken a life."

Throughout their talk, the inscrutable N'si had hardly moved and hadn't questioned anything she'd told him. When she was done, he stood. It was a controlled movement, silky and wrapped in lethal grace. He was no longer looking at her. His eyes fixed on the shelf, and his hand rubbed his chest.

"The meditation stone?" she said. "To be honest, it's an artifact from the Watchers' Den. My friend is an acolyte of the Unraveling. He borrowed it from the Hall of Relics for me to study."

A corner of his mouth curled in the first hint of a smile she'd seen.

"Borrowed?" he said.

Amryn shrugged.

"And what have you learned from studying your relic?"

"Be wary of what we aren't meant to understand."

He gave her a curious look. She wondered if he'd expected a more analytical reply.

"You can sense its yearning," he said.

He asked the question so casually it stunned her. How could...? He sensed it, too.

"It wants to go home," she said, hoping he wouldn't ask how she knew. She'd rather not broach the subject of spells and curses.

Instead, he turned to leave.

"Wait," she said. "Who are you? Where are we going?"

"You did not lie to me today," he said over his shoulder. "Do not start tomorrow."

Chapter 8

Seared

And so, it continued. Hobi returned to sit with Amryn in the mornings. He would question her, each time expecting to catch her in a lie. And she would answer, each time proving him wrong. Eventually, he accepted she had not intended to be on his ship. Improbable as it seemed, the only explanation for Amryn Nisari choosing to stow away on the *Seeker* rather than any other ship anchored in the harbor was his own uncanny good luck.

When Resa caught up to him, and he had no doubt she would, she would find he had a bargaining coin. And while he was not fool enough to consider Amryn harmless—she could kill if she chose to—he shifted his attention to the odd relic. Unfortunately, it was less forthcoming than its keeper.

Hobi called Khaldun, Cora, and Rafael to his cabin. They gathered around his desk, cramped for elbow room. Privacy was hard to come by at sea.

"She says it is an artifact *borrowed* from the Watchers' Den," Hobi told those whose expertise he valued most. "That means Kitsune had access to the relic, yet he never suspected its use."

Kitsune was gone, defeated by the Chalyns, but for thousands of years, the mechanical mind had ruled the Watchers and the seeds of humanity they had sown here. A monster of humanity's own making, Kitsune had turned Earth into his breeding ground, trying to evolve humans he considered worthy of grafting with his consciousness. But Chalyns had proven cleverer than Kitsune expected. They kept their mindgifts hidden until they grew far more powerful than he could contain. Through all those years of waiting, if Kitsune had learned of a hidden enclave of humans he had not claimed, he would have obsessed over finding them.

"Aye, and that means Kitsune didn't look for what he didn't know was there," said Cora. "Just another rusty ole key to an unknown lock. It would've seemed useless to him."

"Kitsune never knew the lock existed," said Rafael. "But we do."

"And I believe the relic might lead us there," said Hobi.

"So, ye think it's attuned to Amryn," said Cora. "Or she's attuned to it."

"Both," said Hobi.

"She told ye it wants to go home." Cora scratched her chin. "Homin' pigeon?"

"The key seeking the lock, yes?" said Rafael.

"Did ye show her Khaldun's map?" said Cora.

"No," said Hobi. "Even if she isn't here to kill us, she is still a Fang."

"You did not show her." Rafael frowned. "Gracia. Does the poor girl even know she is in the Endless Ocean?"

"Poor girl?" Cora rolled her eyes. "Resa's daughter. Fang assassin. Repeat those words until yer head slaps some sense into yer lonely cock."

"Lonely and longing for you, mi amore." Rafael winked.

"Oaf."

Khaldun got up off the floor. He cast them an exasperated glance and gathered his map from the desk. He held it out to Hobi.

"Show her."

# # #

Hobi could not rest that night for thoughts of locks and keys and maps to nowhere. He needed to know more about the artifact and its connection to the prism, yet he couldn't risk telling Amryn why. She had not tried to deceive him, but that didn't mean he could trust her.

The prism reacted to the nearness of the relic. That much was clear. With each visit, he became more aware of the effect. Proximity triggered the heating response and awakened a shared link of some sort. Did that mean Yuji's prism was as ancient as Amryn's relic? How did one end up in the Watchers' Den and the other in his father's hands?

Yuji's hands. Nimble and strong. Forever busy, knotting a rope or raising a sail. Hobi remembered him most clearly with his face to the wind, staring wistfully out to sea. Memories he had thought buried in the past were returning to haunt him. Reading his father's journal had stirred a restless ghost.

Hobi could still see his father lying on the beach. The tide was coming in, and the sea reached for its own. With each wave, the encroaching surf painted blood-red streaks on the sand.

He remembered running down the beach. Frantically trying to wake his father. But death already lurked near. He remembered crying and holding on as Yuji drew his last breath. Too gripped by grief, he didn't sense the change at first. He didn't feel the moment when Yuji's magic passed to him. Only years later did he begin to understand his inheritance and learn what it meant to be a sorcerer's son. By then, he had nearly destroyed Yuji's legacy with neglect.

Hobi's first encounter with the gift left an emotional scar he carried to this day. The silent presence, for that was how he thought of the magic within him, rewound the hours before his father's death and showed him a vision of Yuji surrounded on the beach. Lured and ambushed. Many against one. The presence made Hobi watch the brutal attack at the hands of those Yuji thought were his friends. Then it took Hobi's pain and exchanged it for something he could use. A keen sense of truth. It made sure Hobi would never be deceived as his father had been.

Some time later, with Hobi still clutching the pendant on Yuji's chest, other arms pried him away from the corpse and lifted him from the blood-stained sand. Gar, the nene Hobi would call Father from that day forward, carried him to the fine manor he would call home and to Raik and Kabu, the boys he would call brothers.

Such was the N'si way. Mothers raised daughters. Fathers raised sons. The more sons a nene added to his household, whether by siring or winning them in combat, the greater his status. The Battle of Fathers was considered unassailable law in N'si culture. The challenge, once accepted, was a duel to the death. The fittest won the right to raise the weaker nene's sons as his own. Only Hobi knew Gar's battle with Yuji was wrongly done, and how could a child explain a vision conjured by magic he did not understand?

"I should have tried," Hobi told the shadows.

The shadows answered with a muffled cry. Faint, yet urgent. Hobi sat up in bed, listening, and he heard another cry.

Amryn. It was Amryn's voice. Was she having a nightmare? No, those were not whimpers of fear but cries of pain. Hobi bolted from bed in his long drawers. If any man in his crew had dared to—

Cora was there ahead of him, hurrying to unlock the bolt. Hobi brushed past her the second the door swung open, and his intensity lit every candle in the small cabin. Amryn was on her bunk, clawing at her chest. Blood soaked the front of her tattered gown and streaked the bedsheets.

"Amryn, stop." Hobi grabbed her sleeves to still her flailing. Tears rolled down her face with each shaking sob.

"Sweet Mother of Aurel," Cora muttered, kneeling beside the bloody bunk. She wadded a corner of the bedsheet and blotted the ugly wounds. "Quiet, lass. Let me find what's hurtin' ye."

Cora pressed her hands to Amryn's skin, and the empath's mindgift set about assessing the injuries and soothing the pain. Amryn thrashed under the healer's touch, and Hobi tightened his hold. The prism around his neck burned as hot as a coal.

"There, now. Calm yerself," said Cora.

Cora gently pulled back the shredded gown. Hobi clenched his jaw at the sight of her. From Amryn's neck to her breasts, gouges and burns mottled her skin. At the center of the raw wounds, the ancient relic had burrowed into her flesh.

"Get it off her," said Hobi.

Cora closed her eyes and splayed her palms over Amryn's shoulders. Hobi had seen Cora summon her healing trance before, using her empath's mindgift to sense torn flesh and bone and mend a broken body from the inside. Cora winced at whatever she found. Sweat glistened on her brow. Suddenly she broke off the touch, trembling.

"It's rooted too deep. Tendrils. Spreadin' through her. It's…"

Amryn stopped straining against his grip. She panted for breath. Her wild eyes flitted and focused, and she seemed to recognize he was there. With a glance at the prism on his chest, then down to his hands clutching the bunched cloth of her sleeves, she drew a slow, shuddering breath.

"You can let go," she said.

He hesitated. "Amryn, you—"

"Have a tenuous hold on sanity at the moment. Yes, Captain. I know."

She gathered her wits, proving stronger than he expected. Hobi released her, and her hand went to the relic seared to her chest. She traced its rectangular face with her fingertips, feeling where the edges had fused with her skin.

"You said it's burrowed in deep," she said, steadying the tremor in her voice.

"Aye, for now," said Cora. "I'll need time to study its nature. The tendrils have slowed their spreadin' about. If I can find something the thing is averse to, give ye an herb or oil it dislikes, it may pull back on its own."

"You talk as if it were alive," said Hobi.

"She didn't do this to herself. That... whatever it is... acted on its own accord," said Cora. "If it refuses to leave on its own, I'll have to find a way to wither those tendrils. If I tried to cut it out now..."

"Not an option?" said Amryn.

"Not yet," said Cora. "Are ye hurtin' lass? I am able to ease pain, speed healin' in a body."

Amryn didn't respond. Instead, she closed her eyes and covered the relic with her hand. Communicating with it, perhaps? Hobi sent Cora a questioning glance, but Cora shook her head.

"Let her be," she said and stood to leave.

"What? Walk away and let the thing have her?" said Hobi. "That relic is a menace is on my ship. What might it be doing to her? When it's done with her, who might it come for next? No, I cannot let it leave this cabin."

Amryn stirred from her trance. When she looked up at him, the fear was gone from her eyes.

"It won't leave here, not without me."

"You can't be sure," he said.

"And yet, I am."

Hobi understood that kind of certainty. He'd found it in himself, after he'd stopped running long enough to look inside. Once that doubt was gone, he had learned what it meant to be changed. To carry a sorcerer's legacy.

"Leave me," she said. "Give me time to learn its intent."

"And if it intends evil?"

"You'll know," she said. "Kill me and destroy it."

Harsh words, but acknowledging a reality they both knew they must face. With a nod, Hobi accepted the choice before them. For the first time, he glimpsed the N'si behind the Ari façade of this extraordinary creature luck had sent him. Both nenan and woman. And an unflinching realist, like her mother.

Yes, he would know.

"I will guard the door."

Chapter 9

Intent

Amryn stared at the cabin door after it closed. She stood motionless, counting each beat of her heart and listening to the steady rush of her breath. Both were her own and hers alone.

Having been herself and no one else for her entire life, she was familiar with the feeling of being Amryn. So, it stood to reason. If the relic were turning her into anything other than Amryn, she would know.

She tucked her chin and tried to peer down at the thing. It was hard to see because it had affixed itself just below her collarbone, in the spot where a pendant might rest. She went to the washbasin to look in the mirror and winced at her disheveled hair, torn nightgown, and bloodshot eyes. She stared, searching for traces of herself in a reflection she barely recognized.

"What have you done to me?" she said.

The mirror blurred, and a different reflection looked back at her. This Amryn had translucent skin, and her body glowed as if lit from within. Silver threads spread outward from the relic, blazing trails throughout her body. The tendrils Cora had sensed. An intricate silver filigree traced her heart, spine, arm, and legs. As she watched, tiny tendrils encircled her head like a crown. Then the translucent Amryn winked out in a flare of silver light, and her bedraggled reflection returned.

It had answered her, she realized. She asked a question, and the relic answered.

Belatedly, she noticed the bedraggled reflection had changed, as well. The cuts crisscrossing her chest were already fading. Little remained of the ugly injuries besides a few fading scars. Was that the work of Cora's healing gift, the relic, or both? Amryn shuddered, recalling the pain searing her chest, the icy fire burning through her bones. But as the aches dulled and wounds faded, her horror turned into curiosity.

"Why? How?" she asked.

It offered no answers this time. So she tried a less esoteric question.

"You wanted to go home," she said. "Where is home?"

Again, the mirror blurred. A new Amryn appeared, fully healed, healthy, and strong. She was standing on the ship's bow with her face to the wind, vibrant and alive. The sun felt warm on her skin, and she breathed in the salty air and smiled. A familiar rush of yearning swept her, and she recognized it as the relic's yearning. The yearning soon passed, replaced by an invigorating new sense of purpose. The relic had found its home.

"Me? Why me?"

Again, it offered no answers.

# # #

Hobi stretched muscles stiffened by a night and morning spent with his back against the cabin door. Neither Amryn nor the relic had attempted to pass him. Instead, the cabin he guarded had gone quiet. For a while after taking his post outside the door, he had heard her muffled voice. Talking to the relic or to herself—if the two were still distinguishable one from the other. But hours had passed without a sound.

Demon came crawling down the narrow hallway, his black tongue darting out, tasting the strangeness. Blood and sweat and tears. All except the sweat were rare on the *Seeker*. He wondered whether the old lizard sensed predator or prey.

"What do you make of it, my friend?" said Hobi. "Danger or opportunity?"

Demon crawled up beside him. He lowered his scaly snout to the thin gap under the door. For a few moments, his forked tongue flitted underneath and sampled what lay beyond. Then he climbed over Hobi's outstretched legs and continued on his way, his claws clicking against the planks and his long tail swaying in his wake. Headed to the kitchen for Cook's morning handout, no doubt.

"Unimpressed, eh?" said Hobi. The creature had avoided Amryn since their first tumultuous meeting. Pummeling fists had not endeared her to him. But whatever now lurked behind that door, Demon seemed to find no cause for alarm.

Hobi stood and rested his hand on the bolt. Was she even still alive in there? Had the relic claimed her completely? What sort of monster might it have made of her? And could he look into her eyes when he killed it?

A knot rose on his shoulder and rippled down his arm, rolling under his skin. The presence was manifesting itself in a way it seldom did. The magic that dwelt inside him urged him to slide the bolt and see for himself. Hobi steeled his resolve, and the door creaked open.

Amryn was lying on the bunk with her back turned to him. She had a blanket pulled up to her chin. He stilled in the doorway, watching until the rise and fall of her shoulders confirmed she was alive. The relic had not killed her, apparently. That bitter task might yet be his.

For now, she was sleeping, healing, and becoming whatever she would be. He could draw his blade and end the threat before it grew stronger. A sudden flash of heat burned his chest, warning him off. If the prism and relic were connected, if these artifacts from a world long gone shared a bond, would the memento he carried of his father turn against him?

Amryn sighed in her sleep. It didn't sound like the sigh of a monster.

Hobi hesitated, then stepped back and closed the door. He would not make that choice yet.

# # #

When Amryn woke, it was late afternoon, and she found a tray of bread and cheese waiting beside the bunk. Someone had ventured in to feed her. They may never trust her to leave the cabin, but at least they hadn't decided to starve her. She sat on the bunk and nibbled the bread, her mind darting from one improbability to another.

The yearning she had sensed from the relic. Was it for her or for where it might lead her? Why her? It had established it wasn't the talkative sort, but she would get no answers if she never asked.

"You might have just as easily latched onto Ottah," she said.

Nothing. Was it always listening? Did she need to do something to get its attention?

"Would you have bonded to Ottah if he had kept you instead?"

Still no response. She pushed a bit further.

"No? What was the difference between Ottah and me? What about me mattered?"

Amryn drew back as a new Amryn appeared beside the bunk, a ghostly mirage taking shape in thin air, so close she could have reached out to touch her. Not wanting to scare away any response at this point, she resisted the urge to test the vision's substance. This Amryn seemed as robust as the image the relic showed her last night in the mirror, and it took a moment to notice the difference. Faintly, almost hesitantly, delicate markings began appearing on her neck.

Amryn watched in awe as the silver, tiger-like stripes painted the other Amryn's skin. Pale silver etched patterns on golden brown. N'si markings. Beautiful and mysterious. Drawn by an invisible hand, the graceful stripes swept from behind her neck and down her throat and shoulders, then encircled the relic on her chest in a bold flourish.

She could only stare, mesmerized. She had never seen her N'si stripes, the one-of-a-kind patterns each nene bore from birth. Her mother had told her the few faint birthmarks she'd been born with had faded before she reached her first birthday, as her stronger Wodian heritage absorbed the N'si shadows. Watching her stripes reappear, she felt as if she'd found a missing limb she hadn't known she'd lost.

"So, you needed an N'si," she said. "Sorry to disappoint, but I'm only N'si by half. Admitting to even that much can make a person's life difficult these days."

The dreamlike image before her didn't waver. N'si outcast or not, the vibrant, silver-marked Amryn was as real as any other the relic had shown her.

Amryn was Wodian, born to House Ari, daughter of the mighty Gyakari. No doubt, she was her father's child. Her place in his empire and her value to his dynasty had never been challenged. At least, not until Habibah dared launch her scheme. But Amryn was also her mother's child. Resa, the exotic beauty with a razor-sharp mind and sharper blade, sent to the Ari to seal an alliance in the days when N'si oaths could be trusted, was just as powerful in her own right. Her cunning and charisma won the heart of an ambitious young prince, and together, they kept a wary Ari court bowing down in respect. That was Amryn's heritage, too.

"So, you decided to make do with what little bit of N'si you had," she said. "It took you a while. I must have seemed quite the gamble."

Whatever it was, it had an underdeveloped sense of humor.

"What of the others of your kind? Did you all have N'si of your own?"

The Amryn mirage faded to nothing. The yearning and sense of purpose faded with her. Then, like storm clouds gathering on the horizon, an ancient and terrible sadness crept from the void.

What had been, was lost.

Disjointed feelings blew through her like a desert sandstorm. Dry shards of grief and longing. Scattered echoes of pain. Trying to convey what images could not. Ceaseless watchfulness and slow-burning hope. Sadness that stretched beyond time. The wrong not yet set to right. The determination to endure, to outlast the other.

Amryn rubbed her forehead. She could make no sense of what it was trying to tell her. Then, with a pang of frustration, it retreated. Many questions still clamored to be asked, but Amryn silenced them all. She had learned enough, for now.

Chapter 10

Branded

Hobi paced outside the cabin. He had heard her voice again during the past hour. Though too muffled to understand much of what she said, her tone was calmer than the circumstances warranted. Perhaps that meant the relic had robbed her of reason. He had to know.

He slid back the bolt and froze at the sound of footsteps. Amryn flung open the door, and he braced for the kill he didn't want to make.

"It serves rather than commands," she told him hurriedly. "The relic is a servant, an ancient device crafted by Watcher science. Created with one purpose, to belong to the person it bonds with. And it has an affinity for—"

Amryn stopped when she spotted the dagger in his hand. With a deliberate step closer, she locked eyes with him.

"If I were not the Amryn you know—"

"You would be dead now."

"So the dagger is a token of endearment?"

"A test," he said. "To see if the relic can be provoked to attack."

Hobi had no such test in mind. He'd been so stunned by her appearance, he forgot he had been preparing to kill her. Amryn seemed transformed. Healed, healthy, and... well, stunning.

"You look... your drakmu...."

"My what?"

"Drakmu. Your stripes," he said. "The N'si word for our birthmarks is drakmu. Well, the actual word is longer than you can say in a single breath, but it's seldom used. Our drakmu set out our fate, chronicle the lives we're destined to lead. From the moment we're born, we're marked by the dragons, N'in and N'si, in their language."

"Dragons, of course. I must have overlooked the dragons during all the pandemonium last night."

"I suppose yours are the relic's doing. The silver is... different."

Amryn reached to cover the markings that now graced her neck.

"Different. I've been called worse," she said. "I thought it was only showing me how I might look. With the mirage, I mean. I didn't realize the stripes were real."

"No, I didn't mean... it's only... our drakmu are a shade darker than our skin. Yours are lighter."

"And that's bad," she said.

"No, it's good. It's..."

Whether woman or nenan, no female had ever flustered Hobi, and he had no experience at being clumsy with words. On the contrary, being blunt had always sufficed before.

"Your drakmu are mesmerizing," he said.

Amryn smiled, and for a moment, he forgot to breathe. Had he lost his mind? A mysterious Watcher artifact had claimed and branded her, and Hobi chose *now* to want her for himself? Wanting her was pointless. He could never allow himself to touch her. Never.

"Get back in the cabin," he said. "Rest."

"I'm not tired."

"Barely a day ago, you were screaming like a banshee while a relic crawled under your skin. Now you're talking about it as if it were merely an intriguing specimen of Watcher science. It's unnatural to be so calm."

"Scientists are an adaptable sort," she said. "We're generally quite rational."

"We will discuss this when your mind is clearer," he said. "Return to your cabin."

Amryn seemed disinclined to follow his command. But, of course, she was. Who followed orders from a flustered N'si who blathered on about a few stripes on a neck?

"Captain, why did you follow me to the sea crypt?"

Hobi frowned. She was questioning *him* now. This newfound familiarity would not do. Not when they had the entire expedition ahead of them. But at least it confirmed she was undoubtedly still Amryn.

"I did not follow you," he said. "I was there before you."

"You still have not told me why."

And he never intended to, but the truth might restore some of her fear of him. He'd squandered that advantage when he turned into a tongue-tied boy at the sight of her transformation. *Mesmerizing.* Damn it all. Had he actually told Amryn Nisari he found her mesmerizing?

"Resa had something that belonged to me," he said. "I planned an exchange. Something of mine for something of hers."

"So you went there to kidnap me."

"Yes."

And yet, he had allowed her to leave. And he had gone emptyhanded to the N'si enclave to steal back Yuji's journal. Hobi had wagered his life on having the skill to penetrate the N'si stronghold hidden deep in the Janlin jungle, the last bastion of their kind, founded and guarded by Resa and her most loyal Fang. After the Chalyn War, little effort went into sorting N'si who had sided with the Ari rebels from N'si who had aided the Ari Empire. Instead, most in Wodi considered it an opportunity to be done with their age-old neighbors and rivals—the wily and unpredictable nenes of Tokju.

Resa, fortunately, had managed to hide those who opted not to take their chances in the sorting. She insisted her band of refugees would bide their time, training and planning until they were strong enough to reclaim their homeland.

Hobi, unfortunately, had an overdeveloped sense of purpose since his change. He was determined to find the homeland they had lost long before the Ari Empire crept across the desert sands and cornered them on the narrow strip of jungle and sand they named Tokju. To complicate matters, the change had also burdened him with a conscience.

That had left them at an impasse.

"How did you find the crypt?" said Amryn. "I told no one. I was careful never to be followed."

"I noticed you setting out from the harbor one night," he said. "Years ago, on that little dhow of yours. A young woman setting out alone at night struck me as odd. It was my turn at watch duty on one of Nefekari's ships anchored in the harbor, so I saw you return a few hours later. Months passed until I noticed you leave and return again."

"And you wondered why," said Amryn.

"A few questions. A little luck." He shrugged. "Learning you were Resa's daughter fit most of the puzzle together. Sailing the coast and asking myself where I might hide a corpse answered the rest."

"The turtle's head rock. You found it on your own."

"As did you. It was the logical choice for anyone looking for a place to hide the dead."

Amryn smiled again. It was not the response he expected. So much for instilling fear.

"Did you get it anyway?" she asked.

"Get what?"

"Whatever my mother had that belonged to you."

"I did."

"Good," she said. "I don't believe I have ever met anyone who got the better of her."

"Envious?"

"I was eight years old when Resa first took me on a kill. At ten, she taught me to cut up a corpse and roll the barrel into the river. When I turned twelve, she handed me the knife and left me to deal with the dead on my own. Telling her I'd rather not never mattered."

Hobi studied her anew. He hadn't considered what life must have been like for her, growing up as Resa's daughter. No wonder her self-control was damned near unbreakable. She had learned to ignore what she found too dark to dwell on.

"Perhaps rest is a good suggestion, Captain," she said. "Though I'm no longer afraid of losing myself to this... whatever it is... I need to learn more of its intent. For the sake of the crew."

She would follow his order and return to her cabin. But on her terms. A typical contrary N'si, he noted with grudging respect.

"And may I suggest you take your own advice?" she said. "Bolt my door and go get some sleep. I'll be here when you return."

"That may be your intent, but the relic may decide otherwise."

Amryn started to argue but stopped herself. She was, after all, a realist. Instead, she nodded in acquiescence.

"As you think best, Captain."

# # #

Amryn propped her chin on the rim of the porthole, watching dusk darken the sky. Despite her attempts, she'd learned little more of the relic or its intent. The few theories she now considered established facts she could count on one hand.

One, the relic was sentient. Two, it was not of flesh and blood but a metalmind, a creature created by Watcher science. Three, it existed to serve. Four, it now served her. That wasn't much, but it did convince her the ship and crew were in no danger.

Her list of unknowns was much longer. What sort of service was the relic designed to provide? How did it determine when or what service she required? Was that up to her or the relic to decide? And most importantly, how did she get rid of her unwanted guardian?

Those were questions she could pursue without fear of hurting anyone. Yes, she could report her findings without worrying the captain's uncanny nose for truth would smell her doubt. Perhaps then, he would dare a night's sleep in his own cabin again.

As she waited for the nightfall and the dinner tray that would follow, she passed the time listening to the whispers of the sea. She would have sworn she heard the captain sigh from beyond the door. It was a pensive sigh, soft and private, and not meant for her. Yet she heard him as clearly as if his breath had warmed her cheek.

And not only his sigh. She heard the little orange cat yawn. She heard Demon's scaly tail scrape against a plank. She heard Cook stirring a pot and Rafael setting a plate on a tray.

"Relic, I hear what I shouldn't be able to hear. Is this your doing?"

Amryn drew back as a disembodied ear materialized in the porthole glass. The ear, which she assumed to be her own, glowed as its skin peeled away, as if flayed by an invisible blade. Her new and ever-present companion showed her the silver spirals it had added to her ears to augment her hearing. Without asking her, of course. She rubbed her ear and turned away from the grisly mirage. There had to be less morbid means of communicating with this thing.

"Relic, do you have a name?"

Though she expected no answer, it seemed polite to ask. If she wanted to negotiate its retreat, convince it to retract its silver tendrils and let her be, she needed to get it to the bargaining table. To do that, she had to get it talking.

"Ufa, then. I will call you Ufa."

Ufa was the oldest Ari she knew, the eldest elder of all the Gyakari's kin. No one recalled his lineage, exactly. Ufa had simply always been there. Bent, bony, and grey-bearded, he had outlived his cousins and their progeny by keeping quiet and being content with being overlooked. He harbored no ambition other than continuing his solitary life and performing whatever tasks the latest Ari on the throne required of him. It seemed a dull existence, but it did ensure longevity.

The approval the relic shared was quick and clear. So, it was pleased to be given a name. A small step, but at least they were on the same path.

# # #

Three days passed in a fog of waiting and watching. Khaldun and Cora took shifts guarding the door long enough for Hobi to eat, wash, and see to the tasks a captain owed his ship. When Hobi unbolted the door for Rafael to carry trays in and out of the cabin, they sometimes found Amryn asleep. Other times, they found her in a trance, sitting on the edge of the bunk. Rarely did she acknowledge or even seem to notice them. He began to wonder if she ever would.

Then, when he unbolted the door on the third night of their vigil, Amryn spoke to him.

"No harm will come to you," she said in a voice raspy from disuse. "Any of you. And no harm to your ship. Not from the relic or from me. You have my word."

Hobi waited for the prickles up his spine that signaled a lie. None came.

"And you? Are you as safe as the rest of us?"

"Safe from the relic? Yes," she said. "Free of the relic? That's another matter."

"Cora has been brewing concoctions that might repel it. She can try if you're willing."

Amryn nodded. Neither of them expected it to work.

"I appreciate your concern," she said. "But confining me to this cabin is a choice I hope you reconsider. I gave you my word. I ask only to be allowed on deck for a while. To feel the wind and the sun again."

The conscience he wasn't supposed to have jabbed him again. Amryn was no more a killer than he was a kidnapper. There was a chance the relic may yet point them in the right direction. And that analytical mind of hers might prove helpful to the expedition. It was tempting to trust her and her newly acquired guardian.

"Call for me to accompany you in the morning. The door will be unbolted," he said and turned to go. "Good night, Amryn."

"Captain, wait," she said. "May I know your name?"

Hobi hesitated. He could not want her. He could not want anyone. Everything depended on him staying true to his purpose.

But Amryn had proven the strength of her will. So would he.

"My father named me Hobi."

Chapter 11

On Deck

Amryn paced, waiting for the first glimmer of light on the first day she would spend as she wished, not locked away like a thief. Sleep had eluded her the entire night. Whether it was her awareness of the relic or restlessness to be free, she couldn't say. After washing herself and combing the tangles from her hair, she buttoned on the loose cotton trousers, white shirt, and vest Rafael had altered to fit her. Well, fit wasn't quite the word, but the clothes were clean and covered what needed covering.

By now, dawn was breaking. The familiar sounds of the crew setting to work filtered down to her cabin with far more clarity than before. Though her keener hearing was Ufa's doing, and she resented the relic meddling with her senses, it was a small boon after all she'd been through. If Ufa served her, she could command it to remove its unsolicited "improvements" to her body, couldn't she? Perhaps she would do just that. After she was free from this prison ship.

The sun was well above the horizon. What was she waiting for? She was a scientist, not a criminal. And she was ready to know more about this grand expedition she had accidentally joined. The more she learned about her captors, the more easily she could plan her escape. Resa was alive, and that meant she was already chasing the *Seeker*. When her mother's ship appeared, Amryn would be ready.

She crept barefoot to the door and tried the latch. True to his word, Hobi had left it unbolted. She stuck her head out, relieved to find he had posted no guard, and hurried to the steps before he had a chance to change his mind.

When she reached the deck, she threw out her arms and laughed aloud. Glorious sunshine. How she had missed its warmth on her face. The wind smelled salty and sweet, and the sky was sapphire blue.

"Does the captain know yer wanderin' about?" Cora sauntered up to her.

"Oh, he won't mind."

"Is that so, lass? Because it sure looks like he minds."

Cora nodded past Amryn's shoulder, and Amryn turned to face a scowling N'si.

"Call for me to accompany you," said Hobi. "Were those not my words?"

"Yes, Captain. Your exact words," she said. "And conveniently, here you are, accompanying me."

"Do not make me regret my lenience," he said. "You may not be a killer, but you are still a stowaway."

"Guilty. So, I must earn my keep," she said. "Consider me one of your crew."

"My crew would have me consider otherwise. They were already wary of having Amryn Nisari aboard. For many, wariness turned to fear when they heard a mysterious relic had claimed your soul. On the open sea, those who are feared meet with unfortunate accidents."

Amryn glanced at the crew gathering around them. Suspicious frowns darkened more than a few faces, and a row of narrowed eyes met hers. Reflexively, Amryn reached to cover her silver markings. They must find her transformation disturbing. To them, she would seem an aberration.

"Back to work," Hobi ordered. Grumbling, they dispersed. Hobi waited until they were alone. "Come with me. Stay close until they learn you are no monster."

He headed for the helm, and Amryn followed without debate. He was protecting her, and whatever his reasons, she needed the shield his authority carried, for now. She climbed to the quarterdeck behind him.

At the wheel stood a giant.

"Amryn, meet Khaldun, our navigator."

Khaldun stared down at her, his dark eyes taking her measure. His was an unapologetic stare, without the veil of deference she was accustomed to receiving, and his sheer size made him a man to be taken seriously. Luckily, the tiny gold spectacles propped on his incongruously large face took some of the edge off the menace. Besides, he reminded her of Ottah.

"To where are you navigating us, Khaldun?"

Amryn's smile seemed to catch him off guard. Khaldun cast his captain a questioning glance, and Hobi nodded and took the helm. Khaldun drew a scroll from beside the ship's wheel and spread it on a bench.

It was a map, extraordinarily well-drawn and scaled to match the oversized cartographer's hands. Amryn stepped in beside him, taking in the fine detail and trying to get her bearings.

"Where are we now?" she said.

Khaldun's fingertip and Ufa's glowing dot answered in tandem. Khaldun seemed not to notice the green speck blinking on his fingernail.

"And where are we going?" she said.

Khaldun's hand brushed an arc over a rather large section of the map. Amryn did the quick calculations. They were headed for a vague stretch of open ocean hundreds of leagues wide and at least two weeks away.

"You don't quite know, do you?"

"We're searching for the lost city of Maurya," said Hobi. "*Lost*, as in not easily found."

Khaldun shrugged.

"Only one person ever found Maurya and returned to tell the tale," said Hobi. "His name was Yuji. My father."

Amryn nearly laughed, but the looks on their faces stopped her. Maurya was a myth, a fanciful old tale nannies told children too young to know better. So, this was their grand expedition?

"And Yuji told you where to find this elusive city?" She suppressed a grin.

"Not directly. He died when I was young," said Hobi. "A few years ago, I learned he had kept a journal he intended to give me when I was older. Yuji's journal was my inheritance, and I would have its secrets. But, first, I had to reclaim it from Resa."

"Why would my mother have your father's journal?"

"You would have to ask her."

Amryn had learned to be leery of coincidences. Reason said the odds of Resa and Yuji being tied up in some delusional search for a mythical lost city were statistically infinitesimal. Her mother was far too practical for such nonsense.

"Yuji was a dreamer, a poet at heart," said Hobi. "Rare enough, I admit, but even N'si dream. His descriptions of his time in Maurya are compelling. The details he chronicled, fascinating. His recollections have such clarity I am convinced Maurya exists."

"But Yuji was bad at math." Khaldun gave a deep chuckle. It was the first time Amryn had heard him speak, and the rich rumble in his voice made her want to hear him again. If the *Seeker* would soon be crisscrossing leagues of empty sea in search of a legend, they should have plenty of time for conversation. But their expedition to nowhere also meant escape was not an option. Not until they admitted Maurya didn't exist and headed back for land. Or until Resa's ship crested the horizon.

Amryn studied the map for a moment. Might she nudge them towards that conclusion a bit sooner? It was worth a try.

"Ufa, where is Maurya?" she said.

To her surprise, a glowing green dot promptly set to blinking on Khaldun's map. The relic did have a sense of humor, after all.

"Ufa?" said Hobi.

"The relic. I named it," she said distractedly. "Show them, Ufa. Can you?"

Hobi and Khaldun exchanged dubious glances. Apparently not. Amryn touched her fingertip to the green dot.

"Here," she said. "Ufa says you can find your lost city here."

Chapter 12

Barrels

Another week passed before she discovered his secret.

"Captain, we're runnin' low on water." Cora wiped a sleeve over her sweaty brow.

"How low?" said Hobi.

"Down to the last barrel," she said. "Come tomorrow, we'll be parched."

Cora pushed back her hat and walked away, unconcerned, as if she hadn't just delivered the dire news that they were all about to die of thirst. Hobi set aside the nets he'd been mending and, without a word, headed for the bow. Amryn followed, more than a little bewildered.

The crew lowered empty barrels into the sea and hoisted them back filled with seawater. Cora rolled an empty barrel across the deck and positioned it beside one filled with brine. Then she set a wooden trough atop both barrels, balancing an end on each, and stepped back.

Hobi rolled up his sleeves and dipped his hand into the seawater. Methodically, he drew his hand from the barrel, and a trail of waterdrops darkened the dry trough. A trickle of water followed his hand, like ducklings following a hen. The trickle swelled to a stream, and his hand led the water down into the empty barrel. Hobi stood with his hand in the slowly filling barrel, focused on the water flowing over the trough. Sweat beaded on his face.

When the barrel was full, Cora hammered on a lid and rolled up the next barrel. She noticed Amryn's frown and laughed.

"Never seen an elemental work his magic?" she said.

"Magic? You cannot be serious."

"Nah. Naught serious about a wee bit of sorcery."

Amryn rolled her eyes. "Honestly, Cora. What is he doing?"

"Callin' the clean water out of the brine."

Amryn remembered what Rafael had told her. *The Seeker never runs out of fresh water.*

"Comes in handy, so to speak." Cora winked. "Make yerself useful and roll up another barrel."

After filling the last empty barrels, Hobi retired to his cabin for the afternoon. At dinner, he reappeared as if nothing had happened. He darted glances at her over his cup, looking like a child caught at mischief. Around the table, the others drank and dined, unworried they served a captain who commanded the sea itself to do his bidding. Instead, they chatted over trivialities, as if it were perfectly normal to be trapped on a ship that could sail forever, never needing to return to port. Well, perhaps not forever. Even with food barrels filling the storage space water barrels would typically occupy, their food would eventually need replenishing. Eventually.

Unless he could simply turn fish into cabbages.

No wonder he had stopped bolting her door. She was his captive all the same.

Sorcerer. No, it had to be a trick. She refused to consider such nonsense.

Amryn left the table. She needed air. Needed to see the world still existed beyond this ship sailing to nowhere and its spellbound crew. Most of all, she needed to find some shred of science that might explain the inexplicable.

Instead of making for her usual spot, balancing her way out the bowsprit to sit and watch another nightfall claim the horizon, Amryn went to the stern instead. She needed to hold on to the last golden rays of the sun sinking in the west. Tonight, seeing where she was headed seemed too unsettling. She longed for the comfort of where she had been.

Gripping the railing, she stared down at the ship's wake. The sea roiled beneath the hull, agitated by something unnatural passing through its usually empty expanse. Red and gold rays from the sunset battled the frothy black water. The *Seeker* left chaos in its wake, and how could it not? Even nature followed rules. Life adhered to logic. But from the moment she jumped off the wharf in Ealim, she began questioning whether she had ever known what was real.

"Another gift from my father." Hobi leaned beside her. "Perhaps I should have prepared you."

"Could he not give you something normal? A plot of land. A bag of gold. A nice signet ring?"

"Yuji was not normal."

Amryn bit back a retort. Nothing she could say could be any blunter.

"But then, neither are you," said Hobi. "Not anymore."

"Ufa may be hard to explain when I return. At first," she said. Muttering to an invisible guardian. Mirages only her eyes saw. They would think she had lost her mind. "But one can always explain science."

"So, explain me." Hobi propped against the rail and crossed his ankles.

Of course, there was an explanation for his ability. Accept his challenge, explain away the inexplicable, and she would set the world he had turned upside down right again.

"What else can you do besides separate clean water from brine?"

"Swim underwater for as long as I wish," he said.

"An impressive feat of endurance," she said. "Achievable with sufficient training."

"Bend a current to send fish into a net," he said.

"A matter of timing. Luck. Coincidence."

Hobi picked up a coil of rigging rope from the deck. He held up the neatly clipped end, and his lips twitched in mischief again.

"And I can do this."

Sparks crackled between them, and tiny fireflies danced on his fingertips. The tip of the rope lit like a candlewick. Amryn blinked at the flickering flame, and the world she thought she understood took leave of its senses. Science laughed and abandoned her, beguiled by the magic shining in a sorcerer's amber eyes.

#   #   #

After a sleepless night spent wrestling doubts she would never have doubted before, the stars faded too soon. Morning dawned red and surly as her mood and storm clouds gathering in the west stalked the ship like hungry jackals. The sea's foul temper infected the crew, as well, and they set about the day's chores with none of their usual chatter.

Amryn busied herself with cleaning the starboard cannons. Distracted, but not careless. She polished brass, oiled carriage wheels, and replaced fraying tether ropes. Though Hobi had yet to declare her a member of his crew, she worked beside them daily, trying to allay their fears of the royal-blooded, Fang-trained, silver-striped, half-N'si stowaway with a sentient Watcher artifact burrowed into her flesh. After several weeks of refraining from murdering them in their sleep, she found most of them could look at her without scowling.

"Lash down that cannon, lass. The storm's upon us," Cora said as she strode past. The busy empath and ship's quartermaster was one of the few Amryn considered unlikely to toss her overboard, even if no one were watching. Cora had a keen sense for the weather and its whims, and she had no sooner passed than the wind whipped across the deck.

Amryn secured an end of the lashing, tightening the knot as Nefekari had taught her. She felt the first drops of rain on her neck and stood to thread the rope through the carriage bolts. Rafael caught her hand.

"I will finish for you, m'sita. Get below. The captain will answer to Resa if he allows you to be swept away, yes?"

Amryn hesitated. The task was hers to see done, but Rafael might take offense if she refused. She needed no new slights to atone for, so she let him have the rope and turned to leave. The wind gusted with the storm's fury, and the rain came pouring down.

"All hands, brace," Hobi shouted above the shrieking wind, through rain so heavy, Amryn could no longer see him at the helm. The ship lurched, and the slick deck rumbled beneath her feet. As she struggled to right herself, she glanced back to the sound of creaking metal.

The cannon was rolling towards her. A half-ton of brass on the loose. Amryn dove out of its path and landed hard. The awkward fall knocked the breath out of her. The ship pitched on another wave, and the cannon's charge slowed. Amryn scrambled to her feet as the deck tilted again and sent the cannon careening.

Its blunt brass nose crashed into a stack of barrels. Splintered wood scattered in the wind. A roar of anguish rose from amidst the debris. Amryn crawled towards the cries. The rain let up on its pummeling, and she wiped her eyes. An arm's length away, a knot of mangled, twisted barrel staves had jammed a carriage wheel.

Beyond it, Cora was wedged between the cannon and the foremast. Khaldun came staggering across the deck and put his shoulder to the cannon's nose, straining to free Cora's leg. Amryn got to her feet and shouldered in beside him. An eerie calm enveloped her, slowing time and numbing senses until she was hardly aware of the storm raging around her. As her hands tightened on the carriage, Ufa rippled under her skin. Silver threads wove a mesh of tendril and muscle down her limbs, and her arms shone like candlewands. Together, Amryn and Khaldun hefted the carriage and cannon. They held it firm until the ship steadied and the wind ceased its shrieking.

The weight left her hands as others came to secure the loose cannon. The surge of strength coursing through her body began to wane, and time seemed to resume its flow. The storm had passed, she noted, as her awareness returned from whatever distant star it had gone.

"Amryn," a voice drew her back. "Amryn, look at me."

Focusing took more effort than it should. Warmth brushed her shoulders, and a blanket quieted her chattering teeth. Hobi was there, she sensed from the *rightness* his presence brought. Until she and Ufa had done what needed doing, he belonged with them. *What?* It was a random thought, either her own or Ufa's, she would try to make sense of later.

"Masterful sailing, Captain," she said. "I see we still have a ship to stand on."

"Though not all of us are standing."

"How is Cora?" she said.

"She'll heal," he said. "Quicker than most. She has a knack for it, you know. And you?"

"Fine."

"Amryn."

"I am cold, wet, and exhausted. Rattled and bewildered. Oh, and I forgot. Famished," she admitted. "Need I go on?"

Hobi picked her up, blanket and all.

"What are you doing?" she said.

"Fixing you."

He carried her to his cabin and left her to change into dry clothes. The Ari robes were his own, she supposed, and the sleeves hung down to her knees. Because, of course, they did. Goblin meowed her disapproval, and Amryn had to agree, but it felt good to be out of wet trousers. Hobi returned in dry clothes, carrying a tray of food— flatbread, cheese, and olives—and a carafe of wine. Demon slithered in after him, or more likely, after the olives.

"We dispensed with cold and wet," he said. "Our next challenge— famished."

They sat together at the small writing table, as if it were meant for dining, and shared a quiet meal, as if they did so every day. Though eating took precedence over talking, talk came easily enough, and Goblin and Demon found they preferred having two sets of hands offering them tidbits.

Amryn set down her cup. No more wine. She was feeling far too comfortable.

"I should go," she said.

"You should lie down and rest. Exhausted was next on the list of complaints I was to fix."

"I will rest, Hobi, but not here."

Amryn caught herself too late. Hobi, not Captain. She had called him by his name. He must have noticed. How could he not? He let her familiarity go unremarked.

"I wish I could continue giving you that choice," he said. "But after today, I cannot. You will share my cabin."

"You can't decree something like that. It's unseemly."

"Only if you make it," he said. "I was not asking you to be my lover."

"Asking? I'm sorry, did I miss the part where you *asked* me anything?"

"Then let me start over. Amryn, will you please allow me to keep us both from having our throats slit?"

"Share my cabin, or we'll die." Amryn rolled her eyes. "Tell me someone didn't actually fall for that line before."

"That's irrelevant." He ran a hand through his hair. "Amryn, a captain's authority is tenuous. More so on the Endless Ocean. Ports grow distant, and challengers are as close as a single lapse in judgment. Lose the confidence of the crew, and mutiny is not far behind."

"The crew defers to your every word. I have seen how—"

"How they obey an N'si sorcerer? How I command their loyalty and respect?" Hobi shook his head. "They defer to the power they believe I hold, and the magic and luck I bring to our expeditions. Today, they saw you wield magic to rival my own."

"Ufa is not magic," she said. "And I am not your rival."

"Power is relative to the power in its proximity. Another imperfection in man's perception of the world. Your strength diminishes my own in their eyes. Just as my strength lessens their estimation of yours. In that sense, we are rivals."

"To be pitted against one another," she said. Growing up in Ari palaces meant she was familiar with the nuances of power. "They choose a champion, and the other falls from favor."

"And both are weakened," he said. "For your sake and mine, until this expedition is over, they need to see your strength belongs to me. You belong to me."

"Why not the other way around?"

"My ship. My rules."

Amryn hesitated, which she at once regretted. Hesitating implied she might agree with him, which she had no intention of doing. Ufa distracted her with a mirage of Hobi bound and gagged in his chair, and Goblin and Demon beseeching her with their pleading little eyes. That was hardly fair. The traitor was arguing Hobi's case for him.

"I could kill you in your sleep," she reminded him.

"Your first kill?" Hobi shrugged, a casually seductive rise and fall of his shoulder, as if he knew no other way to shrug. "Is that my thanks for not tossing a stowaway overboard?"

"Stowaways *intend* to leave with the ship. How was I to know you'd go sneaking out of port before the break of dawn?"

Hobi busied himself at the desk, failing to hide the amusement playing on his lips.

"You will not kill me, Amryn Nisari," he said. "Because I will give you no cause."

He was right, and it irked her that he knew her weakness. She was no Fang.

"Very well, then. But let us be clear about the arrangements. If I am to—"

"The bed is yours," he said. "I will take the floor."

#   #   #

Amryn slept the afternoon away. Hobi was stretched out in the sunny window seat when she woke, absently scratching Demon's chin and reading his father's journal. With his long hair unbound and wariness not tensing his brow, he seemed too young to be captaining his own ship. Nenes aged more slowly than men, of course, but N'si tended to get themselves killed before their longevity matched others of their kind. She wondered how long Hobi had been trying to survive alone.

"How old are you?" she said.

Hobi glanced up and set aside his reading. He shifted Demon to the cushion and stood in one fluid motion, no small feat considering the lizard was as big as his leg.

"Ah, we can mark exhaustion off the list," he said. "That only leaves rattled and bewildered. Though I should leave you a little something to deal with on your own. It might boost your self-esteem."

"Oh, my. I may succumb to hysteria at any moment. Do you have fainting salts ready?"

"Hysterical and disheveled after an afternoon with me." Hobi tossed her a hairbrush. "Not the impression we want to give at dinner. Your trousers are dry. Tidy up, and I'll return for you."

"That was overly blunt."

"I see no point in dancing around what can be said directly," he said. "It is time for dinner. You are not presentable. Fix that."

"Do you ever ask instead of command?"

"Why would I ask you to do what obviously needs doing?"

"Demon has better manners," she muttered.

"Oh, I've tried corrupting him." Hobi sighed. "I'm afraid he's hopeless."

Chapter 13

Pushed

Hobi pretended to find something that needed doing on deck, but his mind was on Amryn and the murderous look in her eyes as he left. He had pushed her too far, presumed too much. But damn the fates, he had no choice.

He needed her.

Luck had put her on his ship. The prism's reaction to Amryn and her relic meant he had to do whatever it took to keep them cooperating. Amryn's growing connection to Ufa and her ability to tap into ancient Watcher power might hold the key to his search.

But he had lived alone for too long, detached from those living their lives around him. The few he relied on, and only because he must, he kept at a distance. Even Khaldun, who he might have counted a friend if his life were not consumed by chasing a dream. Had he forgotten how to live with someone else? Not that he'd been particularly adept at it before. He had despised and feared Gar and found his brothers tediously stupid. When he was young, it had been hard to be a loner. Though he tried to blend in with his kind, they continued to disappoint him.

Hobi had always been drawn to the sea. He would stand on the beach, staring out at the horizon. His brothers had never stared out at the sea in yearning. They had never known there was anything to yearn for.

"They're waiting." Khaldun stuck his big head up from below deck.

Hobi returned to his cabin. He raised his hand and paused. He was uncertain whether to knock at his own door. *Strength evokes, not provokes.*

Amryn opened the door while he stood debating his conscience. She was transformed, yet again. The simple sailor's garb accentuated her lithe body. He was amazed at how quickly she tamed her glorious hair into braided perfection. She was everything he could not have.

"You are perfect," he said. "Come."

"Wait," she said. "Against my better judgment, I am about to face the crew and allow them to believe you bedded me today."

Hobi tensed, and for a fleeting moment, he wondered what it would be like to hold her. He squelched the reckless urge.

"We'll be making a pretense," said Amryn. "However, you and I know nothing happened."

"We came to an understanding. We made a pact for the sake of the expedition. I do not consider that *nothing*."

"Nor do I," she said, chagrined. "Understanding is more enduring than lust. But thinking things through is what I do, and preparing to face the crew set me wondering. How would I behave if you had? Would I smile? Touch your hand?"

"No, you cannot," he said too quickly. Then, to cover his lapse, he grasped at the first idea to dart through his mind. He went to the wardrobe and opened a drawer.

"Mystique," he said, pulling on doeskin gloves. "Let them wonder whose touch must be contained. Is it your power or mine that is too potent to risk sharing an inadvertent brush of skin?"

"You would make a good charlatan, Captain," she said. "Should you ever tire of hunting lost treasure, you have a talent for trickery."

Amryn took his gloved hand and led the way. The sound of voices stalled her steps, and she stopped just out of sight of the dining crew.

"I am not comfortable with this," she said.

"I can tell," he said. "Your drakmu tinge to pink when you blush."

"Was that supposed to be helpful?"

"No, but this is." Hobi lifted her chin with his finger. "Hold your head high, Amryn Nisari. You're stronger than you know. This ship is our realm. Rule it."

Amryn bit her lip and walked on, and a hush fell over the crew as they entered. Forks paused, and eyes fell on the possessive hand he held at her back. The chair beside his cleared, and Amryn claimed her place, poised and regal as a queen taking her throne. Hobi sat at the head of the table, covered her hand with his for a moment of reassurance, then took off his gloves and folded them beside his plate.

Dinner resumed, subdued at first, then with the ease of seasoned adventurers adapting to new circumstances. The *Seeker's* crew adapted with the ease of having survived strange circumstances before. Their expeditions with Hobi had given them abundant practice.

Cora was at her place to his right. The walking cane propped against her chair was her only concession to her injury. Broken bones did not heal overnight, even for an empath of her skill. Khaldun sat beside her, silent and brooding as ever, casting frequent and unsubtle glances at Amryn. Their charade did not fool him, but his silence did not betray them.

"Captain, I can hold my tongue no longer." Rafael pushed back his chair. "Dio mio, such an unpleasant matter. But I must have it said or cannot take another meal at your table."

Hobi narrowed his eyes. He had expected a challenge, but not so openly or so soon.

"Dire words, M'ser d'Ortega," said Amryn. "I'm afraid you may spoil my appetite."

"Pardon me, M'sita. To distress you distresses me doubly," said Rafael. "But if I may beg your—"

"Speak your mind," Hobi said curtly.

Rafael nodded and took a long sip of wine. Whatever this was about, he was drawing it out.

"The loose cannon," said Rafael. "M'sita Amryn was lashing it down when the storm struck. I took the rope. I told her I would finish." He hung his head. "I am to blame."

"It happened so quickly," said Amryn. "Who can say whether either of us could have secured the carriage in time?"

Hobi tapped her knee under the table. Had Resa taught her so little? Mercy granted without penance was soon forgotten. A confession without accountability was an opportunity squandered.

"Rafael took the rope," he said. "He took the responsibility, as well."

Amryn's look disagreed, but she didn't press the matter.

"You will serve Cora," said Hobi. "See that she wants for nothing. Tend to her tasks so that she may recover in leisure. She will decide when you have toiled sufficiently to compensate for her pain."

"My own manservant." Cora laughed. "I rather like the sound o' that."

"Gracia, Captain. I humbly accept your penance." Rafael bowed, then looked up and winked. "Cora, mi amore. I shall tend to your every desire."

Guffaws and whistles went up around the table. After another round of wine, Rafael stood again and lifted his cup.

"To the *Seeker* and her good fortune," he said. "An empath who can stave off death itself. A sorcerer with the cunning of a fox and the wisdom of a sage. A princess who can summon the strength of the gods. My friends, we sail in the company of the finest witchery on the seas!"

#   #   #

Later that night, Khaldun came to their cabin. After a perfunctory knock, he let himself in, unconcerned he might be interrupting a tryst. Khaldun was not fooled in the least.

Without preamble, he handed Amryn a short coil of rope. She unwound it and frowned at the knotted end.

"Nefekari's shackle hitch," she said. "I tied this knot."

"Your knot held," said Khaldun.

Amryn looked again, and her frown deepened. She offered Hobi the rope.

"It was cut loose," she said. "I had finished knotting this end to a carriage bolt. Even with the storm, with one corner secured, if the knot did not fail—"

"The cannon might have shifted in its bay, but it would not have gone careening across the deck," said Hobi.

"The moment you turned your back," said Khaldun.

"Someone meant to kill you," said Hobi. "And might have succeeded if Cora hadn't shouted a warning. And if your reflexes were not quicker than most."

"Rafael was there," said Amryn. "He might have seen someone else near the cannon."

Khaldun looked at Hobi. The same suspicion occurred to them both. Amryn caught the exchange, and her eyes widened.

"It can't be," she said. "Khaldun, why didn't you say something earlier? We might have questioned him at dinner."

"I sometimes regret my words, never my silence," said Khaldun.

"Rafael took the blame for the accident," said Hobi. "A killer wouldn't call attention to himself so brazenly. Our suspicion may be misplaced."

"Whoever did this doesn't know we have evidence," said Amryn. "The schemer is probably feeling smug tonight, convinced he has us believing it was an accident."

"An advantage we will keep, for now," said Hobi.

Khaldun studied Amryn. "Your relic did not warn you."

"If he tried, I didn't understand him," she said.

"Yet, you knew which way to leap," said Khaldun.

Amryn touched the relic fused to her chest. Hobi had grown so accustomed to seeing its onyx glint, he sometimes forgot it had not always been a part of her. Her silver drakmu paled as she considered Khaldun's observation.

"Perhaps Ufa did guide me. Nudge me somehow," she said. "It's hard to know, thinking back. We are still rather inept at understanding one another."

"We are nearing our destination," said Hobi. "Ufa seems to know where we are going. And with more precision than my father's journal. We need you and Ufa on speaking terms."

"We're making slow progress at that, I'm afraid," said Amryn.

"Then we must assist you. Practice begins tomorrow." Khaldun stood to leave. "Keep her close, Captain."

Chapter 14

Lost

Amryn immersed herself in crafting a language both she and an ancient Watcher device could understand. Khaldun proved a tireless practice partner, methodically recording their trials and devising new exercises. Hobi often joined them for the repetitive drills and was the first to coax a few consistent responses out of Ufa. Soon, they were agreeing on such rudimentary symbols as ship, sun, cat, and dagger.

Though far from discussing the existential questions of life, they were at least communicating. Amryn formed the signs with her hands. Ufa replied, forming the signs as silver runes on her skin. She had abandoned trying to speak to Ufa aloud. Though she sometimes got a response in the form of a mirage only she could see, Ufa more often seemed perplexed by her words. Their unique new language of symbols was proving more reliable than writing words on paper, then waiting for Ufa to shape mirages in response. Amryn needed only her hands, Ufa needed only his silver tendrils, and Khaldun and Hobi could share in the conversation.

Ufa was downright giddy over their breakthrough. And after a few weeks, it was hard to get him to hush.

There had been no further accidents, and she and Hobi had settled into a comfortable, though wary, routine. At times, he even seemed to enjoy her company.

Amryn pretended to anticipate discovering the lost city as eagerly as the rest of them. It was possible they would find something before Resa caught up to them. A sunken Watcher airship, perhaps. A craft larger and older than the few skimmers left behind from the last Cycle. But finding an entire city no one noticed floating in the Endless Ocean? Hobi's father had a vivid imagination.

When Khaldun declared the evening practice session done, Amryn tucked her jambiya in her belt and headed for the bowsprit. She no longer dreaded what might lie ahead, only the disappointment Hobi and his crew would feel once they got there. Though she was slow to admit it, she had also stopped scanning the horizon for Ari ships coming to her rescue. Oh, they were coming, of that, she had no doubt. But somehow, it seemed less urgent than her curiosity over what might be waiting ahead.

The night was clear. Twinkling pinpoints of starlight filled an endless velvet canopy of sky. At sea, the sky made her feel larger. On land, she was just another speck, settling in the dust with all the other specks. As she balanced her way out the bowsprit, a movement startled her, and she reached for her jambiya. It was Hobi, waiting for her. She slid out to meet him.

"She prowls my ship with the grace of a tiger," he said with a side-eyed glance.

"The sea must draw the N'si out in me," she said.

"It's always been there. You just didn't see it in yourself."

They sat in the quiet for a while, listening to water lapping against the hull and sails luffing in the breeze. Water and wind. Companions for as long as the earth had been spinning. Perhaps even longer.

Eventually, Hobi stirred beside her. He reached and took off the pendant he wore around his neck. The diamond prism caught the starlight. Like the fluff of a dandelion scattering on the wind, the light burst into specks of color. His prism intrigued her, as always. Swirling patterns and shifting colors. It never looked the same twice.

"Here, hold this," said Hobi.

Amryn wavered. She would never forgive herself if she dropped it into the sea. It was Hobi's dearest memento of his father. Carefully, she took the prism and wrapped the silver chain around her thumb.

"Closer," he said. "Bring it closer to Ufa."

She lifted the prism to her chest, and it grew warm in her palm. The lights flickering inside it grew brighter, and the usually dark face of the relic lit in response. She watched, mesmerized by the exchange of patterns and colors. And so, it continued, flicker and response, between prism and relic.

"What does that seem to you?" said Hobi.

"A conversation," said Amryn. "How is that possible?"

"I don't know. The prism reacts to Ufa and has from the start. It's time we knew more."

"What do you suppose they're saying to each other?"

"Ask him."

Amryn held her empty hand between Ufa and the prism. She signed the question.

"Ufa and necklace talk? Words?"

The flickering lights continued. If Ufa saw the question, he was ignoring her. She was about to form the signs again when the lights winked out. Ufa and the prism went dark in tandem, and Ufa's silver reply appeared on her arm.

"No words. Eyes."

Ufa summoned a mirage in her empty palm. The images shifted in rapid succession, denser and clearer than any Ufa had shown her yet. Scenes flitted past, one into another. A closed door morphed into a veiled face. Palace walls rose and crumbled. A child hid under a bed, frightened and alone. Minnows darted into the reeds, hiding as a crocodile swam past. A crystal key turned in a lock. A black mountain took on the face of a beast. Shoulders and limbs formed from the mountain's stone, muscles bulging. The stone beast rose from the earth and reached for the sky, devouring all the stars in the heavens.

The mirages faded, leaving the emptiness of a thousand dying worlds and the sadness of hope forever lost. Tears stung her eyes and trickled down her cheeks. Fingers tightened on her sleeve, and she looked up. Hobi's cheeks were wet, too.

"What Ufa showed me—"

"I saw," he said. "The face of the beast. The face carved on Kitsune's mountain."

"Kitsune rose up against the Watchers," she said. "Conquered them here, then claimed their empire in the stars."

"The Watchers created Ufa and his kind. So, it's understandable their demise distresses him. But my father's pendant? I saw Ufa's mirages because the prism mirrored them for me."

"Because the Watchers created the prism, too," she realized.

"But how did my father end up with a Watchers' relic? And why didn't he tell me?"

"He may not have known. Without Ufa to get it talking, we wouldn't know either."

Hobi took the prism back. He stared at it for a long moment, then hung it around his neck.

"What we saw," he said. "The images of veils and people hiding."

"Watchers hiding from the beast," said Amryn. "What if some of them are hiding still?"

"Those who hide don't think they are lost," said Hobi.

A chill tingled Amryn's neck. The lost city Yuji found. The relic he took from there.

"The Watchers. They're hiding in Maurya," she said.

Chapter 15

Ordinary

The lost city awaited them, and only days away, Khaldun and Ufa agreed. Hobi had grown quieter, and Amryn's sense of unease grew with each passing sunrise.

At night, Hobi came to the cabin after she had fallen asleep and often left before she woke. Even when he was there with her, he wasn't. Preoccupied and distant, he retreated to the window seat with Demon, where he read Yuji's journal from beginning to end, and then again. Goblin soon grew tired of his moods and shifted allegiances. Amryn was hers now, instead.

So, when Amryn woke one morning to find the cabin empty but for herself, she worried. On deck, she found the entire crew gathered at the rails.

"What's wrong?" she asked Rafael.

"Ah, m'sita. He has only just begun. You have not missed much."

Goblin clawed her way up a barrel and leapt to Amryn's shoulder. Her tiny growl tickled Amryn's ear and drew a chuckle from Rafael.

"Come. Tell your guardian to spare my life, and I will show you a wonder. Your handsome young captain makes more sorcery to delight."

Rafael led her through the milling crew, brushing aside elbows and squeezing his way past shoulders.

"Make way," he said. "You see this before, my friends. Make way for our captain's companion. Let her witness this wonder."

With a grand sweep of his arm, Rafael motioned her to the rail. The others were leaning out, pointing, and chattering. Amryn stepped in to see what had them so excited.

Hobi was down there, beside the ship, sitting in the waves. Not swimming or treading water—no, that would have been normal. No, he was sitting cross-legged *on* the water, hands resting on his knees, bobbing in the waves like a pelican. And naked as a seal. In a circle around him, yellow buoys marked the edges of a fishing net.

"Tuna," cried one of the crew.

"It's a big yellow-fin," another shouted.

"What on earth is he doing down there?" said Amryn.

"Fishing," said Rafael.

In under an hour, the net was teeming with fish, prawns, and lush green kelp. Cora blew a whistle that seemed to shake Hobi from his trance. He caught the grapple line Cora tossed him and fastened it to the net, then stood upright and walked towards the ship. *Walked?* The waves rose and reshaped beneath his feet. The water spiraled and flattened to receive each footstep, matching his stride.

Khaldun began hauling up the catch, and others hurried to help. Hand over fist, Hobi climbed the grapple line and hoisted himself over the rail.

Standing barefoot on the deck, wet and sleek as a creature from the sea, Hobi scanned the crew, searching until he locked eyes with her. Something primal lurked in his gaze as he stood there, breathing hard from the exertion. Something wild and untamed. Barely human.

Amryn stepped back, and someone tossed him a towel he tied at his hip. When he looked up again, his eyes held the deepest weariness Amryn had ever seen. Without a word, Hobi turned and left.

Amryn started after him, but Rafael caught her arm.

"Let him go," he said. "The captain must... be alone... until he is himself again."

Rafael joined the crew, already preoccupied with admiring and sorting the bounty in the net. Amryn watched them, more worried now than when she woke in the empty cabin. If Hobi was not himself, who was he? What was he?

"Not a sight for the fainthearted, was he?" Cora came up behind her.

"He looked ill," she said. "Go tend him, Cora, please."

"Aye, summonin' takes the wind out of his sails for a few hours. Sometimes more." Cora sighed. "Every mindgift takes its toll. And an elemental's gift is one of the hungriest. I've scolded him to take care, but he pays me no mind."

"But why now? We have food. We're nearing our destination. There's no reason to expend himself at this point in the expedition."

"Captain says it's the N'si way. Celebrate before the big event, not after. If fate turns sour on us...." Cora shrugged. "At least we ate well before we died."

Amryn was incredulous such fatalism came from someone optimistic enough to be searching for a mythical city. Hobi couldn't expect to fail, could he?

"Don't look so horrified, lass," said Cora. "N'si humor. Ye get used to it."

Amryn doubted she would ever get used to anything about this N'si. But they were bound by a pact of pretense, one she could hardly abandon in the middle of the Endless Ocean. Still, Hobi would have to be more forthcoming if he expected her to keep up this charade. She wanted answers.

Amryn slipped away unnoticed. Outside their cabin, she stopped to question her judgment. *The captain must be alone.* She pushed the door open a crack and peeked inside. It was dim, and the curtains were drawn. The window seat was empty. Hobi was lying in bed, his back to her. She held her breath, watching as his shoulder trembled.

"Go away," he said, his voice hoarse with pain.

Amryn stepped inside and drew the bolt. She went to the wardrobe for a blanket, draped it over him, and sat on the edge of the bed.

"Leave me," he said. The tremor in his voice was almost a sob.

"Would you leave me like this?" she said.

He didn't answer. He didn't have to. They both knew he wouldn't.

Amryn did what Hobi had done for her. She sat with him. Knees curled to her chest, listening to each shuddering breath, she sat beside him, offering him her silence. Not questioning, not chiding, just being there.

Eventually, Hobi rolled to his back. Her heart leapt to her throat at the sight of his face, wet with tears. To know he was accustomed to bearing such pain alone, enduring the burden in silence, was heartrending.

"I did not want you to see this," he said. "But you make a habit of not doing what I want."

"How long does it last? The pain?" she said. "Let me get something to ease you. I'm sure Cora has—"

"It's not what you think." Hobi heaved a sigh. "It isn't pain, but a melancholy that overcomes me. Devours me. A darkness of spirit that is not my own. It passes."

She reached to brush his cheek, and he recoiled as if her hand scalded him.

"Amryn, no," he said. "I cannot give in to a touch—even yours."

The puzzle came together. The gloves on his hands. The times he held her sleeve instead of her arm. When he wrapped her in a blanket before carrying her. *Let them wonder whose touch must be contained.*

"Whatever I name this thing, be it magic or curse, its presence passed from my father to me. I sensed the change come over me... while holding on to my father as he lay dying. My arms went numb, and then everything went black. When I came to my senses, I was no longer myself. Or not only myself. Something... left my father and passed to me."

"Are you afraid this presence might harm someone?" said Amryn. Was that why he had feared Ufa would leave her and attack another?

"No, I fear it might leave me," he said. "And then, I will be what I was before. Ordinary."

"Hobi, you are the least ordinary person I know."

"The change set me on a path I couldn't have followed on my own. It made me something more. And without it, I'll be unable to finish the task I started. I cannot let that happen."

"The task is finding Maurya?"

"The task is seeing N'si survive. Doing so means finding the homeland we left behind."

Hobi sat and ran a hand through his hair. He looked too young to be carrying the survival of his people on his shoulders. The N'si were her people, too. Maybe there was a reason she had chosen his ship of all the ships in the harbor.

"In Maurya, Yuji met others like us. Better than us, or better than what we allowed ourselves to become. What we were meant to be before we lost our direction."

Hobi studied her, deciding whether to say more.

"When Yuji returned, he went to see Resa in Naré. He told her what he had found."

"Your father told my mother about Maurya." Amryn frowned. "Why her?"

"Because there was a time when they mattered to one another. Long ago, before whatever happened to make them part ways. Yuji knew Resa would believe him, and he trusted her with the secrets he had sworn to keep."

Amryn had to ask. "Are you their child?"

"No. I'm certain of that. They had both moved on with their lives by then," he said. "But after I was born, Yuji went to see her again. He warned her Ari rebels were visiting Tokju. Stirring discontent. Recruiting allies. He feared being on the wrong side of a rebellion would be the end of the N'si houses."

"He was right to worry," said Amryn.

"That's when he gave Resa his journal. For safekeeping, I suppose. She was to give it to me when I was older, should anything happen to him. But, instead, she kept it from me."

"How did you learn of it?" said Amryn.

"Before the war, some of us were working with Fang agents in Tokju."

"Fang? I find that hard to imagine," said Amryn.

"We knew the rebellion was doomed, and N'si would bear the brunt of the defeat. At the same time, Kitsune's hold on us was slipping. It was our chance to be free of him, if we survived."

"So you chose sides," she said.

"I chose the side I knew would fight Kitsune."

"Over those who sold him their souls for the promise of power."

"A promise Kitsune never intended to keep," he said. "One night, when I went to meet my Fang contact, Resa was with him. It was the first time I met her and the only time I have seen her lose her composure."

It wasn't hard to guess why.

"You look like your father," Amryn surmised.

"She didn't expect to meet Yuji in a dark alley that night," said Hobi. "After she realized I was his son, she sent the others away. We talked for hours. She seemed to crave reminiscing with someone who had known him. The tales Yuji had told me were true, she said. Maurya was real."

"And the journal?"

"If she hadn't told me, I would never have known it existed. Maybe it was nostalgia. Maybe it was a lapse in judgment. But she told me. She said it was better if she kept it hidden while times were so unsettled. But after we dealt with the rebellion, I could claim what my father had entrusted to her care."

"And you believed her," said Amryn.

"After the war, she said I wasn't ready. Yuji would have wanted her to see me settled and independent first. So, I joined Nefekari's fleet and saved every coin I earned, adding it to what I inherited as the last heir in Gar's lineage. Within a few years, I had the experience I needed. And I had accumulated enough wealth to buy the *Seeker*."

"What did she say to that?"

"Seeking Maurya was not the path she had chosen for me," said Hobi.

"Sounds familiar," she said. "But my mother believed Maurya was real?"

"Yes, and she would decide when and how to begin *our* search. In the meantime, I was of greater use smuggling supplies to the N'si refugees she was hiding in the Janlin."

So, it was true, what Habibah claimed. Parts of it anyway. Feeding refugees was a far cry from inciting N'si rebels.

"Not the path she chose for you," said Amryn. "That's what she said when I told her I wanted to be a scientist."

"What your mother is doing may be well-intentioned, but it's risky. Despite what Habibah accuses her of, Resa would never betray the Gyakari. But if he discovers she has been hiding runaway N'si from him, her choices may be hard to explain," said Hobi. "Resa is running out of time, and our people are running out of options."

"So, you took what belonged to you."

"What my father meant for me to have. He trusted I would understand what to do when the time came and that I'd be strong enough to see it through."

"With me, you are," she said. The time had come for her, too. And the path she chose was her own.

Hobi leaned his face to hers until only the space of a shared breath lay between them. Exquisite as any touch. The wish of a kiss he dared not give. His sigh sent a rush of warmth over her skin.

"Wait for me, Amryn," he said. "Someday, I can be ordinary again."

Chapter 16

Summoner

On the open ocean, one league of water looks like the next, and the next like the one before. Eventually, the sun is compelled to point out you are sailing in circles.

Khaldun knelt on the deck, his thick shoulders hunched over his maps and a compass and sextant in each hand. His mouth thinned in consternation, or maybe it was from muscle cramps. They'd been at this a while. Cora scowled down at the giant cartographer and his fickle maps.

"Well?" she said. "What next?"

"Stop," said Khaldun.

"Stop?"

"You heard him," said Amryn. "Here is as good a spot as any."

Cora rolled her eyes and took the wheel. There was no point in arguing if she could offer no better options. They'd circled this water enough, and no one wanted to admit the obvious.

There was nothing there.

"Heave to," Cora shouted to the crew.

Their mutters were soon drowned out by the sound of sails reefing. Amryn was certain, from that day on, she would remember it as the sound of defeat.

Maurya was not where Maurya would have been, if it were real.

"Go to him," said Khaldun.

Amryn forced herself to look to the bow again. Hobi was still there, sitting on the forecastle deck as he had been for days. Alone and entranced. Determined to summon what wasn't there to be summoned.

Everything he was, was bound to this search, to finding a myth his father convinced him was the last hope for his kind. Amryn had wanted to believe it with him, and then, somehow, she had believed it on her own. They could not be wrong. And yet...

"Handle the crew," she said. "Buy me time."

She made for the bow and walked up behind him. He heard her, of course, but his summoner's pose didn't waver. To break the trance would be to admit he was wrong.

"We will try again," she said. "When we find whatever piece of the puzzle we're missing."

Hobi clenched his fists, and the heat of his anger radiated off him. He was not taking this well. With his rage simmering, he stood to face her.

"Try again? There is no *again*. I'm done playing the fool. He lied."

"Yuji wouldn't have lied to you, Hobi."

"And why not? Everyone knows we can't help ourselves. N'si revel in mayhem. We thrive on spite. Oh, what grand mischief he left behind. A fitting inheritance for a dull-witted son."

Hobi snatched the prism from around his neck.

"We cheat ourselves, time and again. N'si killing N'si for sport. Betraying our kind to the highest bidder. There can be no redemption for us, Amryn. Go home and forget everything but the Ari you were."

Hobi drew back, ready to throw the prism into the sea. But, quick as light, Amryn caught his fist in her hand. Ufa's silver bands bulged from her flesh and shackled Hobi's wrist to hers. Hobi stared in disbelief that hardened to menace.

"Do not test me, Amryn."

"Water. Water." Ufa formed the runes on her arm, then hurried a mirage above their linked wrists. In a quickly rendered scene, Hobi splashed into the sea, and Amryn jumped in after him. Once they hit the water, lights flashed between the prism and relic.

"Talk to the water," Ufa signed and waited.

"That's it." Hobi's anger faded, and hope lit his face. "The puzzle. Ufa, let go. Hurry."

Amryn signed the command, and Ufa drew in his shackles. The moment he was freed, Hobi hung the prism back around his neck and ran to the rail. He knotted a grapple line and swung down. When he let go and jumped to the waves, Amryn drew back the line and swung down after him.

When she kicked back to the surface, Hobi was waiting for her, treading water, and not using his water magic. After seeing what it did to him, she understood why. Straight away, Ufa and the prism sparkled with patterns of light as they had earlier. But this time, they weren't talking to each other.

Their ancient Watcher light-speech reflected through the azure waters, casting colors and patterns like a net. Rapid and shifting, the rays streaking from Ufa brightened into a dazzling display of the confidence Amryn felt surging inside her. Hobi dove beneath a wave, and Amryn watched him swim deeper, knowing she couldn't keep up with him in his element. Heartbeats passed, drumming in her ears as Hobi vanished into the sea. Ufa's dancing lights narrowed to an intense red ray that followed his path, then winked out.

Amryn looked down as she treaded water. Ufa's face had gone dark, like the sea beneath her feet. She dove under, uncertain whether to go after him. A speck of silver glinted in the darkness below, then disappeared. It flickered again, and then a silver streak headed for her.

Hobi emerged from the depths, sleek as a shark on the hunt. The prism around his neck glinted like starlight on his coppery skin. His eyes shone with the iridescent glow she hadn't seen since that night in the sea crypt. He belonged to the sea.

"Up," Hobi signed as he swam closer. "Up. Up."

Amryn spun and kicked. She surfaced, gasping for breath. Hobi rose from the water as if he were climbing steps to the deck. Water or air seemed to make no difference to him. His expression immediately squelched her curiosity.

All around them, the water began churning. Bubbles rose in swirling pillars from the sea below.

"They're coming," he said.

Chapter 17

Descent

Something had answered. Summoned from the timeless fathoms of the sea, from the endless water set in endless motion, it had answered. Whether he had summoned Maurya or something else entirely, there was no undoing it now.

He needed to get Amryn back to the ship. She'd be safer there than in the water. He couldn't bear losing the one person who'd seen him for the freak he was and not abandoned him. She surfaced beside him, heaving for breath, and the conscience he'd tried to ignore stung him. He had put her at risk yet again. There was no undoing that, either.

The water churned with bubbles rising from the depths. He was out of time.

"They're coming," he said. "Stay close."

Shouts clamored from the ship, and a few hundred feet off the bow, a creature rose on the crest of a wave. Though human in shape and size, with recognizable limbs and torso, its head was a monstrosity. Bulbous, hairless flesh protruded from its oversized skull, and fleshy bands wrapped its face where a nose and mouth ought to be. Peering above the bands were intelligent, human-like eyes, with a strong jaw set below. The rest of its skin had a reddish-brown hue, lighter than Hobi's, though not by much. The creature's arms were bare, but snug black cloth covered its muscular chest and legs.

Nearby, another of the creatures surfaced, and then another, until dozens of the strange beings encircled the *Seeker*. The first of the creatures raised a gloved hand and touched the bulging mass on its head. The mass moved, detached, and slid down the back of the creature's head. Hobi saw tentacles on the bands retracting from its face, exposing a nose and mouth.

It was not one creature but two. The smaller one was none Hobi had ever seen—not quite sea ray or squid, but a bit of both, and something else he couldn't begin to name. The larger creature wore it like a cloak. When it fell back from its head like a hood, it exposed undeniably human features.

A young male was floating before him, rising and falling with the waves. Without tentacles covering his face and with his black, wavy hair pulled back, the faint lines of drakmu on his neck stood out more clearly. Hobi was looking into the face of his ancestors.

The Mauryan spoke. He hailed them in a strong, clear voice and seemed to be asking a question—or posing a challenge. Something about a dare and a signal. Hobi recognized a few words from a language he had not heard in years, but frustratingly few. Children learned Old N'si by rote and recited it in ceremonies, but not in conversation. It was a dead language. Dead as the N'si soon would be if he didn't find them a home.

"We bring an urgent message for your people," Amryn answered the Mauryan.

Hobi managed to hide his astonishment. He understood little of her reply beyond the first few words, but she spoke Old N'si with convincing aplomb. The Mauryan acknowledged her with a slight nod and said something more about a council, or maybe an empire. His words carried a tone of both urgency and command. Amryn nodded, and the Mauryan motioned for them to return to the *Seeker*.

"We're to follow him," she said.

Amryn started swimming for the ship. Hobi was disinclined to obey a stranger's command or anyone's command, for that matter. Obedience traded away power without reward. But, Maurya was a reward worth risking a temporary shift in the balance he would later reclaim. With a sweep of his hand, he willed the seawater to shed its salt and drew the thickened brine beneath Amryn and then himself, shaping a current and lifting them both. They would walk back to the ship. Let the Mauryans see who they were dealing with.

Amryn caught her balance as he lifted her from the sea with the innate grace her heritage bestowed. Then, with scarcely a wobble, she glanced over her shoulder.

"Power is relative to the power in its proximity." She gave him a sly grin.

It pleased him not to have to explain himself.

The crew gathered and tossed down a rope. Amryn had no sooner started up when the sea began roiling beneath her feet. The water moved in eddies and swirls around the ship, as if uncertain where it should go.

"Be quick," Hobi called to her as he tried to calm the rebellious currents.

An odd vibration hummed beneath the surface and echoed through his bones. Near where the Mauryan had vanished, a thin arc was rising from the waves. Translucent as glass. Sleek and rigid. The ring rising from the sea was of no substance he recognized. The humming arc soon encircled the *Seeker* like a fence. Hobi tried willing it to dissolve back into the sea, but it wasn't made of water and ignored his command. Instead, the fence rose higher, sending frothy sheets of brine cascading off its surface.

As the strange substance stretched higher and dryer, it seemed to dissolve, until Hobi could discern its rim only by the slightly darker shade of blue against the pale sky. Then, it seemed to alter its course, bending and curving inward like a pair of shadowy hands cupping the ship.

Amryn had made it back to the deck and leaned over, looking for him. He should have started up after her. But he'd been too preoccupied to climb. Well, that and the fact he was still chafed at being told what to do by the Mauryan. His obstinance would likely kill him someday, but it was a flaw he had given up trying to master.

"What are you waiting for?" said Amryn. "Climb!"

The anxiousness in her voice got him moving. Just as he reached the deck, a shadow crossed the ship's bow. Hobi vaulted over the rail. Shouts erupted from the bow as the Mauryan's fence snapped off the *Seeker's* bowsprit and sent it splashing into the sea.

Someone panicked and bolted past him. The youngest of his crew, Sparky was barely old enough to grow whiskers. But he had a knack with gunpowder and played a fine fiddle. Before anyone moved to stop the boy, he had clambered down into the dinghy. The razor-edged Mauryan fence sliced the dinghy in half. Sparky screamed and clutched what remained of his arm. Khaldun reached and grabbed the boy by the collar and hauled him back aboard. Blood trickled down the fence as it continued rising, arching over the ship like a dome.

"Dowse the topsails!" Hobi ran for the helm.

The crew hurried to protect the precious canvas, climbing out yardarms and freeing sheetlines, just ahead of the encroaching dome. It clipped a topmast as if it were straw and sent the crow's nest tumbling down its glassy back.

"Roll out the canons, Captain?" Cora ran after him.

"No! They didn't intend to hurt anyone or the ship," said Amryn.

Hobi spun to face her. "The Mauryan told you this?"

"No, Ufa did."

"How the hell would Ufa know?"

"He's one of them, remember?"

"Watchers and their arrogance. Damn them!"

"They have to hurry!" said Amryn. "If we put up a fight, it will only slow them down."

A shadow passed overhead, and the ship rolled to port as the dome caught the mizzenmast. The deck swayed as the *Seeker* righted herself on unexpectedly placid water, trapped inside a windless bubble, bobbing on the Endless Ocean.

One after another, their eyes turned to him. Unspoken challenges hung in the stilled air, and accusations simmered behind their stares. Khaldun stepped up beside him, then Amryn and Cora. The scale of power tilted decidedly towards the helm.

"We set out in search of a legend," said Hobi. "Will you now fret over discovering what wished to remain lost? The *Seeker* never returns emptyhanded."

"Have you forgotten who sails with you?" said Amryn. "The djinn does not worry while he waits inside the gem. He laughs at the fool who thinks it can hold him."

"Sparky's not laughing," someone said.

"Because fear got its claws in him," said Cora. "Will it take ye, too? Ye knew the risks when ye signed on to this expedition. Sailin' with the *Seeker* ain't for the fainthearted. We go where others dare not even dream!"

Mutters gave way to a few cheers, and a renewed bravado swept the doubters.

The ship shuddered, and Hobi sensed a tug, like a fish taking a hook. Then, the dome began sinking into the sea. Waves splashed against its sides as it carried the *Seeker* down. Air traveled down with them, trapped under the dome with the ship. Hobi soon realized the dome was actually a sphere, and they were trapped inside a Mauryan bubble. It carried them down into the sea, away from the wind's caress and the sun's warmth, until the shrinking circle of pale blue sky disappeared above them.

"We go where you go, Captain," said Rafael. "Who else can sail us *under* the sea?"

"Here, here!"

"We found the lost city!"

"Treasure!"

Their cheers went quiet as the sea and its eerie silence enveloped the ship. No bird's cry. No luff of a sail. Only a slow, ominous drumming. The heartbeat of the Endless Ocean.

Hobi's eyes itched in warning. As the sea embraced his ship, he felt the change tugging at him, too. Though it would sharpen his vision underwater, the iridescent eyes that made him look not quite human would not help settle a jittery crew. He fought to hold it off. Even inside the Mauryan sphere, the water beyond it beckoned him, knew him, yearned for him. The sea won the battle of wills, as it always did, and his vision shifted, adjusting to the diffused, blue-green light of the ocean realm.

The Mauryans were swimming ahead and somehow compelling the sphere to follow. Trails of air bubbles rose from the swimmers and the creatures that were once again clinging to their heads.

"They use the smaller creatures to breathe," said Amryn.

He looked at her, surprised she had seen what he could. Silver glinted around the pupils of her eyes. Ufa was augmenting her vision, too. Once again, Hobi was relieved at not being the only odd one aboard.

"How much of what the Mauryan said did you understand?" he said.

"Everything," she said. "He wanted to know why we dared summon them. No one has used the signal in thousands of years."

"The signal. The patterns of light we saw flitting between Ufa and the prism?" said Hobi. "It was a signal meant for them?"

"Apparently so. The empire forbids using the signal. He was quite emphatic about that part. Who were we to take such a risk, chancing it might be detected?"

"Detecting it didn't mean he had to respond."

"He had no choice but to silence us."

"Sounds like a threat," said Hobi.

"The conversation headed in that direction," said Amryn. "But Ufa had me say something more. And it got the Mauryan to stand down."

"What was it?

"Gibberish," she said. "Perhaps an old N'si saying you'd recognize. I mean, I was speaking Old N'si."

"A skill inexplicably acquired," said Hobi. "So, what was this saying that needed saying?"

"Wisdom for the ages, no doubt," Amryn smirked. "Put out the tea lamp. The tiger with no wings dances on the edge of dawn."

Hobi blinked. It made no sense at all.

"That's it?"

Amryn shrugged. "It sounded better in Old N'si."

"Which you now speak fluently," said Hobi. "If Ufa speaks Old N'si and you understand Old N'si, why bother with sign language all this time?"

"How should I know?" she said. "When I spoke to the Mauryan, the words flowed to fit the meaning. I knew what I was saying because Ufa knew. But if I tried coming up with anything on my own, I'd sound like a blithering idiot."

Khaldun joined them at the helm with his maps and compass. To chart the sphere's course into Maurya would be crucial to finding their way back. They had little choice but to accept the escort, but no one intended it to be a one-way voyage. Comparing calculations with Ufa and charting the path out seemed prudent.

"Will Cora be able to heal the boy?" said Amryn.

Khaldun nodded. "He will live."

"With one less hand and wiser for the loss," said Hobi.

The sphere's descent slowed and leveled no deeper than two ship's masts below the surface. A capable swimmer could still make it up for a breath, even without the aid of the Mauryans' head-riding creatures. Hobi often swam deeper and for far longer on his own, yet their escorts were swimming above the sphere now, at a more comfortable depth for a human.

So, water was not their natural element. They didn't seem to have the same affinity for the sea that the change had given Hobi. He wondered how they managed. And why they chose to.

Chapter 18

Starheart

Questions flooded Amryn's mind. Did the sphere have substance? Was it a transmutation of water? How long before it began to entropy?

A flicker appeared in the water ahead. A spot on the sphere's surface sparked and widened into a circle crisscrossed by tiny arcs of white lightning. The circle expanded, and flickering arcs became a ring, traveling across the sphere. The Mauryan sphere had encountered something more significant, a barrier challenging its approach.

"We've reached the city walls," said Hobi.

One by one, the Mauryans swimming above them began to disappear. As they reached the unseen wall, it seemed to consume them whole. Then a school of fish materialized, darting out from where the Mauryans had vanished. All the while, the flickering ring grew wider, and the sphere passed into the wall like a fish swimming into a leviathan's maw.

Amryn held her breath as she strained to glimpse what lay ahead. The wall was not a barrier, but a veil. Merely an illusion like Ufa's mirages. Soon, they and the ship had passed through unscathed. The wall was a mirage of empty ocean, and it veiled what lay within its boundaries.

The sheer magnitude of the undersea mountain sent a shiver down her back. Stark and imposing, it rose sharply from the ocean floor, and its peak stretched past the waves above. If seen from above, it might seem a small island, but the mountain hid its greatest treasure below. The legendary city of Maurya.

The city seemed to have grown from the solid rock of its crags. Its buildings were not squared like all other cities she had seen. Instead,

Maurya was rounded, a hive of turrets and saucers, flatter than tall, with thousands of little windows. The pinpoints of light peered out from expanses of grey, blinking from weathered steel like a thousand eyes watching their approach.

Amryn held her breath as the illusion shifted to substance. The arbitrary limits she had once known as reality shattered yet again. The vast reach of human possibility stood before her. Evidence of what mind and skill could attain. To have mastered such engineering, advanced beyond comprehension, Mauryans indeed must be descended from the Watchers. But why would people so advanced choose to live in isolation, hidden beneath the sea?

She reached for Hobi's hand, and his fingers curled around hers. For one shared moment of awe, they chose not to think of what he risked for her touch.

"Is it as your father described?" she said.

"No, it is not."

Hobi drew back and sunk into a brooding silence. Whatever his father had led him to expect, what they were seeing as they approached had made him wary. With Goblin crouched on his shoulder, Demon hissing at his feet, and his eyes glowing amber, Maurya couldn't be blamed for being wary of him, as well.

Amryn let him retreat. He'd share his concerns when he'd sorted them out for himself and not until then. She turned her attention back to the city, trying to learn what she could on her own. She studied the weathered steel structures again. Metal corroded faster in seawater than fresh, and Maurya supposedly was ancient. On the other hand, perhaps the city wasn't made of steel or even metal at all, but of a substance known only to Watchers.

"Ufa, what are the Mauryan dwellings made of?"

She felt the familiar tingle, and Ufa's tendrils traced runes on her arm.

"Star heart. Ship."

"Ship?" she said. "Ships sail on the sea, not under it."

"Star heart ship," Ufa insisted.

Amryn frowned and studied the city anew. Stars with hearts? Hearts in ships? Ships crafted from the hearts of stars. That must be it. The substance was not steel but starheart. It was the best she could make of it yet. It painted a beautiful scene, though. Filtered sunlight turned the grey saucers and turrets to silver, and their smooth design did remind her of a ship's hull. She tried to image such a ship in the sky, descending through cloudbanks, voyaging from the stars above. What a sight that would have been.

But these randomly connected structures didn't look fit to float, much less fly. A starship with no wings? Anchored to a mountain beneath the sea? Amryn shook her head. Surely, she had misinterpreted Ufa's meaning.

They passed more translucent shapes as they drew closer to the undersea mountain. Some were flat and rounded, almost pillow-shaped, and floating at the end of tethers. Others were wide, low domes, and crouched on the seafloor like crabs. None reflected the glint of glass. Were these wrought by the same science as the sphere encasing the *Seeker*?

Their outer shells were of a transparent substance. Similar to the dome that had risen to capture the ship. But, if the metallic material was starheart, the crystal-like surfaces must be something different. Inside the bubbles and domes, rows of crops reached for beams of sunlight, and specks that might have been sheep or goats dotted green pastures. Extending from the mountain like spokes from a hub, the tethered beads appeared to be farms. Scattered between the farms, a few cylindrical columns rose taller than the rest. Outposts, she decided. Watchtowers guarding the city.

It was magnificent. And she was seeing only a portion of the city as they approached. If these structures extended around the entire mountain, Maurya might be as large as Ealim, perhaps even Naré.

The people milling about inside the bubbles had noticed their arrival and found it alarming. Everyone seemed to be running, even hiding. Lights in windows began winking out.

"We're makin' the locals jumpy." Cora came to stand beside her. Blood still splattered her sleeves, but if she was on deck, it meant the injured gunner was alive and resting.

"I'd say Maurya doesn't make a habit of pirating ships," said Amryn. "Or hauling home the bounty."

As they neared the submerged city, sharper details tarnished her awe. Algae streaked the silver walls. A broken window lay unrepaired, hidden behind a vibrant coral fan. Breached hulls gaped in the shadows of a giant kelp forest. Compared to the sea life teeming around it, the city was old and tired. A relic of another time resigned to its fate. Fading into the past.

If Maurya had ever sailed the stars, it would rise no more. The Endless Ocean had chained a dragon with broken wings.

Chapter 19

Ring Island

Hobi remembered the day he met the sea.

His father woke him early that morning and lifted him out of bed. He carried him down the stairs and through the quiet streets of Tokju, stopping to buy a sweet morsel from a vendor just rolling out her cart.

They walked away from the city, towards the beach, beneath the shadow of Kitsune's mountain. The gargoyle carved in its black cliffs snarled down over the city. The blood of countless sacrifices stained its grotesque tongue. Even as a child, Hobi knew the blood was not shed willingly.

N'si bowed to no one, not even among their own. They worshipped no gods, for why would they imagine faraway deities greater than themselves? Why would anyone barter free will to win the favor of an unseen god? And yet, N'si served Kitsune, or at least placated his whims. The blood on the mountain came from those whose lives were unimportant, those with no one to avenge them, sacrificed to appease the monster within the mountain.

"Turn away." Yuji's hand gently guided his chin. "Look to the sea instead."

Hobi turned, wondering why his father had brought him to the beach. He had seen the Endless Ocean before, many times. Everyone in Tokju had. But he had never watched the golden sun rise from its depths.

"Ah, the sun awakens," said Yuji. "She grants us another day."

"Where does the sun sleep, Father? Is the sea her home?"

"Of course. Everything begins and ends in the sea, Hobi."

Yuji took his hand, and they waded into the water. As the surf caressed his bare feet, Hobi sensed the presence for the first time, seeping through his father's hand to sense him. Hobi felt its warmth as the presence whispered to him.

The sea is good, it assured him. The gentle surf swirled to welcome him. He would be safe in its boundless and timeless waters, the presence promised.

From that day on, the Endless Ocean spoke to him as a companion. And after his father died, the sea claimed him as a son. The presence stayed and kept its promise, and the change sealed the bond.

As the sphere neared Maurya, the intense longing the sight awakened in his heart unsettled him. He had to reach the mountain—needed the mountain—with an urgency he couldn't explain. Blanketed by the sensation of coming home, and without knowing how, Hobi understood he belonged somewhere he'd never been.

A twitch fluttered in his side. Not painful, but insistent, as if in anticipation.

Amryn had asked whether Maurya was as his father described. He had answered tersely but truthfully. Yuji's journal described an island, not the undersea city Hobi saw now. Though he no longer questioned the journal's credibility, there were pieces to the puzzle Yuji had either been unaware of or had intentionally omitted. But why?

Abruptly, the deck shifted beneath his feet. The *Seeker* pitched inside the sphere. Both ship and sphere lurched downward, rushing towards the mountain, careening for the rocks.

"Amryn!"

Hobi lunged to hold on to her and braced for an impact that didn't come. Instead, the sphere streaked between the rocks without slowing. The sphere sped into a narrow crevasse and plunged them into total darkness. Amryn's heartbeats drummed against his chest. The muscle in his side twitched again, and he recognized it as the presence—reassuring him.

"There's nothing to fear. Stay calm," Hobi called to the crew, then whispered to Amryn in the darkness, "Hold on to me."

She locked arms with him, sleeve to sleeve, even now taking care not to touch his skin. How he had won her trust mystified him as much as anything ever had in life, but he was determined he would not lose her to the sea. As the presence protected him, he would protect her, too.

The ship moved through darkness so totally void of light, even his eyesight could not pierce the inky black water. Moving through the void was disorienting. A deafening rush of silence filled his ears, and time unraveled wrong. Swallowed in the belly of eternity, they hung trapped in the moment, racing time while standing still. Adrift in the vacuum.

Eventually, the *Seeker* shuddered, and the sphere began to rise towards a dim glow. Faint shadows revealed the sheer rock walls of the crevasse as they passed in a blur of speed. Then, almost imperceptibly, the sphere began to slow its ascent, and light revealed fish and kelp in the passage they traveled from inside the mountain. Shafts of sunlight sent flickering fingers through the turquoise water waiting beyond.

The sphere continued rising to greet the sunlight with the exuberance of a breeching whale. Ship and sphere burst to the surface and splashed back down. The ship swayed and righted itself, and settled into calm blue waters. The sphere began dissolving at its crest, sending seafoam raining down over the decks. Their translucent transport retreated until it was only a thin ring, rippling outward across a lagoon.

The *Seeker* floated alone in a secluded harbor. Several leagues broad, at least, and placid as a lake, the lagoon filled the center of a crater-shaped island, ringed by ridges and cliffs. Ribbons of white sand stretched along the shoreline. Beyond, hills of windswept grass met sun-dappled forest. Beyond the green hills, the land rose outward and upward to crest the island ring, crowned by a circlet of timeworn mountain peaks.

Home.

A chorus of birds chirped in alarm over the oddity of a ship drifting in their lagoon. A lazy breeze stirred the moist air, carrying the fragrance of ginger lilies and jasmine and the earthy scent of ferns. The idyllic island and the abundance of life it sustained bore not the slightest mark of humankind's touch.

"*This* is the Maurya my father described," said Hobi, feeling an instant kinship with the place.

"But there's no one here," Amryn said. "Why abandon such an island and live underwater?"

"Oh, look closer. Mauryans are masters of illusion." Hobi pointed to the trees. "What do you see? A forest. Wild and untouched. But walk with me beneath its canopy, and you'll discover an orchard—almond trees, cashew, orange, breadfruit, and more. Further up the slope, you'll find silk floss, eucalyptus, and cacao."

"Bounty masked by design," said Khaldun.

"Mauryans farm the island but hide the farming," said Amryn. "But why—"

"Look there." Hobi pointed astern. "See that row of old stones on the sand? Nature didn't set those in place. Those are standing stones, the same as I saw in Rhynn." Tall and thick as a Rhynn warrior, the stones on the shore were cracked, and their tops weathered smooth. But they served the same purpose as those in lands far away. "Standing stones mark passageways used by the ancients. Beneath the feet of those stones, you'll find the crevasse our ship passed through. The way in and the way out."

"Nothing here is what it seems," said Rafael.

"Except for us," said Cora. "Trapped like a ship in a bottle. Not a Mauryan in sight."

"And no treasure spilling into our hands," said Rafael.

"Oh, it's here. Waiting to be found," said Hobi. "We're right where we wanted to be. And now, we do what we do best."

Chapter 20

Council

Vishal climbed the sea ramp with purposeful strides, not bothering to change from his seaskin. He left his patrol to see their lomloo settled back into the nesting pool. The council would be apoplectic over the Republic's long-awaited arrival and anxious to hear his report. Or ready to feed him to the sharks for bringing outlanders to Maurya. It could go either way.

If the strangers on the ship were Republic envoys, assuming the Republic still existed, they could not have picked a worse time to reappear. Tensions were running high between Trads and Progs, and extremists in both factions would spin news of the strangers' arrival to suit their cause. Win the rumor war and sway the opinion pendulum. Truth be damned, so long as the polls ticked higher.

But if the strangers were opportunists who had somehow discovered the signals and code phrase not used since ancient times, Vishal's mistake might bring down the worthiest leader Maurya had known in generations. He would not let that happen, even if it meant some truth-twisting of his own.

"What do they look like, Vish?" asked Quan.

The spry, white-bearded fellow wrung out a white rag and stood beside his white pail, taking a pause from polishing the glass on the council doors. Quan was as curious as everyone else, Vishal supposed, but the old man's judgment was far sounder than most.

"Like us and not," he said. "No two alike. Marked and unmarked."

"So, they appear as they wish to be seen. As does Maurya." Quan shrugged and went back to polishing. "Tell me when you find what's under the veil."

That was it, the spin he needed.

Vishal flung the doors open wide and marched into the Assembly Hall. As he'd expected, all twenty councilors were in their appointed chairs, gathered and waiting, and every eye locked on him as he entered.

Historians generally agreed that the Assembly Hall had once been the bridge of a starship. Vish supposed it could be true. Every nook and cranny in Maurya boasted some claim to former glory, touted by bronze plaques as plentiful as the historians who wrote and rewrote the past to suit the sentiment of their day. Out of respect for the past, the commander's chair had been left intact and in its original position, though bracketed now by twenty councilors' desks and rows of seats in the People's Theater beyond. But over time, the commander's chair had lost its sleek, utilitarian form, as had most everything else in Maurya. A few centuries spent trapped in self-imposed isolation tends to foster creativity, if only from the sheer boredom of seeing the same walls year after year, generation after generation. Coral and mother-of-pearl had adorned the dull, metallic bones of a starship bridge, upholstered in cobalt and blue damask woven from the silk of the weebul, and surrounded by a veritable forest of potted orchids and ferns.

Maurya was caught in a trap of its own devising. Comfortable and complacent. Locked away by their own key, hiding from their own shadows. Pretending there was not an entire world beyond their illusionary walls. Occasional discomfort might have reminded them they didn't belong here.

Vish stepped up to the Speaker's Deck. Ignoring the councilors' eyes boring into his back, he stared ahead, his attention fixed on the one person whose opinion mattered.

The Rajin of Maurya leaned forward in her chair. Her movement summoned a tinkle of golden bells and rustle of silk from the ceremonial garb she hated. Chandra stilled and dared the slightest sound to challenge her dignity again. Unsurprisingly, none did.

From his earliest memories, Vish had been aware Chandra's beauty was different. Not delicate, but fierce. From the henna tattoos darkening her bold birth-markings to the defiant black waves of hair and kohl-rimmed eyes, Chandra commanded attention whether she wished to or not. To her chagrin, she had passed the curse she rued down to her son. Her unwavering stare reminded Vish of his duty. He, too, was born to lead.

"Explain yourself," she said.

# # #

"What part of my report was unclear, Gagan?" Vish glared at the Traditionalist Leader, annoyed by his grandstanding. Gagan would find fault with the color of the sky if he thought it might bolster his polls. "We were patrolling in the west. The signal pattern unique to the Return activated our transceivers. Every prism around every neck lit in answer to its call."

"And, of course, you took the bait," said Gagan.

"Ignoring a greeting we've waited centuries to hear is illogical."

"Rushing headlong to answer it was reckless," said Gagan. "Did you stop to consult the council? Vet the source of the signal? Weigh the risks? No, you did not."

"I responded according to protocol. Need I cite section and subsection for you?"

"Vishal, mind your tone," said Janak. "We are here to share information, not to judge. The Assembly weighs facts presented to us in good faith."

Vish nodded curtly. His father had no temper to lose.

"We'd been scouting the ship for days, undetected. There was no doubt it was traveling alone," said Vish. "And no doubt the ship was where the signal originated. As prescribed for patrols encountering a potential Return, we circled and contained the source for further vetting."

"And what did your vetting reveal?" asked Chandra.

"An outlander ship, same as the others. Except two of the crew were in the water, and their transceivers were emitting the signal. When challenged, they provided the designated passphrase in our language."

"So much for the possibility they're common Breeders pulling a ruse," another Trad said, dragging the derogatory epithet into the debate. "Their kind is too backward to cobble together a coherent thought."

"Objection." Lalima, a first-termer eager to climb the Progressive party ranks, sprang to her feet. Vish generally counted her as an ally, though her votes aligned with ambition more often than conviction. "May the record show the esteemed councilor referred to the subjects in question as outlanders, not Breeders."

"Make it so," said Chandra, her sharp glance skewering the offender. Her ruling needed no affirmation. The records must be unblemished, circumspect in every nuance when the Watchers eventually returned and reviewed the diligence of their stewards. Any disparaging of the very races the Watchers had planted here, the raw material Mauryans were assigned to nurture and evolve, could hardly be expected to garner the Republic's approval.

"My friends, we fret over nothing." Gagan laughed. "Commander Vishal would have us believe that, after a long journey through the stars, rather than descend from the clouds in an awe-inspiring Return, the Watchers simply bobbed out our way in an old wooden sailing ship, masquerading as the common Breeders... sorry, *outlanders*... they left behind. I should hope not. It would be rather anticlimactic."

Chuckles and guffaws rippled through half the Assembly Hall. Gagan was a master of irony. Damn him.

"But, of course," said Vish. "Why would the Watchers choose *not* to call attention to themselves? Why have we not dared poke our heads out from this damned turtle shell in—how many generations now?"

"Because we might draw the enemy's attention," said Lalima. She had a penchant for speaking, even when it meant stating the obvious.

"Watchers are no less clever," said Vish. "We appear as we wish to be seen."

"Watchers or outlanders, we can determine their motives and identities later," said Chandra. "For now, our greater concern must be whether today's events alerted the enemy."

"Or whether the Commander of the Watch invited the enemy into our midst," said Gagan.

Janak rose from the chair to her right. General of Defense and a power in his own right, he garnered respect for more than being the rajin's husband. Few dared question his command, and none dared challenge them both.

"Gagan, go. Consult the Elders," said Janak. "Rather than stand there and speculate on our doom, you can be of service by bringing back any insights they have to offer."

Vish suppressed a grimace. Of all the councilors who might have been selected as the Assembly's envoy to the Elders, Gagan was the worst possible choice to represent them. But he'd campaigned for the honor and won the votes. What was done was done.

"Rekha, compare details of the encounter with the protocols recorded in the archives," said Chandra. "Scour the histories. Find us a means to verify this potential Return is authentic."

Quicker than many her age, the gaunt and humorless Minister of History gathered her books and left. Her apprentices scurried after her like ducklings. For a Trad, Rekha was relatively rational. She still valued fact over fiction—as long as the archives supported her interpretation of the facts. He was confident she would find nothing in them to challenge the encounter's authenticity.

"Captain Atharvan, tell the Monitor Corps I want them on high alert," Janak ordered his aide. "Double shifts. Watching every quadrant. If they detect so much as a ping against the network, inform me at once."

"Yes, General."

"And divert nonessential power to the walls. If the signaling drew the enemy's curiosity, he must find nothing but dead space when he looks our way."

"Of course, Sir."

Atharvan hurried off to make it so. Like most in the Watch, he had opted for inside duty, spending his entire life caged inside Maurya's walls, pretending it was enough. Vish would have gone mad long ago without the freedom of the patrols.

"Councilors, I expect you to inform your constituents of the situation," said Chandra. "Get out there and get ahead of the rumors. Responsibly so, with no theatrics. Anyone inciting panic will answer to me. Do I make myself clear?"

Murmurs swept the Assembly Hall, then faded to uncharacteristic silence. Chandra governed by consensus, not decree. On the rare occasions she threatened them, they knew to take her seriously. The somber gathering began to disperse, and Chandra locked her attention on the source of the trouble brewing in her domain.

"Commander Vishal, to my office."

# # #

Chandra tossed her rajin's robe over a chair and waved Vish to sit with her on the jhula. Compared to the Assembly Hall, her office was almost austere in its simplicity. The only concessions to extravagance were the natural sunlight piped through refraction tubes and the seater swing that dominated half the room. Carved of teak and ladened with cushions, the jhula was a family heirloom, passed from mother to daughter. The design was a reproduction, inspired by nostalgia for the distant stars Mauryans had once called home. Figures of exotic creatures Vish could not name climbed and slithered throughout the lacquered carvings, and shiny brass chains suspended the swing from the ceiling. It was easy to lose track of time when sitting in the jhula, surrounded by plump bolsters. Vish had often done so as a child. While his mother worked at her desk, he swayed to the soothing rocking of the jhula, reading tales of the Republic's glory and dreaming of the worlds beyond Maurya's walls.

Over the years, he'd also been summoned to sit with his mother, to be scolded for one offense after another. As a boy with a penchant for testing his boundaries, Vish had come to appreciate the family heirloom on a more practical level. It was hard to stay angry in a jhula.

Chandra handed him a cup of mint tea and settled back on the bolsters.

"Now, you may tell the rest."

Vish took his time answering. The report he gave the Assembly had included only irrefutable facts. She wanted his perspective, even his conjecture. He was still sorting it out for himself.

"The one who spoke the passphrase," he said. "She is Wired."

"Impossible." Janak snorted, seated at the rajin's desk. "The last augmenters were deployed generations ago."

"Which proves she must be from the Republic," said Vish.

"Wired. Are you certain?" said Chandra.

"I got close enough to notice the glint in the sun," said Vish. "Silver markings on her bare arms. No attempt to hide her augmentation. There's no doubt she's Wired."

"That complicates matters," said Janak. "She can communicate. Will our walls dampen any signal she tries to send?"

"I suppose we'll find out," said Vish.

"It would be reckless of her to risk the attempt," said Chandra. "What are the odds she is unaware the enemy might be listening? Intercepting? Tracking?"

"Zero," said Vish. "The Republic has been fighting Kitsune for a long time."

"Yet, she openly signaled us." Janak frowned. "Does that sound like someone aware of the enemy's reach?"

"Or someone who finds the enemy irrelevant?" said Vish. "Have you considered the possibility the Republic may have finally defeated him?"

"We would know," said Chandra.

"How?"

She didn't answer.

"There's more." Vish rubbed his neck. "Her companion. I haven't decided whether he's her guard or a fellow envoy. He didn't speak but seemed to understand our conversation."

"Another Wired?" said Chandra.

"No, not unless he was hiding the same clues she flaunted. His stripes are considerably more pronounced than ours, but not unnaturally so. Distinctive patterns. Covering more skin than normal. But not a trace of silver."

"Tattoos? Vanity?" said Janak.

"Maybe. Who knows what the Republic fashion is these days?" said Vish. "His appearance is not what bothers me. He marshaled a feat not recorded in our archives. Commanded water itself. Transformed the waves, shaped them into a conveyance with a wave of his hand."

"With a power fielder? A shielding device?" said Janak.

"Not that I saw, but he must have one on him." Vish shrugged. "An intentional display of their superior Republic technology? Harmless theatrics to inspire a bit of that awe Gagan expected."

"You were right not to mention this to the Assembly," said Janak. "No need to give Gagan more fodder for stirring up fear. We need time to shape the message. How do we tell Maurya we have Republic envoys floating in the lagoon?"

"First, we need Rekha to authenticate the encounter," said Chandra. "If she does not... Gagan will find something sinister in their arrival. Inciting paranoia is the only way he can turn this to his advantage."

"And we'll prove him wrong, as we have before," said Vish. "Why pass up an opportunity to let Gagan make a fool of himself?"

"Never underestimate a sufficiently determined fool," said Chandra. "Vish, we must be certain about them. You may be right. They may be Republic envoys bringing word of the Return. But it is also possible they are spies sent to infiltrate our defenses."

Whether they were imposters or not, they were not Mauryan. That was enough.

"Vish, return to them as my representative," said Chandra. "Deliver my greetings but be clear they are to remain on their ship. I need to know if they are who they seem before I allow others to judge for themselves."

"And if they are not?" said Vish.

"You will eliminate the trouble you brought us," she said.

Chapter 21

Dare

Cora bounded up to the helm with a yellow orchid stuck in her hat, whistling like a child. If not for her robust frame, he would have suspected she was part fae folk, dancing to music only she could hear. But then, every mindgifted Hobi had ever met was a bit tetched in the head.

"Rafael repaired the dinghy, I see," said Hobi. "He took you out on the first jaunt?"

Cora blushed, and her hand flew to the orchid.

"Just doin' my duty, Captain. Keepin' wily little Laradians out of mischief."

Hobi had doubts about Rafael after the cannon incident, but with no proof and no further mishap, he had shelved his suspicions. The crew had stuck by him so far, and Rafael was well-liked. His was a voice of support he would rather not lose. But, soon enough, the crew would be pressing for answers about the treasure he had promised they would find. Then it would be their doubts, not his own, he had to worry about.

"So, what do we do next?" said Cora. She rested her hands on the ship's wheel. Habit, he supposed, even on a ship going nowhere.

"We wait for them to come to us," he said.

"How long will that take?"

"Not long," he said with more certainty than he felt. Their arrival had caused a stir in such an isolated realm as this, of course, and it would take time for Mauryans to agree on their next move. He hoped that move brought talk rather than cannons. "In the meantime, no more jaunts. Keep to the ship. I want no misunderstandings with the locals."

A flicker in the water beneath the standing stones caught his eye. A shape darted from the shadows. A swimmer from Maurya. Barely a heartbeat later, Amryn took the quarterdeck steps in fluid leaps, like a silk scarf riding the breeze.

"They're back," she said breathlessly, her eyes wide with the insatiable curiosity that never seemed to leave her. Too often lately, Hobi caught himself watching her, struck by how lovely she was while pacing back and forth, mumbling to herself, sorting out her latest puzzle.

How long, indeed? The line between choice and duty no longer seemed so clear.

"Looks like this one's alone," Cora said, lowering a spyglass.

"Lower a ladder," said Hobi. "Everyone on deck. Let's show we know how to behave."

Amryn accompanied him to the foredeck, claiming her place beside him without being asked. Her days of waiting to be asked to do what obviously needed doing were over. The few hours they spent practicing his rusty N'si language skills were not enough. Amryn and Ufa would have to do most of the talking.

The lone Mauryan approached the ship and climbed from the water. It was the same Mauryan who had spoken to them before, but with no strange creature on his head this time. By their standards, the lagoon might seem a short swim and require no breathing aids. Or perhaps the squid-like creatures were skittish of the unknown. Other animals on the island had gone into hiding, wary of the strange ship floating in their midst.

The *Seeker's* crew gathered on deck, in lines closely approximating discipline, or at least as close to such as a bunch of antiquity hunters, adventurers, and opportunists cared to attempt. The Mauryan stepped over the railing, and a slight hesitation betrayed his wariness. For all their mysterious illusions and ship-devouring spheres, they were not invulnerable. Hobi cataloged the observation and recalibrated the gambit.

"When power meets power, the first act betrays the weaker," he said quietly. Amryn acknowledged with an indifferent nod and lifted her chin. She was becoming unnervingly good at N'si games.

"Greetings from our honorable Rajin." The Mauryan pressed his palms together and bent in a stiff bow. "I am an envoy of Rajin Chandra. You may address me as Commander Vishal."

Hobi and Amryn acknowledged him with nods but did not return the bow.

"I am Amryn Nisari," she replied in Old N'si. "This is Captain Hobi of the *Seeker*. We are bemused by your belated greetings. Bringing guests to your home in restraints is... a unique custom."

Commander Vishal stiffened, and shame darkened his paler cheeks. During their encounter at sea, Hobi had recognized him as kin. But, standing closer, under the bright morning sun, his Mauryan features seemed a faded watercolor memory of N'si copper and amber. The commander's few faint drakmu were plain and covered less than half his neck. Countless generations spent hiding in the shadowy depths had leeched away some of the vibrance their ancestors had shared.

If Mauryans indeed had more Watcher than N'si left in them, he'd have to recalibrate again.

"Guests do not barge in uninvited," said Vishal.

"An unusual interpretation of the circumstances." Amryn arched a practiced Ari brow. "I am curious. How is one expected to deliver a message other than by arriving at the prescribed location and *delivering* the message? Does Maurya have other counterintuitive customs of which we should be aware?"

"One in particular," said Vishal. "We do not try the patience of our hosts."

"An admirable quality in any circumstance, Commander Vishal." Amryn smiled. "We expect to continue our business here as welcomed guests of Maurya."

"The signal," said Vishal. "Is the source still on the ship?"

"Yes," said Amryn, declining to elaborate in the pause that followed.

"Do not attempt to use the device again," said Vishal. "All outbound communication is prohibited, and violations will be dealt with swiftly. Until Rajin Chandra and the Assembly determine what is to be done regarding the message, you are to remain on your ship."

"As prisoners or hostages?" said Amryn.

"Guests, for now," said Vishal. "Do not think to escape. The ocean is vast."

Hobi let a smile spread over his lips—slow and sly—and edged with the promise of trouble. N'si trouble. He turned and walked away, tugging his shirt off over his head.

Amryn sighed. "You had to challenge him, didn't you, Commander Vishal?"

"What is he doing?" said Vishal.

"Daring you to stop him," said Amryn.

Hobi climbed the rail and dove into the lagoon. Warm, brackish water enveloped him, embracing a son of the sea. He drifted where the current's whim led, and a splash soon announced Vishal had taken his dare. Good.

Hobi swam ahead, taunting pursuit. He led the chase away from the *Seeker*, down into the cooler, deeper waters away from the shore. *Home.* An inexplicable joy returned again to wash over him, drawing him onward. With no destination in mind, he swam for the pure delight of swimming. He glided through the water with streamlined limbs and unencumbered muscles, lightened by the buoyancy of the element his body craved. Vestigial gills awakened to draw life's breath from the water as effortlessly as his nose drew it from the air above.

He glanced back, gauging his pursuer, and testing his limits. Vishal was a strong swimmer and quick for an ordinary nene. But the Mauryan showed no signs of shifting and kept to shallower depths than the change allowed Hobi. With a pang of disappointment, he flipped and circled back. As Hobi rose from the depths, Vishal kicked to the surface for a breath.

Hobi swam up beneath him, watching him from the water, aware his eyes shone the glow the change wrought. Vishal stared down in slack-jawed astonishment. When their eyes met, Hobi realized finding others like himself among the Mauryans had been a wasted hope. He dove beneath Vishal's feet and headed back for the *Seeker*, to the only one he'd ever known who was as different as he was.

He waited beside the ship until Vishal reached the ladder. The Mauryan clung to the bottom rung, frowning down at him through the water's surface.

Slowly, Hobi rose to face him. As water trickled off his shoulders, the change shifted him again. He drew an effortless breath and echoed the warning Vishal had given.

"The ocean is vast."

Chapter 22

Gambit

Hobi had no sooner jumped overboard when Cora came running from the helm.

"More Mauryans headed our way," she said. "A sloop full of them."

"They are not swimming out?" said Rafael. "Ah, these must be the wealthy ones. Salt stains are nearly impossible to wash out of silk."

Amryn scanned the lagoon for any signs of Hobi. She would have to handle these newcomers on her own.

"Khaldun, take the captain's place beside me," she said. "You've studied Old N'si."

"I understand the words," Khaldun conceded. "Do not expect me to speak any of my own."

"Perfect," she said. "Just stand there looking large and disgruntled."

A trio of Mauryans boarded with the same brisk efficiency as Commander Vishal, though their readied weapons conveyed an uncertainty he had not. That Vishal had faced them alone and unarmed raised him a notch in Amryn's estimation. Their weapons were odd. Not quite muskets. Hilted like swords but thicker and blunted. Different from the harpoons she'd seen the Mauryan sea patrol carry.

"Greetings, travelers." The next Mauryan stepped aboard with his arms spread wide and a smile oozing charm. "I am Councilor Gagan, Speaker to the Elders of Maurya. I am honored to be their envoy on this momentous occasion."

Gagan instantly reminded her of Rafael, from his undersized stature to his oversized swagger. Dressed more elegantly than any

131

Mauryan she'd seen, he moved with the self-assurance of those who've been told they're handsome their whole lives. Charisma wafted off him like perfume, wrapping any fool he encountered in his almost tangible aura of persuasion.

Amryn knew his kind well. Equal parts allure, cunning, and bluster. After years spent in the Ari palace, she'd encountered many Gagans in the pit of vipers preening for the Gyakari's favor. But instinct whispered this one's bite could be dangerous.

Gagan stopped and scanned the deck, sniffing for pockets of power. His shrewd eyes swept Amryn, and his smile faded.

"You are Wired," he said. Menace coiled beneath his velvet voice.

Wired? Had she misinterpreted his words?

Amryn's skin prickled under the intensity of Gagan's gaze. His eyes were riveted to her neck and the silver drakmu that branded her as different. The warmth on her arm drew her attention to Ufa's hurried signing.

"He sees. Ufa in your service."

"No servant," Amryn signed back. *"Companion."*

"Companion." The silver rune shimmered on her brown skin, then faded.

Amryn narrowed her eyes and held Gagan's stare. He blinked first and took an involuntary step back, startled by the silver glow she felt warm her eyes whenever Ufa sharpened her sight. She lifted her chin and trusted Ufa with her voice.

"Wired? How quaint," she said. "Wired is such an archaic term. I cannot recall hearing it spoken. It comes from a time long ago when the ignorant among us feared augmentation. Surely, Maurya no longer holds such primitive views."

"Augmentation is the polite word for your condition," said Gagan. "But on the tongue, it tastes as tart. So tell me, what is it like? Surrendering your body and will to a lifeless master."

Sparks crackled in the air between them. Gagan shielded his face as flames licked his sleeves. The Mauryan guards screamed and cursed as the weapons burned red-hot in their hands. They threw down the smoldering metal, and Gagan staggered back, shaken and singed.

"Empowering," said Amryn.

Before she could toss them overboard, Commander Vishal climbed over the rail. Considering the murderous scowl on his face, it might be more entertaining to let him deal with them. Hobi vaulted to the deck behind him, seeming bemused by the gathering storm.

"Gagan, what are you doing here?" Vishal demanded.

"Speaking for the Elders, of course," said Gagan.

Amryn studied the subtle dance. She was well-versed in the slope of shoulder or angle of chin that conceded unspoken deference. The two were not equals. She gauged them by the measure of the Ari court, by degrees of distance from the highest source of power, the Gyakari. The younger commander had the standing of an Ari prince. Gagan's deference was the same as the palace climbers grudgingly offered one of his birthright.

"On whose authority?" said Vishal.

"Are you suggesting the Elders' authority is insufficient?" said Gagan.

"When it bypasses the rajin, yes. You know the protocols, Gagan."

"Enjoy your swim?" Amryn signed over the Mauryans' posturing.

"When do I not?" Hobi's smirk said the rest. He'd delivered his message to Commander Vishal, and quite clearly. *"Rajin? Check the meaning."*

"Queen leader," she or Ufa replied. It had ceased to concern her who found which answers first. *"Selected. Chosen. Not birthright."*

Amryn shifted her attention to the petty squabble unfolding on deck. They'd gone from sniping to calling down sinister threats.

"You failed to mention she is Wired." Gagan paced around a fuming Vishal. "Such a glaring omission calls your entire report into question. What if she's a spy? Even now, she might be echoing our every word to the enemy."

"The shields would not allow—"

"—the enemy. What enemy? Who do they fear?" Amryn wondered.

"Who sent them into hiding?" said Hobi.

"Kitsune."

"Yes."

"They don't know he's dead," Amryn realized. How could they? Hiding here for centuries, cowering behind their illusions, and afraid their own shadows might betray them. That was no way to live.

She bit her lip. Was she actually considering this? Maybe she did have mischief in her blood.

"This charade grows tiresome," she said, interrupting their argument. "Giving you the benefit of the doubt and adhering to first contact protocol have proven fruitless. Continuing the pretense will only strain my patience and indulge your ineptitude."

Vishal and Gagan abandoned their barbs midsentence. She had their attention.

"Well played. Run the gambit." Hobi quirked his brow in a dare.

"Nearly eight years ago, we received a hail." Amryn closed her eyes and read from the image Ufa summoned. Chalyns had sent the desperate hail at the height of the war and forgotten about it not long afterward. To this day, it remained unanswered, lost and abandoned in the vast nothingness between the stars.

> *On behalf of the races of Earth, we hereby challenge any decision to end this Cycle. We claim the right of self-determination and will defend against any enemy attempting to deny us the freedom to forge our own destiny. Our people and yours can set a new path together. We welcome allies in the fight against oppression. Join us in the cause of liberty.*

She studied their reactions. Much as it disheartened her, it was apparent they'd heard the words before.

"So, you received the message." Amryn paused, staring down each Mauryan in turn. "Yet you failed to respond."

"Responding would have drawn the enemy's wrath down on our heads instead of theirs," said Gagan. "There would be no Maurya left for you to saunter in and second guess."

"Chalyns and the Ari Empire faced the enemy you feared," said Amryn. "They fought, bravely and valiantly, while Maurya cowered."

She paused, gauging whether they were capable of chagrin. Vishal had the decency to avert his gaze. Gagan might have been carved from ice. It was time to find out what it took to rattle that one.

"They defeated your monster," she said. "Kitsune is no more."

Vishal's head shot up, and the guards shifted uneasily. Gagan stood gaping, and his eyes flicked from one face to another like a loose kite searching for a tether.

"You were right," Hobi signed. *"They didn't know."*

Amryn steeled her composure, though the implications sent her mind reeling. It was too incredible. Was Maurya burrowed so deeply into hiding they couldn't tell there was nothing to hide from anymore? And if Maurya was the last bastion of Watchers on earth, what did that say about their empire scattered throughout the stars? Had no one told them?

Ancient images flooded her mind again, as on that night on the bowsprit with Hobi, when Ufa and the crystal prism mourned. *The emptiness of a thousand dying stars and the sadness of hope forever lost.*

Was Maurya all that remained of the Watchers?

If they were, how would they know?

"They think we're Watchers. Returned from the heavens. That must have been the signal." Amryn sent Hobi an uncertain glance. *"Here to judge them? Or to save them?"*

"To take them home. An overdue changing of the guard." Hobi frowned. *"This complicates the plan. Stall."*

The Mauryans still seemed stunned by her world-shaking revelation, so Amryn opted for a righteous glare to buy time. Sooner than she wanted, Vishal regained his wits.

"Why sail out to tell us this?" he said. "Can the Republic not spare a starship these days?"

The Republic. So, Watchers and Mauryans and the stars from which they came were part of a broader alliance. On one world or many? By consent or decree? Where did their loyalties lie?

"Come, you know better," Amryn shot back. "Rules of engagement. Or have you forgotten the protocols governing the Cycles you are tasked with administering?"

Vishal's mouth thinned, and he held whatever retort wanted out.

"You seem flustered." Amryn pressed the advantage. "Have you never been called to account before?"

"Often and deservedly, by those whose authority I respect," he said. "But your accounting is not for me to accept or refute. Remain on your ship. When the rajin wishes to hear more, she will send for you."

# # #

"We'll take dinner in our cabin," Amryn told Cora after the Mauryans rowed away, and Hobi offered no objection. They needed time to strategize.

"Don't let him talk ye into anythin' rash," said Cora. "I don't know what ye said to those fellas, but they looked mighty shaky when they left."

"Your confidence in me is underwhelming," said Hobi. "We merely informed them they may come out of hiding. We killed the monster under the bed and stole his loot."

"Monster?" said Cora.

"Kitsune," said Amryn. "They didn't know he was dead."

"As if a metalmind can die." Cora grunted. "But the Chalyns clipped his wires to the quick, and he can't grow them back. How could these folks not know the beast is gone?"

"Improbable, isn't it?" said Hobi. "Even when fear becomes a way of life, the hunted keeps an eye on the hunter. There must be something else in play here."

"Well, try not to get us tossed in a Mauryan dungeon while ye figure it out." Cora gave a shrill whistle to the crew. "Quit standin' around. The show's over, lads."

Amryn scooped Goblin from the deck and carried the little hellcat to the cabin. Lazily sunning in the window seat, Demon opened an eye at their footsteps, halfheartedly gauging the likelihood of food in the offing. Hobi sat on the floor and scratched the old lizard's scaly chin.

Amryn smiled. They made a contented little band of misfits.

"Impressive gamble," he said. "What tipped you off?"

"Gagan recognized Ufa. But his reaction was one of fear, not familiarity. That told me Mauryans are aware of augmentation, but there are no Augmented among them."

"So, you could only be from somewhere they assumed the Augmented still exist," said Hobi.

"I guessed that would be the worlds the Watchers came from." Amryn shrugged. "So, that's where we're from."

"Clever," he said. "They don't seem particularly fond of their fellow Watchers."

"Would you be? Imagine being sent here and abandoned. Left to survive on your own. No contact for generations. Then, to have those who abandoned you show up after all this time."

"A bit of resentment seems natural."

"Their resentment seemed to be festering into something uglier," said Amryn. "So, I tried putting them on the defensive instead."

"You shamed them for hiding while the sheep they were to supposed shepherd were the ones who killed the wolf."

"I think I hit a sore spot."

"That you did."

Hobi launched into analyzing the encounter with the Mauryans, parsing every word for nuance and noting every subtlety of body language. Then, remarkably observant, he challenged her with his questions and listened intently as she reasoned through a few theories.

Rafael brought a dinner tray at some point, but they left it untouched. They puzzled well together, and his respect for her intellect raised her expectations of herself. A few short months ago, the assassin who couldn't kill and a scientist who couldn't pursue her passion wouldn't have dared the gambit she had raced headlong into today.

"How do you do it?" she said.

"Do what?"

"Coax the daring out of me."

"Coaxing what's clamoring to escape is hardly a challenge."

The sunset was fading, and Hobi got up and stretched. He carried the untouched dinner tray from the table and sat it on the floor between them, and with a casual flick of his fingers, a flame lit in the lantern on the wall. Science took leave of its senses every time Hobi coaxed magic out to play. She'd never stopped wondering how. He sighed and leaned back on his hands, staring at nothing.

"Do you still believe Maurya is the haven you're looking for?" she said.

"It'll have to do," he said with a shrug. "There's no time to start searching anew."

Mauryans didn't seem the hospitable sort. She tried to imagine them welcoming boatloads of N'si refugees to their secluded enclave.

"Then we have work to do here," she said. "Attitudes to change. Horizons to expand."

Hobi gave her a long look. "You're joining the cause?"

"Securing N'si a place in the world sounds worthwhile to me."

"You're serious."

"Yes. You're surprised."

"Well, I suppose I expected it to require a bit more convincing. You know, we can be unconventional," said Hobi.

"Yes, I noticed."

"And our reputation for being devious, vain, and, by most standards, utterly amoral, is not entirely undeserved."

"I suggest we work on your sales pitch."

"All right, then," he said. "We're also clever. Survivors. Individualists who have always considered slavery an anathema, bowing to kings naïve, and fighting for land or power a sorry waste of time."

"Better," she said. "Keep going."

"We're the crows, collecting shiny treasures because we can. We're the foxes, surviving on wit and thriving on beating the odds. We're the cobras, hunting alone and striking when cornered."

"Cobras?" Amryn shook her head. "The cobra is the mark of the Fang."

"By whose choice?"

Resa, of course. A lone N'si established her territory within the Ari court.

"N'si fight alone, in self-interest or defense, but rarely conquest. We will never raise an army, and we take to a battlefield only when we choose a side in a fight someone else started. We have no appetite for building empires. No obsession with imposing our will on the world. And no religion to justify doing so."

"Children of the dead gods," Amryn's voice dropped to a whisper, remembering the rare times her mother had spoken of her kind. "We make no promises, and we ask for none."

She was ever the realist. Whatever happened in Maurya, the events that brought them here would not bind them for long. Amryn liked who they were together, but this window in time would close, and they would go where the wind beckoned next, even if it meant going in different directions. No promises.

She slid beside him, half expecting him to retreat. But the memory of one shared breath had shaken his resolve as thoroughly as it had hers. Temptation darkened his eyes with the portent of amber skies before a desert storm. Amryn drew closer, shifting her gaze to his sensuous lips, following the sculpted line of his jaw to his lean neck and muscled shoulders and the distinctive drakmu that tempted her fingertips to trace across his skin. For a long moment, she simply studied him, memorizing such rare beauty.

She met his eyes again, wondering how to begin. Hobi gave her no hint and waited for her to make up her mind. The wildness he had kindled in her urged her on. Bold and curious, she pressed her mouth to his, and he cupped her face, kissing her in earnest. Sensations she'd never imagined flooded her body, and the magic she'd denied existed ran rampant. The world shifted, going velvet soft and silent but for the shared heartbeats drumming in her ears. Hobi curled his fingers in her hair, keeping pace with her curiosity until she paused for breath.

"Amryn, I have never wanted anyone more." His thumb gently brushed her lips. "But I must send you back to your mother as intact as I found you."

"But you said—"

The crash of shattering crystal cut off her objection. She turned to the frenzied clanking. Demon lay sprawled across the silver dinner tray, claws clenched tight and tail whipping madly. Hobi reached for the old lizard, and Demon hissed.

"What's wrong with him?" Hobi gripped Demon by his spiky ridge, trying to still the poor beast's thrashing.

Amryn crawled towards them, and a half-eaten banana squished under her palm. A sharp pain shot up her arm and knocked her back on her heels. Ufa's hurried signing prickled her skin.

"Bad. Bad. Sour. Bad." The runes scrolled a frantic warning.

"Poison," Amryn cried. "He's been poisoned."

Hobi cursed and lifted the convulsing lizard in his arms.

"Get the door," he said. "I need to get him into the water."

Amryn threw back the bolt and cleared the way up the steps. Hobi staggered across the deck, carrying the writhing, frothing beast. He hit the rail with an awkward lunge and toppled over the side. Hobi and Demon disappeared in a splash below.

"Get Cora!" said Amryn.

Rafael appeared and tossed down a ladder. Rope and rungs flew, unfurling and clacking against the hull. Amryn half-slid and half-climbed, anxiously searching the dark lagoon for any sign of them. As she reached the bottom of the ladder, Demon broke the surface like a fish striking a lure, then sank back under the water. The old lizard's spiked head crested the surface again, lying limp in Hobi's grasp. Demon hung like dead weight, and Hobi strained to keep him afloat.

Amryn swam for them. Hobi went under again. When she reached them, he surfaced again, and her heart nearly froze. His sunken eyes held none of the iridescence the change usually wrought. He was in his element, yet struggling for breath.

"Take Demon. Go," he rasped. "Go."

She dove and shouldered the lizard's weight. In a curtain of swirling bubbles and dark limbs, Rafael was there with them, lifting Demon beside her. Together, they swam for the ladder.

She felt the weight leave her shoulders and kicked up for air. Rafael hung on the bottom rung with Demon clamped under his arm. Amryn clawed her way up to them, and rung by rung, they started up with Demon clutched between them. Then, a scratchy thump brushed her shoulder, and she looked up.

Khaldun was rappelling down the hull with a net slung over his back. Stronger than either of them, he secured Demon in the net and shouted up to the deck.

"Heave ho!" Cora called the cadence. The crew hauled Khaldun and Demon up the rope.

Amryn looked back for Hobi. He had made it to the ladder. He hung there in the water with his arm crooked over the rung. Head down. Barely moving.

"Go, M'sita," Rafael urged her. "The captain will follow when he catches his breath."

"No. Not yet."

Amryn slid back down to him. Something was not right. Hobi lifted his head at her touch. His sallow skin confirmed her fear. He'd leeched the poison from Demon, but the poison's taint had sickened him. For once, sorcery had no cure for the sorcerer.

"Hold on to me," she said, forcing the panic from her voice.

Hobi clasped her arm and winced. A strange knot rose on his forearm. She watched as it bunched under his skin and traveled up his arm like a living thing. The misshapen bone—or claw—rolled across his chest and disappeared into his flesh. What was she seeing? Hobi tightened his fingers on her arm, and Amryn fought the instinct to shove him away. She stared at his chest, unsettled and searching for whatever it was that lived under his skin.

"Don't let them see it," Hobi pleaded. "Please."

Amryn pushed his stiff hand to the next rung and curled her fingers around his. Whatever it was, she wouldn't let it have him.

"Blanket! He's going into shock." She shouted to anyone listening.

Hobi coughed and spit bile. He was fading.

"I'm going to need you to climb, now," she told him. "Trust me to cover you before we reach the top."

Hobi gave a weak nod, and his white knuckles gripped the next rung. He shivered and turned to heave whatever the poison left churning in his gut.

"You are not allowed to leave me on this damned island alone," said Amryn. "Do you hear me, Captain?"

They climbed together. Hobi grunted with the exertion. One hand, a foot.

A blanket sailed down from above. Amryn snatched it as it passed and wrapped it around his shoulders. Next, she tied a knot under his chin and around his waist. Khaldun swung down again and caught Hobi under his thick arm, blanket and all.

"Heave ho!" Amryn cried.

She dragged herself onto the ship as Khaldun set Hobi down on the deck. Cora ran from Demon to Hobi, cursing up a storm. Hobi gripped the blanket around his neck and pushed to his feet. He swayed in the path of Cora's indignation, his red-rimmed eyes sunken and his knees trembling.

"Sit down, ye blasted fool," said Cora.

"Stand aside," he said.

"Captain, ye been poisoned!" Cora planted her fists on her hips.

"Rather ineptly, if I'm still alive," he said. "Stand aside."

Cora stepped back, shaking her head, and let him pass. Then, she walked over to Amryn.

"This is the worst I've seen him," she said. "Stay close."

Amryn caught up to Hobi and slid under his arm.

"Lean on me," she said.

"No one can see it," he said, his voice growing distant as he wandered the poison's labyrinth alone.

"No, Hobi. No one."

# # #

Hobi drifted into a restless sleep. Amryn sat on the bed beside him, watching moonlight and the lantern's glow shift the shadows on his face. She rested her hand on his chest and stilled her breath. Was it still there? She waited.

A knot rose under her palm, and she drew back. Its shape was unmistakable now, a knob of flesh not his own, living inside him. The presence Hobi had spoken of wasn't some esoteric notion. Not a vague voice in his head. It had substance, or assumed substance when it chose. When it deemed a tangible manifestation of its existence necessary. Tentatively, she touched her fingertip to the being nestled under his skin. It shied away, then returned, seeking contact. Seeking reassurance Hobi was going to be all right.

"What is it?" Amryn signed.

"Unknown," said Ufa.

Amryn stretched out beside Hobi and rested her head on his chest, needing the same reassurance herself. She fell asleep with the presence under her palm, both of them counting the quiet drumbeat of his heart.

# # #

When she woke, Hobi's hand was stroking her shoulder. She rolled over, and he met her with a tired smile.

"Thank you," he said.

Simple and done. Making it clear he wanted no questions about what she'd seen. It was yet another of the fragile threads they wove in their unlikely tapestry of trust. He wouldn't lie, and he would tell her when he was ready or not at all. Amryn tried the less direct route.

"How close have you come to dying because you couldn't accept anyone's help?"

He didn't answer. That was answer enough.

"Well, your color is better this morning, so I suppose you'll live." Amryn sat up. "Can I get you something to drink?"

"No. Stay and rest with me," he said. "Cora came to check on us. Demon is awake and surly, as usual. Khaldun is certain he's discovered the villain who poisoned our dinner."

"Rafael again?" she guessed.

"The likely suspect."

With the excuse of testing repairs to the dinghy, Rafael had made a few more forays to the island. The fruit he foraged offered a rare treat for a crew tired of fish and dried rations. Cook had made banana pudding for the crew the previous night. No one else had fallen sick. Rafael had been the first into the water to help them. If he had wanted them dead...

"He didn't do it," she said.

"No, but someone did," said Hobi. "Until we discover who, Rafael is confined to your old cabin. Khaldun was adamant we make a show of dealing with the threat for the morale of the crew."

"And the killer is free to try again."

"Would the Fang?" he said. "If a knife missed its mark?"

"Not for a while and never with the same weapon," she said. "The mark is on high alert after a miss. It's the worst possible time to strike again."

"It's been weeks since the last attempt. Poison instead of a cannon." Hobi shrugged. "Or the cannon truly was an accident, and we have a poisoner with some new grudge. More than one Mauryan left with his pride bruised today."

"I'd sooner suspect bruised Mauryans than believe a murderer is hiding in the *Seeker's* crew," said Amryn. "We know these people. But the Mauryans—"

"Are not what I expected. We can toss any hopes of sweeping in here and being embraced as long-lost kin. They're going to take some convincing."

"All the more reason to press the gambit," said Amryn.

"As emissaries of the Watchers."

"Keep them on the defensive."

"When a challenger falters, power presses the advantage," said Hobi.

"Another pearl from your trove of truisms?"

"It's an enviable trove." Hobi smiled. "You can use borrow from it when we meet the elite and powerful of Maurya tomorrow."

"Tomorrow?"

"Rajin Chandra summoned us while you were sleeping."

"And you didn't wake me?"

"I told Commander Vishal we were indisposed, and his rajin would have to wait. She'll send a sloop for us in the morning."

Chapter 23

Maurya

A translucent sphere rose to envelop the Mauryan sloop and sank into the lagoon. Less disconcerted than the first time a sphere had swallowed her, Amryn managed to focus on the conveyance itself. She wondered who controlled its coming and going. Commander Vishal and a few Mauryan guards were on the sloop with them and more wary of Amryn and Hobi than a simple transport bubble they'd been using all their lives. The likelihood of the water breeching its walls and drowning them seemed of no concern.

They traveled a maze of passageways into the mountain itself. Narrower than the crevasse the *Seeker* had traversed and faintly lit rather than pitch black, these routes seemed more frequently used, sized for smaller Mauryan vessels going to and from the lagoon and wherever else the maze may lead.

Amryn steadied herself as the deck shifted angles yet again. The sphere rose and dissolved on command, leaving the sloop floating inside a vaulted chamber hidden somewhere within the mountain.

Grand, towering arches of metal and stone filigreed the expanse of glass overhead. Muted sunlight cast blue-hued rays over a canal wide and deep enough to accommodate the dozen boats plying its still waters, passing in and out of the shadows between shafts of sunlight, propelled by neither sail nor oars. Though longer than wide, Amryn could see the entire canal from end to end.

Stone-like columns, almost as tall and broad as those in the Gyakari's palace, stood sentinel above a honeycomb of porticos and brightly lit plazas lining the harbor. Like the grand foyer of a forgotten city, the waterside plaza was painted in subtle shades of blue, white, and green, depicting scenes from the earth above—lush landscapes and majestic creatures—memorializing the world Maurya had tended and then abandoned.

Though subdued by Ari standards, the marketplace was not empty. The few vendor stalls not shuttered had a sparse scattering of customers. Those who had dared venture out for a look at the strangers cast furtive glances at the approaching sloop before scurrying for cover.

"What are they so afraid of?" said Amryn.

"Meeting the gods they gave up for dead," said Hobi.

Vishal gave them a long look. Perhaps in disapproval because they were not speaking Old N'si. Perhaps in consternation over what he might be bringing into his city. He was a hard one to read. Yet, he had let slip one bit of information she might use. When coming to collect them, he had pulled the sloop alongside the Seeker and hailed them as Emissaries of the Republic.

Interesting. Did Mauryans consider themselves independent or subjects of the Republic? Given their careful dealings with them thus far, she suspected there was some lingering deference to the greater alliance of starfolk she'd always known as the Watchers. Amryn surreptitiously signed the question, and Ufa confirmed her theory.

As the sloop neared the dock, Vishal motioned them to follow. He waited while the crew secured the mooring. His jaw clenched when the whistle sounded, and he turned to face them.

"Do no harm," he said.

"Give us no cause." Amryn swept past him.

Arrogance was both a shield and a blade, a skill born of entitlement and honed to its sharpest edge over her years at the Ari court. Authority was a more nebulous commodity, one many discovered they lacked only after their bluster crumbled to a challenger's strength.

Amryn had never relished the deference others considered their due merely for being members of the Gyakari's favored kin. But she'd grown accustomed to the silken armor her blood and her name bestowed, and she stepped onto the Mauryan plaza like the Ari noble she was, aware of every eye following her.

Hobi fell in beside her, matching her step for step, and looking as regal as any Ari prince. He'd made sure they both looked the part.

Dressing to meet a queen had presented a quandary. Amryn had only the clothes he'd found her in and the sailor's garb she'd been wearing since. Neither were particularly awe-inspiring.

Hobi had surprised her by digging around in a trunk and pulling out finery of his own. Tailored to hug like a second skin, the sleeveless N'si vanlors buttoned from breast to hip, with embellished hems that barely brushed the ankles. Swirling vines, dragons, and moons in shimmering threads of copper and gold adorned his collection of silk brocades. Not one, but several, in crimson, white, and midnight blue. Amryn wondered anew at the estate he'd inherited from the house whose name he disdained.

Vanlors were cut to accommodate the renowned N's dexterity, as were the loose-fitted breeches in deeper shades of linen or silk worn underneath. Exquisitely and unabashedly sensuous, vanlors flattered the body, set off by wide, tasseled sashes to accentuate a lean N'si form. Cut to expose more drakmu-marked skin than she would have dared in Wodi.

"I'm not sure this is what Watchers would wear," she had said, eyeing the finery.

"They wear whatever we say they wear." Hobi had shrugged off her doubts. "Maurya has been in hiding for a long time. Tastes change."

A few hours later, Rafael had tailored a vanlor to fit her perfectly. He even altered a pair of suede slippers, which impressed her almost as much as his willingness to do so. He cut off her apology when she went to the cabin where he had been confined and retrieved his handiwork.

"No sorry, M'sita," Rafael said with a quiet laugh. "I find that I have time on my hands. Go, so I may imagine their faces when they see your beauty."

# # #

Vishal and his pack of guards, each practically indistinguishable from the next, led them through the plaza and past the few Mauryans still in sight. One young merchant trailed after them until Vishal stopped to shoo him away.

"Not all sheep," she signed.

147

"Yet not one lion," Hobi replied.

Beyond the plaza, featureless glass doors slid open at their approach, unattended and unbidden. When they had passed, the doors closed behind them with the hushed sigh of duty done. After the spaciousness of the harbor, entering the corridor felt like stepping into a closet. Though wide enough for dozens to walk abreast, its windowless walls and lowered ceiling seemed to press too close, and light took on a strange starkness.

Leeched of the sun's warmth or lantern's glow, the sterile white light washing the corridor made the mosaics on the walls, crafted in the same colors and motifs as in the harbor, seem harsh, even brittle. Yet, Amryn realized this was the same unwavering light Ottah had told her banished the slightest shadow from the Watcher's Den in Ealim. Its nature was one of many puzzles they would have worked together to solve had she been allowed to dedicate herself to the Unraveling instead of the Fang.

Amryn noted the slight incline in the walkway and squared angles not carved by the sea. Precise in form and function, the thoroughfare between harbor and city could be sealed and flooded if attacked. It would be a shame to ruin the artwork, though turning the corridor into a gallery seemed as pointless as draping silk over a marble statue to give it a semblance of life.

Along the way, Mauryans pulling carts or shouldering crates stopped to watch them pass, and whispers nipped at their heels along the way. At each checkpoint, more indistinguishable guards joined their procession. By the time glass doors hissed apart at the end of the corridor, their escort had swelled to the size of a small army.

Vishal stopped and turned to face them again. From the moment he'd answered their signal—and the long-awaited message even they didn't understand they were sending—he'd committed to bringing them to this hidden city.

"You are the first outsiders to pass through these doors since... ever."

Amryn glanced at Hobi. From his expression, he had understood every word and the implications. Had Yuji not been here years ago? Vishal either did not know or was lying.

"Your ability to secure your city is not in question," said Hobi in careful but precise Old N'si.

"We are more interested in your rationale for doing so," said Amryn. "When you might have been engaging the enemy instead."

Vishal blinked. She'd hit a sore spot.

"Ask those who make our decisions," he said.

With that, he led them to a waiting carriage and held open the door. Carriage was a generous term for the small conveyance. The pair of unupholstered benches might seat six, eight at most. Amryn ran her hand over the half-shell of the carriage itself. It was rough to the touch. Porous but sturdy.

"What is this material?" she asked.

One of the guards accompanying them opened her mouth, then hesitated. Taller than the others, with cropped grey curls and more gold bands circling her sleeve than any but Vishal, she had the aura of a warrior, despite her city's cowering.

"Enlighten her, Captain Nira." Vishal nodded consent.

"We call it coralesk," said Nira. "A composite of coral, copper, and sand. We learned to work it to conserve the remaining starheart for structural repairs. As you know, we have been on our own for quite some time."

Resentment simmered beneath Nira's answer. Amryn could hardly blame her. If she'd been waiting on aid from the Ari empire for as long as Maurya had awaited the Republic's, she'd be testy, too.

The carriage shuddered and lurched ahead, not drawn by beasts but propelled by some unseen force. It took all her willpower not to clamber over the side to study the contraption. Instead, she kept her eyes on the path ahead as the carriage clattered along, seemingly compelled to follow the parallel metallic rails stretching before them.

The suffocating sense of confinement fell away as the rails guided the carriage from the station and set it clattering towards a village. Well, it was more than a village, but nowhere near the size of Naré or even Ealim. For a fabled lost city, Maurya was a bit underwhelming.

On either side of the ribbon of rails, tall buildings rose in uniformity. Dwellings stacked one on another. Chairs crowded onto modest balconies. Shared catwalks and tubes connecting a beehive of homes and shops. Straight lines and angled bones lay beneath layers of softer dressing, attempting to soften the rigid sameness, to distinguish one cubbyhole from the next. Each window, the same. The distance from one door to the next, the same.

And above the buildings, clouds drifted across a teal blue sky. The same clouds, drifting one after another. The same birds soaring on nonexistent winds in an endless parade, a wishful charade. More illusions.

In the center of the town, a massive tree trunk stretched from the artificial ground to the artificial sky. Structural support, perhaps? Amryn noticed grates and pipes that seemed intended to blend into its otherwise bark-like surface. The column masquerading as a tree, though rather unconvincingly, supplied air and water to the town, sustaining life through one giant vein grown through the town itself.

Maurya smelled of sandalwood and salt, like incense left sitting too long on a shelf in the bazaar. Shadowed faces drew back from the windows. Wary habits honed by generations spent in hiding muffled the sounds of life any town should have. The laugh of a child, the clank of a skillet, the slam of a door sounded hushed and furtive. Like echoes of the waking world intruding on a dream.

The carriage slowed before a hollow tower of glass and tarnished metal. With a shudder, the rails retreated into the ground and left the carriage sitting inside the tower. A guard latched a door behind them, and the sudden leap upward took Amryn's breath away. Sealed inside the glass tower, the carriage rose rapidly, catapulted from the village in a dizzying ascent. Hobi clutched her hand as they barreled towards the illusionary sky.

Then suddenly, they were in another village like the one below. Sandalwood and salt-scented cafes. Shops and dwellings crowded one against another, huddled around a giant tree to claim their share of air and water. The same dressing over all the same bones. And another glass tower waiting beyond a ribbon of rails.

They ascended three more hollow towers before the bones began to vary. Angles lost some of their stiffness, and silks draped more artfully. Manicured gardens dotted common grounds, layering flowers and citrus scents over the ever-present sandalwood. Not every window was a twin to the ones beside it, and the rows of buildings occasionally parted, conceding precious footing to windows framing views of the cerulean sea beyond. Wealth lived here. If not wealth, then whatever determined status in Maurya.

The last tower carried them to the pinnacle of the city. Nestled beneath a glass dome covering its entire expanse, the buildings here stretched unrestrained, uninhibited by the shoulders of their neighbors, each with a uniqueness lacking in the bland towns beneath. The lower boroughs huddled inside the shell of an ancient ship from the stars. But the pinnacle had grown atop that sunken grey hulk like a coral reef.

On the leeward side of the sunken city, sunset-hued coralesk manors clung to a craggy black mountainside. To starboard, the halo of sunlight rippled over gardens, fountains, and open pavilions, and the tree trunk carrying air and water through the lower boroughs finally sprouted limbs and spread a silken green canopy of handcrafted leaves over parks filled with potted palms and ferns.

The ring island above was the crown on the brow of an undersea mountain emperor. When looking down from here, Maurya and the mountain seemed inextricably melded, like a moth snared after it passed too close to a spider's web. The starship had dared too close. Caught and drawn in closer by the mountain. As if curious about the strange creature trespassing on its domain.

The juxtaposition of human-crafted design disappearing into unyielding stone removed any doubt in Amryn's mind. This was a ship where ships did not belong. And however it got here, it would never break free. This ship from the stars would never fly again.

Chapter 24

Read the Room

As a homeland, Maurya would need a bit of work. The place was too quiet. Too complacent. Generations spent cowering from an enemy they couldn't see had turned his Mauryan cousins into sheep. N'si would sweep through the herd like wolves.

How had Yuji met these people and considered them kin? Hobi had trouble even thinking of them as nene. And how did such an insular community not remember Yuji? Another puzzle to complicate his plans.

A clutch of onlookers had gathered on the steps of a grand, columned hall. As Vishal led their procession, the crowd tightened and waved placards. Each wore a bright red armband and a murderous sneer. Finally, someone here was showing some nerve.

"Imposters," one yelled, shaking her fist. "Servants of the beast!"

"Lock them up," the man beside her snarled and lunged their way.

Amryn's arms shone silver as Ufa readied to strike. A flash of light, and the air crackled. Nira stood between them with her weapon raised and flickering. Her shield pushed back the protesters, muffling angry shouts behind an unseen wall.

"Gagan's rabid fools," said Vishal. "Pay them no mind. They live for the lies he feeds them."

"Gagan, again," Amryn signed.

"A pest we will deal with," Hobi replied. But the encounter tossed another challenge into the mix. Identifying the opposition was only the beginning. Neutralizing Gagan's influence could take time Hobi didn't have to waste. Especially if Gagan led the only Mauryans with fire in their bellies.

One last Mauryan blocked their way. An old fellow in a white robe and carrying a white pail. Nira sheathed the baton, and Vishal paused. This one was no threat.

"Not the time, Quan," Vishal told the old nene with more patience than he dealt others.

"Time can wait."

Quan opened his arms. Something in his expression caught Hobi off guard. He grasped the old nene's forearm, bewildered by the compunction to do so. His hair stood on end as he felt the knot rise beneath his skin. The old nene felt it, too, and his grip tightened on Hobi's arm. Hobi felt the brush of another knot as one seemed to greet the other. Shaken by the unexpected, Hobi drew back.

Quan gave him a smile ladened with meaning he couldn't decipher. Hobi would have sworn the old nene's eyes held a faint iridescence before he looked away. The white-robed window washer bent to pick up his pail.

"The path stretches on," Quan said and walked away.

Hobi fought an irrational urge to go after him, and the sadness that often overwhelmed him rose unexpectedly in his throat. Amryn touched his shoulder. She'd seen enough to raise concern. Hobi shook off the sensation, and, for once, the presence let him go without penance.

"Interesting fellow," he said lightly. "But we have a rajin to meet."

Nira crossed the portico ahead of them and opened yet another glass door, taller and wrought with more attention to aesthetics than the others they'd passed. Hobi took it as encouragement the sheep had not entirely forgotten the pleasure of beauty rendered for beauty's sake.

He hung back and leaned his head to Amryn's.

"We go in as equals," he said. "Read the room. Let it decide."

Amryn nodded and walked ahead. Hobi would accept her judgment as to how to handle the crowd. What her own considerable insight didn't tell her, Ufa's would. Vishal frowned at him for speaking in an unknown tongue again but stopped short of a challenge and led the way.

The meeting chamber fit the grand hall like a hand-me-down shoe. Clunky tables bracketed an oversized and equally utilitarian metal chair. As in the hive dwellings below, valiant attempts at artistry painted over the stark bones. But function was function. Art was art. One had yet to make the other's acquaintance. The potted palms were nice, he supposed, but the rajin's choice of décor was irrelevant.

Hobi read the room instead. The subtle art of discerning attitude from appearance was one at which N'si excelled. The brush of a shoulder. Restless hands or the tilt of a head. A fidget, a blink, a tug on an ear. Hobi sampled the room like a spider tasting each dewdrop on its web.

Vishal stepped up to a railed box. A platform designated for speaking, Hobi assumed. He followed Amryn into the box and studied the assembled as Vishal spoke.

Sameness. One like the other. Dressed in the same prim robes and scarves, covering birth-markings so faint as to be undetectable. Pretty people. Squishier than N'si. Tamed. Malleable.

"In accordance with protocol, and at the behest of the Assembly...."

Hobi listened disinterestedly while scanning the assembled Mauryans. These were supposedly the most influential among them. Finally, his glance settled on one particular stare among the many.

Power is drawn to power.

Rajin Chandra radiated the confidence true power fuels. Now, this was one Mauryan he could imagine descended from the same ancestors as the N'si. From her coppery skin and high cheekbones to her kohl-rimmed eyes and henna-darkened drakmu, she made the other Mauryans seem like faded watercolors. Draped in swaths of blue silk fringed with gold rings and bells, with an armored white shawl circling her shoulders and a gold-and-sapphire breastplate on her chest, she embodied the last trace of fierceness left in Maurya.

The spark of recognition in her eyes unbalanced him, and the flash of joy she swiftly extinguished. Her fingers curled on the arm of the ugly chair, and an attendant closed in protectively at her shoulder. Tall and broad with the coiled readiness of a seasoned soldier, the attendant followed his rajin's gaze, and his brow creased when he saw Hobi.

Vishal was still talking, repeating the message Maurya received eight years ago.

"The Republic received the message, as well," said Vishal. "They have come to respond."

"How have talks with the Chalyns progressed thus far?" said Amryn. She drew no ready replies. "You have engaged their representatives on our behalf, of course."

Her question hung in the awkward silence like steam after a rain. Downcast eyes. Fidgeting hands. None dared voice admission of their failure or acknowledgment of their cowardice. Rajin Chandra fixed on Vishal with an unreadable stare, then blinked.

"I see from your faces you did not." Hobi spoke in the Ari common dialect. He paused, then shook his head in disdain. "You cannot even understand the language of those we assigned you to nurture. What is your excuse for failing in your duty?"

Amryn translated, and scandalized murmurs rippled through the Assembly. Vishal turned at her words, and puzzlement clouded his face. But clever as ever, with instinct honed by her upbringing, Amryn had taken note of the rajin's interest in Hobi. Chandra's was the only regard that mattered.

"Rajin, you are honored by the presence of Prince Hobizadi Ir'Ravadaron." Amryn conjured him a name. "You will answer His Grace as you would our Emperor who sent him."

Amryn offered the nod she'd perfected watching the Gyakari, absolute authority deigning to allow a lesser to speak. Chandra's eyebrows flashed in interest. A challenge of equals? Hobi wagered on Amryn.

Chandra blinked first. Resolutely, she drew back her shoulders and rose from her chair. A sudden compunction to reach out welled up in him, as it had with the old window-washer. But this time, the sense of familiarity carried another scent. Intimacy.

"I am Chandra of House Ajagara," she said. "Rajin of Maurya, Earth Station Seven of the Kishar Republic. Since last the Republic took note of us, securing their interests from the enemy's conquest has kept us preoccupied."

"With hiding to protect yourselves," said Hobi.

"What of your charges?" said Amryn. "Did you secure them, as well?"

"There was no time," said Chandra.

"A few thousand years was not sufficient?"

Hobi caught the subtle shift in Amryn's voice. Ufa knew facts time obscured.

"The Republic cultivated this planet for the fullness of an age. We seeded eleven Cycles and watched ten fall. The science frigate Maurya arrived 4628 years ago to clear the remains of the last failed Cycle and to shepherd in the next. To *shepherd*, Rajin Chandra. Shepherds risk their lives to safeguard the flock."

"Ten," said Chandra.

Amryn, or Ufa, hesitated.

"The Republic seeded ten Cycles," said Chandra. "Before we could plant the eleventh, a rogue AI rose to attack us all."

"The AI we now know as Kitsune," said Amryn. "Created by humankind near the end of the ninth Cycle. A mistake. An aberration lacking the safeguards the Republic sears into all AI protocols."

"And yet, it survived the apocalypse that killed its maker. It hid when we came in to clear the wreckage. We seeded the tenth Cycle with dragonkind, in accordance with the Kazera Convention. While their empires rose and fell, Kitsune skulked, schemed, and grew stronger. He wormed his way across the farthest reaches of the Republic, corrupted our AI, and conscripted an army to serve him."

"Kitsune declared war on the Watchers," said Amryn. "His rebellion swept the Republic. Incapacitated us. Nearly destroyed us."

"Kitsune infiltrated every system on this planet," said Chandra. "Earth Stations Alpha and Gamma fell first. We heard them die. We heard the cries of the worlds he conquered as he attacked."

"And you ignored their cries," said Amryn. "Rather than fight for the Republic, you hid. Rather than follow your duty, you chose to save yourselves."

"You would rather we died like the others?"

"Not all of them died," said Amryn. "Some, he had a use for. He scoured their minds and forced them out into an unclean world, into the barrens you had not yet rendered fit for habitation. After that, Kitsune started the eleventh Cycle on his own. And for four thousand years, he tormented the breeding stock he stole. Sent adversity after adversity to weed out the weak. Cared only for the survival of the fittest."

"And you fault us for not nurturing the seeds Kitsune sowed?" said Chandra. "For not risking our lives for the creatures he bred?"

"Creatures." Amryn stiffened. "They were once citizens of the Republic."

"Corrupted by the enemy, just as he corrupted—"

"Kitsune is dead!" said Hobi. "The *creatures* you abandoned killed the monster you feared!"

"That cannot be—" Vishal's face had gone ashen.

"Eight years ago," said Amryn. "You ignored a message. The children of the Republic, the brethren you disdained as *creatures*, defeated Kitsune without you."

"Lies!" Gagan leapt to his feet. "If Kitsune were gone, Maurya would know!"

"How?" Vishal challenged him. "How can you know the monster is gone if you're afraid to peek out of the closet?"

"Commander, tread lightly," Gagan warned. "Traitors pay the price for consorting with the enemy."

The lights in the Assembly Hall flickered. Amryn's relic and Hobi's pendant flashed and pulsed in a tandem display of warning. Councilors rose at their tables, exclaiming in confusion, and a few made for the door. Hobi spread his arms and called out.

"Your accusation is an insult to the Emperor!"

Gagan's face purpled in rage. He had the look of a nene about to do something he'd be sorry for after. Gagan took one step, then his hand flew to his throat. The stench of fear thickened the air, roiling over the hall like smoke billowing off a pyre. Stilling feet and choking off cries. Unrelenting and insidious in its demand. He tasted the syrupy blanket of paranoia spreading over the Mauryans.

Hobi's side twitched in revulsion. The presence he knew loathed this new force he did not. Amryn swayed beside him and caught his arm. She felt it, too. The Mauryans quieted under its suffocating will, and the air grew lighter. The mysterious force came and went, silently, efficiently.

"Stand down. Enough." Chandra shook free of its influence. "Maurya, hear me. For generations, we have waited. If these envoys are not who they claim, we will expose their trickery. If they are, their arrival is cause for celebration."

"Confine them. The risk of allowing them to roam free is untenable," Gagan objected. "Even now, the Wired could be signaling the enemy. The Elders will hold us accountable if—"

"Prince Hobizadi and Ambassador Nisari are guests of Maurya," said Chandra. "For those who have forgotten what that means, I suggest you do not challenge the protection of House Ajagara."

Chapter 25

Pendant

Chandra returned to her office in a daze, her heart still racing from the shock of seeing his face. After all this time spent convincing herself he was dead, he had materialized before her again, as miraculously as the first time.

Lost in thought, she hardly noticed Janak close the door behind her. Even shaken as she was, she realized he must be reeling as well. The secret they could never reveal had cemented their bond through the years.

"He is not Yuji," Janak said bluntly.

"No," she admitted. "The years would have aged even him by now."

Chandra sat at her desk, seeking the familiar comfort of control, determined to hold together the world she felt dissolving beneath her feet. If only he *were* Yuji, she would have willingly borne its loss. She drew a steadying breath and looked at Janak.

"Prince Hobizadi is a mirror image of the Yuji we knew. To the smallest detail, he is a replica of Yuji in his youth. You may remember our youth. It was long ago, when we were reckless, and dreaming was not a curse."

"The resemblance is unnerving, I grant you. But it must be coincidental," said Janak. "Time fades the clarity of our memories. The image you locked away shifted to fit the image of someone standing before you."

"Shifted instantly and identically for both of us?"

Janak paced before the window. The view the window framed was an illusion. Birds flew above trees swaying in a soundless breeze. Precisely one hour from now, the same birds would fly beneath the same clouds, as they had for years. Mauryan had grown accustomed to their comforting illusions. Chandra hated that window.

"What if some caught in the other stations came from House Ravadaron? What if the bloodline runs strong?" said Janak. "You resemble the portraits of your Ajagara forebears."

"So, Yuji and his N'si are descendants of the Ravadarons. Conscripted by Kitsune from the other stations he seized. And after four thousand years of breeding with their fellow conscripts from throughout the Republic, they are still indistinguishable from Prince Hobizadi? That is highly improbable, my dear."

"I suppose you have a more likely explanation," said Janak. "Share it."

Chandra hesitated. The alternative could destroy them both.

"Yuji made it back," she voiced the possibility they were both avoiding. "Hobizadi is his son."

"And this son now returns to Maurya, masquerading as a prince of the Kishar Republic, having somehow acquired both the signal and passphrase, as well as a Wired companion. Do you know how improbable *that* sounds?"

She wished she could allow him the pretense. Janak deserved every accommodation she could offer after years of standing by her side, keeping her confidences, and sharing the emptiness Yuji left in their lives. But improbable did not mean impossible.

"The pendant," she said.

Janak stared back, unblinking. He, too, had felt the heat of the attunement. The heirloom transceiver prism, of no practical use with its energy depleted, had been gifted to Chandra by her mother, Srilata. Besides the diamonyte itself, clear and well-cut but of average size, the relic's only value came from the artisanry in its design and nostalgia for the faded glory of the past. Chandra had fitted the old pendant with a power bead attuned to the rings she and Janak had exchanged the day their families declared them betrothed. Locator bands in the rings grew warm in the paired wearer's proximity. It was a silly little endearment incorporated into Mauryan culture over time.

Attuning their rings to the diamonyte in the old pendant had served no purpose other than giving her hands something to do while she tried not to think about the inevitable. But the day arrived anyway, and, too soon, Yuji left. She gave him the pendant that day, knowing the attunement would be useless once he passed beyond Maurya's walls. It hadn't kept her from hoping she'd know when he made it home.

"You felt it," she said.

Janak nodded.

Chandra leaned her head back and sighed. It was a choice she had never regretted, though the memory was a constant whisper in the back of her mind and followed her through her days like a shadow. One forbidden mercy with the power to bring down her entire house. All because she looked into a stranger's amber eyes.

"Send for Vish," she said. "I hoped never to burden him with knowing of our crime, but that is no longer an option."

# # #

"What do you know of others who have come here?" said Janak.

"No one has found Maurya and lived," said Vish.

"One did," said Chandra.

She poured tea and carried a cup to Vish on the jhula. She plumped a bolster and settled beside him. Having made up her mind, she wanted to confess and be done. Regret could wait.

"I see much of myself in you, son," she said. "I was once young and longing to go beyond the walls, to feel the unfiltered sun and taste the wild wind. The world I was forbidden to explore filled my daydreams. Like you, I leapt at the chance to join the patrols as soon as the captains would have me."

"Ajagara are not content in a cage," said Vish. "The horizon calls us still."

"One day, while out scouting alone, I noticed an odd lump of driftwood floating in the distance. A flutter of white snared my curiosity, and I swam to see what it might be. What I had thought was driftwood was the splintered mast from a small ship. Nothing extraordinary. Patrols had encountered bits of broken ships before. But I was eager for any glimpse of the outside world, so I swam closer."

"What did you find?" said Vish.

"A man clinging to the wreckage, lashed to the mast with his shirt. He was unlike anyone I had ever seen. Yet, even so near death, he was beautiful. Skin burnished to a deep copper. Birth-markings so bold, so intricate. Their patterns covered his back and arms."

Chandra swirled the tea in her cup. She could live a thousand years, and the memory of that day would never dim.

"By Mauryan law, I should have left him to die," she said. "But then, he opened his eyes. Amber eyes, a shade I would never have imagined eyes could be, lit with amusement. His parched lips twitched in a smile."

Vish was watching her intently. He had always been a bright child, quick to piece together any puzzles she gave him.

"Dusk was setting in. I cut his shirt from the timber. He didn't fight, just let go and let me pull him away. Maybe he trusted me. Maybe he had nothing left to lose. But I swam with him to the island and hid him in an abandoned grotto in the raveler caves. I picked some fruit and left him there with my canteen."

"Elder's teeth, Mother." Vish swept a hand through his hair. "If anyone found him—"

"We would both have been executed," said Chandra. "I returned the next night, half expecting he would have succumbed to dehydration or fever. Instead, he propped on his elbow and laughed. He assured me his kind were too stubborn to die."

"His kind?" said Vish.

"N'si, he named them. To hear him tell it, the N'si are elves, wizards, and djinn rolled into one. A people not lacking in confidence, I can assure you. For days, I snuck away to spend time with him. Learning about his world. Talking about ours. Reveling in meeting someone who had seen so much more than I ever would. And yes, knowing that each day he stayed, the risk of being discovered grew."

Janak stirred from his stance at the window. He had listened in silence while she told a story they both knew. He had his own part to tell.

"Chandra came to me," he said. "We were to be married the following month, but we had been friends our entire lives. Your mother had a habit of bending the rules, and I was accustomed to extracting her from the traps she laid for herself. She took me to meet Yuji."

Janak sat at her desk and folded his hands. For a while, Chandra wondered how much he would be willing to say about those few weeks that had shaped them both. Lost in reflection, deciding whether he dared release emotions he had kept locked away for so long, he chose to say no more.

"Weeks passed," said Chandra. "Yuji healed. We knew he could not stay. He had to leave Maurya, but we kept finding one more reason to delay that day. Then the matter was decided for us."

"If you'd been discovered, I wouldn't be here," said Vish. "So, what happened?"

"Ravelers found him."

Vish sucked in a breath. The creatures seldom ventured from the labyrinth of caves and crevasses they hollowed throughout the mountain, riddling stone from its crown to its core. Ravelers were distinctive beings, neither octopus nor ray, and their cunning surpassed any creature in the sea. Named for their peculiar ability to unravel elements of their surroundings and weave new designs, ravelers had always lived here and seemingly nowhere else on earth. Though, who could be certain with masters of shapeshifting and camouflage?

"I found him in the grotto, covered in ravelers, his amber eyes glowing. I will never forget the sight." Chandra rubbed her head. "I foolishly had not given him the bitters, but they had not taken anyone in so long. When I found him, it was too late."

"It changed him, of course," said Janak. "Not in the ways we have always been told."

"He was still Yuji," said Chandra. "Only more so. Everything about him more... potent."

"Oh, the wonders he could do." Janak smiled faintly. "Shape water as he wished. Make clean water from brine. Charm any fish in the sea to do his bidding."

"Swim without drawing a breath?" said Vish.

"Yes, that, too." Janak's brow flicked in surprise. "How did you know?"

"Hobizadi challenged me to a swim," said Vish. "On the second day he was here. His endurance was inhuman. Could ravelers have gotten to him so soon?"

"Possibly," said Chandra. "The change in Yuji was quick. In an instant, a mischievous young N'si grew wise beyond his years. Yuji decided the risks to us were too great. He had to go back to his people. We had to stay to lead ours."

"When he set out alone, I was certain it was to his death. No ship. No food," said Janak. "But I could not deter him."

"On the day he left, I gave him an Ajagara heirloom, a diamonyte pendant that had been my mother's. A memento, I hoped," said Chandra. "We never saw him again."

Vish stared at her for a long while. He weighed the terrible danger of the truth.

"Why tell me now?" he said.

"Hobizadi bears a remarkable resemblance to Yuji in his youth," said Chandra.

"The similarity is eerie," said Janak.

"So, the only stranger you've seen since arrives, and he has a few similar features. Enough to stir old memories," said Vish. "As you said, it has been a long time. Hobizadi and Yuji cannot be the same person."

"He is wearing the pendant I gave Yuji," said Chandra.

"His transceiver? Mother, you cannot believe...."

"I don't *want* to believe," said Chandra. "But if the outlander we sheltered has returned, and if he gives us away—"

"Gagan wins," said Janak.

"All the progress we have made will be erased," said Chandra. "The Trads and Elders will cement their hold over Maurya."

"Or these people may be from the Republic, as they say. The physical features, even the pendant, can be like those you remember without being the same," said Vish. "You're reading too much into this."

"Prove us wrong," said Janak. "Help us uncover the truth before anyone else does."

"Stay close. Ask questions. Watch and listen," said Chandra.

"I *have* been listening," said Vish. "Have you? Did you not recognize the words Hobizadi spoke when he accused us of failing those we were assigned to nurture?"

Chandra and Janak exchanged glances.

"No," she admitted. "Should we?"

"It isn't exact. I might not have noticed if I hadn't overheard a few of their exchanges earlier," said Vish. "But the language is enough like Tehut to be intelligible. With time, listening to some of the classics again, a bit of practice—"

"Tehut." Janak snorted. "No wonder you understood them. Always the dreamer, with your poetry and plays."

Vish tensed at the tired barb, but he would make no apologies for his love of the classics. A lovely but discarded language, few bothered to study Tehut anymore. Historians had translated nearly all the ancient literature into Mauryan long ago. But the original Tehut had a mystical, musical quality no translation could capture. Vish had taken time to learn its beauty.

"Why would they speak Tehut?" said Chandra.

"Yuji did not?" said Vish.

"Not to us," said Chandra. "His Mauryan was stilted. An odd dialect. Not unlike how the Augmented one speaks."

"It could be the Republic still speaks Tehut," said Vish. "They used Mauryan only for our benefit. That would explain why their accent was so strange."

Chandra mulled over the contradictions. One image of Yuji wearing her mother's pendant and an identical image speaking Tehut? Both could not be real. What if she *was* wrong about the outlanders? They might be from the Republic.

"We cannot risk a mistake," she said. "We must learn more. Hobizadi's companion, the Augmented female. Vish, I want you to win her trust. Find out what she knows about the prince or the pretender she serves."

"Probe her for answers," said Janak. "Did Yuji send them? What does he want?"

"Leave Hobizadi to us," said Chandra. "We will spend time with him, convince him we believe he is who he claims. He gave no sign of recognizing us. Let us see whether he maintains his composure after we jar loose a few memories."

"If there are any to be jarred," said Vish. "What if they *are* pretenders?"

"I wish I could say that depends on their intentions," said Chandra. "But too much is at stake. I will not be as slow to make a difficult decision this time."

"What will you do?" said Vish.

"Expose them without exposing ourselves."

"Gagan will feed them to the Elders," said Vish. "You know this."

"And I will sign the warrant."

"Even if we find common ground?" said Vish. "If Kitsune is gone, that leaves only the Elders. You said Yuji gained exceptional abilities from the ravelers. I saw what Hobizadi can do, and Amryn is the only Augmented in Maurya. They could be the allies we've been waiting for, whether they're fresh from the Republic or not."

"Or our demise," said Chandra. "Our secret is a blade that can slice us in half. Unless we keep our grasp on the hilt, we won't survive long enough to change that."

Chapter 26

Pact

"Ye appear to be alive," Cora noted as they climbed aboard the *Seeker*. The crew gathered on deck, eager to hear more about the fabled city beneath the waves.

"Someday, I will hire a crew that doesn't greet me with that observation every time I return," said Hobi.

"Only because they absconded with your ship while you were gone," said Cora. "Well? What happened?"

"Amryn crowned me the Prince of the Republic," said Hobi. "And I broke the news the monster under the bed is dead."

"We left them contemplating their next move," said Amryn.

"So, what's down there?" said Cora. "Any treasure worth comin' here for?"

"Aplenty," said Hobi. "You can retire to Rhynn and raise cattle and barley."

"The locals may object to parting with their pretties," said Cora.

"Minor details," he waved off their questions and crossed the deck. He looked back at Amryn and reached out his hand. "Might we talk, please?"

Amryn smiled. She made a grand show of taking his hand, if only to encourage this fledgling habit of asking her instead of commanding. Once they were in the cabin alone, he drew the latch.

"Tell me what you saw, what you heard," he said. "All of it."

"You were with me the entire time," she said.

"And I may have noticed a few details you missed." He paced the cabin with the restless energy he'd been slow to recover after the poisoning. "But the same is doubly true of you and Ufa. So, please, indulge me."

He had a point. Fang agents honed their perception skills with such tests. Failing to notice one tiny detail might mean springing a painful trap. Amryn reflexively rubbed a scar from one such early mistake. The years had made her much more observant.

"Something about you rattled the rajin. Considerably more so than I did," said Amryn. "And the rajin is not easily rattled."

"What do you suppose it was? My appearance? My words?"

"Definitely your appearance. By the time you spoke, she'd recovered her wits."

Amryn thought for a moment.

"When you first met Resa," she said. "In a dark alley, she thought for a moment you were Yuji. You resemble your father that strongly."

"Yes." Hobi frowned. "You think she may have known Yuji."

"Probably not. Considering how they reacted to us, Yuji would have also seemed dangerous. Yet he was allowed to leave. Someone in her position couldn't have dared such a risk."

"That was many years ago. She may not have been rajin then."

"What if only those at the highest levels of authority are privy to the most scandalous breach of security in Mauryan history? The breach was discovered after Yuji was gone. Someone confessed. Reports recorded the details. You matched Yuji's description in ways no Mauryan could."

"The rajin would know what others may not."

"It's possible."

"Yet she said nothing to challenge our claims."

"Would she? Based solely on secondhand descriptions of an event she can't reveal happened?" said Amryn. "Was there anything in your father's journal to give us a clue as to who aided him?"

"Nothing specific," he said. "He wrote of *them*, so more than one. Dark-haired angel. A silent warrior. I believe he meant to protect them should the journal fall into the wrong hands. Could be anyone in Maurya, if they're even still alive."

"That's a tenuous *if*," she said. "Especially if someone discovered the truth after Yuji left."

Amryn didn't need to say the rest. If those who had aided Yuji paid with their lives, what mercy would Maurya have shown Yuji if he hadn't escaped in time? And what did it say of the *Seeker's* fate if anyone discovered their ruse?

"What else did you notice?" Hobi set aside the troubling implications. "Anything less open to interpretation?"

"Yes, plenty. The route we took from the lagoon is one of several in and out of the harbor chamber. Others may lead to the sea beyond the island or to the farming domes outside the city."

"How can you tell?"

"After we surfaced in the sloop, a fishing trawler appeared across the harbor. Distinctive scent. It wasn't there before us and didn't follow in after us."

Hobi kept pacing. "Go on."

Amryn recounted what she recalled of their passage into the city and ascent through rising levels of comfort and social status as each glass tower lifted them higher. She skimmed over the obvious details anyone with eyes or ears would have noticed.

"The unnatural white light. The mechanics of the doors and towers. The city isn't powered by windwheels or waterwheels." Amryn paused to study the symbols flickering on her arm. "Ufa names it a *sun seed*. Not the precise term, but a close enough analogy. Imagine capturing a speck of the sun and locking it away to serve you. Never to escape and never to fade."

"Maurya siphons power from this sun seed to feed their mechanics," said Hobi. "And to breathe."

"Ah, so, you caught the scent of sandalwood. Yes, the scent comes from the steel lungs that breathe for Maurya. The most important mechanics of all."

"The column running down the city's spine," said Hobi. "The poorly disguised tree covered in grates. It hides the air vents and water pipes."

"Yes, I believe so. Without the sun seed to fuel the steel lungs, the city would drown."

"With it, they have little need to leave their bunker. That's how they've stayed hidden for so long."

"It may explain how but not why," she said. "Mauryans have lived in fear for so long, they've forgotten how not to. Coaxing them out of hiding will be..."

Amryn left it unsaid. She hesitated to name his dream an impossible one. But after sensing the stench of fear blanket the Assembly Hall and feeling the grip of paranoia wielded by an unseen force, she wondered if they were up to the challenge.

"Was I wrong to bring you here?" Hobi sat on the edge of the bed. "They will not allow us to leave, you know."

"We haven't decided we wish to yet," she said, unsettled by seeing his confidence in himself waver.

"Amryn, I can't explain how, but I feel it in my bones," he said. "This is where I belong."

Months ago, she might have dismissed his declaration as emotion twisting reason. But with Hobi, emotion and reason were inseparable. She sat beside him and sighed.

"Then I suppose we will have to make this place ours," she said.

Hobi cut her a sideways glance. A familiar glint of mischief lit his eyes, and the reckless N'si confidence came creeping back.

"You're proposing we conquer Maurya?" he said. "That's the good old Ari spirit."

"Not conquest. Consider it a liberation of the oppressed," she said. "It sounds more appealing to the conquered."

There it was, then. Emotion and reason were hopelessly twisted. She had just calmly decided to help a rogue sorcerer take over a small country because she disliked seeing him sad. She wondered if this was how the Ari had come to rule an empire.

"You *would* make a formidable ally," he said. "I accept your proposal, Amryn Nisari."

Hobi sealed their pact with a soft, slow kiss. Amryn knew then she would never go back to the life others had planned for her. The path she walked snaked through the unknown, and her name no longer paved the way, but at least the journey was her own. She had never felt stronger.

Amryn combed her fingers through Hobi's long, sleek hair and drew him down to the pillows with her. The warmth of his body stoked her curiosity and awakened feelings she'd been taught to repress. After so many nights lying alone in the dark, listening to one another breathe, her in the bed he had sacrificed for her and him from his pallet on the floor, their fragile walls of restraint shuddered in their rolling waves of yearning.

"Amryn, tell me to stop. Be the wiser of us. Because I am a fool."

She drew back. The desperation in his eyes said it all.

"You're still afraid it will leave you," she said.

He had yet to talk about what she had seen the night of the poisoning, the presence she had *felt* living under his skin. The living magic without which, Hobi believed, he would be ordinary again. The physical manifestation of the mysterious sorcery that had somehow come to inhabit him. The legacy he had inherited from his dying father.

"Hobi, I held you while you struggled to fight off the poison," she said. "The presence sought me out during the night. We reassured one another, Ufa and I, and the magic that lives in you. Because we all feared for you. Because we all care for you. Whatever this presence is, it won't abandon you any more than Ufa would abandon me."

"It told you this?"

"In its own way."

"Ufa spoke with it? Is it an augmentation device, like him?"

"No. Ufa is as perplexed by its nature as you and I are."

Hobi leaned his forehead to hers and breathed a deep sigh.

"But it is real, isn't it?"

"Very much so."

"Then all of us together must be damned near invincible," he said. "I wonder if that's why it led me here. I suspect it did, you know. Though you and Ufa must have been an unexpected bonus. For that, I can only thank luck."

Hobi abandoned restraint and kissed her in earnest. Eager hands cast aside clothing and caressed bared skin, exploring pleasures they'd denied themselves until now. She tingled at his touch, gentle and coaxing at first, then insistent as desire burned brighter. They came together as if their bodies were made for one another, reveling in lovemaking so exquisite she wished it would never end. Late in the night, tangled and content, they slept.

Where they belonged. Under a Mauryan moon.

# # #

Amryn woke to find Hobi studying her, as if trying to memorize her to the tiniest detail. She stretched in the warm morning sunlight and smiled at him.

"What are you thinking about so intently this morning?"

"If luck brought you to me," he said. "I am wondering how I can make you want to stay."

"Kisses. Your kisses are quite nice."

"I'm serious," he said. "I need you, Amryn, and I am unfamiliar with needing anyone. There must be something expected of me. How do I ensure you remain content?"

"Respect. Trust. Honesty," she said. "All you have shown me so far. Keep doing that."

Hobi frowned. "It can't be that simple."

"Would you rather have my list of demands?"

"It would help, yes."

"Very well," she sighed. "I demand we share our cabin with a cat and a lizard. You are to dine with me in the evenings. Share your fancy wardrobe with me. If I plot to take over a country, I will require your allegiance. And when I wake in your arms, I expect to be kissed."

"There, you see? Every alliance comes with demands." A sly smile curled on his lips. "Never let it be said I reneged on a bargain."

Hobi pulled her close and kissed her soundly, stirring memories of the night's lovemaking. A brisk knock on the door interrupted them.

"Not now," Hobi grumbled.

"Message from the rajin," Khaldun announced, his deep voice reverberating through the door. "She marked it urgent."

A letter slid through the crack beneath the door. With a frustrated sigh, Hobi rolled away and went to retrieve the message. As he read it, a scowl darkened his face.

"The rajin demands an exchange," he said. "A prince for a prince."

Chapter 27

Commander

Amryn tapped her fingers on the railing, fighting the urge to shout out. She could stop him. The sloop hadn't gone far. Agreeing to the rajin's proposal felt wrong. But it wasn't as if she had a better idea.

They set out the gambit. They had to make the moves.

"Don't worry so, lass. The captain outwitted the Fang. He can handle a few island folk," said Cora. "And I've yet to see a Mauryan big enough to get past Khaldun."

Hobi had called Cora and Khaldun to their cabin after reading Rajin Chandra's message. Hobi was invited to be her houseguest. Only Hobi and one guard. In an exchange of mutual trust, Chandra would send Captain Vishal, her son, into Ambassador Nisari's remand on the *Seeker*.

Refusing would have fueled suspicions. Agreeing may let them learn more than if they insisted on staying together. They'd debated their options, but the opportunity to pry open some closed Mauryan minds had won out, and Hobi and Khaldun headed back to the city.

"Get Rafael," Amryn told Cora. "If I'm a Watcher and you're playing bodyguard, someone has to be captain of this ship."

"Aye, Your Grace. Or whatever we're callin' ye now." Cora broke into a grin. "Try to figure that out while I tell the little Laradian he's Captain d'Ortega now. This should be entertainin'."

Cora left as another Mauryan sloop made its way across the lagoon. Commander Vishal stood on its deck with his arms crossed and feet braced as if headed into battle. Amryn suppressed a smirk. A single company of Ari soldiers would conquer what she'd seen of Maurya without breaking a sweat. A few Fang would send them fleeing into the sea. Somehow, these people had managed to survive on their own, unassisted and undiscovered for thousands of years.

Yet imagining boatloads of N'si arriving to join their timid kin made her smile. Maurya would never be the same.

"Ambassador Nisari," Vishal hailed her. "Permission to come aboard?"

Amryn sighed. Making him wait would improve her mood, but the tickle of curiosity was more compelling. This may not be the Watcher's den she had yearned to study, but Maurya held scientific treasures of a different sort, and there were still people here who might know how the ancient marvels worked.

"Granted, Commander," she said. "On behalf of Captain d'Ortega, the hospitality of the *Seeker* is yours."

Vishal arched a brow. "How many captains does the *Seeker* have?"

Damn it. She had introduced Hobi as the captain earlier.

"When Prince Hobizadi is aboard, the ship is his. When he is not— need I explain the maritime chain of command?"

"No, I grasp the concept," he said, a twitch of amusement on his lips.

"Good, then I will consider further questions rhetorical," said Amryn. "Since you're here, and I'm tasked with keeping you occupied, let us be frank. Being ordered to stay behind while my prince goes to meet your rajin annoys me. His wellbeing is my responsibility, and I am less than impressed with His Grace's reception thus far."

"Noted," said Vishal.

"Noted? What an uninspired response. Have Mauryans lost the ability to express anything but platitudes?"

"I don't give a damn whether you're impressed with His Grace's reception," said Vishal. "There, is that better?"

Amryn suppressed a smile. At last, one lone spark flickered in the embers.

"Much better," she said. "Now that we are speaking freely, tell me why you are here."

"My rajin sent me."

Amryn pursed her lips. The deflection didn't merit a response.

"Because I want out of this cage," Vishal answered evenly, but the tremor in his voice snuck through. She recognized desperation all too well. Fenced in by someone else's obligations. Suffocating, grasping for a window of escape. The *Seeker* could find itself with another stowaway.

"Come," she said. "I'll show you to your cabin."

"Wait," he said.

Amryn glanced back at him. Whatever debate he was waging with himself, he settled.

"Let us begin with honesty," Vishal said in heavily accented Wodi. "I understand your Tehut words."

Amryn had no idea what Tehut was, but Vishal was speaking Wodi. What had he overheard while they had assumed he did not understand them? Could she even remember when she and Hobi had spoken Wodi instead of using Ufa's sign language in Vishal's presence? What did the Mauryan commander know, and what did he want?

"How convenient," she said lightly. "What you call Tehut is an older form of the Wodi language commonly spoken in this region. Your accent might become intelligible to them with practice."

"The *Seeker* crew," he said, ignoring her slight. "They are not from the Republic."

Amryn was ready with a response. She and Hobi had agreed. Expecting the entire crew to pretend they'd swooped down from the stars was asking for trouble.

"Certainly not," she said, shifting back to Old N'si. "We needed to reach Maurya without attracting attention. That meant engaging a sailing ship common to this region. Few had the courage or expertise to voyage into the *Endless* Ocean." Amryn smirked. "But the *Seeker* had a reputation for going where few dared. Captain d'Ortega and his crew are adventurers, antiquity hunters known to have ventured into parts unknown. Conveniently, they were open to the right opportunity."

"The opportunity to sail with gods who fell from the heavens?"

"We could hardly tell them that, could we?"

"So, you posed as wealthy patrons of the antiquities. Eager to fund a daring expedition to find the rarest antiquity of all."

"The Ari Empire has many handsome young princes. In fact, few could even name them all. When one appears bearing sufficient gold...." Amryn shrugged. "He says he is Prince Hobizadi, you pocket his gold and call him Your Grace."

# # #

They dined well that night. Of the many crates the crew hauled from the sloop that had delivered Vishal, only one held his personal belongings. The rest were filled with sweets, soft breads, pickled fruits, and other delicacies a crew months away from any port found irresistible. A clever offering, it cleared a path through a briary welcome as intended.

"The Borlag!" young Sparky called out, raising a mug in the hand he had left. "Tell him about the Borlag."

Amryn had heard this favorite *Seeker* tale retold many times, each time a bit more preposterously. She settled back as Rafael launched into the story of a fire-breathing leviathan and its golden hoard off the coast of the Barrens.

To be fair, the *Seeker* had salvaged some impressive relics on that expedition. Some of the artifacts even made their way into the museum halls of Naré. But the purported monster from whom the treasures were stolen had yet to be verified.

Rafael made a splendid storyteller, and from the corner of her eye, Amryn studied their Mauryan guest. Vishal leaned in, caught up in the tale, soaking up every word as eagerly as a child. How hungry he must be for a taste of anything from outside Maurya's suffocating shell. Despite herself, a twinge of pity colored her judgment of these reclusive folk.

Having a rapt audience, even of one lone Mauryan, sparked more stories and kept the crew gathered around the table far longer than usual. Eventually, Rafael caught her glance and stood to call an end to the evening.

"A toast to our guest, a gentleman of discerning taste and delightful company," said Rafael. "Commander Vishal, welcome to the *Seeker*."

"Thank you, Captain," Vishal returned the toast. "Honored I am to meet adventurers of your great height. To the *Seeker*!"

Cheers went up at Vishal's awkwardly phrased Wodi toast, as did the bottoms of many mugs, and not for the first time that evening.

The night was warm and muzzy, and everyone's Wodi was sounding a little slurred.

"Ah, my friends. Dawn will be upon us too soon," said Rafael. "Our tales will continue on another evening. I bid you good night."

"Good night." Vishal rose a bit unsteadily. From the rosy tinge on his cheeks, Amryn would have sworn the commander was tipsy. Was he unaccustomed to the effects of wine or just enjoying a rare night of freedom?

Amryn escorted him to the deck without comment and strolled with him to clear his head. He'd have a headache in the morning, but at least he wouldn't fall down the steps on the way to his cabin. She stopped near the broken bowsprit and leaned her arms on the railing.

A pale blue moon hung over the lagoon, and a salty breeze herded silver ripples across its ebony surface. Sequestered inside the bowl-shaped island, it seemed a world apart, disconnected from the laws of time and place that ruled the earth beyond. A faint warmth tingled her arm, Ufa's subtle summons, and she noticed Vishal was watching her. He drew back, almost imperceptibly, when she caught him.

"What is it like?" he said. "To be... wired."

Wired? Amryn puzzled over the mishmash of Wodi and Old N'si. Oh, he meant Ufa.

"Well, I suppose—"

"I'm sorry. That was..." Vishal searched for the word. "That was rude of me. Unfortunately, my curiosity oversteps my manners."

"Commander Vishal, I am—"

"Vish," he said. "I command nothing on this ship."

Amryn was trained in the arts of a spy, the cloying skills used to set a target at ease, the feigned familiarity meant to secure an enemy's trust. Whether tipsy or sober, his technique could bear some refining.

"My augmentation is not a sensitive topic," said Amryn. "I am quite comfortable with being *Wired*, as some of the less informed still refer to us. Ufa is a companion, an advisor, and a guardian whose prime concern is my wellbeing."

She believed that was true, mostly.

"The device has a name?" Vishal seemed surprised.

"The *device* thinks and feels, just as you do," she said. "Why would I not call a fellow being by name?"

"A creature of metal crawling around under your skin? How can you—"

Vishal caught himself before finishing the insult. He lowered his head and sighed.

"Again, I apologize," he said. "It has been so long since the last of our Augmented died. Once all the devices were deployed, we made no more. We forgot how—extraordinary—the Augmented had been."

"Intentionally?" she said. "How can you miss what you convince yourself isn't worth having?"

Vishal studied her, searching for answers he'd given up finding.

"I don't know," he said. "But you're here, and we have not killed you. That's a start."

Chapter 28

Weebul

The following day, Amryn rose early. She climbed out the broken bowsprit and worried over how Hobi might be faring below. They had made a pact to make Maurya their home, and she didn't expect they would win Maurya's acceptance overnight. Patience was not her problem. However, being separated from someone who had come to matter a great deal to her was. She brushed the empty timber beside her, and Goblin crawled into her lap. The animals were restless without him, too.

A quiet cough drew her attention. Vishal was there at the bow rail. She hadn't expected to see him up before noon and was in no mood to endure his artless attempts to ingratiate himself. Let him wait.

"I could show you more of the island," he said. After a moment, he tried again. "You could see how we adapted, learned to survive on our own. The Republic might find something we've done of interest. I mean, of use in future settlements. Future Cycles."

There would be no more Cycles because there was no Republic. There would be no more Watchers swooping down from the stars, clearing fields, and sowing seeds. Earth's children were on their own.

But Amryn couldn't tell him that. Not yet.

"Our science may not have progressed as quickly as yours," said Vishal. "But we have not been sitting idle, either. Many of the first Mauryans were biologists. Some were environmental engineers. The Republic may find—"

"You may show me," Amryn cut off his insistence. She walked down the bowsprit, balancing her way along the narrow timber without giving the effort the slightest thought.

"Are all Augmented so agile?" Vishal hurried to offer a hand she didn't need.

Amryn wondered. Would Ufa's protection mean anyone could balance a bowsprit? Or was it her N'si blood that guaranteed each step fell true? She wasn't sure, but Vishal expected an answer.

"Yes," she decided. "Balance of one of many senses Ufa enhances. It's no different for any who accept the bond."

"Then I look forward to the Republic replenishing our devices," said Vishal. "Perhaps I wouldn't have stumbled over my own feet last night if I had Ufa to steady me."

"For that, you should blame the wine." Amryn smiled. "Go easy on the refills tonight, Commander."

"Vish."

"Vish, then," she relented.

# # #

"Sweet Mother of Aurel," Cora cried. "Get me out of this damned mess!"

Vish waded into the shallows and slashed at the sticky web Cora had wandered into. He balled up the long white strings as he went along, laughing as Cora sputtered curses.

"Such a fuss," he said, offering Cora her hat back. "The weebul should be upset you ruined his web."

"What the hell is a weebul?" Cora shook the water from her hat.

"One of our adaptations," said Vish. "Web worms. Segmented like centipedes, with many legs for swimming. They spend most of their time in the water and weave webs like spiders. Their webs are sticky when wet but pliable once they dry. We weave the threads into silk."

"It must take a lot of worms to clothe Maurya," said Cora.

"We have a saying. Busy as a weebul." Vish grinned. "The worms would cocoon the entire island if harvesters didn't keep the webs cut back. During mating season, males weave night and day, spinning fancy webs to attract mates. At night, the hum of their strings echoes over the island like music."

"What do these critters look like?" said Cora, squinting at the water around her knees.

"They are easier to spot at twilight," said Vish. "Weebul grow segments as they age, in pale shades of blue and green. An older weebul looks like a strand of opals whipping through the shallows."

"Ye bred these worms to be as they are?" said Cora.

"We engineered them," said Vish. "They breed themselves."

Amryn found the notion fascinating. To engineer a web worm as if one were building a house? The possibilities were intriguing and horrifying in equal measure. She wanted to learn the science behind these adaptations, but an ambassador from the Republic should have at least a basic understanding of the skills the Mauryans had mastered. She dared not ask the many questions popping into her mind.

The morning passed swiftly and wondrously. Vish showed them the sea cows Mauryans tended for their milk. Big as walruses, with udders like cows, the sleek-pelted creatures Vish called bantee grazed the abundant marsh grasses and reeds in the shallows where the forest met the lagoon. Adapted to land and sea, the fat grey bantee used their strong front flippers to propel their bulk through the water and drew their hind flippers under their bellies to walk the banks and the forest's edge almost as well as four-legged cows.

"More like goats, if you ask me," said Vish. "Bantee will eat anything—kelp, palmettos, even tree bark. And they're a frisky lot, despite their size. Take care." He winked. "They have a mischievous streak."

Higher up the slopes, swaying in the tall bamboo, the tarchu munched contentedly on leaves, slowing baring each stalk and climbing to start their next meal. Sloth-like creatures with menacing, razor-sharp claws, the tarchu had been engineered for their long, shaggy, white coats. Mauryans sheared the docile beasts often, which seemed merciful considering the island heat, and used the water-repellant hair for rugs, ropes, brushes, and scrubbing cloths.

"Remarkable work," Amryn said carefully. "And, I admit, some may be of potential use to the Republic. But, who here has the expertise to recreate such adaptations? If modifications were required?"

Vish looked away. "No one. Not for a very long while. I thought the Republic might...."

"Replenish your biologists after replenishing your augmentation devices?" said Amryn.

For some reason, the words came out gentler than earlier.

Vish led them back to the lagoon. He knelt on the shore to show Cora yet another creature crafted by skills lost to time. Amryn left him poking in the sand with his dagger and walked down the beach, lost in thought. The more she learned of Mauryans, the more lost they seemed. The science that had brought them here as gods had long since left them behind. Isolated, afraid, and unsure.

"Wait," Vish called. "We do not go there!"

Amryn realized she'd strayed farther than she intended. The urgency in his voice stilled her feet. Just ahead, the strip of beach she walked on narrowed, and white limestone cliffs jutted out into the water. Weathered caves laced the vine-shrouded cliffside, deepening into an endless honeycomb of passages, each turn, each arch more shadowed until the maze disappeared into midnight blue darkness deep inside the cliffs.

Vish ran up, gripped her arm, and dragged her back.

"Raveler nests," he panted. "You have not eaten enough yet. The bitters."

His hurried warning, delivered in a frantic jumble of Old N'si-Mauryan and Tehut-Wodi, made no sense at all. Amryn frowned and pried his hand off her arm.

"Vish, I am listening. And not tempted in the least to make a bolt for those caves," she said. "So, you may slow down and tell me why you're apoplectic about the chance I might do so."

"Ravelers." Vish ran a hand through his thick hair. "Creatures one does not encounter without precaution. The food I brought to the *Seeker* is laced with a powder we call the bitters. Tasteless to us, but ravelers find it disagreeable. Until you have enough bitters in your system, avoid the caves."

"Ravelers? More of your adaptation?" said Amryn.

"No, the ravelers were here before us," said Vish. "Learning to coexist was... not without its price. Do not ask me more, Amryn. I would rather not lie to you."

Amryn nodded feigned acceptance. She glanced over her shoulder at the raveler caves, another mystery she must solve before Maurya became the N'si homeland Hobi sought. But she would not solve it with Vish fretting over her every move.

She followed him back down the beach, to the dinghy that had brought them from the *Seeker* that morning. Cora's pack was bulging with balls of weebul web and tarchu shearings. No doubt, Rafael would craft such finery from her samples, even a Mauryan would be envious.

As they neared the dinghy, Amryn noticed a lone figure standing motionless on the sand. An old man, vaguely familiar, waded knee-deep into the water, eyes closed and seemingly oblivious of their approach. Along his outstretched arms, shreds of white cloth hung dancing in the breeze, like laundry flapping on a clothesline. Amryn recognized the old window-washer who had waylaid them outside the Assembly Hall.

"Quan," Vish greeted the old man, as if accustomed to his spontaneous appearances. "Laundry day? You could use the washing machines like everyone else, you know."

The water frothed around Quan's feet, and trails of ripples fanned out across the lagoon. Quan sighed and opened his eyes. After a moment, he turned and greeted them with a smile.

"Vish," the old man said fondly. "Show me the machine that scrubs tarchu wool as well as I do. I see you've been showing our guests our home. Take the big one and keep her occupied. I wish a moment alone with the Augmented."

To Amryn's astonishment, Vish and Cora simply walked on, as if unaware they'd been ordered to do so. The tingle on her skin said Ufa had noticed, too. She felt the silver coalesce in her fingertips like claws and the sharpening vision that always rimmed her eyes with a silver glow.

Quan tilted his head, reminding Amryn of an inquisitive owl studying a mouse.

"My, aren't you a rare one?" he said.

"What are you?" she said, trying to steady the quiver in her voice.

"An interested observer."

"A Mauryan?" she said.

"More so than you."

Quan picked the freshly laundered wash rags off his arms, folded each with care, and stowed them in his pail. In his own due time, he straightened to face her. She met the eyes of ageless wisdom and faltered.

"May I?" he asked, holding his palm up in invitation.

Without considering why, Amryn pressed her palm to his. His gaze held her fixed, and her hand thrummed as Ufa rushed to protect her. They met, eyes locked and skin to skin, in a cautious dance of curiosity. A tiny knot rose under his skin, explored her palm, and traced its way out each finger. She had felt its like once before. Amryn drew back her hand, and Quan smiled.

"Rare, indeed," he said. "Why are you here, child?"

Amryn felt compelled to answer, though it was a question she had not answered even to herself yet. What did she want from Maurya? What did she want from Hobi?

"Because a dreamer went searching for a dream," she said.

"How splendid," said Quan. "If we cannot dream, every sunrise is the same."

Quan picked up his pail and turned to leave. Amryn started after the old man, uncertain what she expected but sure more needed saying. But Quan kept walking, and Vish and Cora headed back towards them. He stopped to pat Vish on the shoulder.

"You should take Amryn to the city," Quan told him.

"Chandra said she was to stay up here," said Vish.

"As you wish." Quan shrugged. "You were about to tell them about the lomloo," he prompted, then walked on alone.

"Ah, yes. The lomloo," Vish picked up the conversation, oblivious to the fact he'd just been shooed away and summoned back again. Cora gave her head a shake, looking a bit bewildered. Amryn recalled the suffocating waves of paranoia she'd felt sweep the Assembly Hall. Was that Quan's doing, too?

"You've already seen them, though," Vish went on, oblivious to the effect Quan had over him. "On our heads. The lomloo have an extra funnel growing from a chamber their gills fill with air. They can hold or expel air to control their depth in the water." He grinned. "Though sometimes, I think they just like blowing bubbles."

"So, when one of those critters grabs hold of yer face—" said Cora.

"We breathe the air it shares with us," said Vish. "It's hot, humid, and smells like fish, but we find it preferable to drowning."

"Another of your adaptations?" Amryn asked. A chill prickled her skin as Quan disappeared in the distance.

"No, the lomloo were here when we arrived," said Vish.

"Living alongside the ravelers," Amryn noted.

"Well, yes." Vish frowned. "Ravelers are a similar species, but lomloo are harmless. Easily tamed and trained."

Like you? Amryn wondered.

# # #

That afternoon, Amryn went to the food stores and had Ufa sample each of the crates Vish had brought aboard. Soon enough, they identified the extract of eucalyptus, cinnamon, and castor bean rendered into a tasteless powder lacing the Mauryan food.

The bitters.

"Repels ravelers. Not lomloo?" she signed.

"Unlikely," Ufa replied. *"Similar species."*

The facts didn't fit. She'd seen lomloo. Small and squishy. If they were similar species, how could ravelers be so monstrous? Vish refused to dare even a brief encounter in the caves.

But if not to keep the ravelers away, what purpose did the bitters serve? Why was Maurya so thoroughly dosed with the stuff? They obviously considered the extract necessary. They even sent bitters to dose strangers they did not trust.

"Can we remove it from the food?" she asked. *"As Hobi cleanses the water?"*

"No. Tainted."

She had to do something before it spread some unknown effect over the entire crew. She might toss the crates overboard, but she'd have to explain why. After the poisoning incident, telling the crew Maurya was now feeding them a suspicious potion might incite them to try fighting their way off the island. Now was not the time. An accident maybe? Setting a fire on a ship was unthinkable.

"Antidote?" she tried.

"Researching."

# # #

Amryn ate alone that evening. The dried fish, flatbread, and fruit Ufa had declared untainted by the bitters, she shared with Demon and Goblin. She needed to talk to Hobi, but he was in Maurya, eating what the rajin put before him.

She brushed crumbs off her hands, went to his desk, and sat to write a warning message. Whatever she sent would be intercepted, of course. But only Hobi and Khaldun could decipher the runes they used with Ufa. Painstakingly, Amryn sketched a decorative border around the paper's edge and hid the warning runes within its design. When the ink had dried, she wrote the letter more likely to pass the rajin's scrutiny and make it into Hobi's hands. Amryn recounted their tour of the island and the *adaptations* Commander Vishal had shown them. She mentioned the crates and told him the crew was enjoying the Mauryan delicacies.

She sat back and reread the letter. It was certainly dull enough, even written in the expressive flair of the Wodi language, or rather, Tehut. Amryn gave Demon and Goblin a sly wink.

"Make her for work it," she said. "She'll summon a scholar to translate, only to find it wasn't worth her effort."

She folded and sealed the letter. Convincing Vish to deliver it was a challenge she could manage. She hoped. The others should soon be done with dinner, even considering the likely extra round of wine and bold tales, and Vish would eventually wander to the deck.

"Amryn? Are you awake?" The quiet knock startled her. It was Vish.

"Yes," she said. "Is something wrong?"

"Are you not feeling well?" he said. "When you weren't at dinner, I—"

"I'm fine," she said. If he was waiting for her to invite him in, he would just have to keep waiting. "I was about to go up to the deck. Go ahead. I'll be right there."

Amryn listened to his footsteps as he climbed the steps. Before Quan and the bitters, she had no qualms about being alone with him. But today had brought too many unanswered questions. She cast a rueful glance at the vanlor she'd shed as soon as she returned to the cabin. Its elegance had served its purpose, but brocade was miserably hot on a muggy night. Ambassador of the Republic or not, she wasn't putting on the vanlor again. Instead, she slipped on a simple white sailor's shirt and tied it over the crimson silk breeches. Half as elegant, but it would do.

Vish was waiting at the bow rail. The way his eyes swept her, she wondered if she'd forgotten to fasten a button or two. Fighting the urge to look down and check, she pulled the letter from her pocket instead.

"My report on the adaptations. I would like it delivered to Prince Hobizadi tomorrow," she said. "I assume, as guests, we aren't forbidden from corresponding with one another."

Vish took the letter and turned it over, running his thumb over the seal. A faint smile curled his lips.

"Quite impressive," he said. "The handwritten missive. The parchment. The wax seal. All done precisely as an authentic Ari princess might have, I'm sure. The Republic prepared you well for your mission, Ambassador."

Mauryans didn't write letters? How was she to know? Ufa had some explaining to do later.

"Can you see it delivered?" she said. "When you're done admiring my handiwork, of course."

"Swear you aren't plotting an insurrection behind my back?" Vish winked. "Yes, of course. I'll see your report reaches your prince."

Vish tucked the letter into his vest, and Amryn let out an anxious breath.

"I'm flattered you found some of our work worth reporting," he said. "I often wondered whether Maurya would seem backward to you if you did finally return. Tell me, what *are* the Republic's geneticists using these days to accelerate recombinant transduction?"

"Are you testing me?" Amryn arched a brow. "You aren't very good at this subterfuge business, you know."

"Am I that obvious?"

"Your subtlety is atrocious," she said. "And your tactics could use improvement. Test me with a question." She held out her arm, and the glow of silver runes danced over her skin. "Perhaps I know the answer. Perhaps Ufa does. What have you proven?"

"That I enjoy dueling wits with you."

Amryn smiled and leaned against the rail. She should stop while she was ahead. He'd agreed to deliver the letter. But she'd never been able to walk away from a puzzle.

"Who is Quan to you," she said. "A relative?"

"A friend. One whose counsel I value above most others."

Amryn waited, as any well-trained Fang would. Silence hurries a hesitant tongue.

"I was raised in the ways of Maurya. Aware of the role likely to pass to Chandra's son as leader of House Ajagara. Aware of the likely challenge from Gagan and House Silhad. I could worry over Gagan, or I could prepare to govern. It was not a hard choice."

Amryn understood all too well. Being born to wield the authority one's parents had earned meant carrying their expectations, as well.

"When I was young, I didn't feel the weight of my name. Children see children. As my friends and I grew older, that changed. Deference crept in, and distance. Games and pranks became fewer. Shared secrets fewer still. With passing each year, I became less Vish and more Ajagara."

"That must have been difficult," said Amryn. Being half N'si, she grew accustomed to other children keeping a wary distance, even at a young age. Would it have been harder to have lost what she never had?

"Finding myself with more time alone, I studied," said Vish. "I prepared by learning about maintaining the walls, about fishing and farming—all that goes into sustaining Maurya and keeping us hidden until the Return. That meant exploring Maurya to see for myself whether what I read in the books would be enough."

Amryn imagined the serious young boy leaving the comfortable, manicured levels where Maurya's elite dwelled and traveling down into the crowded hives, out to the farming domes, and beyond.

"On one such excursion, I met an old man," said Vish. "Dressed all in white and washing the glass in a farming dome. He struck up a conversation, and I sat down to talk with him."

"Quan?" said Amryn.

"Yes, Quan. That day, Quan asked the questions I'd kept pushing aside. I talked through my doubts. We reasoned through the unreasonable, picked apart inconsistencies Maurya's most revered scholars had assured me were irrefutable facts. With a window-washer's common sense and unindoctrinated insight. Quan helped me see not everything is as we are taught."

"A valuable lesson," said Amryn. "And an unlikely mentor."

"Needless to say, I returned to talk with him again," said Vish. "Over the years, I've come to value his friendship as much as his advice. What is he to me? He is... Quan."

More importantly, Quan was the ally they had to win. Though Vish seemed oblivious, Amryn witnessed Quan's control over his young friend. Quan had made no attempt to hide his power. What did he want? Vish said he wanted free of the cage. Was he voicing Quan's wish or his own? With Quan's guidance, perhaps Vish might sway Chandra to open Maurya's doors to their N'si kin and rejoin a world that no longer included Kitsune *or* the Republic.

"What do you want for Maurya?" she said, wondering whether it was Vish or Quan she was asking. "You must have thought about it."

"Often. But wanting does not make it so."

"But we can."

Vish stared back at her. A flicker of hope faded, and bitter resignation darkened his eyes.

"They will not let you," he said. "You don't understand. No one leaves Maurya."

"They?"

Vish looked away. He didn't mean Quan. Who was it he feared? Who or what held more power than either of them?

"We will finish the mission that brought us here," said Amryn. "And then, we will leave. I hope it will not come to a battle. Maurya would lose."

Vish gripped the rail, and his entire body tensed in sudden and silent fury.

"Do not be so sure."

Chapter 29

Proclaimed

Hobi pushed away a cup of over-sweetened lemon tea, waiting at the small table near the café's windows while their Mauryan handler paid for the midday meal. At Chandra's request, Hobi and Khaldun had ventured into the city daily, escorted by Janak or Nira. They dined, browsed shops and galleries, and strolled parks. Tedious, but it drew the intended attention, giving skittish Mauryans an opportunity to gawk at the outlanders in their midst and begin acclimating to the notion that entire worlds might exist beyond their cloistered perspective.

Meanwhile, the rajin continued meeting with the Assembly, placating their fears while historians scoured the archives for even the most obscure references to the Return. Seemingly endless speeches, speculation, and debate between Traditionalist and Progressive factions had delayed Chandra's declaration recognizing Hobizadi as a legitimate Returned Prince of the Kishar Republic.

As the debate dragged on, a palpable uneasiness had blanketed the city, setting even inscrutable Khaldun on edge. Some met them with wary curiosity, and others with undisguised hostility. Hobi soon learned Mauryan opinion on this, as most everything else, split along political lines. Gagan seized every opportunity to challenge Chandra and stoke Maurya's already pervasive paranoia. Their competing houses of Ajagara and Silhad, as leaders of the Progressive and Traditionalist parties, had been feeding the flames of distrust for generations. The cauldron was nearing the boiling point even before the *Seeker* appeared on the horizon.

Though tensions simmered all around him, Hobi's sense of purpose grew more resolute by the day. The presence he'd dared acknowledge and that Amryn had named real lurked in the corners of his mind, repeating its unspoken assurances. Hobi belonged here. He had returned in time. In time for what? He wished he knew.

As Janak headed back to their table, a young courier with an Ajagara emblem on her sleeve rushed up to intercept him. Janak's expression turned pensive, and he dismissed her with a brisk nod. Khaldun rose and took a guarding stance beside Hobi's chair.

"We are returning to the manor," said Janak.

"Trouble?" said Hobi.

"Its resolution, I hope," said Janak. "The voting is underway. The rajin will call you to the Assembly Hall before announcing the results."

And the gambit would continue or fail. Hobi had already considered how to get out of Maurya alive if the vote did not go his way. Tricky, but a little shy of impossible. By how much depended on what the ramifications of failure were here.

"Will the results go as she hopes?" Hobi asked.

"Chandra doesn't close debate until she believes she has the votes," said Janak. "More often than not, she's right."

"More often than not." Khaldun scowled. "Poor odds for a wager."

"Politics is seldom worth the gamble. Yet few can taste its power and walk away from the game," Janak said, an undercurrent of bitterness in his voice.

Janak's disdain for politics was obvious, but he'd stayed in the game for his wife's sake. He might even be relieved to see the Republic take over the burden of ruling and leave the table to new players. As long as Gagan wasn't among them. Yes, Hobi could envision Janak joining in their liberation of Maurya when the time was right.

As he often had since their arrival in the city, Hobi realized Janak was watching him, studying him. Janak seemed on the verge of saying more or perhaps expecting more. But then, he shifted his gaze and motioned them towards the door.

Outside the café, a small group of Mauryans had gathered. By now, Hobi recognized the Trad emblem on their placards. *Keep Maurya Secure*, said one. *Protect Our City*, said another. Reasonable enough sentiments. Nothing overtly threatening. But the gatherings were growing larger each day that passed without the Assembly acknowledging the authenticity of the Return.

# # #

The young courier intercepted them again in the gated courtyard outside the manor. Flushed with excitement, she ran up and caught Janak by the hand.

"Uncle, there's news," she said.

"Sera? But you just left us." Janak's brow furrowed.

"The vote was decisive," she said. "The Assembly recognizes the Return is authentic."

"Rekha swayed the doubters," said Janak.

The resemblance was unmistakable when Sera quirked a corner of her full lips. The fast-footed young courier was Janak's kin.

"Took her sweet time with the research, but her historians presented compelling evidence today," said Sera. "Five Trads crossed the aisle in support."

"And what of the Elders?"

"Still no opinion on the matter," she said. "At least, none Gagan could twist to his liking."

Janak nodded. "Is she ready for us?"

"Give her an hour. She's writing the declaration, and we're readying a reception for the...." Sera gave Hobi a shy smile. "For Your Grace. House Ajagara is hosting the reception to welcome the Prince of the Republic to Maurya."

"The Republic has an abundance of princes." Hobi smiled in return. "I'm one of many to bear that title, but I'm honored to be the first welcome in Maurya."

"Quite the distinction," said Janak. "Sera, tell Chandra we'll be there."

Sera hurried off on her errands, and Janak clasped Hobi's shoulder. Relief swept aside the tension that had etched his face the entire time Hobi had known him. Janak had been worried... about him? About the risk Chandra took by giving credence to his claims?

"Go, dress in your finest. You must look the part, Your Grace."

Janak gave him a wink and walked away.

# # #

Chandra read the proclamation before a chamber packed with councilors, dignitaries, and staff. In a show of sheer petulance, Gagan and several Trads walked out when she acknowledged Prince Hobizadi as a legitimate envoy of the Republic and long-awaited herald of the Return. She ignored his petty theater and reminded everyone of Maurya's duty to a vast empire in the stars, one Hobi doubted still existed. Then she called on her fellow Mauryans to celebrate the Return they had been anticipating for generations.

It was an inspiring speech, filled with optimism and themes of heritage shared between Mauryans determined to survive in a world far from home and the Republic that had sent and stranded them there. Chandra spoke so eloquently, no one suspected how little she believed her own words.

Hobi took to the Speaker's Deck and accepted their welcome with grace. He made no mention of its belatedness or the Republic's demands all knew would be forthcoming. Time enough for that later. If he was to coax them back into the world, he had to win their trust.

N'si can be charming when it suits their purpose. Hobi had been raised with that understanding about himself and his kind. Charm was a survival skill when everything in life was a transaction. Some small part of him knew life could be so much more. His kind could be so much more.

# # #

Hours later, Chandra sought him out in the crowd at the reception. Khaldun nudged him as she approached. If he ever tired of navigating ships, Khaldun was a natural at playing the attentive bodyguard.

"You've mingled enough," said Chandra. "And made no new enemies. Shall we take our leave while we're ahead?"

Though phrased as a question, Hobi recognized the command. He had nothing to gain from challenging her when she was right. For Chandra, wielding authority was merely a habit.

"A well-timed suggestion," he said. "Never be the last to leave a celebration in your honor."

Extricating themselves from the crowd took another half-hour because ending such things takes longer than beginning them. But after sufficient handclasps and platitudes, they eventually left the

Assembly Hall and returned to Chandra's office. The rajin cast off her ornate robe and heeled slippers as soon as she was through the doorway. She climbed onto the jhula and went straight into analyzing the political intricacies of the day.

Did she never rest?

Hobi poured himself a glass of papaya wine. Overly sweet, of course, but Mauryan wines were generally terrible in one way or another. On the other hand, the climate was amenable to vineyards, and table grapes were plentiful. If he managed to open Maurya's doors, he would have to recruit better vintners to come here.

"But he squandered an opportunity by leaving," Chandra was saying. "If he'd stayed for the reception, he could have dampened the mood. Snide little comments. Whispers and smirks. All the pettiness at which he excels. Why would Gagan pass up the temptation to spoil my party?"

Hobi assumed it was a rhetorical question, but her puzzled expression appeared genuine. Were these people truly so naïve in the art of the dodge?

"Proximity to power," said Hobi. "Such a decisive victory raises your power considerably. By comparison, his power can only appear smaller. Quite obviously so, to anyone observing the two of you together. By removing himself from your proximity, he avoids the comparison while the imbalance is so pronounced."

"Power seeps from the defeated like water," said Khaldun. "Leaving removes the siphon."

Chandra replied with a thoughtful nod.

"Gagan will try to refill his bucket," said Hobi. "Before others notice its emptiness."

"Of course. He must be desperate," said Chandra. "Janak, turn on the news."

Janak went to a blackened panel on the wall. At his touch, the onyx glass lit with an image from the city's lower levels. Blocky letters scrolled across the bottom of the image, too fast for Hobi to decipher. Chandra left the jhula frowning and stood before the news panel. With a press of her finger, Gagan's voice rose to a shout.

"... to those who abandoned us!"

The crowd pressed closer as more stopped to listen.

"The Republic is weak. Debased by centuries of servitude to the enemy. My friends, Maurya is far stronger than the Republic! We neither need nor want their Return!"

After failing to discredit the envoys, Gagan resorted to demonizing the Republic that had sent them. In the gathering crowd, angry mutters grew louder and fists raised in defiance.

"Demand the rajin keep our walls secure. Keep the barbaric outlanders away from our children," Gagan shrilled. "Defend our way of life. Defend our independence. Patriots, rise in defense of Maurya!"

"Get the Watch down there," Chandra ordered. "Arrest him for incitement."

"That is what he wants," said Hobi. "Recognition of his power after you lessened it. Arrest him for speaking, and you give his words credence. You refill the bucket for him."

"And what would you have me do?" Chandra shot back. "Stand by while he incites an insurrection? The Republic of old would never tolerate such dissent."

Hobi clenched his teeth. Telling her the Republic was as weak as Gagan claimed, assuming it still existed in any form at all, would make matters worse. Standing by while Mauryans fought Mauryans ran counter to his plans, and he *would* find a way to ease tensions before broaching the matter of welcoming a return of N'si rather than the Republic. What happened then mattered more than what happened now.

"Do what you must," he said and turned away.

Janak tapped the medallion on his chest and gave the orders. Within moments, guards swarmed the image on the news panel, dispersing the crowd and leading Gagan away.

"Return to the manor," Chandra told Hobi. "Do not leave there unnecessarily."

"Confined to quarters now?" he said.

"Under my protection, until calmer heads prevail," she said. "Seeing you moving freely about the city will add fuel to the fire I am trying to extinguish. Discontent in a closed world such as ours can be lethal. The desperate have nowhere to run."

"Unless you lower the walls."

Chandra stared at him for a long moment.

"Do not leave the manor," she repeated.

Hobi turned to leave.

"Wait. Before you go." Chandra went to her desk and pulled an envelope from the drawer. "A letter arrived for you from Ambassador Nisari."

# # #

Hobi walked the few short blocks back to the manor in silent contemplation, flanked by Khaldun and Captain Nira. He glanced up at the inky blackness beyond the dome overhead. The dark of a moonless night enveloped Maurya so utterly, the world above disappeared. Suspended alone in the Endless Ocean, without even the soothing lap of water to remind them anything existed beyond their own small lives, the city drew contentedly and obliviously into its shell for yet another solitary night.

The eerie white light of flameless street lanterns cast motionless shadows on the sidewalk. The light waned as they walked a stretch of sidewalk between the lanterns. Leaves rustled, and one of the shadows moved. A blade glinted in the dark.

Khaldun noticed the glint a heartbeat before Nira. He took a step and drew his sword. A suffocating wave of paranoia rolled out of the darkness, and Khaldun froze where he stood. Nira lunged once, then stumbled.

The shadow lurched from the bushes, and a sharp pain pierced Hobi's side. He knocked away the next jab and gripped the arm wielding the dagger. Hobi's throat tightened in instant and visceral revulsion as he touched the cold, pale flesh. The assassin's shrill cry snapped Khaldun and Nira to their senses, and they swung in tandem at a ghostly blue form. With a gurgled cry, the creature fell at their feet.

Human in shape and features, the assassin's pale blue skin was unlike any race Hobi had encountered. And he had encountered them all. The blood oozing from its wounds was a deep, iridescent azure. Instinctive loathing for the creature rose bile in his throat.

"What is that thing?" he said.

"Elder." Nira wiped her brow. "A lesser one. They never venture out. Never."

Footfalls came pounding down the sidewalk behind them. Janak stopped short, staring down at the blue stain darkening the sidewalk.

"What happened here?" he asked quietly.

"It waited in ambush," said Nira. "Prince Hobizadi fended off its attack."

Hobi pressed the pain burning in his side, and his hand came back bloody. Janak drew a sharp breath.

"You're wounded."

"It's nothing," said Hobi. "Barely grazed."

"Get him to the manor," Janak ordered. "Leave me to clean up here."

Nira took Hobi's arm and swept him down the sidewalk. Khaldun opened the courtyard gate and covered their retreat inside.

"Let me bind that wound," said Nira. "I'll staunch the bleeding until Janak sends a physician we can trust to keep this quiet."

"I said, it's nothing." Hobi pressed on the cut. Deep enough Cora would have insisted it needed stitching, but Hobi trusted a bandage more than any Mauryan physician at this point. The presence was already healing him, and he'd rather not explain a miraculous recovery to anyone just now.

"Janak stayed behind to hide the evidence," said Hobi. "Why such secrecy?"

Nira cast a nervous glance over her shoulder.

"Because that was an *Elder*," she hissed. "And it broke the treaty even by being in the city, much less attacking you. If word gets out—"

"You fear them," said Hobi. "What *are* these Elders?"

Nira tightened her lips. He'd get no more out of her, but the implication was clear. Maurya lived in terror of these creatures, under a treaty that laid out rules for a tenuous coexistence with them. Hobi thought back on what he'd heard earlier. Gagan was the designated liaison with the Elders. The Elders had offered no opinion on the Return.

Well, they had now. If word got out, Chandra's proclamation would be questioned.

"Secure the manor," said Hobi. "Khaldun, come with me."

Throughout his exchange with Nira, Khaldun had hovered nearby, ashen and shaken by the effect of the Elder's mind-poison. Dark emotions seemed to hang over him still.

"Khaldun. With me," Hobi said firmly.

Khaldun shuddered and met his eyes. The glaze of fear seeped away, and the big man gathered his wits. With a brisk nod, Khaldun followed Hobi to their suite. There he latched the window and ran a shaking hand over his braids.

"Elders control them, don't they?" said Khaldun.

"To a degree," said Hobi. "Selectively. Perhaps when threatened."

"Its fear still sours my mouth. Coppery and bitter," Khaldun admitted.

"Here." Hobi poured a glass of wine. "It will settle your nerves."

Khaldun rarely drank, but he took the wine and sunk down on the sofa. Hobi left the man to recover himself and went to the study. It was a small but comfortable room and seemed a luxury in a city where living space was limited. Though no one had said so, Hobi suspected the suite had been Commander Vishal's before he'd traded it for hostage duty on the *Seeker*. Hobi had taken to using its library tablet and news panel as he became more acclimated to Mauryan technology. He settled behind the desk and pulled Amryn's letter from his pocket.

The wax seal was broken. The rajin had made no pretense of privacy. Amryn would have anticipated as much. Hobi read her account of bantee and web worms. He turned the letter over, expecting something more. Why bother to write such a bland report? Did he miss reading between the lines? A familiar shape in the vines sketched along the paper's border caught his eye. Hobi chuckled. *What a clever mind.*

He deciphered the runes she'd hidden for him. Strange spice in the food. Suspicious of its effect. Mind whispers. Ufa searching antidote.

Mind whispers.

Hobi got up and carried the letter to the parlor. He handed it to Khaldun without a word, cautious of invisible eyes and ears. He did not point out the border. Khaldun would notice it in time. Sure enough, Khaldun set the letter down, then picked it up again. His eyes darted over the runes, and he looked up wearing a scowl.

Since their first night here, something in the food had set Hobi's stomach on fire. He didn't draw attention to his adverse reaction, not wishing to offend, but he had been selective in what he ate since then, subsisting on uncooked fruit, vegetables, and nuts. Olives, plain rice, and the occasional flatbread. Khaldun had eaten as the Mauryans ate.

Was that why fear froze Khaldun tonight? And why had Hobi been unaffected by the Elder's mind-poison? He wanted to talk to Amryn, to learn what more she dared not write. He fingered the prism hanging from his neck. Mauryan technology might detect if he tried to contact her. There was too much he did not understand yet.

Coming here had always been a gambit. It was time to make his next move.

# # #

By morning, the protests had spread, creeping upward through the city's boroughs. Trads demanding Mauryan independence hurled insults at Progs waving banners in support of the Republic and hailing the envoys of the Return.

No one was listening to anyone but themselves.

Gagan was relegated to watching from the confines of house arrest. But the sparks he'd tossed had fallen on dry kindling, and the discontent burned on without him. Not even he could stop it now.

Hobi walked into Chandra's office unannounced. She glanced up sharply at the sound of his footsteps. From the looks of her, she'd been at her desk all night.

"I told you to stay in the manor," she said curtly.

"And yet, I am here," said Hobi. "We have trouble on our hands."

"How perceptive." Her voice dripped sarcasm. "I hadn't noticed. Fortunately, I have a Prince of the Republic here to point out the obvious."

Hobi sat on the edge of her desk. Chandra frowned at his impertinence.

"I am here to help," he said. "Let's start with you being honest with me."

"Because one of us must? Why don't you go first? Show me how it's done."

"Such a suspicious mind," said Hobi. "For someone who staked her rule on a stranger being who he claimed."

Chandra had no ready retort for that one. It was the cautious dance they'd danced from the start. Questions and deflections. Waiting to catch the other in a lapse. He'd gambled Chandra held the key. If his hunch was wrong, he had no time to waste. He wagered it all.

"All right, I'll start." He stood and folded his arms. "You recognize me."

To her credit, she didn't flinch. Chandra held his gaze and stood.

"You may remind me of someone I once knew," she said carefully.

"Someone the Rajin of Maurya cannot admit to remembering. Someone she should never have met."

"And will never forget. Why did he send you?"

"As I said, I came to help."

"Help do what? Tear my country apart?"

"I came to bring your country out of hiding. I came to free Maurya from this prison of fear. Look at me, Chandra. Tell me that is not what you want."

Chandra turned her back. Heartbeats passed as Hobi's challenge hung in the silence. Just when he thought he'd gambled and lost, she faced him again, and tears glistened in her eyes.

"Freedom is all I have ever wanted," she said. "He made me believe we could make it happen."

"Then help me help you. I need answers."

"Ask, then."

"What are ravelers?"

From the look on her face, it was not the question she had anticipated.

"You expect me to believe you don't know?" she said.

"Unless you'd rather me invent the truth like Gagan, yes."

Chandra came to a decision.

"Come. Out the back."

Chapter 30

Elders

Amryn gave up trying to sleep and lit the lantern. Yuji's journal lay open on the desk where she'd left off reading. Hobi had left it in her care and entrusted its mysteries to her, as well. Though he had read every word a dozen times, the cryptic mixture of fact and fable left him wondering whether he had missed some crucial key to unlocking Maurya's secrets.

She had examined the exact words through the lens of a scientist. Before Vish had escorted her around the island, she would have discounted Yuji's tales of web worms as fiction. But weebul existed, as did bantee and tarchu and lomloo. The only creature Yuji omitted from his chronicle of Mauryan wildlife was the raveler. The only creature Vish refused to let her meet was the raveler. Logic screamed that was not a coincidence. But what did it mean? It was one of many questions haunting her sleep.

Amryn got out of bed and dressed, unwilling to give the journal the last hours left in the night. With Goblin tucked in the crook of her arm, she propped the cabin door open for Demon to follow if it suited him. The beasts were out of sorts with Hobi away, and her restlessness was wearing on them all.

She carried the cat out onto the bowsprit and sat, swinging her legs above the water. The night was warm and muzzy, and the breeze stirred ripples on the surface below. A luminescent strand of opals whipped beneath her feet. A lone weebul returning to the shallows after feeding. She smiled. Despite the uncertainty ahead, she had come to treasure this magical place.

Whether it would take conquest or liberation to open Maurya's gates, she hesitated to press forward with either attempt. Even the best of plans needed refining, advancing, and recalibrating. With

Hobi gone, she had to make decisions for them both, knowing the wrong decision could put him in danger. Had her message even made it into his hands?

Her thumb traced the edge of the relic where it fused with the base of her throat. Ufa communicated with Hobi's prism when he was close, but at what distance might they lose contact? She'd been warned not to signal the Republic. Vish said communications were monitored, and any outbound message would raise an alarm. What if a message stayed inside Maurya's walls?

Goblin hissed at a dark shape breaking the surface below. Sleek black hair glistened in the faint light of dawn just creeping above the ridge. Amryn frowned down at the tanned limbs rising to tread the water. Vish lifted his head and spotted her.

"Permission to come aboard?" he said.

"He asks innocently. Hoping she'll forget he didn't ask permission to leave."

"I take that as a yes," he said, starting up the ladder. Vish climbed aboard wearing his seaskin and walked barefoot to the bowsprit. "Sorry, I couldn't sleep. Thought a swim might burn off some restless energy. I guess I miss not going out on patrol."

"How often did you go out?" she asked, curious.

"As often and as far as I could get away with. Which was never as much as I wished."

Amryn bit her lip. He could be testing her again, trying to draw her out. But Vish was no Fang, and his earlier attempts had lacked finesse. Instinct nudged her to tempt him a little farther.

"Then I must put that restless energy to use," she said. "I wanted to go ashore again today. Gather fresh fruit for the galley. Milk a bantee or two. How many bantee does it take to fill a barrel? Of course, *you* get to haul our bounty back to the ship. I expect you'll need to swim a few laps."

"Forced labor? The Republic shall hear about this, Ambassador," he grinned.

"Please, *do* file your complaint promptly," she said. "May I open a channel for you now?"

"Nice try." Vish wagged his finger. "How about I call home instead? I'll have a few more crates of treats sent up, and we can pretend this little duel of wits never happened."

It was the opening she'd waited for. She slid from the bowsprit and faced him.

"Keep your crates. The crew and I will keep our wits," she said. "Did you think I would not detect being drugged?"

Vish blinked. "Drugged? Are you accusing me of—"

"The powder in the food you brought. A blend of eucalyptus, cinnamon, and castor bean extract."

"Oh, that," he said, relieved. "The bitters. The name's misleading, I suppose, since it has no taste. At least, to us. We add it to everything."

"Why?"

"As I told you earlier, it's a natural repellant. Perfectly harmless to humans, I assure you."

"Remind me. It's a repellant against what?"

Vish hesitated. "Ravelers and their ilk."

"The creatures in the caves you warned me away from," she said.

"Yes, in their most common form. There are others," he said. "But it doesn't matter. The bitters keep them from getting too close."

"So you all take it willingly."

"Why would anyone refuse a preventive?"

Amryn had her answer. Vish honestly didn't know its effect. The bitters he believed protected him from whatever ill ravelers threatened instead turned Mauryans into obedient sheep. But who or what wielded that control? Was it Quan alone? An unanswered question nagged at her.

"The Elders," she said. "Who are they? *What* are they?"

An unreadable mask crept over his face even as she voiced the question. Vish faded into the background as another consciousness eased forward. Ancient and measuring in its approach.

"Why do you ask?" Vish asked vacantly.

"Because it intrigues you that I would," she answered the presence.

"The Elders are Lahr. What is not Lahr, is Quan. So it has been since before your kind fell from the sky."

Quan and Lahr. Two puppeteers haunted Maurya, then. At least two. But not thousands. The fact she considered that a plus when dealing with invisible, mind-controlling, epoch-spanning beings should have made her question her sanity. Ufa prickled her skin, and she glanced down to read the runes.

"Thank you," she said. "I understand. We should be negotiating with you instead. We will await an invitation for the time and place of your choosing."

The mask lifted, and Vish shuddered after the abrupt shift. He blinked again, as if he'd lost track of his point.

"Yes, um. As I was saying..."

"Give me your hand," said Amryn.

"My hand?" Vish frowned. "Oh, yes. Of course."

He extended his hand as if sealing a bargain, and Amryn extended the handshake into an arm clasp. She pressed her forearm against his, and Ufa pierced his skin to inject the antidote.

"What the hell was that?" Vish jerked away.

"Liberation. Give it a minute. Ufa isn't sure how soon it will take effect."

"You drugged me!"

"Un-drugged you. Don't be so melodramatic."

Vish glared at her in silence, which she considered an improvement over the shouting. After a moment, she tried again.

"Tell me about the Elders."

"We don't talk about them. It's bad luck."

"Superstitious rubbish," she said. "Vish, you don't talk about the Elders because the bitters keep you from doing so."

"No, you're wrong. The Elders are what happened before we learned the bitters kept ravelers away."

Amryn sighed. *This may take a while.*

"Start there. The ravelers before the bitters. Tell me what *that* has to do with the Elders."

Vish looked over his shoulder. He seemed bewildered when his mind remained his own and scanned the lagoon for... what? Elders coming to stop him?

"Not here," he said.

Amryn didn't debate. She led him to her cabin, drew the bolt, and waited. Vish looked around, and if he noticed Hobi's belongings, he refrained from remarking on the obvious. The Prince of the Republic shared a cabin with his Ambassador. She stifled an objection when Vish settled in Hobi's chair. It didn't matter. She needed answers.

"Ravelers, Vish," she prompted. "Ravelers."

"They're creatures like the lomloo, but a bit larger and far more cunning. They are keenly attuned to their surroundings and can unravel whatever interests them, dissembling even this ship into its elemental components, then reassembling it into an entirely new design. Ravelers have the tentacles of a squid and the wings and tail of a ray. That's their natural form. But they can shift into any form, mimic any creature they observe... or consume."

"So, they're carnivores," said Amryn.

"In a way, yes. Ravelers don't eat other creatures, really. They absorb them. Crawl under their skin and whittle away at their bones and flesh. Replacing them, bit by bit, with raveler."

Amryn shivered at the thought. What a horrible way to die.

"And then?" she said.

"It depends. Usually, the raveler keeps a new form for a while. Almost as if it enjoys the novelty of being something else. A raveler could be the dolphin chasing your ship's bow or the sea turtle paddling up to give you a look. Eventually, it tires of the game and shifts back into its natural form. Until it feeds again."

"You said ravelers are not Mauryan adaptations," she said. "How can you be sure they aren't an experiment gone wrong?"

"They aren't. I'm certain. Maurya's biologists were scrupulously ethical in their work. Ravelers cannot be their doing."

So far, she detected no inconsistencies in what he'd told her earlier. Though it was the stuff of nightmares, this much of the story, it seemed, was not considered taboo. Even while under the effect of the bitters, Vish had told her most of what he repeated now.

"So ravelers were here when the first Mauryans arrived," she nudged.

"They selected the islands in this area as optimal for the science station before the ship even left the Republic. Remote and easily shielded. Modest resources, but nothing of particular value. Far enough from the major continents and the most likely trade routes."

"A perfect hiding place for Watchers," said Amryn.

"Exactly," said Vish. "It wasn't until the engineers began welding the ship into place that they discovered the island was riddled with caves. Above the waterline and below. From the lagoon to the seafloor. Some broad enough for a bantee, but most no wider than your shoulders. Shaped by creatures no scientist of the Republic had ever encountered."

"Ravelers," Amryn surmised.

"Quite the discovery for a bunch of star-weary biologists. The creatures seemed equally intrigued by them." Vish paused. "I suppose you can guess where this is headed."

Amryn imagined the excitement of the Mauryan scientists, eager as she would be to study a unique new lifeform, and their curiosity turning to horror.

"A raveler tasted human flesh," said Vish. "But unlike its other prey, humans retained an ember of self-awareness even after the raveler consumed them. It found it could access their memories, experience their emotions, and even communicate with the essence of the individual that human had been. In other words, the raveler absorbed the flesh, but the spirit lingered. It found the experience compelling."

Living hell. Ravelers took on the form of their prey. That meant Mauryans saw the faces of their dead, and their anguished spirits looked back at them from behind raveler eyes.

"They are the Elders," Vish said quietly.

"Wait. That was thousands of years ago. And the same ravelers kept the same faces all this time?"

And the same trapped souls.

"No, the ember dims after a few decades," Vish said, his voice quieting to a whisper. "When an essence begins to fade, the Elder calls for a replacement. And Maurya sends one."

"No," said Amryn. "No, that can't be right. That's barbaric."

"After a few generations of attacks and retaliation, Maurya negotiated a treaty with the Elders. They would appoint a Mauryan to represent the Elders' interests in the Assembly—"

"The role Gagan fills today," said Amryn.

"Yes. And in return, the Elders agreed not to venture into the city. They are free to roam the caves and swim in the sea. And only the appointed Mauryan liaison is allowed into the chamber the Elders call the Well."

"And?"

"Maurya sends willing replacements, and the Elders no longer prey at random."

"You send sacrifices to appease the monsters." Amryn couldn't believe what she was hearing. "Condemning anyone to such a hellish existence is unconscionable."

"The governing houses accepted the duty long ago." Vish avoided her eyes. "Ajagara, Silhad, and five others with permanent seats in the Assembly. When it was last our turn to answer an Elder's call, my grandmother chose to go. Rajin Srilata named Chandra as her successor and left us. Elders prefer replacements of greater age and wisdom. Their memories are richer, and their essence fades more slowly. By going, my grandmother ensured it would be longer before the next Ajagara had to answer the call."

Amryn stared in disbelief. The thought of Elders feeding on any Mauryan stirred her to anger, but Vish spoke of Srilata's sacrifice with a detached resignation. Generations of living under the fear of ravelers, the threat of Kitsune, and the constant, insidious paranoia clouding their minds... had left these people numb.

Vish had yet to meet her eyes in the silence that swallowed the dreadful truth. He clenched his fists, and with no bitters to suffocate his emotions, he began to tremble. As his mind remained his own, uncaged anger flushed his face. When he lifted his head, his eyes were clear and cold.

"I will not rest until every raveler is dead."

Vish stood and headed for the door. Rage had broken free and raced past reason. He couldn't stop himself. He never had to before. Amryn darted around him and blocked his way.

"Vish, stop. You aren't thinking straight."

"Get out of my way."

"Try to fight this war alone, and you die."

"I don't want to hurt you, Amryn. Get out of my way."

Vish tried to push her aside. Amryn dodged his reach and caught him by the shoulders instead. She shoved him against the cabin wall, and silver bands sprouted like vines from her hands. Ufa curled around Vish's arms and burrowed into the planks to trap him. Vish bellowed in frustration as he struggled futilely against the shackles.

"Release me!"

Amryn held his shoulders, letting his fury burn wild. It had plenty of fuel. So, it took a while. His shouts turned to curses. Rafael kicked open the door, wielding a pistol, and Cora shouldered in behind him. They stopped short when they saw Amryn wasn't the one in need of rescue.

"Ah, Commander Vishal," said Rafael. "Perhaps I should have warned you. Only a fool draws the ire of the daughter of—"

An elbow from Cora ended Rafael's slip of the tongue with a gasp.

"Republic," said Cora. "Daughter of the Republic."

"Get her off me," said Vish. His glare would melt iron, but a sliver of reason was creeping back into his eyes.

"Intervene in your diplomatic negotiations?" Rafael shrugged. "It is bad business to annoy a client who has paid in advance. Ambassador, you will cover any damage to the cabin, yes?"

"I have the situation under control, Captain," said Amryn. "You may go."

Vish abandoned a losing plea. He thinned his lips and watched them leave.

"If you're done shouting, perhaps we can discuss how we're going to liberate Maurya," said Amryn.

"We?"

"You and I. We."

"Why make this your fight?"

"We both know we won't be allowed to leave here. From the moment you brought the *Seeker* through the walls, we were Maurya's. That makes this my fight as much as yours."

"You're right. The Elders can't risk letting anyone escape," said Vish. "Sentencing you to this prison was not my intention."

"But since I'm here, I may as well make a few improvements," she said. "Starting with bringing down those walls."

"But that would expose us to—"

"An entire world beyond this lagoon, much of which is quite lovely. People and cultures you might find appealing. Trade, allies. The sharing of knowledge and exchange of ideas."

"The Republic sanctions revealing ourselves to the seed population?"

Amryn weighed her choices. It may be time to risk recruiting another ally to the cause. She was finding it harder to keep up the pretense with Vish. Ufa loosened the shackles, and the silver vines curled back into her hands and retracted under her skin. Vish stepped away from the wall, rubbing his arms.

"Sit down and hear me out," she said.

"Do I have a choice?"

"No, so save us both another wrestling match."

Vish returned to Hobi's chair. The short time his will had been his own seemed to have sharpened him. Hardened his resolve. He'd need that and more.

"There is no Republic," Amryn cut to the point. "At least, not enough left of it to attempt a Return. Kitsune's conquest of the Watchers was total."

She expected denial, a rush to refute her, anything but the utter apathy that met her revelation. Instead, Vish stared at her for a moment, then shrugged.

"Makes more sense than the alternative," he said. "Prince Hobizadi of the Kishar Republic shows up wearing my grandmother's pendant and bears an uncanny resemblance to the only outlander ever to leave this island."

The ruse was up. Hobi was in danger.

"You knew," she said.

"We suspected," he said. "You made it damned hard to tell which improbability was closest to the truth."

Who suspected, and how much did they know? It couldn't be Gagan. He would've fed a ship full of outlanders to the Elders by now. Vish was too young to have known Yuji when he was here. So someone else had to have told him about the resemblance. *His grandmother's pendant.*

Chandra. She had to be one of the Mauryans who sheltered Yuji and let him go all those years ago. The prism Hobi took from his father... Chandra must have given it to Yuji when he left. *Her mother's pendant.*

"Chandra dared not dispute our claim because we might have exposed her," said Amryn. "Because if anyone learned what the rajin had done—"

"Gagan would destroy her," said Vish. "And the walls would never come down."

Amryn thought quickly. This changed the gambit considerably.

"That's why Chandra needed to get Hobi alone. And why she sent you here."

"To learn whether we could trust you," said Vish.

"Do you?"

"That depends. Tell me what you want."

"Open your doors to your kin. They've fallen on hard times out there. Bring them home."

"Kin?" Vish frowned. "From the Republic? Did some from the other stations survive?"

"No, you're the last of the Watchers. I don't know how nenes ended up outside your walls. Maybe a few of you escaped before the Elders enslaved you. Maybe a few were out scouting when Maurya cut communications and shielded from Kitsune. Maybe some were in the other stations Kitsune raided for breeding stock. We may never know. But surely you see Hobi is more like you than not."

Vish couldn't argue. Of course, he had noticed Hobi's distinctive drakmu, coppery skin, and jet-black hair. And he recognized a reflection more vibrant than the original.

"Nenes are few in this world, and N'si are fewer still," said Amryn. "Many took to the losing side in the Chalyn's War and died for their stupidity. But others joined in the rebellion and fought to defeat Kitsune. Hobi was one of them."

"So, at least one Mauryan had the spine to fight back," Vish said with a hint of pride. "There may be hope for us yet."

Not exactly an invitation to launch shiploads of refugees, but she would deal with the details later. It was the concession she'd been waiting for.

"Allies, then?" she said.

"Allies." Vish offered his hand. "How do we get the antidote distributed?"

"Ufa says it can be effective when inhaled. The effect is slower than an injection, but the first breath weakens the bitters' control. Take me to the lungs."

"The what?" Vish looked confused.

"The mechanics that breathe air into the city. Where the sandalwood scent comes from."

"Ah, the refinery," said Vish. "Most of our air and drinking water runs through the purifying equipment there. We have a few substations as backup, but targeting the refinery would get it out to the most populated boroughs."

# # #

Vish dove from the *Seeker's* deck and led her away from the harbor passage, swimming beneath the rocky shoreline, and navigating through an underwater passage until her lungs burned. They surfaced in a dark chamber to the sound of dripping water. Amryn sucked in a deep breath, and cool air filled her lungs as Vish swam ahead. Dim pinpoints of light woke to his presence and outlined a barnacle-crusted ladder.

Vish held a finger to his lips and waved her to follow. He climbed the ladder with a sack of antidote vials clinking against his back and reached back for her hand. Amryn wiped seawater from her eyes and stood beside him before a featureless metal wall. He tapped the prism on his chest, and a door she'd not detected hissed open.

"They'll know I'm here," he said. "Hurry."

With that uplifting bit of news, they were running down hallways, through catacombs of steel and starheart deep beneath the city. At each dead end, another undetectable door parted for the Commander of the Watch.

Their footsteps echoed in the emptiness of the catacombs beneath the city. The unwavering white light shone less starkly, and no mosaics or tapestries shrouded the bones of the old starship. Though time had dulled its sheen, the ancient ship had not yet crumbled to dust. That alone was a testament to the engineering mastery of a Republic that had once been.

They ran on silently, intent on reaching the refinery. Vish could be leading her anywhere, but she had little choice but trust he wasn't betraying her. Even so, the puppeteer's words haunted her every step.

The Elders are Lahr. What is not Lahr, is Quan.

Whether it had been intended as a confession or a warning, Amryn couldn't say. She had chosen not to repeat it to Vish. Not yet. Quan was his mentor and friend. She couldn't have him flying off into a rage again.

There was only so much truth a freshly liberated Mauryan could handle.

Chapter 31

Ravelers

Chandra led Hobi down through the levels of the city, taking to alleyways and avoiding guard posts. They skirted the marketplace and turned course before reaching the harbor. Beyond the farthest market stalls, the starship's hull disappeared into the ancient rock of the island, and shadows stretched where stark white light never reached.

Chandra skimmed her hands over the rugged stone, searching. With a glance over her shoulder, she beckoned him to follow and vanished into a narrow crevasse.

Hobi slid into the darkness after her.

"Stay close," said Chandra. "If the tide comes in, I'm not turning back for you."

Rising tides never concerned him, but he kept quiet. They inched through the darkness, feeling their way along walls of timeworn stone. Their hands met and stuck in a slimy stretch of rock.

"Blasted weebul." Chandra snorted in disgust. "Whoever thought creating webworms was a good idea was an idiot."

"Keep moving." Hobi wiped the sticky web from his hand. "Tides, remember?"

"Don't make me regret bringing you."

Their climb took a steeper incline. Hobi sensed a halo of sunlight in the distance, and some while later, Chandra noticed it as well.

"The shore," she said and quickened her pace.

The passage widened as they neared the sunlight and led to a shallow cave. Hobi dropped to his knees and crawled out onto the sand. A wandering wind swept off the Endless Ocean to greet him. Its salty breath brushed his face, curious and untamed, tasting his substance and recognizing one of its own.

Chandra appeared beside him, brushing sand from her hands. The sight of her there on the shore rekindled a memory that was not his own. She'd been younger then and restless as the wind. An ache of forgotten regret rose to tighten his throat. Time had moved on, and so had they.

"I discovered the passage as a child," she said. "I wasn't supposed to go outside alone, but I was never one for following rules."

She waded into the surf, then turned to look at him. Testing his response to the surroundings. For a brief moment, her eyes softened with a hint of affection as sand and sea called forth another memory. *Black-haired angel.* Could she be the Mauryan who had found Yuji adrift and dying? Was Chandra the black-haired angel from his father's journal?

Though Yuji had guarded their secrecy and not risked recording their names, Chandra and Janak could be the young nenes who had defied their laws and sheltered him here. It was hard to be certain. Mention of them was made sparingly, and the descriptions were vague. But whoever they were, Yuji had carried a fondness for them long after he left their hidden island behind.

"The ravelers," Hobi brought her back to their reason for coming. "Is this stretch of shoreline theirs? Do they burrow in the sand? Hunt the shallows or deepwater?"

"You truly do not know," she said, slowly coming to accept the fact.

"Chandra, this is important."

"To whom?"

"Yuji."

Hobi made his choice. It was a stretch of the truth, at best. But when he spoke the name she'd artfully avoided, he passed her final test. The balance of their dance shifted as Chandra recognized the power the name held. Hobi held the power, and her fate was in his hands.

"What do you want?" she said. Fear sharpened the gravel in her voice.

"Take me to where you hid him."

Hobi had stopped wondering why this urge to see ravelers would not let go of him. He'd spent years fighting the magic within him, pretending not to hear its silent whispers, and suspecting any decent thing he did came from the prodding of its unwavering honor. The presence had given him a conscience, whether he'd wanted it or not.

He would never betray her secret, but he would let her wonder.

Chandra returned to the cave and made for another gap in the rocks. Tucked between the boulders was a crevasse like the one that had brought them here. Yet this one was wider by a shoulder's breadth and worn smooth by time and use. Instinctively, he recognized purpose in its placement and form rather than the randomness of nature.

Chandra started up without a backward glance. Hobi trailed her through the passage of polished stone as the light dimmed and her breath grew heavy. After a while, she stopped to rest in a quiet stretch of the tunnel that smelled of moss and rain.

"It took us longer then," said Chandra. "Yuji was too weak to climb. But I'd already succumbed to an outlander's smile. I'd decided he would not die alone, so I pulled him along. To the only place I knew they would not find us."

She started crawling again, and they made their way deeper inside the mountain, beyond the light, into a realm of shadows only eyes with magic could perceive. Hobi watched her wistful smile flicker and fade.

"His rescuer," he said. "He wrote what he remembered of you and of this passage."

"Wrote? There is a record of—" Chandra stopped and turned in the darkness.

"One journal. In safekeeping on the *Seeker*."

"Safe in the hands of your partner," she snorted. "Leaving her there seemed a clever move at the time."

Hobi ignored the bait. Not having Amryn by his side troubled him more than he cared to admit, and he had no reason to prolong this pretense. Time to move the gambit along.

He lifted his finger in the darkness and lit a flame on its tip. Her face illuminated by its flickering glow, Chandra gaped. To her credit, she stifled a scream as, one by one, flames sparked on each of his fingertips.

"What *are* you?" she rasped.

"My father's son," he said. "And whatever he was, this island made him."

"Was?" she said. "But he sent you. Yuji cannot be..."

Chandra stopped, refusing to pronounce her cherished memory dead. Hobi couldn't fault her. He had clung to denial for years as a child. Until slowly, the elemental magic that had been his father's legacy pulled him from a pit of grief and set him on the path that led him here.

Back to where the magic began.

"He died when I was young," said Hobi. "Never betraying you or your people. He guarded your secrets, even from me. But he knew a time may come when he needed your help again. That's why he left me the journal, to send me back in his place."

Chandra stared into the flames on his fingertips, and shadows of sadness closed in around her.

"Yuji was a star I plucked from the sky. Rare and beautiful as a dream. I suppose this world could not hold him for long." She studied Hobi anew. "You have his beauty, but not his spirit. Yuji was never serious, and you wear duty like a cloak. What is this burden he left you to bear?"

"Like Maurya, our people are also in hiding. Refugees driven from their land. Persecuted for wrongs they did not commit. We are few and growing fewer." Hobi extinguished the flames in turn until only one flickered on his fingertip. "We are N'si. Children of Maurya stranded in the world beyond your walls. We are your kin, and we are ready to come home."

Chandra's lips thinned. She did not challenge his claim. Damn her. Damn them all. They knew the N'si were their own. They'd closed Maurya's doors and shut them out anyway. Abandoned them to a monster to save their own skins.

"You wouldn't have risked so much to save a mere outlander, a Breeder," said Hobi. "You recognized Yuji as being from the nenes your ancestors cast out."

"Do not judge in ignorance," said Chandra.

"Sorry, but we lack the luxury of accessing the archives of the entire Republic whenever we wish. There must be more to the story. Care to enlighten me?"

"You inherited his sarcasm in double."

"Not his patience, though."

"I could offer more practice."

"Chandra."

"It's no great secret," she said. "Our homeworld of Endath was one of many the Kishar Republic colonized. Not all of us looked as Mauryans do now. Those in the southern continents tended to have lighter skin and pale hair. They recruited scientists from all over Endath into service, filling quotas expected of all the worlds of the Republic. Many came here to staff the biology, engineering, and monitoring stations."

N'si were not the only nenes on earth. Their estranged, pale-haired cousins, the Nunyaehi of Tallu and the Firstborn of Rhynn, had their own quirks and challenges. Nenes trying to survive in a world overwhelmingly populated by men might have banded together if they didn't distrust one another so thoroughly.

"When Kitsune took control, we shielded our station and cut off all contact. Some of us were out on scouting expeditions that day. Those, along with Endathns in the other stations, were already beyond our help."

"At least you were safe," said Hobi. "Too bad for the rest of us."

"Kitsune's conquest was thorough."

"Yes, it was. And a few thousand years later, so was his defeat. We destroyed him for you, Chandra. You can open the doors now."

"Your world would curse the day I did."

Chandra turned her back and crawled away, vanishing again into the darkness of the passageway ahead. Hobi curled his fingers and put out the last flame. He would convince her yet.

They crawled along in silence, feeling their way along polished stone as the tunnel took dips and rises and turns. After a while, he began to hear them. The whisper of silk falling behind him as he passed. A soft sigh of breath near his ear. And he began to feel them. Tentative touches brushed his cheek and combed through his hair. A feather-light tendril curled around his ankle and then retreated.

Ravelers. Somehow, he knew them. Felt them gathering. Smelled their curiosity.

Chandra had climbed ahead, widening the distance between them. He could still hear each pant of her breath and her hands patting the stone. Yet, she seemed unaware they were no longer alone. The ravelers were uninterested in her. Because she reeked of the bitters? If he called out, she might discover he had avoided the stuff. He wasn't ready to explain someone or something was using the bitters to control her. Not until he knew who was holding the reins.

Hobi swallowed and continued crawling. Fear would make him smell like prey.

The darkness seemed to dissolve into nothingness, expanding around him in a vast, inky void. Into an existence with no beginning and no end. Into endless journeys of forgotten purposes. Hobi felt the prism slip from beneath his shirt. It dangled from its silver chain, and its faint glow caught the glint of wet grey flesh slithering out of sight ahead. Behind him, he felt another brush, another touch.

Suddenly, the weight of a wet cloak fell across his back. The weight clung to him, and damp seeped through his shirt. Icy pinpricks pierced his skin, shoulder to shoulder, trailing down his spine, numbing and burrowing into his flesh. Hobi rolled and kicked out at the darkness and flung himself back against the tunnel wall. The wet slap of skin hitting the glassy stone was not his own.

Hobi's side spasmed as the magic within him manifested. The knob rolled over his ribs and around to his back, flattened, and blanketed his shoulders like a shield. Elemental heat sparked a thousand tiny embers, pinpoints of fire melting away the ice burrowing its way inside. Reclaiming him as its own.

He gritted his teeth and pushed to his knees. He inched out a hand and winced as pain seared his back. He forced himself to move. Each movement brought fresh torture. Around him, the tunnel echoed with slapping skin, huffing breath, and snapping teeth as the creatures abandoned their prey to fight one another.

Hobi choked down bile and kept crawling. His tattered shirt fell and twisted around his knees, and he ripped the tangled remnants away. Creatures brushed past him in the dark, rushing to the fight he left behind. Intentionally or not, they covered his retreat. The fighting began to grow fainter, and the tunnel abruptly went quiet.

While straining to listen for pursuit, he hurried ahead. His hands slipped from under him as the tunnel took a sharp decline and sent him sprawling to his belly, sliding down the polished chute with no handholds to slow his fall. A maw of light in the distance came rushing at him.

He tucked his head, curled his knees, and held tight. Suddenly, he was airborne and falling. Then arms of warm, salty water embraced him. A smile tugged at his mouth.

The sea never failed him.

Hobi surfaced to find Chandra pacing on a strand of pebbled sand beside a pool in a dimly lit cave. Her hair was wet, which he took as consolation. At least unceremonious plummeting into the pool was the expected manner of arrival. He glanced up at the chute. Nothing followed him out, so he swam over and lifted himself onto the pebbled ledge.

"I was beginning to think you had turned back," she said. "What happened? Your back is scratched raw."

"I hit a rough stretch. Glad you seem to have missed it."

"Rough enough to rip your shirt off." She gave him a skeptical frown.

"It wasn't one of my favorites." Hobi shrugged. "Stop frowning. Stings a bit, that's all."

Chandra pursed her lips and let the deflection stand.

"I brought him here, to the far fringes of the raveler caves." She looked around as if seeing the place anew. "It's only a short swim from the lagoon and secluded enough no one was likely to happen upon him. Enough nooks and crannies to stash him in if anyone did."

Hobi walked the ledge circling the pool in the shaded grotto, trailing his hand along the time-worn limestone. Arches opened into other chambers, large and small, and others beyond those, in a labyrinth of caves, pillars, and pools honeycombing the mountain along the tideline. Wind sang through the labyrinth like ancient spirits playing flutes. The crescendo of a cresting wave, the harmony of lapping currents, and the deep bass drum of the tides echoed an aria to the Endless Ocean.

And the scents. Salt spray and the sweet portent of rain. A night breeze luffing sails. Jasmine and citrus and ferns. And fog rolling in with the sunrise.

Serenity he had never known. Yet had always known.

"If you wait here alone, ravelers will come."

Chandra's voice drew him from the siren's song. He wanted much from this place, but it would wait until he had what he needed.

"You left Yuji here for the ravelers?" he said.

"Not defenseless," she said. "I marked him as protected."

"What does that mean?"

"Ravelers are a threat we dealt with long ago, with bitters and a treaty to coexist. I cut my hand and painted his forehead with my blood. Any creature marked with bitters-scented blood is forbidden prey. We protect newborns with the bloodmark until they can take solid food."

It was the stuff of nightmares. They smeared blood on their babies to keep beasts from eating them. Trapped on an island, they couldn't escape without facing another monster named Kitsune. No wonder Mauryans were paranoid.

"This treaty you speak of," he said. "Mauryans negotiated terms with ravelers. How does one negotiate with a beast?"

"Ravelers communicate when they wish." Chandra shuddered. "Through telepathy or by using the mouths of Mauryans they claim. When our ancestors sat down to negotiate, they were met at the table by one raveler in its true form and another in the pale blue shell of the Mauryan it had devoured."

"So, you bloodmarked Yuji and went to Janak for help."

"Janak had no part in it," she said. "The crime was mine alone."

"You're lying."

"And you have lied to me at every turn." Chandra glared at him. "Prince of the Republic. Son of a sorcerer. Here to help us. Here to beg us for help. I don't know what you want, but you will not have it at the price of Maurya's safety."

"An unseen enemy prowls this island, Chandra. Feeding you fear and paranoia. Keeping you hidden away here for itself. You'll never be free until you open the gates."

"To let others like you inside?" she scoffed. "No. I left a city in turmoil. The turmoil you created by coming here. I indulged you for Yuji's sake, but enough. Either expose my crime or don't. I need to return to my duty."

"Then I will go with you."

"Your presence would only make matters worse," she said. "Return to your ship or stay here. You wanted to meet ravelers. Meet them."

With that, Chandra dove into the pool and swam away. Hobi fought the urge to defy her, to dive in after her, but he knew he had overplayed his hand. Even if he won Chandra's support now, it wouldn't be enough. Liberating Maurya meant he had to first rid them of the force that had imprisoned them here.

He glanced up again at the empty chute. As he spread his arms, a ring of fire sprang up to encircle him.

"Come out," he dared them. "I am the new power on this island. If you are as wise as they say, you will negotiate with me while you still can."

No response. As he expected. Acknowledging a taunt only grants it power it did not earn. A reckoning was coming, but not until they had more to lose than to gain. It was always a matter of shifting the balance.

Hobi let the flames flicker out, and the labyrinth's song took a somber tone. A warning in return? Possibly. But the music of this place resonated with him in a way he couldn't quite name. Once again, a rush of conviction buoyed him. He belonged here and would liberate it from whatever claimed it now.

"Until we meet again."

Hobi nodded a salute to the empty chute and dove into the pool. For now, he would return to his ship and to Amryn. They had much to discuss, and he was anxious to hear her perspective on ravelers and bitters and liberating Mauryans.

He had barely cleared the cave when a splash broke the surface above him, and a tangle of rope descended. The net trapped him and tightened. A fierce jerk sent him sailing from the water and crashing into the rocks. A sharp blow to his head sent pain skittering down his limbs, and shadows crept over his eyes.

# # #

Hobi blinked away the blur. His face was in the sand, and the magic within was trying to wake him. He rolled to his side and coughed seawater, but sitting proved a feat beyond him. Ropes bound his hands and feet, and the fishing net held him fast.

Khaldun stood a wary distance away on the pebbled ledge of the raveler grotto. A silver pistol glinted in his grip.

"It would have been easier on us both if you hadn't come to."

"Why, Khaldun?" Hobi stared. "Why?"

"Because you will likely succeed in conquering Maurya," said Khaldun. "And in making it the N'si haven you intended. If you had failed... moved on to the next scheme as your kind always does... I wouldn't be forced to stop you."

Another man with a grudge. Reckless and hedonistic N'si such as Hobi's brothers had created an abundance of those through the years. The Chalyn War had killed off the worst of them, but N'si survivors were left to bear the consequences of their stupidest kin. But Khaldun?

"I trusted you."

"Because I needed you to," said Khaldun. "The N'si war hero. Favored by Nefekari. Your cunning earned you a ship, and you set out on your impossible quest. It should have ended after a few months of wandering the Endless Ocean, but that unnatural luck of yours led us here instead."

The loose cannon. The poison. Khaldun had nearly killed them both.

"Amryn is Ari," said Hobi. "She bears no blame for any N'si wrongs you're avenging."

"When I return Amryn's jambiya to the Gyakari, I will tell him how Captain Hobi raped and murdered his daughter. Perhaps then, he will remember why every Ari emperor before him hated N'si," said Khaldun. "Resa, the seductress, blinded him to their wretchedness. But when I lead the Gyakari into the jungle, to the nest of N'si vermin Resa has been hiding from him, the world will finally be rid of your kind."

"Your hate runs deep."

"My love runs deeper," said Khaldun. "My brother's blood stained the sands of Tokju."

"He fought in the Chalyn War," Hobi surmised. "Many men died in battle that day."

"Asim died without honor. He fought beside the rebels."

"A poor choice on his part."

"They deceived him. Blinded him with lies, as they did the others," said Khaldun. "N'si spread the lies. N'si stoked their unrest. Manipulated Ari into fighting Ari. Turned man against man. Brother against brother. As you always have."

"That is not what happened," said Hobi. "Sanjakari plotted to overthrow the Gyakari. Ari son rose against his Ari father. Because Ari ambition never wanes. Sanja sought out N'si allies. Not the other way around."

"Silence! No more of your lies!"

Light pulsed from the prism hanging from Khaldun's neck. It was a Mauryan transceiver. He must have stolen and used it to track Chandra to the caves. And he'd seen her leave alone.

Amryn. Khaldun wouldn't risk leaving her alive to reveal his crimes. Hobi strained at the ropes binding his wrists. He tried lighting a flame, knowing the fire would burn skin and rope both. Magic manifested, and the familiar twitch rose a knot in his side.

Watching his futile struggle, Khaldun edged closer. The cold silver of the pistol pressed against Hobi's temple. The knot slid up his chest. Too late.

Water erupted behind Khaldun. From the raveler pool, great, arcing waves and sprays of foam rained down over them. Brine blurred Hobi's eyes, but their slapping skin and snapping teeth closed in around them.

Khaldun stumbled back. The pistol fell to the pebbles, and Khaldun fell across Hobi's legs. From beneath a blur of foam and flesh, he cried out. His cries turned to gurgles, and Hobi felt the big man's weight being dragged off his legs. A riot of splashing drowned out his last desperate screams.

Hobi lay panting. He pleaded with the elements to light flames for him one last time. Heartbeats counted out the seconds. And still, no attack came. Were the ravelers feeding on Khaldun? How long until they had their fill?

The grotto grew quiet.

Chapter 32

Inside

The last doors hissed open, and they entered the refinery. Vish stopped at a panel and tapped a rapid pattern. A red light blinked above the closing doors.

"We're sealed in for now," said Vish. "Few can override my commands."

"Don't tell me. Gagan is among the few."

"All right, I won't," he said. "But you'd best use the time I bought us."

Amryn scanned the chamber. The refinery was vast. It was larger than the largest warehouse she'd ever seen, larger even than the Gyakari's throne room. The cavernous bastion of Watcher technology seemed a living thing. Hulking beasts of metal grazed a mesh floor, fenced by ribbons of pale blue light. The refinery itself was a leviathan that had swallowed the beasts. Ladders and catwalks formed its ribs, and veins of wire and cable fed it sustenance.

"The lungs," said Amryn. "Take me there."

Vish climbed a flight of metal steps and crossed a railed platform skirting the refinery. They passed beneath square-faced lights suspended at precise intervals, glaringly bright and shining down on the machinery below like the eyes of gods watching mortals for misdeeds. A bank of observatory windows along the outer walls revealed how deep they were beneath the sea. Deeper than the lowest of the living levels. Deeper than the harbor and marketplace. Beyond the windows, massive intake culverts pumped water and air into the refinery.

"This way." Vish started down another set of stairs.

He took her into the belly of the leviathan. Everywhere, images flickered from an endless array of panels. Most blinked with shifting charts and graphs, monitoring the status of whatever they were supposed to care about. Others displayed grainy, colorless scenes of the empty corridors they'd run through to reach here. Nearby, a barrel-sized mechanic with a domed head and pincers for hands scaled a ladder. The metalmind servant went about its assigned tasks, ambivalent about their presence.

The refinery pulsed with power. Amryn felt its energy thrumming in the air, making the fine hair on her arms prickle.

"The sun's seed is here, isn't it?" she said.

"You feel the weirdness," said Vish. "The sunseed chamber is beneath the refinery. Its effects are disorienting. Stay too long, and your mind plays tricks on you. That's why we have bots do all the work here."

"Lovely. You might have warned me." Amryn rubbed her arms.

"Would a warning have kept you away?"

"No."

"Then why waste my breath?" he said. "We have a half-hour or so before the hallucinations start."

Vish cut a haphazard path through the machinery. Cables crisscrossed overhead in purposeful webs, and pipes curled like serpents' coils around fat, sweaty cylinders that smelled of seawater. Eventually, they reached a row of boxy equipment that huffed instead of gurgled. Like a passel of giant warthogs snuffling for grubs, the air filtration machines were noisy beasts. Troughs of blinking lights fenced the area.

"The control panel is over here," said Vish.

The machine's angled face, sleek and featureless, lit to acknowledge their approach. The runes glowing in the onyx glass reminded her of Ufa, only larger. The familiarity set her a bit more at ease. However ancient its mind, it was likely more concerned with serving its design than toppling empires. Amryn ran her fingers over its surface, and Ufa sent runes flickering up her arm.

"We need to empty the vials into the equipment," she said. "Ufa can mix it with elements he needs from the seawater. Take me to whatever part of this contraption adds the sandalwood scent."

Vish started off, and Amryn stopped him. She risked the next move in the gambit.

"Wait, we'll need inside its mind, too," she said. "Ufa says there's a wall keeping us out. A wall on fire."

"A firewall." Vish grinned. "Like a moat around a castle but for metalminds."

"Can you get us around it?"

"I can."

And he would because he trusted her. He would forgive her someday for not telling him her intent. She hoped.

"There, done." Vish stepped back from the panel. "You have elevated privileges. Be quick about it. That command will trigger an alert, and if someone's bored enough to notice, they may come to investigate."

Amryn touched the control panel again. This time, the silver runes gave her the confirmation she'd wanted. Ufa could get in. The glow of their silent conversation faded, and Amryn waited with her hand pressed to the glass.

She barely contained a gasp when Ufa tapped into the metalmind network. Vast beyond belief. Cold and sterile, yet rich in depth and patterns. Infinite paths to take in a world not of substance but of thought. Predictable. Analytical. Rational.

Ufa paused on the threshold of his homeworld, and Amryn sensed his hesitance.

"You are my purpose," he said. *"I cannot leave you."*

"Companion, not servant, remember? We are allies," she signed. *"These may be the last of your kind, Ufa. Convince them to open the gates."*

Ufa flickered meaningless dots up her arm. The choice was difficult for a being created for defense, not conquest. She hoped Ufa's time with her had convinced him some battles were worth waging.

"Go, my friend."

Amryn felt the emptiness the moment Ufa left her. And yet, he wasn't entirely gone. They were inseparable, and the silver thread binding them existed beyond any tangible manifestation. But his attention had shifted elsewhere, and Amryn needed him to stay focused on his mission. She stepped back from the control panel.

"Ufa will ready the equipment," she said. "We can move on to the sandalwood tank."

Vish nodded and set off again. They climbed a service ladder to what looked like a water tower amidst the snuffling filtration beasts. Vish strained to turn a stubborn wheel on a tarnished metal hatch. It seemed refinery bots seldom needed manual access to the tank.

"I suppose you triggered another alarm." Amryn coughed as a potent cloud of sandalwood wafted from the hatch.

"Sure, I did." Vish shrugged. "But it takes a while for anyone to make it down here. The weirdness would get to us first. Start pouring."

Amryn unbuckled the sack from his back, and they emptied vial after vial into the filtration tank. The pungent blend of sandalwood and sulfur made her eyes water.

"Whew, that's strong." Vish hurried to seal the hatch, and the transceiver on his chest chirped, demanding attention. He held the prism to his ear, and as he listened to the muted voice, his face turned ashen.

"Vish?" she said. "Vish, what is it?"

"Damn him. Damn the arrogant, reckless fool." Vish started for the ladder. "I have to get back to the city. Gagan was upset the Assembly recognized Hobizadi and the Return as legitimate, so he's inciting Trads to revolt against the Republic. Nira says the Watch has been breaking up skirmishes all morning."

Amryn hurried after him. Hobi was in the city, and Gagan made him a target.

"So, the rajin must have Gagan arrested," she said. "Surely treason is a crime here."

"It is, and she did. But house arrest was the most she could manage without the Elders' sanction. Gagan is theirs to discipline."

Amryn shuddered, knowing the sort of discipline Elders meted out, and so would Gagan. That must mean he was acting with their consent. She jumped from the ladder and landed in front of Vish.

"The Elders are inciting this," she said, blocking his way. "They've decided we're a threat."

Vish's mouth set in a thin line. He knew she was right.

"Go back to the *Seeker*," he said. "You won't be safe in the city."

"Hobi is there."

"The Watch can protect him."

"Not like I can." Amryn started for the doors.

"I could command you to go," Vish called after her.

"But why waste your breath?"

Amryn stopped at the sealed doors, trying not to pace while she waited for Vish to open them. When he didn't, she turned and found him stubbornly holding back.

"Vish, we don't have time to argue," she said. "Open. The. Doors."

Amryn wondered if she could force the steel apart without distracting Ufa.

"Maurya has never known war," said Vish. "There's a logistical problem with firing cannons inside a sunken ship you don't want to crack open."

"You don't know how to fight," Amryn realized. Of course, they didn't. No one had ever shown up and tried to conquer them before, and the Elders could squeeze the heart out of any rebellion before it disturbed their little paradise. Unless they were the ones who started the rebellion.

"That's why you'll be safe on the *Seeker*," said Vish. "You and the crew can defend your ship from any of Gagan's malcontents rabid enough to venture out there. You're battle-hardened warriors compared to the rest of us. Give me time to get the city under control, and I swear, I'll bring him to you."

"And then what?" she said. "You'll help us leave? Escort us out as you escorted us in? The Elders would destroy Maurya before they allowed us out with their secrets. You know that."

"Once the antidote clears enough heads, we'll negotiate with them again," he said.

"For what?" Amryn threw up her hands. "To lower the quota of Mauryans you agreed to sacrifice to them? Or to allow us to stay in their prison with you?"

"You don't understand. We have to negotiate. There's nowhere to escape them."

"Yes, Vish. There is." Amryn caught his shoulders. "Open the walls. Send the message. Speak my name, and the entire Ari war fleet will come."

Well, she hoped it would. She was *one* daughter out of many, but the Gyakari did not come to rule an empire by ignoring threats to those he considered his own. Belatedly, she noticed the stunned look on Vish's face. She probably should have left out the war fleet part.

"Who *are* you?" he said warily.

"Amryn Nisari," she said. No point in dancing around the rest. "My father is the Gyakari, Emperor of Ari. It's a big empire. The largest left on this world, in fact. The Laradian Empire fell apart after the war. And the Rhynns... well, that's beside the point. My mother is Resa Nisari, commander of an assassin's guild known as the Fang. They were both rather annoyed I wanted to be a scientist instead of a killer, but family is family."

"They sent you here?"

"No."

"Then how—"

"I ran away."

"With Hobizadi... Hobi."

"Not exactly. That part was an accident." Amryn gave up. Explaining was taking too long. Hobi was in the city, and Gagan wanted him dead. "Vish, I promise to continue this and any other confessions of interest after we deal with these ghouls you call Elders. Now, please. Open the walls. Send the message."

"I can't," he admitted. "I don't know how to override the protocols. No one does anymore. Only the Elders remember. So, you see, we have no choice but to negotiate with them."

Amryn wanted to shake him. He could have mentioned that earlier, and she wouldn't have hesitated over a little guilt at conquering Maurya's metalminds. Ufa was their only hope.

"Well, since opening the walls seems an unreasonable goal at the moment, perhaps you can open these damned doors instead. Once the antidote starts taking hold, we'll have a city full of freshly liberated Mauryans to deal with. If Gagan already has everyone on edge—"

"The Watch has to take control," he said. "Martial law until everyone comes to their senses."

Preferably before some agitated Mauryan decided to fire a cannon inside a sunken ship.

Chapter 33

Quan

Hobi's shoulders ached from struggling to loosen the net. Annoyingly, he'd outfitted the Seeker with only the best equipment, and the net refused to give even a hair's breadth. And for the first time since the change, magic failed him. Instead, the elements ignored his pleas, and the presence abandoned him to whatever dark hungers lurked in the raveler caves.

Khaldun floated face down in the pool nearby. Not eaten. Not dyed blue by raveler blood or reanimated into a ghoulish mimicry of himself. Simply drowned and left to float.

Hobi could see them now, barely visible in the diffused light. Ravelers circled in the dark depths of the pool. Some large. Some small. Graceful, cloak-like wings sailed through the water below. Nimble tentacles curled in patterned gestures as if the creatures were signing to one another.

In curiosity? Menace? Hobi could only wait to discover which had drawn them here. He'd never had the patience for waiting.

"My father knew you," he said. Thirst graveled his voice. "Years ago, Yuji encountered you and survived."

The swirling spiral of ravelers seemed to slow, even as their tentacle gestures grew more animated. He had no clue whether they understood his words, but they had reacted to his voice.

"Meeting you changed him," said Hobi. "I came here to learn why."

A set of grand, sweeping wings materialized from the depths, and the largest raveler Hobi had seen yet rose through the heart of the spiral, scattering the smaller creatures in its wake. Hobi decided then his extraordinary luck had forsaken him, as well. In his impatience, he had somehow summoned an Elder. He strained again at the rope chafing his wrists.

The great raveler emerged from the pool, rising from the surface like an ancient god of the sea. Rivulets cascaded over its opalescent skin, and furled wings draped its shoulders like a cloak of sapphire satin. Where a sea ray's mouth would be, the creature's face sprouted a single thick appendage similar to an elephant's trunk, curled and lifted to delicately sniff the air. Six slender, vine-like tentacles grew from the sides of its elongated knob of a head, each twining in ceaseless motion, tasting its surroundings. Its prominent brow and expressive eyes were reptilian, streaked with sapphire and gold, and fixed on Hobi.

The raveler king hovered at the water's surface, buoyed by the elemental magic that had abandoned Hobi to return to its master. Hobi stared back at the mysterious creature, returning its curious gaze. The twining tentacles began to retract and fuse into limbs as he watched. The raveler sailed towards him, shifting its form as it drew near.

A sudden burst of light blinded him, and a rush of cold chilled his skin. The net froze, trapping him inside an icy cocoon. Instinctively, Hobi lashed out, and his fists shattered the frozen twine. He kicked and twisted his way free and rolled to his knees. Shards of ice lay scattered over the pebbles.

A white-haired nene stood over him. The old custodian Hobi had met in the city looked down at him, wearing an amused smirk.

"Ice breaks things," said the raveler. "It's particularly useful when fire abandons you."

"Who are you?" said Hobi, gauging he wasn't in immediate danger of being devoured.

"I am Quan. We are Quan," he replied with a nod at the pool.

Quan sat on the ledge beside him, scooped a handful of pebbles, and molded a cup. Then his finger filled it with fresh water.

"Thirsty? Go on, take it. We didn't save you in the tunnel just to poison you here."

Hobi felt the familiar twitch in his side. The presence had returned. To take credit for its part in the tunnel rescue, no doubt. *After leaving me alone in the damned net.*

"What was it you saved me from?" Hobi gulped the water.

"Lahr, of course," said Quan. "Elders are Lahr. What is not Lahr, is Quan."

Raveler factions? The creatures were not united in their intentions. It was an opportunity he could use. If he lived through this encounter.

"So, you are Quan. Quan is not an Elder," said Hobi. "Just a regular sort of shapeshifting raveler who walks around in human form, washing windows."

"Ah, a quick wit." Quan laughed. "I liked that about Yuji."

"You knew him."

"Well enough."

"Then you can tell me what happened here," said Hobi. "What changed him? And how did he pass the change on to me?"

"The change?"

"Sorcery. Magic. Elements at my command," said Hobi. "This peculiarity I call *the presence* was once with my father. When he died, it shifted to me."

"Ah, yes. Well, the telling will take a while." Quan waved his hand over the pebbled sand. In seconds, the ledge had melted, smooth as glass. "Sit. You may as well hear it comfortably."

Hobi considered trying to escape and was disconcerted to find he didn't want to leave quite yet. Though his wits seemed his own, Amryn had told him the raveler could warp minds as easily as it shifted forms. But he had come here for answers, so he folded his arms and leaned against Quan's freshly polished wall. As he settled back, the knot rolled its way up his chest and burrowed beneath the prism. Watching? Waiting?

"Where to start? That's always the hardest part." Quan sat cross-legged beside him. "I am many millions of years old, but I did have a beginning."

"Millions? How is that possible?"

"Who knows?" Quan shrugged. "I recall the distant past only from the dim fog of beast memory. Awareness came gradually after I had remade my body-self many times. Eventually, my awareness endured from one remaking to the next, and I began to acquire and retain experiences as creatures that are born to die cannot."

"How could you begin if you were not born?"

"Was the sea born?"

"No, but the sea isn't a living being," said Hobi.

"Yet, without it, there is no life." Quan studied him for a moment. "What you call life is not the only form life takes."

"But there had to be a first raveler," said Hobi. "Now, there are many."

"I am the first. All are part of me. We are Quan."

"I don't understand."

"We don't reproduce as you do. We regenerate. The elements sustain us."

Questioning the nature of life had kept philosophers occupied throughout the centuries. Hobi was pressed for time.

"Very well," he said. "You came to exist. Then what?"

"Not the patient sort, are you?"

"No."

"Good. Patience is overrated," said Quan. "Now, where was I? Oh, yes. Self-awareness. As time passed and other creatures birthed and died around me, I came to understand my uniqueness. And I discovered loneliness. I wondered what it would be like to have more of me. So I began experimenting. When I consumed another creature, I learned to read its design. From its design, I learned how to regenerate its shape."

"Taking another shape doesn't make more of you."

"Frustrating, I know," said Quan. "So, I began studying their eggs. Eggs are strange things. Incomplete. Half a whole. Yet the halves join to form a new creature that is both, yet neither of the halves. Quite intriguing. Yet, I could not halve myself."

"Were there no female ravelers?" said Hobi.

"Perhaps I am not explaining clearly. We are of one gender, or none, depending on your perspective. Quan is simply what I am and have always been. But I discovered that when an egg began dividing and growing, I could replace its design with my own. Finally, I could give birth to more of me. So many and varied, we were. And for a time, we were content. Yet for all our numbers, we were still Quan."

"One gender and one mind," said Hobi.

"One awareness," said Quan. "We think independently, just as your hand can move independently of your foot. Yet, your hand and foot are equally aware of the sun warming your face."

The concept seemed reasonable. And conscripting an egg to carry another's design reminded him of the cloning he'd read about in the strange and wonderful science being uncovered in the Watchers' dens. The early Mauryan biologists might have used the same techniques when they crafted weebul, bantee, and tarchu.

"Then, one day, a ship arrived. A ship not of this world but from worlds far beyond. It brought creatures unlike any we recognized, and they carried the scent of predators, not prey. So, we studied them from a distance and observed their busy ways. They were always busy."

"That's the way of humankind," said Hobi. "We're a restless sort."

"Indeed, you are. When one of you drowned, we consumed its flesh to decipher its design and were astonished to discover its sentience. We had encountered no sentience on this world but our own."

"Even beasts have thoughts of food and mates."

"Of course, but beasts cannot dream of being more than they are. Strangely, though this strange new creature's intelligence surpassed any but our own, each was confined within its own awareness. What one sensed, the others did not. They spent their entire lives as individual grains of sand on the shore. It saddened us to see them exist in such loneliness."

"We had the individuality you thought you wanted," said Hobi. "It wasn't as grand as you thought it would be."

"Still, your kind fascinated us, and we watched as their numbers swelled. The strongest dominated the weaker. They were driven by the quest for dominance and craved individual power above the survival of their kind. The first humans to travel from the stars ended themselves a mere hundred thousand years after they arrived, but they were not the last. Others came from the same and different stars. We watched them repeat the same rise and fall many times. First, humankind, then dragonkind, then humankind again. All ended the same."

"The Cycles," Hobi realized. "You've been here through them all."

"We've been here since before your Cycles began," said Quan. "We unraveled and rewove these islands many times, in many forms, but it is our home. The elements suit us well, so we stay. After the last of the dragons died, your kind returned. The Mauryan ship came here, to our nest. Theirs was the last ship from their worlds. A fleshless being of humankind's own creation, the metalmind they named Kitsune, conquered them, first here and then on all the worlds that sent them."

"That much is familiar to me," said Hobi. "We fought Kitsune and broke free of the Cycles."

"That you did." Quan smiled. "Indeed, this is the last of your Cycles. If you end yourselves again, no ships will come to replant the seeds. Perhaps it would be better if you endured."

"Because you've grown accustomed to us?"

"Yes," said Quan. "We are sentimental old fools, at times."

"But Maurya is more to you than sentimentality."

"Unlike the others, when the Mauryans arrived, they didn't rush out into the world searching for power," said Quan. "They hid and watched and waited. They allowed us to study humankind up close. Shapeshift to walk among them. Learn their language, their ways. We grew fond of them, these intriguing creatures born to die. So soon, their vibrant lives were over. We thought to make them last longer. Share our ability to regenerate. But how? We had many ideas, and for the first time, Quan disagreed with Quan and became Lahr."

"How does one being, after millions of years, divide over a difference of opinion?"

"Your word for our parting of ways is rebellion," said Quan. "Lahr left us. Severed itself from our awareness. It was the darkest time of our existence, and it forever changed us."

"What did you disagree on?"

"Lahr consumed a living Mauryan, then regenerated into its identical design. Unexpectedly, and unlike the drowned human we had sampled before, the replica retained the Mauryan's consciousness, yet it hosted Lahr's, as well. Over time, the Mauryan's awareness faded away, and Lahr was left alone." Quan gave Hobi a quizzical look. "The human consciousness. Where does it go when it leaves?"

"That depends on who you ask," said Hobi.

"I am asking you."

"Some say I will cross into the mists. There, I'll choose to meld into the One or return for another life. Hold on to my sense of self or relinquish it to become part of a greater whole. At least, that's what the Chalyns tell us, and I know of no one who has been there and back but them."

"Hmm. Not so different from Quan. Perhaps we will meet your One someday." Quan shook off his musings. "Back to the telling, for you are not the patient sort. Again and again, Lahr tried to create a human that would endure, one able to regenerate as we do. Each attempt created another Lahr with a stolen consciousness that faded too soon. But in consuming them, Lahr gained their unique memories. Love and hate. Lies and joys and sorrows. Lahr hungered for more, and to this day, demands sacrifices to keep its hunger fed."

"And Lahr continues to make new Elders," said Hobi. "Can't you stop him?"

"Lahr is powerful. The deepest emotions of your kind linger long after the source is gone. The potent residual of your emotions accumulates in the Elders. Lahr wields its power as both a weapon and a restraint."

"Paranoia," said Hobi. "I felt it smother them."

"But you were unaffected."

"I avoided the bitters," said Hobi. "Mauryans are convinced the concoction protects them, but we uncovered the truth. Lahr uses the bitters to enhance his control, to weaken their minds."

"Clever theory," said Quan. "If it were true, there would be no Mauryans left. No, the bitters are my doing, a repellant I created to keep Lahr from decimating the population."

"You're lying."

Quan's brow arched. "Bold, too. Another trait I liked in your father. Yuji would be the first to tell you, a lie is different from an incomplete truth."

"So, you and Lahr are both controlling Mauryans. What is it? A game of rivals? Sport?"

"Certain scents in the bitters help attune my awareness to those who have a sufficient concentration in their blood. I can sense what they sense. Seed thoughts. Suggest actions. But control? No, I can merely nudge them. Forcing Mauryans to do what they would not willingly do on their own is beyond my power or ethics."

Ravelers had ethics. Hobi supposed he should find the possibility reassuring.

"None of this explains what happened to my father."

"I was getting there. You keep leading me on tangents."

For an ancient god of the sea, Quan rambled as badly as an old sailor.

"Our falling out with Lahr. Let me pick up there." Quan refilled the pebble cup. This time, with decent wine. "We had other ideas on how we might share our longevity with humans. Not by consuming and replicating you, but by joining with you. Existing within the body you were born to, sharing nourishment, experiences, awareness. Regenerating you as you aged."

An icy wave of realization struck him, and his hand went reflexively to his chest. The knob. The presence. The magic within him.... Hobi scarcely registered the words as Quan went on talking.

"Trisana was a bright young biologist. He came to our caves often and studied us as we studied him. Eventually, we managed to communicate our offer and gave him time to decide. Tris accepted, but soon after the joining, his mind faltered, overwhelmed by Quan's. Fitting millions of years of existence into the span of a human life... the potency proved too much."

"So, you claimed a Mauryan, just as Lahr had."

"We are not Lahr!"

Quan's temper flashed hot, and for a precarious moment, Hobi glimpsed the force coiled inside an old window-washer's body. A force he dared not challenge. Not yet.

"We grieved Tris. To this day, we honor his courage. When you spoke of the mists... we regenerate this body in hopes Tris may return."

"If you're waiting for absolution, it isn't mine to give."

Quan's amiable demeanor chilled. Who was Hobi to challenge an immortal who had seen mountains rise and crumble? Who had shaped the world to its liking and dissembled it again for amusement?

"Short lives can accumulate only so many regrets," said Hobi. "We are creatures born to die, as you say, but our regrets die with us. When a life has no end, regrets have nowhere to go."

"Profound," Quan smirked. "After losing Tris, we couldn't risk another attempt. And that is where the telling ended on the day Yuji sat with me and listened, as you are listening now."

"Somehow, he convinced you to try again," said Hobi.

"Convinced?" Quan snorted. "Yuji struck a clever bargain. Did your father teach you how to gauge whether a bargain is fair?"

"Both sides give up something they want."

"Yuji agreed to host a raveler and accept its companionship. Quan agreed to send a raveler severed from our self, as we had severed Lahr."

One raveler cut off from the whole like a lock of hair. One lone raveler, not imbued with the overwhelming potency of Quan. Alone, its awareness might attune to Yuji instead.

"My father saw a chance at immortality," said Hobi. "But he would lose his independence. Possibly forfeit his freedom of will."

"Quan saw a chance truly to create another of my kind. But I would lose my child to a human I knew could not stay with us."

"A fair bargain."

"Freely given. Freely received," said Quan. "Yuji purged himself of the bitters. I selected a small raveler from among us to be the first true child of Quan. We named it for Tris and cut it off from us. The joining began at dusk, there in the pool. Tris fused to Yuji's skin, and by dawn, the bonding was complete. Tris had reformed within Yuji."

"And Yuji got access to your magic," said Hobi. "That wasn't part of the bargain."

"They became more than Quan had hoped for. More than Yuji expected. Raveler and human. Symbiont and host. A whole greater than its halves."

"N'si cleverness and raveler magic," said Hobi. "You birthed a sorcerer."

"And we gifted it to the world," said Quan. "Yuji and Tris set out to discover their potential, and I said farewell to a child."

Such a grand adventure. Such a wasted opportunity.

"You failed to keep your end of the bargain," he said. "Tris let my father die."

Hobi got to his feed and stared down at Quan, tempting the raveler's temper, daring it to face the anger he held in reserve. Anger he'd fed since the day his father's blood darkened the sand. Quan sat motionless, and Hobi clenched his fists. He wanted to fight. Needed to fight.

"No time," Quan began mumbling. "Blood. Too fast."

The twitch on Hobi's chest traveled up his neck. Spasms rippled his shoulders, and sweat beaded on his skin. The raveler inside him, the coward, was trying to flee again. Hobi had never wanted a dagger so badly.

"Calm yourself," said Quan. "We are nearly done here."

Quan blurred and shifted form. The aged nene's face wavered, and Yuji stood inches away, smiling as he had in Hobi's memories, holding out his hand. Hobi glared back at the charlatan and its clumsy attempt to placate him. He didn't give a damn about losing the power he'd once craved. He wanted ravelers gone from the world, and he'd die to take one out.

"Beast," Hobi snarled. "You soulless beast."

Hobi lunged for the raveler's throat. Quan shifted again and thrust out his hands. A wind gust tossed Hobi against the cave wall. With another burst of light, ice shackles bound his wrists. Quan held the greater power in proximity.

The raveler stepped up to him, its eyes narrowed in warning. Hobi seethed at its arrogance. But it was a fight he would not win. Not here. Not yet. He stopped struggling and hardened his hate to match the coldness of the ice that bound him.

"There was no time," said Quan. "Yuji was mortally wounded and losing blood faster than Tris could replenish. The attack had weakened them both. After years as symbiont and host, one's health was bound to the other's. As they both lay dying, a choice remained. Tris left Yuji and fled into another host. The only possible host."

"Me."

Hobi had no memory of the hurried bonding, only the dark desolation that followed. Perhaps he'd felt no pain. Perhaps the raveler had erased the memory.

"There is no denying it was wrong. You were a child and knew nothing of the bargain," said Quan. "Tris should have died with Yuji. And you would not be here judging us."

Quan's shame rang hollow, and Hobi had come for more than empty apologies. He intended to claim what belonged to him. The truth of what happened here was his inheritance. And Yuji's legacy.

"Release me," he said. "You proved your point."

Quan considered him for a moment, then lifted a hand, and the ice shattered. Hobi pushed away from the wall, rubbing the cold from his wrists. How the telling ended would depend on his cunning. He had something Quan wanted.

"The Change," he said, calm masking his intent. "That's what I named it. Whatever had happened and left me peculiar. It had its challenges, you know, being young and alone and peculiar. Having someone to explain things might have helped. A companion?" He shrugged. "I had a twitch in my side."

"You were merely a vessel," said Quan. "Necessary, but temporary. A means to return to the nest. You have served your purpose."

"But the magic—"

"Was never yours. Tris used the elements when necessary to keep you alive. Otherwise, you might not have completed the journey back to us."

Another hollow claim. Hobi had no doubt who wielded the magic. The stowaway raveler might be the source of the fuel, but it didn't light the fire.

"Tris told you this?"

"Yes. Soon after you arrived."

"How, if you cut him off?"

"Him?" Quan cocked his head. "Interesting. You refer to Tris as *him*, not *it*."

Hobi shrugged. Seeds of doubt were so easily planted, even in ravelers. But Quan was not the only raveler listening.

"Answer my question," he said. "How did Tris tell Quan anything if Quan cut him off?"

"Being severed from us doesn't change a raveler's nature. Tris can still seek our awareness."

"But not mine."

"You aren't bonded," said Quan. "Out of respect, of course. Tris took care to shield Yuji's child. Your mind was too impressionable. And you were not part of the bargain."

Hobi knew then, the balance had shifted. It was time to call in a debt.

"Now, get in the water," said Quan. "It won't take long. Tris will leave you and return to us. Then you may continue with your life as you wish."

"And if I wish to leave Maurya?"

Quan shook his head. "Adapt."

Hobi glanced at the pool and back to Quan. No need to hurry. Let the raveler see him hesitate. One or the other of them would finish the telling soon.

"Will you try again?" said Hobi. "With another Tris and another joining?"

"Someday," said Quan. "First, we will take time to reflect on what we have learned."

Hobi turned away and went to the water's edge. Without looking back, he jumped into the pool still teeming with ravelers. Their winged spiral circled expectantly as he sank into the cooling depths. Hobi swam deeper and drew a breath. Life-rich seawater rushed through the gills he had trusted would reappear. Descending to the farthest reaches of the light, Hobi stopped.

He focused his mind inward, searching for the presence as he had so many times before. But, this time, the search was a short one. What he sought was no longer a mystery.

I am ready. Don't let me down.

The raveler twitched in his chest. It heard him. And it knew he'd come to collect a debt.

You led me here. You lied to Quan.

Hobi's fingers tingled from a frigid chill. Numbness crept up his limbs as the heat of his body retreated to his core. He fought the fear slithering from the shadows of his mind. Fear signaled prey. He was the hunter now.

"Time to choose, Tris."

Hobi waited, floating beneath the spiraling ravelers, alone with the presence which now had a name. Silent. Measuring. They knew one another. They knew what was at stake.

Without warning, spasms rippled his chest again, just as when he faced Quan on the ledge. Tris hadn't been trying to flee but to hurry a bonding. Hobi's body convulsed as white-hot jolts raced along his spine like lightning ahead of a storm. Helpless to stop the transformation now, even if he wanted, he shuddered and focused on the presence emerging from the corners of his awareness, the guardian who had shadowed him for years.

Images flooded his mind. Scents and tastes. Colors of loves and losses. Vivid memories of a life cut short. Deeper memories of a life that had seen millions of lifetimes come and go. What began as a bargain had forged a friendship of shared purpose. Hobi added his own life to the cause he had not fully understood. Tremors still wracked his body when he first heard the voice of magic.

"I made that choice long ago," it said.

It was a windy voice of rolling tides and cresting waves, of gull wing and whale song. Hobi had heard the voice in his dreams, soothing his fears, daring him to test his limits. Those limits seemed boundless now. He sensed the rich mosaic of elements at his beckoning, felt the steady heartbeat of the sea sustaining him, the sanctuary of the mountain, and the thrum of energy from the sunseed in its belly. Mauryans had brought the seed, and ravelers had kept it hidden beneath their nest, unaware of its value. Years ago, when Yuji and Tris bonded, energy from the sunseed arced through rock and water, drawn to them as to a lightning rod. The strangeness it emitted released a fountainhead of potential neither realized they held. They left Maurya as vessels of magic, attuned to the elements, yet ignorant of the power simmering within them.

"We learned our way together," said Tris. *"Yuji mated with other N'si, and you were born. Child of our hearts. With elements of us both in your design."*

"How did I not know you?"

"You knew me through Yuji. Before he died, we shared in raising you. And together, we settled on our purpose."

"Bringing more N'si to Maurya," said Hobi.

"Repeating an evolution that can only happen here," said Tris. *"Making more of us, so you would not be alone."*

"But I'm not alone. Not anymore."

Hobi hadn't felt alone since luck brought Amryn aboard. What would she think when she learned the sorcerer's son wasn't quite human? Would she find him too strange because of the raveler living inside him? Amryn understood that sort of peculiar better than anyone.

"Shall we stick to our purpose or find another? Time to choose, Hobi."

"We see it through."

Hobi gathered elements newly responsive to his call. He lit the depths with a purple glow, the herald of a coming king. Tris was with him, as always, no longer a silent guardian but a trusted companion. Together, they swam for the surface, ascending through Quan's circling court of ravelers. When Hobi pulled himself onto the ledge, Quan barely acknowledged him, instead peering into the pool and searching for Tris.

"I am here, Quan."

The windy voice echoed through the grotto, like the rumble of distant thunder. Quan spun around, searching for its source. His expression darkened when he saw Hobi and the ring of purple flames flickering at his feet.

"Harm him, and you harm me," Tris warned.

"What hold does this human have over you? Tell me, and I will break it."

"He is mine," said Tris.

Quan's brow furrowed. Understanding was slow in coming.

"I was born after the bonding," said Hobi. He waited for Quan to grasp the significance. "Raveler and human. I am both and neither."

"An unanticipated aberration," said Quan. "Unfortunately, Tris seems to have grown too fond of you. A messy situation, but one I can remedy."

Quan cast a swirling ice net. With Hobi trapped and dragged back into the pool, could Quan finish reclaiming Tris? Not without a fight.

Hobi dodged and sent purple flames flaring higher. The net fell and hissed, melting in a cloud of vapor. With a swipe of his hand, Quan called a waterspout from the pool and flung it at the flames. Purple mist billowed to fill the grotto. When it cleared, Hobi stood within the guarding ring of fire, dry and untouched.

Quan knelt and struck the ledge, shattering the glass he'd polished from pebbled sand. The force sent crystal shards flying for Hobi's flesh. Tris spun a gust of wind, and the shards banked steeply away. Crystal blades rose and coalesced into spears, and the spears rained down into the raveler pool. Blue blood tinged the water.

"Enough!" Quan shouted.

Unaccustomed to yielding, Quan was slow to accept the stalemate. He paced around the circle of flames, studying Hobi, measuring Tris, and tasting their freshly forged strength.

"What do you want?" he said, finally.

"Maurya," said Tris.

The demand reverberated through the labyrinth, and the mountain itself seemed to tremble at the destiny it commanded.

"First, we will rid Maurya of Lahr," said Hobi. "Then the bitters. Maurya will let down its walls, and N'si will return to their homeland. And Quan will carve out more ravelers and set them free."

"N'si and raveler will evolve together," said Tris.

"That wasn't the bargain," said Quan.

"Yet, it's the only offer on the table," said Hobi. "Allies or rivals. Choose wisely."

Quan ran a hand through his tousled white hair. "What have I created?"

"Something new and wonderful. Something more than we were," said Tris. "Isn't that what you wanted?"

Quan leaned back his head and laughed.

Chapter 34

Ascent

Vish pressed a pattern into the tiles outside the refinery doors. Amryn waited impatiently as he repeated a lengthy sequence meant to keep the doors from opening to any authorization but his own. Few would be able to override his code. She didn't need to ask who those few might be.

The first Mauryan they encountered on their way back to the city was a young technician making her daily rounds and too awed by meeting the Commander of the Watch to ask questions. She nodded at him as they approached, and infatuation colored her cheeks. Vish was oblivious, of course.

"This area is restricted," he said as he passed. "Return to your home and remain there."

"But I'm supposed to…"

Vish stopped and turned. The technician looked as if she wished the floor would open up and swallow her.

"There is unrest in the city," he said with strained patience. "The Watch is securing the peace. Until then, it is not safe to be down here alone."

"Yes, Commander," she said, then turned and ran.

Amryn sighed. "You realize she will tell everyone she sees about meeting dashing Commander Vish and how concerned he was for her safety."

"So?"

"Gagan might find out we were here."

"He already can, if he checks the locator grid." Vish tapped the transceiver on his chest. "Stealth isn't an option."

"Can't you get rid of that thing?"

"Not unless you have another way to open doors."

Ufa probably did, but she'd sent him out to recruit an army. When losing the advantage of stealth, a Fang relied on speed.

"Then start moving," said Amryn.

Vish set out at a brisk run, and Amryn kept pace beside him through the brightly light, sterile corridors. At each vacant checkpoint, featureless metal doors slid open at their approach. Their clap of footfalls and huff of breath settled into the purposeful cadence of marathon runners. With the time Vish spent on patrol, he'd built up decent endurance. It had been months since Amryn had awakened at dawn for Fang drills, but the N'si blood in her veins was steeped in the defiance of generations, surviving in a world trying to wash it away.

When one pair of doors parted, Amryn glimpsed movement instead of empty corridor beyond. A clutch of Mauryans gathered beyond the doors stood braced and waiting. Most were common city folk, but a few were uniformed and armed. Gold stars circling their sleeves identified them as the private guard of House Silhad. Gagan's guard.

"It's him," someone shouted.

Vish stepped ahead of her and gripped the stun wand on his belt. A guard with a double band of stars on his sleeve met him in kind.

"Vishal Ajagara, you're under arrest for espionage and colluding with the enemy."

"You know me better than that, Bharad," Vish replied evenly. "Step aside, or this won't end well, my friend."

"Wish I could, Vish." Bharad shrugged. "Nothing personal. Gagan wants you out of the way."

Amryn tensed. She'd never walked away from a taunt, even when it was the smarter response. She rarely backed down.

"Vish is in the way of his ambition," she said. "Gagan wants to take over Maurya, but his ambitions are empty. He will never be raj."

"Try telling him that." Bharad snorted, and his dismissive glance left and returned to her. Realization darkened his glance to a glare.

"Outlander," the mutters rose behind him. "Wired."

"Watch out! He has the Wired with him," cried a rotund Mauryan who looked better suited for a bakery than a militia.

No sooner had he shouted than the acrid stench of fear came rolling through the corridor like a twilight fog. The Elders had come to kill. Their malice contorted faces, stripping bare the pretense, and the knives came out.

Bharad swung at Vish and caught him off balance. Vish staggered back and drew his weapons. To Amryn, the stun wand and deflector rod looked like blunted swords, and Vish wielded them like a two-handed swordsman. He rushed at Bharad, and thin bolts of lightning arced where their stun wands met.

Amryn gripped her jambiya, and the wild-eyed baker charged. She ducked his swipe and spun to thrust the blade between his ribs. A Silhad guard came at her with a stun wand. She rolled and swept his feet from under him, then slashed his throat as he fell.

Fighting had driven her away from Vish. She cut down another rabid Mauryan and searched the chaos of arcing bolts and flashing blades. Bharad was down, and Vish was pressing the remaining Silhad guards. A stun wand swung for his head, and Vish blocked the attack. His deflector rod sent the lightning forking back the hand that wielded it. The guard cried out and fell to the floor, twitching.

"Behind you!" Amryn sprung for the next of the mindless Mauryan fodder.

When they were done, bodies the Elders had sacrificed lay strewn. The acrid stench of fear vanished.

Amryn bent over the dead baker and swallowed bile. With her thumb, she drew his lids over his vacant eyes. A cold sweat swept her, and she forced herself to memorize the face of her first kill. She despised Elders. She despised ravelers.

Amryn looked up to find Vish standing over her, his face as pallid as the dead baker's.

"You killed him," Vish stated the obvious. "Dead. Not stunned. Dead." He looked around the bloody corridor as if unable to comprehend the concept.

Amryn wiped her blade and stood. Mauryans were not a pragmatic breed.

"They attacked with knives," she said. "Not stun wands. Knives. Sorry to break it to you, but knives draw blood. Death is often the result."

He shot her a look of undisguised disgust. Amryn bit her tongue and walked away. He couldn't know how deeply he had hurt her. She wasn't a killer. She wasn't.

"We need to keep moving," she said. "Gagan sent them, but the Elders were pulling their strings. You smelled them. They'll stop at nothing."

Vish didn't move.

Amryn sighed and went back. She remembered when Resa had first forced her to watch as she dismembered a kill. A body emptied of the life that had animated it was just meat. It didn't feel. It didn't hate.

Hate was for those who lived on.

"Vish?" she said. "Please, Vish. I need you to look at me."

He closed his eyes and shuddered a sigh.

"Is this what opening Maurya to the world will bring?" he said.

"It brings choices," she said. "They didn't die of free will."

Vish knelt beside an unconscious Silhad and picked up his lost deflector.

"We will take the back route from here," he said.

# # #

Amryn paced while Vish paused to check yet another monitoring panel. The route he'd chosen was a tedious repetition of stairs and narrow hallways, avoiding the lifts and checkpoints that would have been the quicker ascent. And keeping more mindless Mauryan fodder alive. With each stop, the scenes from the city grew more alarming. Maurya was at war with itself.

After staring into the latest checkpoint panel, Vish slammed his fist on the wall and turned his back on the images. Amryn stopped him.

"Wait," she said. "That group getting on the lift."

One face in the group had a decidedly blue tinge.

"They're coming for us," he said.

Amryn looked for advantages as she studied the dim hallway. The tactical options were limited, with only a few metal barrels to offer cover, but the girders above were well-shadowed.

"Take off your shirt," she said.

"My... what?"

Amryn rolled a barrel on its side. "Your shirt. Dress the barrel as you. The shape is wrong. You're too fit. But with your transceiver tucked under its belly..."

Vish sacrificed a smile. "You are danger itself, Amryn Nisari."

"Not by choice, but Mother is a stickler for practice."

Vish dressed the barrel and hid the transceiver while Amryn climbed a row of bolts protruding from the wall. She locked her legs around a girder and reached down to help Vish up. They settled on a beam to wait.

Vish laid the stun wand across his knees, and his knuckles whitened as he forced a ribbed collar near the hilt to turn. With a few turns and a muted click, the blunted sheath of the wand detached and slid away. Underneath was a finely honed rapier. Like Vish himself, its dulled façade hid a spine of steel. There was hope for these Mauryans yet.

The clack of boot heels echoed down the hallway. Vish glanced a warning, and they held a collective breath.

A silver-haired Elder with the face and form of an aged Mauryan female stopped beneath them. Amryn drew deeper into the shadows. She wondered whether the raveler might be wearing the visage of Vish's grandmother. If she was, his panther-like crouch didn't waver. As the Elder motioned her Mauryan thralls, they filled the hallway behind her. Wordlessly, she raised a pale, slender arm and pointed. A pair of her minions moved as one and started towards the decoy.

"Vishal Ajagara," the Elder raised her reedy voice in judgment. "You are under arrest for espionage and colluding with the enemy."

Vish leapt first, with rapier and deflector in each fist. He landed on the Elder and thrust the blade as she stumbled. Blue blood spurted onto his face.

Amryn jumped from the girders a second later. One after another, throats split and spilled.

A writhing tentacle whipped past her shoulder. The wounded Elder was trying to shift her form. Flames sparked along the tentacle's length. She lashed Vish across his chest with her fiery whip. Vish drew back and stabbed again.

One after another, the Elder and her thralls fell to their blades. Killing came easily, and the dying was over quickly. Mercifully.

Amryn stood in the gory hallway and wiped her jambiya. She ventured a glance at Vish. His eyes were cold, his face frozen in an unreadable mask. They both lost a bit more of themselves with each kill, but neither lingered over the angst this time. They were not who they had been.

"How much farther?" she said.

"Half an hour, at most."

# # #

The last few hallways were the quietest, and the pensive silence hanging between them added to the sense of emptiness. The checkpoint panels they passed showed the Watch pushing back rioters in the city. Ajagara strength seemed to be subduing the threat, for now.

Amryn tried to find the right words. They would soon reach the city, and Vish would again shoulder the duty sworn by ancestors whose name he bore. He would bear the weight. His shoulders were strong enough. But he had one weakness, and it would bring him down if he faced it unprepared. The one blind spot she saw, and he did not.

"Quan is a raveler," she blurted out as they reached yet another flight of stairs.

Vish stopped and frowned, as if she'd spoken in an unknown tongue.

"Quan," she repeated. "Not all ravelers are Elders."

"That's absurd. Quan is as human as you are."

"How can you know?"

"Elders have a look about them. Raveler blood runs blue. You saw them."

"I saw Quan control you, there on the beach. I watched him manipulate you, and he didn't care that I saw."

"You misunderstood."

"No, Vish. I didn't," she said. "The Elders are Lahr. What is not Lahr, is Quan."

Vish hesitated, and Amryn pressed the point.

"You spoke those very words yourself, Vish. Do you remember? No, you don't. Because the words were not your own."

Vish shook off what he couldn't explain and latched onto the only truth he had left.

"Quan is no raveler. He's a wise man born in the wrong part of town, a sage who taught me to question assumptions others fed me as irrefutable fact. I would trust him with my life."

"And perhaps you should," she said. "But Elders aren't the only ravelers pulling Maurya's strings. Prepare yourself in case you're wrong. That's all I ask."

# # #

Janak was there waiting when the last doors hissed open. He rushed up to embrace his son. Amryn stood back, holding the question burning in her throat until they had their moment. Dressed in full combat gear, Janak drew back and rested his hands on Vish's bare shoulders, taking in the burns and blood crisscrossing his chest, and his eyes dropped to the rapier hanging at Vish's side. Janak said nothing. He held his son's steady gaze for a moment, then saluted him with a nod of respect.

"Where is Hobi?" said Amryn. They could continue the family reunion later.

"Ambassador Nisari?" Janak seemed to notice her for the first time. She wasn't wearing a transceiver, and with Ufa preoccupied elsewhere, it seemed they hadn't detected her prowling the corridors with Vish.

"Amryn accompanied me from the *Seeker*," said Vish. "She learned how ravelers are keeping us docile, herding us like sheep. Father, they're using the bitters to control us. The fear, the paranoia..."

Amryn sniffed the air. "Sulfur and sandalwood. That's the scent of your liberation."

"It's a concoction to counteract the bitters," said Vish. "We used the filtration system to disseminate it."

"So that's why you went to the refinery," said Janak. "It explains why the rioters scattered. They were fighting us like demons, then a few began to fall back. Dropped their weapons. Wandered the streets confused for a while. Then they started heading home. We assumed Gagan had called a retreat."

"Gagan isn't in control," said Vish. "Not directly. The Elders know we've discovered their secret, and they're desperate. They'll stop at nothing to keep Maurya enthralled."

"They sent an assassin last night," said Janak. "It seemed Hobizadi was the target."

"Where is he?" Amryn demanded.

"Chandra took him to the raveler caves," said Janak. "He'd be safer there than in the city."

"Safe?" Amryn stared incredulously. "Ravelers want him dead, so sure, let's take him to their caves."

"Elders want him dead," said Janak. "By now, you must know that means Lahr, not Quan."

"You knew." Vish's eyes widened. "Amryn tried to warn me, but I didn't believe her. What is wrong with you? You let me befriend a raveler. You allowed it to gain my trust. Was I to be its next shell?"

"No, of course not. I'd never risk you," said Janak. "Quan and Lahr are enemies. We've been trying to leverage their animosity for years, and you were helping to forge an alliance. With Quan's backing, we might have forced Lahr to renegotiate the quotas."

"No quotas. No more." Vish shook his head. "We can free ourselves, Father. We can be done with Lahr and Elders and quotas. I've tasted freedom from their control and won't go back to living in fear."

"Never cared much for it either," Janak said with a faint smile. "At your lead, Commander."

# # #

Amryn stood by as Vish gathered the Watch. Outside the Assembly Hall, Nira and Janak readied companies of elite fighters on the commons. Gagan and the Silhad guard had barricaded themselves inside the hall after Gagan declared himself raj.

Chandra had yet to return from the raveler caves. Amryn needed to find Hobi. But wandering off on her own would be stupid when magic-wielding Elders were hunting them both. Her fight was here.

The envoy Vish sent to offer terms emerged from the Assembly Hall alone and ran down the steps. Sera Ajagara seemed to have only one gait, and it was a sprint. She rushed up to Vish to deliver her report.

"Gagan refuses to surrender," she said, panting. "He says he's the Raj of Maurya now, and a raj surrenders to no one."

"You did mention we have retaken the city," said Vish.

"I did, multiple times, and paraphrased for good measure. But I don't believe Gagan is in his right mind, sir."

"Not everyone in House Silhad bows to Gagan." Janak approached. "Some are quite rational. We could offer them terms and let them deal with their delusional kin."

"I don't believe anyone will be able to reason with him," said Sera, "You see—"

"So, we will wait him out," said Janak. "He can't stay locked in there forever."

"Actually, he probably can, Uncle," said Sera. "You see, he's blue."

"Elder's teeth," Janak cursed.

"Yes, exactly," said Sera. "They seem to have... eaten him. Perhaps they were disappointed in his performance of his duties as liaison."

Vish rubbed his neck. "The Silhad guards in there with him. How are they?"

"Terrified, sir."

"But not yet blue?" said Amryn.

"No, Ambassador," said Sera. "Just Gagan."

"So, we have one freshly made Elder who's decided he's the Raj of Maurya and a few dozen guards looking for a chance to bolt on him," said Amryn. "No other Elders in sight?"

"No, Ambassador."

Vish stalked away and resumed pacing. Sera hesitated, then called after him.

"Commander, if I might make a suggestion?"

"Yes, Sera. What is it?" Vish said absently.

"We might lure him out. We do have something he wants."

"And what might that be?"

"Me," said Amryn.

Vish looked at her as if she'd lost her mind.

"Me," she repeated. "The wired Ambassador of the Republic. They can't eat me without destroying Ufa, and they won't risk losing his knowledge of the latest Republic technology."

"Ufa is as old as Maurya," said Vish.

Amryn pulled him aside. "They don't know that. By the time the Assembly voted, we had convinced even Gagan we were legitimate emissaries of the Return. He didn't like it, but he didn't refute it. That's why he started railing against the Republic instead."

Vish was unconvinced.

"Sera is still calling me Ambassador." Amryn lowered her voice. "If Janak or Chandra figured out the truth about Hobi, they didn't tell anyone. And if the Elders knew, all of Maurya would be gossiping about the Ajagara family scandal by now."

"You're right," he admitted. "And I don't like where this conversation is heading."

"We can't know how long we'll have the advantage of deception. I need to get close to Elder Gagan while I have the chance."

"He's one Elder. Taking him out won't win the war."

"How many are there?"

"Seven, usually," said Vish. "Sometimes fewer. Never more. There may be a limit to how many Lahr can sustain at once."

"We killed one today. Janak said the assassin died last night," said Amryn. "Take out Gagan, and Lahr cannot afford to lose any more. That is when we negotiate."

# # #

The city lights had dimmed and taken on a golden hue to mimic the twilight of the world beyond Maurya's cloistered domes. Yet, even after so many years in hiding, they still clung to the pretense. Guards of the Watch spread across the commons outside the Assembly Hall, filling the cobbled paths and courtyards between gurgling fountains and potted palms. The faint scents of sulfur and sandalwood, the welcomed perfume of reason, hung reassuringly near.

Vish stood beside her on the broad, columned portico of the Assembly Hall, as rigid as she'd ever seen him. He had on a clean shirt and Watch coat someone had brought him and had washed the blood from his face. But the past day had aged him in ways no rest would ever undo.

Amryn still wore the sailor's garb she'd worn when they left the Seeker. She had left the stains of battle unwashed. Ari warriors painted themselves before going out to fight, transforming their faces into fierce visages of desert djinn. Close enough.

Muted voices sounded from behind the sealed doors. Tall and square, the hall's doors were made of metal, no doubt, though the Mauryan penchant for embellishment had obscured the original utilitarian design. Long-dead artists had etched a vast landscape of spired cities, flying chariots, and exotic plants and beasts Amryn couldn't begin to name, and colored the scenes in countless shades of blue and white. Crafted when Maurya was young, the doors promised a portal back to the homeworld in the stars they had left behind. But what waited behind those doors today was a monster from the nightmare they had stepped into instead.

With a rattle of locks, the massive doors parted, giving a long, low whine of complaint at being asked to open yet again after opening and closing through untold ages.

A blue-skinned ghoul that had once been Gagan Silhad walked from the hall, surrounded by stone-faced Silhad guards. A ring of blue flames sprung up around the raveler's feet in an unsubtle reminder of its newly acquired status. An altered mimicry of the rajin's robes hung loosely over what had been Gagan's shoulders, and a pale hand gripped her stolen scepter. The Elder scanned the gathered Watch companies beyond the portico with disdain. Then its eyes returned to the steps and rested on Amryn.

The insidious pull of the Elder's will tugged at her mind. Even without the bitters, its force was compelling. Amryn shut out a tendril of fear trying to worm its way inside her mind and stared back into the cold blue eyes with defiance. Let it fear her. If all Elders were Lahr, then Lahr was aware they had killed one of its forms today. And they were capable of doing so again.

She wondered if the creature had found consuming Gagan distasteful. What would absorbing such madness do to a raveler? Whether Lahr was still sane or not, she needed it to believe Ufa was guarding her, coiled and ready to lash out at the slightest threat. It was the one deterrent that kept the monster wary of her.

But she had lost her last tenuous thread of contact with Ufa hours ago. That must mean he was focused on completing his mission. Ufa would never desert her, but if he were unable to—

She refused to consider the alternative.

The Elder lifted its hand and beckoned her forward. For a fleeting moment, an unreadable emotion swept the mask the raveler wore. Was an ember of Gagan still lingering within? Rebelling against his tormentor? Trying to warn her away? The pale, hollow face hardened again, and the moment was gone, the rebel spark extinguished.

Amryn stepped forward on the portico. Vish shifted his stance but made no move to stop her. Even he had accepted arguing was pointless, and he could offer no better options. As agreed, Amryn would accompany the Elder into the Assembly Hall. There she would spend her days answering its questions. Then, when satisfied with the information she had provided, it would allow her to leave, and it would return to the Elders' lair.

Amryn doubted Lahr had any intention of honoring the agreement, but a minute alone with the beast was all she needed. The blade hidden in her braid would do the rest.

The ring of flames parted at her approach. As she drew nearer, the scent of evil swept out to greet her. Amryn gagged at the stench and drew her arm over her face. At her first movement, the Elder threw the scepter aside and thrust out a fist. Icy malice streamed from the emptiness of time, rising like a gale, drowning her in a tidal wave of malevolence. Ancient hatred. Contempt and bitterness. Loathing for all those born to die.

"*Vengeance,*" the hatred sneered.

"Reason survives," she whispered, shutting her mind to the raveler's voice.

She tasted its pique before a burst of white light blinded her. She felt for the quill blade in her braid. Relying on instinct to guide her aim, she flung for the unseen mark. The clank of steel against tile said she missed. Not for long. She stiffened her hands for a khanti strike, squinting to make out the shapes moving within the dazzling light. Too late, she saw the swarm.

"You will die now, puny human."

Amryn staggered back. No, she had come too far to die at the feet of a monster! She ran into the onslaught with a fury all her own.

"Ufa," she cried. *"The battle is here!"*

Amryn stumbled as the first shards pierced her skin. Lahr. She had to reach Lahr. Kill Lahr. Vish shouted, and bolts arced from behind her. She was not fighting alone. She raised her bloodied hands and charged into the pain of a thousand bites.

Chapter 35

War

They finished the brisk swim to the harbor and found the marketplace eerily empty of vendors, with not even a Watch guard at the checkpoint. An elderly woman sat alone on a rug outside a draped stall. She was the only Mauryan in sight. Gold bangles clacked on her wrists as she beaded a silk shawl, and thick white hair fell over her shoulders. She glanced up and set her handiwork aside as they approached.

"Elder's teeth, Quan. Are you daft?" she chuckled. It was a pleasant sound, and pearly teeth shone from her sun-weathered face. "Look at you, walking around dripping wet. You'll catch your death of cold. Then who will sit with me and share my wine?"

"Ah, sweet Liya. I would not dare depart this life without your consent," Quan stooped to kiss her cheek. "But I pray your wine will wait another evening. My young friend and I have an appointment in the upper city. Why is the market so quiet?"

"Because fools abound," she said with a sigh. "First, they fight over nonsense. As if the Republic cares what shopkeepers think about the Return. Then a raj wrestles a scepter from a rajin, and they run to hide under their beds. I tell you, my friend, the entire city has taken leave of its senses."

"The rajin," said Hobi. "Someone challenged her?"

"Not much of a challenge," Liya snorted. "Chandra leaves for half a day, and Gagan sashays in and takes her chair. Mark my words, when the rajin returns, she'll toss the scrawny weasel to the street. Wrestling over a scepter. I'd give my best bottle to see her floor him."

"We must go." Hobi started for the doors and left Quan to deal with the pleasantries.

"Chandra should have returned by now," said Tris.

"Perhaps she wanted some time alone," said Hobi.

"I left a city in turmoil. I must return to my duty. Those were her words. Does that sound like someone planning to take some time alone?"

No, it didn't. But he would search for Chandra later. First, he needed to see Amryn. Then he would deal with Lahr. Hobi had gone straight to the *Seeker* after leaving the raveler caves, only for Cora to tell him Amryn and Vish had left for the city that morning. Frustratingly, Cora had no idea why they left, and Rafael was wearing his captain's hat.

"Such impatience. Wait up," Quan called. "Liya had more to tell me. She says—"

Hobi turned and saw Quan stagger and fall. As he hurried back to help, Quan cried out. By the time Hobi reached him, agony contorted his face.

"Quan!" Hobi knelt and grabbed him by the shoulders. "Quan, what's wrong?"

"Lahr has gone mad," Quan panted. "We must hurry. They... Lahr damaged your mate."

"Amryn," Tris murmured. *"We must hurry."*

Hobi's throat tightened. He would kill Lahr, every last Lahr that breathed, for daring to hurt her.

"Where is she?"

"Assembly Hall," said Quan, still shaken by whatever his awareness witnessed. "The Watch is fighting. Vish... fighting. Silhad. Lahr."

Hobi ran for the thoroughfare that would take him to the lower city and the lifts. He forced away an image of Amryn lying hurt. There had to be a quicker way to reach her.

"Brace yourself," said Tris.

The clatter of metal and whipping canvas echoed across the marketplace. A waterspout summoned from the harbor cut a swath through a row of stalls, sending crates, fruit, and pottery flying. It dodged Liya and set a path for Quan.

Quan dove into the waterspout as it passed. Spiraling winds lifted him upward, then the spout veered for Hobi.

"Get us into the eye," said Tris. *"Let me navigate."*

A wall of water knocked him down and scooped him up. He wasn't sure how one got oneself into the eye of a waterspout, but he let the force of the water take him where it would. The salty water lashing his face began to ease its sting, and, to his astonishment, he looked up inside the whirling funnel to find Quan hovering above him, his white hair whipping in the wind, grinning like a child.

"Try not to break anything I'm going to have to pay for," Quan shouted over the pandemonium.

"I know what I'm doing," said Tris.

Hobi chose not to point out that Tris had no actual experience navigating waterspouts through cities. How he came to know that seemed far less relevant than the fact they were moving towards Amryn quicker than he could manage on his own.

Hobi had just begun to wonder how he might gauge how far they'd gone when the waterspout slowed and wobbled, spinning in place over a spot of cracked tile. He looked around to get his bearings and spotted the giant column masquerading as a tree trunk.

"Get the grate, Quan."

Tris steadied the waterspout while Quan leapt headfirst through the funnel wall. Hobi winced. Landing was going to hurt. Survival probably wasn't the strongest motivator in a raveler who'd outlived everything else on earth and had plenty of spare copies of itself. However, one would think pain avoidance still held some appeal.

A now-familiar burst of light illuminated the wall of water, and moments later, ice shards rained down from above. The tree had one less grate to camouflage.

Tris slowed the spinning and wrapped them inside a tight pillar of water, then launched it into the open vent. Quan lunged in after them, and the geyser lifted them through the heart of the city. Flashes of light through vent grates punctuated long stretches of darkness as they sped upward through the air ducts. The dizzying ascent made Hobi's head ache and proved beyond a doubt, the human body was not meant to move at such speeds.

An abrupt turn sent him hurtling towards the farthest spot of light. The last grate at the top of the tree loomed ahead. Hobi braced for impact, but the force of the water sent the grate flying. He went tumbling as the spent geyser shot them from the vents and dropped them beneath the tree's sprawling, coralesk limbs. Wet and bruised, Hobi wiped a clump of damp silk leaves from his face. They were on a cobbled path in the commons, within a stone's throw of the Assembly Hall.

"I'm somewhat surprised that worked," said Tris.

Watch guards who had scattered at the exploding water and tree grate rushed back with their stun wands drawn. They circled warily as a smaller pair of shoulders pushed through their ranks.

"Quan?"

"Ah, Sera, my dear." Quan got to his feet. "You've met Hobi, I believe."

"Prince Hobizadi." Sera's eyes widened. "How did you—"

"Where is Ambassador Nisari?" said Hobi.

"She was to meet with Gagan outside the Assembly Hall," said Sera. "Commander Vishal escorted her. Then the fighting broke out. No one will let me near the hall now. Please, I need to get through. Uncle Janak is there."

Hobi parted the guards with an arc of fire and ran for the hall. His heart raced when he saw the battle raging between the columns and down the steps of the portico. Near the center of the fighting, tongues of flames whipped above the melee, and dying guards screamed. Thin bolts of lighting answered the flames, and the clash of fire and lightning glinted off thrusting blades.

"Lahr." Quan growled and shifted form. The scaled beast he became was as big as a bear, with claws and fangs, and a barbed tail like none Hobi had seen. It screeched and bounded for the hall. As it ran, more beasts like it sprouted where its claws hit the cobbled paths. Each monster Quan conjured forth raised its head to roar and run with the pack.

Hobi rushed the steps with his dagger in one fist and a fiery whip in the other. He charged into the first skirmish he reached. He swung and slashed, clearing a path to a Watch guard set upon by Silhad rebels.

"They smell of Lahr," Tris warned.

The sting of a stun wand grazed his cheek, and the bared blade on its tip sliced a ragged gash down his arm. Hobi spun at the attack, and his fiery whip circled the Silhad's arm. The man screamed and fell, and another Silhad rushed him from the side. Hobi dodged a bolt from a stun wand and lunged for the man. He drew back a slick red dagger.

A feisty whirlwind whipped through the chaos, but the fighting pressed in on the narrow swath it parted up the steps. Tris was tiring. Even ravelers had their limits. As Hobi watched its shrinking path, Janak appeared on the edge of the portico. He was dragging a fallen guard. Amidst the haze of smoke and confusion, a limp head lolled, and Hobi glimpsed silver stripes on a bloodied neck.

"Amryn!" Hobi stumbled on a step slick with gore.

A flaming spear appeared above Janak. It pivoted and thrust downward. Fire plunged through Janak's back, searing him through. As blood trickled from his lips, with a last defiant lurch, he fell and covered Amryn.

Behind them, a pack of scaled beasts set upon the fire wielder in a fury of fangs and claws.

Hobi saw only Amryn. Single-mindedly, he made his way to her. Dodging and weaving, he pushed his way to the portico. He rolled Janak's body aside and cradled her.

She was covered in cuts. Ice shard wounds. Telltale silver threads crisscrossed her skin like a spider's web. Ufa desperately tried to knit her wounds. But there were too many still weeping her lifeblood. Hobi pressed his hand over a gaping wound.

"Help me, Tris. Please."

"I'm too spent for summoning," said Tris. *"Can you trust me to do this the raveler way?"*

"I cannot lose her," said Hobi.

The familiar twitch in his side rippled over his ribs and down his arm. Icy pinpricks numbed his hand, and he watched in detached pain as his fingers began to thicken. His forefinger fused with its second, and the fused fingers lengthened. Hobi steeled his nerve as a raveler tentacle uncurled from his hand.

Tris brushed over her skin, assessing the damage. Hobi felt the ragged flutter of torn flesh, and bile rose at the coppery taste of blood. He clenched his teeth and steeled his nerve. He could not bear to feel her die. He would rather die in her place.

Tris probed the deepest wound, sealing veins and binding torn flesh. Then his tentacle moved on to the next. Ufa and Tris worked their healing together, racing to staunch the bleeding while Hobi cradled her. Around them, the sounds of fighting began to wane. He glanced up as a Silhad guard stumbled into him and fled.

When Hobi looked down again, Amryn was watching the tentacle burrow into a bleeding gash on her thigh. Her eyes traced a path up his arm, and Hobi turned his face away. He couldn't bear to see her revulsion at what he had become.

Amryn settled in his arms and rested her head on his chest. Even if she shunned him, he had to try to reassure her, let her know he cared. Finally, he forced himself to meet her eyes. She gave him a weak smile.

"Missed you," she said in a broken whisper.

Relief swelled a lump in his throat, and tenderness he never expected he could feel misted his eyes. Had he feared she'd get squeamish over a little thing like hands sprouting tentacles? Not Amryn Nisari. He pressed a kiss to her forehead.

"I'm here now," he said. "Lie still."

"Are we winning?"

"Seem to be."

The Watch was commanding the battle now. Another Silhad tried to flee the portico. A white bolt crackled over Hobi's head, and the man fell writhing. Nira charged up the steps, battle-stained and brandishing a blade, and more fleeing Silhads raised their hands in surrender. Lahr's control was weakening.

"How did Lahr manage to attack you?" said Hobi. "Ufa is too quick."

"Ufa was away," she said. "He couldn't shield me in time."

"Away? He's part of you."

"I sent him. To recruit. An army."

"Of course, you did," he said with a smile.

When Ufa and Tris had healed the worst of her wounds, they began regenerating lost blood and smoothing torn skin. Hobi had no words for the sort of beings they had become—he and Amryn, Ufa and Tris. But he knew with certainty, they had many years ahead together.

Heavy footfalls shook the planks behind him. The clack of claws stopped at his back, and a wet snort of breath warmed his neck.

"Lahr dead?" Hobi asked without glancing back.

"This one is," said Quan. The cracking, squishy sounds of a raveler shifting shapes followed. "What's left of them is utterly insane and hunkered down in their lair. Ah, I see she's lucid. You picked a sturdy one."

"Sheer luck," said Tris. *"Granted, he did have the sense to recognize his good fortune."*

"Quan is on our side?" said Amryn. "Does this mean I have to stop wishing all ravelers dead?"

"An hour ago, I wished the same," said Hobi.

"How horrifying," Quan said dryly. "Get her to the manor and rest. We will set out for the lair in the morning."

"We should go after him now." Amryn sat with a wince.

"Lahr is cornered. We have time," said Hobi.

"I'll find you in the morning," said Quan. "Someone needs me."

Quan left them, back in his old window-washer form, and approached a group of somber guards circled nearby. One of them stepped aside.

Vish was kneeling beside Janak's body. Hobi had felt that pain, grieved beside a father who would never rise again, and knew too well the anger that would follow. Quan rested a hand on Vish's shoulder.

Hobi noticed then, Chandra was not with them.

Chapter 36

Choices

The next morning, a strange stillness startled Amryn awake. Accustomed to the gentle rise and fall of the ship, waking to its absence was disconcerting.

"Five hours and eleven minutes of deep sleep. Vital signs within acceptable ranges."

Amryn tossed aside pillows and stretched, surprised to find her muscles stiff but not as sore as one might expect after being skewered by a crazed raveler hurling ice knives. She swung her legs off the bed and sat, searching for whoever was speaking Ari in the rajin's manor in Maurya.

Its movement startled her. A silver orb, no larger than her fist, hovered before her face. Seams in the sphere gave it a mechanical appearance, and Amryn decided it was a Mauryan apparatus tasked with alerting someone if she'd taken a turn for the worse during the night.

"Shoo," she said. "Tell whoever sent you I appreciate their concern, but I have no intention of dying yet."

"That is a relief to hear," said the orb, "Though you must admit, it will not be from lack of trying. Perhaps you should dress. Hobi went to the trouble of raiding a rajin's wardrobe for you."

Amryn blinked. She recognized the smirk beneath that advice.

"Ufa?"

"Cognitive abilities unimpaired," the orb noted.

"Ufa," she cried. Amryn caught the orb and cupped it in her hands. "You can speak." She glanced down to confirm the relic was still affixed to her chest. "How did you manage it?"

"My task was to engage the local intelligences."

"Yes, to find your kin."

"Task accomplished. Thus, the auxiliary device," said Ufa. "Had our activation been administered by certified technicians, they would have provisioned and attuned the customary accessories at the time. This com ball is from the local inventory."

"Well, it's quite handsome," she said. "I approve."

"To my immeasurable relief. Now, if you would dress, I believe we are to raid a raveler lair today."

#   #   #

Amryn slid off a nightshirt she barely remembered putting on after Hobi had introduced her to the Mauryan luxury he called a steam shower. Then, after managing to eat some flatbread and cheese Hobi pilfered from somewhere in a manor seemingly empty of anyone but themselves, she slept.

She sorted through the folded clothing at the foot of the bed and held up a pair of plain black trousers far too small for her, and certainly too small for the rajin. To her surprise, the fabric stretched and reshaped itself. The trousers fit quite comfortably. The purple weebul-silk tunic was oversized, but wrapping the fringed sash made it as workable as any of the sailor's garb she'd taken to wearing.

"Where is Hobi?" she asked.

"Awaiting you in the study. Reading a news tablet when last I checked," said Ufa. "Commander Vishal has declared martial authority, and the Watch has restored order throughout most of the city. Rajin Chandra is still missing. A search is underway."

"And Quan?"

"Scheduled to arrive in approximately forty-three minutes," said Ufa.

"Tell me more about your kin," she said. "Can we count on them?"

"I have informed them of the circumstances. The Kishar Republic is defunct. Kitsune the Usurper is defeated. We are likely the last of our kind."

"How did they take the news?" said Amryn.

"Undetermined as yet. They were tasked with securing and sustaining the station," said Ufa. "That is their sole purpose for existing. Give them time to consider what that purpose means now."

"Sounds like a definite maybe."

"Perhaps you should dress and take nourishment. Hobi awaits you in the study."

"I heard you the first time, and you're changing the subject," she said. "Cognitive abilities unimpaired, remember?"

Amryn studied the suite with a Fang eye for detail. The bedchamber was not much larger than the cabins on the *Seeker*. Of course, Mauryan had started out as a ship, so private living space would be limited. Yet the rooms here were far from ordinary. The rooms were uniformly lovely, from the intricate geometric patterns carved into the polished coralesk bedposts to the colorful mosaic landscape in the steam shower, depicting the strangely shaped trees and pink seashore from some faraway world. Plush rugs and silk-draped ceilings completed the uniquely Mauryan style that started with function and mellowed into art. Utility adorned for the sake of adornment.

A drawer in the washing credenza held an assortment of combs and brushes. Amryn chose one and worked her hair before the mirror. While Ufa's pet orb hovered impatiently at her shoulder, she wondered if these were Vish's rooms. Even in a rajin's manor, keeping a guest suite seemed an indulgence, considering guests never traveled from farther than a few boroughs away. She hoped she was wrong. Vish ought to have the comfort of his own home when he was grieving.

She would set that right today, after they killed the last monster in Maurya.

# # #

"Ah, Ufa let you out," said Hobi. "That must mean you're fit for mischief."

Hobi set aside his reading and held out his arms, and Amryn claimed the embrace she had missed. An unhurried kiss erased the distance too many days of separation had put between them.

"I feared I had lost you," said Hobi, his breath warm against her cheek.

"We made a pact," she said. "Allies don't leave allies behind."

"In that regard," whirred the orb hovering over their heads. "Continued proximity would be advisable."

"What do you make of the gadget Ufa adopted?" said Hobi. "He says all the ancient Augmented had them."

"I think we'd best get used to being advised. Often. By the way, where is Khaldun? Did he return to the ship?"

"No, he did not," said Hobi. "There's a breakfast tray waiting and much I need to tell you. Come, will you sit with me?"

"You asked," she noticed.

"A new habit I'm trying out," said Hobi. "For you, at least."

"In that case, lead on."

Amryn followed him to a dining nook. It was a pleasant space beside a window, with plush bench cushions and a small table. Hobi uncovered a tray of berries and cream, almonds, and mint tea.

"The bitters?" she said.

"Not a trace," he said. "Everything is fresh from the market and bitters free."

Because, of course, a raveler would know. There was much he needed to say and much more she needed to question. She sat across from him and spooned berries into a bowl. No point in dancing around the matter.

"The presence. The magic under your skin. It's a raveler, isn't it?"

Hobi hesitated, then nodded. "You saw it healing you."

"Yes."

"And this troubles you?"

"Not in the way you mean," she said. "But I do have questions."

"Ask."

"If your raveler isn't Lahr, then it must be... Quan?"

"Tris isn't mine and is neither of them," said Hobi. "Tris is the first and only raveler of its name."

Haltingly at first, Hobi began an account of the raveler history he had learned. He told her how Chandra had found and hidden Yuji, and about the bargain between Yuji and Quan. He told her what he'd learned about Tris, how the raveler had fled from father to son, then spent years guiding and guarding him, sharing its magic. Yet unable to communicate through an imperfect bond. When Tris and Hobi returned to the raveler caves, they each had a choice to make.

Amryn listened, giving him time to tell what he felt needed telling, and came to some conclusions on her own. The gentle presence she had met the night Hobi lay poisoned, and had worried with her until he recovered, wasn't some mystical being. It was a raveler, and it had a name. Separate and distinct from Hobi, it neither controlled nor replaced him. Instead, it augmented him, as Ufa augmented her. The similarity somehow felt right.

"Can I speak with Tris?" she asked.

"You already are," said Hobi. "What I hear, Tris hears. A one-sided conversation, I admit. Tris sometimes speaks on his own, shapes sounds from our surroundings into words. But the shaping takes effort. Since repairing the bond, it's been easier for Tris to echo his words into my mind."

"Telepathy."

"As good a name for it as any."

Amryn was certain, that night on the *Seeker*, Vish had voiced words Quan had put in his mind. But Quan had been using the bitters then.

"I'm curious," she said.

"Of course, you are."

Hobi reached for her hand and held it to his chest. Then, with an uncertain sigh, he lowered his eyes and stilled. Soon, a reedy voice whispered from the shadows.

"May I have permission to speak to you in this manner, Amryn?"

"You may," she said.

"Interesting. You are able to hear me."

"Clearly. Should I not?"

"The healing. I would not have expected…"

"What's wrong?"

"Nothing. I'm sure it will pass. In time."

"What did you do?"

"Nothing. At least, nothing I intended other than preventing your death." Tris hesitated. *"Part of me remains with you after the healing. Repaired flesh. Grafted skin. Elements of my design woven into yours."*

"You left a raveler growing in me?" said Amryn. "That's—that's—"

"It's hardly an entire raveler."

"Access violation," Ufa whirred. "Initiate purge routine."

"That's rich, coming from you," said Hobi. "Shall I remind you how Amryn came to be Augmented?"

"Wait, please. I need to consider the implications. This is new to me."

"How can it come as a surprise?" said Amryn. "Have you never healed anyone before?"

"Not to such an extent. Scrapes and bruises when Hobi was a child."

"Yuji's wounds were as severe and worse," said Hobi.

"Yes, but any elements of myself left behind then died with him. I would not have known. You were my sole concern from that moment on."

"Undo it," said Hobi. "Amryn did not ask for this."

"Neither did you."

"Can you or not?" said Amryn.

"You are his mate, and I will guard you with my life," Tris hedged.

"If I choose not to be guarded? Can you leave me?"

"Possibly. Wounds will open. Scars will mar your skin."

"Most should be within my ability to repair," said Ufa. "But necessitating such repairs before considering the alternatives would be irrational."

"Whose side are you on?" said Amryn.

"Damn it, Tris." Hobi pounded the table. "Wasn't it enough to ask of her, accepting what we are? You had to wrap her into this with us."

"I don't believe either of you is suffering, frankly. Being able to speak with her will be useful."

"Obviously, the raveler was unaware its healing assistance would leave any lingering effects," said Ufa. "There was no time to consider otherwise. Neither of us could have saved Amryn on our own."

"If Yuji had such a device as your Ufa..." Tris trailed off. *"But he did not, and he died. I did not ask Hobi to host me when I needed sanctuary. I did not ask you to carry the remnants of a healing that created this connection between us. In this, I failed you both. Hobi has chosen to accept me, to allow me to remain with him. I can only give you the same choice, Amryn."*

Amryn pulled back her hand, and the raveler's voice faded.

"Amryn, I... I'm sorry," said Hobi. "I should never have brought you here."

"And yet, here we are."

Somehow, on the night she stowed away on the *Seeker*, without even realizing it, she had stopped running from the life others had planned for her. Instead, she had begun searching for a life that fit her. Hobi had been searching, too, and what they found had changed them both. Bound them to each other and to this place.

Amryn had no regrets. She slid around to the bench beside him.

"You once told me, when you finished here, you could be ordinary again. But when given the chance, you did not choose ordinary."

"No, I did not."

"Neither do I."

Hobi looked at her hopefully. She rested her chin on his shoulder.

"We will make an odd family, you and me, Ufa and Tris," she said. "But we will never be ordinary."

Hobi leaned his head to hers. "I swear, I will make you glad you stayed."

"I'll take that promise."

"Quan has entered the manor," Ufa announced. "It came alone."

"Good," said Hobi. "Tris will convey our whereabouts. We can pour another cup of tea."

"It seems to be in a hurry," said Ufa.

"Quan has news of Chandra." Hobi frowned. "Come, this may not be good."

They hurried out and met the old raveler on the stairs. His usually amiable expression was gone, replaced by grim resolve.

"Chandra has little time left," said Quan. "Lahr sent word. They have her."

"If they sent word, they want something," said Amryn. "They may not have consumed her yet."

"They have not. At least, not yet," said Quan. "Lahr is holding her hostage. They captured her as a contingency, in case you proved more resilient than expected. To barter for your cooperation. Now they are cornered and desperate. Her fate is less certain."

"Lahr knows we are coming, and we have given them cause to fear us," said Hobi. "They will not harm Chandra as long as they can use her as a shield."

"If they were rational, yes," said Quan. "But Lahr is beyond reason. They were seven, and now they are three. Adding Chandra to their numbers may prove too great a temptation."

Wind whistled up the stairs and set the chandeliers swaying. Tris spoke from the tinkling crystals.

"Let us teach Lahr what the child has become."

Chapter 37

Bargains

Amryn suppressed a wince but failed to hide her limp. Hobi frowned, and she frowned back. He'd given up trying to convince her to stay behind and settled for shadowing her every move instead.

They took the lifts down through the city. Quan remarked on the slower pace of their descent, but Amryn's headache squashed any interest in hearing how they'd gone up any quicker. No one was in a talkative mood.

Descending through the boroughs, she absently noted the hint of sulfur beneath the pervasive sandalwood. Already, Maurya seemed to have acclimated to the scent of freedom. People were venturing out of their homes and opening shuttered shops. Though their faces were solemn and a bit wary, a tenuous calm had settled over the city.

Vish stared out the glass shell of the lift, ignoring Quan's attempts at conversation. He hadn't spoken since they met him at the Assembly Hall, yet he made no effort to push his former mentor away. Perhaps he took comfort in the raveler's presence despite learning his old mentor was not what he had seemed. After all, none of them were, not even Vish.

The last lift whined to a stop in the lowest level of the city. Vish led them again through doors that parted for only a select few, and down the empty corridors Amryn had run with him only the day before. He kept to the direct route this time, avoiding the dim hallways where they had jumped from the girders and attacked an Elder. When they neared the refinery, the blood of their first kills still stained the floor, though someone had removed the bodies.

Vish stopped and met her eyes for a moment. The respect was unspoken, and the friendship genuine. When he was ready to talk, she would listen.

They passed the refinery and traveled the narrowing corridors beyond. The transition from starship to mountain was subtle, gradual. Mauryan metal and raveler stone met and intertwined, as inseparable as their lives. Amryn felt the palpable pulse of energy—refinery, sunseed, and lair. The connection between them now seemed so clear. Mauryan and raveler hearts beat in proximity to the power that fed them both. If Mauryans had not descended in their starship and settled here, ravelers might never have ventured from their caves. Thousands of years later, they were still trying to find a way to coexist.

They passed the last barnacled arch of starship hull. No doors blocked their path or hissed open at their approach. The starship passage was now a raveler-hewn tunnel of smooth stone and fading light.

"Air ducts terminate ahead," Ufa informed them. "Water pipeline extends to our destination."

She had missed his company and had not felt whole without him. As for his mission, Ufa had simply said he was done. Whether that meant the metalminds in service to Maurya could be counted as allies or had merely agreed not to interfere, Ufa had yet to determine.

Inside the tunnel, light continued to fade until Amryn could just make out Quan's white hair in the darkness ahead. The passageway descended in a series of sharp turns and switchbacks, each segment obscured from the next, intended to separate companions and slow unannounced arrivals. Hobi drew in closer, and they soon lost sight of Quan and Vish.

From somewhere, Quan began whistling. It was an oddly cheery tune. Yet, it served its purpose of keeping them together. A greenish glow began to dissipate the darkness, and after another sharp turn, Amryn stumbled into Quan. The tunnel had ended abruptly, depositing them inside the Elders' lair. They had entered the Well.

Hollowed from the mountain, the chamber was too artfully crafted to be called a cave. Like a beautiful vase of blown glass upended and softened, its walls curved and swayed to form patterns, and the jeweled ribbons of color blended like melted candlewax. The Well glowed with a natural luminescence and was large enough to have held the *Seeker* in full sail.

A lake stretched from edge to edge, freshened by water trickling from the pipes that protruded at various heights on the walls. The

Mauryan water pipeline Ufa had detected supplied the Elders' lair, though why creatures of the sea would prefer freshwater over brine was a mystery. Fish, oysters, and crabs provided an abundant food source and suggested that even Elders needed to eat.

Seven columns rose from the depths of the lake, arrayed in a circle. Pedestals for each Elder, it seemed. Atop the pedestals, cupped nests of crystal had been shaped into unique forms, perhaps for whim, perhaps for comfort.

A glint above the pedestals caught Amryn's eye. Where seamless walls curved to meet the domed ceiling, rows of narrow ledges rimmed the chamber. Shelves displayed the Elders' treasures. Her blood chilled when she realized the glint came from the emerald eye of a skull. Human skulls lined the shelves like mementos. The image of bones entombed in a sea crypt flashed from a memory she had tried to erase. But these were not bones. Lahr consumed bones and flesh. Instead, the skulls were replicas of those it had consumed, sculpted from abalone, gilded in silver and gold, and adorned with gems. The shelves filled with skulls paid gruesome homage to the bodies and souls Lahr had relished through the centuries.

Eerie green light filled the chamber, from the dome to the water's depths, and mist obscured much of the lake. Silence blanketed the lair, but for the faint trickle of water from the pipes. The lair seemed detached from reality, a cocoon of time and space trapped in eternal meditation. Yet, beneath the serenity churned a maelstrom of emotion, raw and barely restrained. Jealousy and rage chittered on a wire strung taut over a chasm of sorrow. The shrill whine of resentment slithered through a charred forest of hate. Raveled souls, condensed and leeched, until at last, awareness faded and found release. The lingering energy was the worst in them and was the retribution they left behind.

Snickering whispers swept from the shadows like beetles scurrying from the light. The green mist thinned and revealed three Elders standing atop their pedestals. All were elderly in appearance, but far from frail. Not empty shells, as Amryn expected. Empty would have been merciful. The three hollowed Mauryans were fading echoes of the women they had been. Their bodies and then their spirits were consumed and drained by Lahr. They moved in a strange synchrony of tics. Each husk licked its lips, and curled and uncurled its hands in tandem with the others.

"After assaulting us, Quan seeks us out?" The Elders spoke in chorus.

"We seek a reckoning," said Quan.

The last shreds of green mist vanished. Beneath an empty pedestal, Chandra hung in chains. The rajin still had red-blooded color in her face, though four ravelers circled the water at her feet. Four to replace the fallen Lahr had lost. Chandra spat in the water. She would not submit.

"Mother, are you harmed?" Vish called out.

"I am chained to a post in the Well. What do you think?" she said. "One of these aberrations still wears your grandmother's face."

"Let the rajin go, Lahr," said Quan. "We will settle this between ourselves."

"We will. Oh yes, we will." Lahr laughed with each mouth in turn. "Make us a bargain. Quan made a bargain with a clever outlander. Lahr thought you a fool because you bargained and lost. Yet, we may have discovered why."

"What do you want?" said Quan.

"Whatever it wants, refuse," said Chandra.

"The child. The beautiful child." Lahr's bodies swayed in a macabre dance. "The child you bargained away. Bargain it to us instead, and we will give Maurya its rajin. And we will declare every quota they promised us met in full."

"Or I can kill you and achieve the same end," said Quan.

"You can certainly try," chanted the Lahrs. "But can you kill us all? Before we raise the seed as our shield?"

The cryptic threat seemed to unsettle Quan, and the rival ravelers took their battle of wills to a plane of awareness only they shared. The chittering shadows grew louder and multiplied. Oily shapes seeped from the ribboned colors in the walls like demons climbing up from the abyss.

"Lahr is threatening to explode the sunseed," Hobi relayed what Tris could decipher from their argument. "Fragments of a key... stolen from many minds... over many years. Lahr pieced together the fragments."

"That must be about the destruction sequence," said Vish. "The code to destroy Maurya, the ship—the entire island chain. It has always been a last resort. One final defiance if Kitsune came for us. No one house holds the complete key. Each would have to provide the portion of the sequence entrusted to them. The fragments pass from generation to generation."

"Seven governing houses," said Amryn. "Each answering the Elders' call in turn. How many generations of scouring minds until Lahr collected the fragments from every house?"

"So, it's no bluff," said Hobi. "Call Quan back, Tris."

Though the old nene's form stood only a stone's toss away, Quan's awareness was fully engaged with Lahr. Anger flushed his face as they argued. Sparks crackled in the air between them. Then, abruptly, Quan threw up his hands and walked back to them.

"Damned coward," said Quan. "Lahr says it will end itself if it doesn't get its way. And it has no qualms about taking us with it."

Lahr wanted Tris and would not be dissuaded. Before Amryn could argue that Tris was not theirs to give, Hobi pressed a hurried sign to her palm. *Gambit.*

"Come now, don't be greedy," the Lahrs cajoled. "You made one. You can make another."

"The child is not mine to give," said Quan. "They are their own."

"We accept." Tris spoke in a voice summoned from the mountain, and his declaration echoed throughout the Well. It was a voice both young and ancient, born of wind and tides, with the timbre of the sea and the resonance of time. The power it carried swept her with a rush of resolve, knowing she was connected to this magnificent creature.

When Tris spoke, the Lahrs went still.

"Do not do this," said Quan. "Lahr may infect you with its madness."

Ufa hovered close to her ear. "Message relayed."

Amryn gave Hobi the nod. Hobi walked to the edge of the lake.

"Release the rajin," he said.

Chandra's chains cracked like brittle twigs. She fell into the lake, and the circling ravelers swarmed her. The Elders swept their hands in tandem. The ravelers convulsed as if stung and returned to circle the empty pedestal. Chandra swam for the shore.

Vish waded into the lake to meet her and guarded her back until she reached the shore. Chandra stalked up to Hobi, dripping and swearing.

"Are you a fool?" she said. "Lahr is a monster. I would see Maurya destroyed before I would let him loose on the world."

"That is no longer your decision to make," said Hobi.

"You came to free Maurya from a prison of fear. Instead, you join our captors."

"You have made your opinion clear."

"Duty sent you. Duty to your people and to Maurya," said Chandra. "Do not abandon it now."

"I did not come to destroy."

"Leave him! Be gone!" shrilled the Lahrs. Watery whips rose from the lake and knocked Chandra off her feet. Vish rushed in and dragged her from their reach.

"Go, Quan. Get them out of here," said Hobi.

"No. I should have finished this long ago."

"You lose again, Quan," the Lahrs cackled. "Do as the child commands, or we may change our minds. The rajin and her offspring have such tempting flesh. And this one, the Augmented. We find her... intriguing."

"She is our mate," Tris' voice rumbled. "Lahr will not touch what is ours."

The Elders swayed in unison, licking their pale lips.

"Of course, precious one. Of course," they cooed. "We shall respect your wishes."

Amryn didn't believe them for a second. She turned her back and spoke hurriedly to Quan.

"Go. Let nothing out of this lair. Nothing. Destroy us with it if you must."

"You are fools. You cannot fight them alone."

"Then, when we fail, you will have the consolation of being right."

Quan shook his head and turned to leave. He had no better options.

"Children," he muttered. "Why was it I wanted children?"

# # #

Hobi stood on the shore with his hands clasped behind him. Amryn hung back, playing the role of the dutiful mate. They waited.

The lair had gone silent again, but for the gurgle of water pipes. The creatures on the pedestals surveyed their prize.

"Come to us, child," said the Lahrs. "Beautiful child. Come to Lahr."

"In due time," said Hobi. "First, we will hear your intentions."

"Intentions, he says," the nearest Lahr snickered. "Let us slip under your skin and learn how you are made. Then we will decide our intentions."

The utter madness in the creature's eyes chilled her. They had to rid the world of this abomination. One last gambit, and the conquest was won. She readied a shield and waited. Hobi's fingers shaped the signal.

Attack.

In the silence that followed, the gurgling pipes shifted their tone. Ever so slightly. Quietly declaring the battle had begun. Amryn took a step back.

Throughout the Well, water pipes rattled and belched. Geysers of black oil erupted from the walls and rained down over the lake. Ufa's army of Maurya's metalminds had answered the call. The black oil spread over the water like wine spilled from a hundred goblets.

Hobi raised his arms, and flames leapt from his fingers. Fiery arcs reached over the lake. Oily puddles ignited, and fire rippled across the lake. Hungry tongues licked at the Elders' pedestals, and bestial screams rose from the inferno.

One Elder leapt from its nest, risking the flames for safety beneath the water. Tris was quicker, and his sorcery was no longer caged by flesh. A white-hot bolt shot down from above and skewered the fleeing Elder in midair. Lightning seared its body, and its charred corpse fell into the burning oil.

Hobi swung his aim, a second too late, as a second Elder dove through the fire and vanished beneath the water. Amryn ran to the lake's edge, searching for movement beneath the chaos of oil and fire. The creature was already out of reach. If even one survived, Lahr would endure. She paced in frustration as the Elder in the lake shifted form. The other ravelers swarmed in to guard its retreat. She waded in after them. She could make the swim if the shield held.

Abruptly, the mountain trembled beneath her feet.

"Sealed," said Tris, his ethereal voice booming over the lake.

"We are betrayed!" the last Elder screamed. The creature sank down into its nest.

Amryn waded in deeper. She could make it to the nest.

"Cover me, Ufa."

"No time. It is contacting the sunseed," said Ufa.

Desperate to convey what his words could not, Ufa slipped back to old habits. A mirage appeared high above the Well. The flickering image played out a battle in a realm where only metalminds existed. In Ufa's mirage, a glowing orb pulsed on its throne like a queen. The sunseed.

The enemy crested a hill with banners flying, as Ufa depicted the unfolding battle with symbols of human war. Lahr and his ravelers gathered. Each banner they carried was emblazoned with a stolen rune of destruction. The banners formed up the vanguard and charged the wall of fire.

Arrows rained down from the parapets. Flames leapt higher. One banner caught fire, then another. The charge faltered. Metalmind warriors held the wall.

Abruptly, Ufa dismissed the image, and a nightmarish screech curdled the air. Wailing atop its pedestal, the last Elder contorted. Grotesque in its frantic shift, it shed its human shell. Tentacles sprouted from its limbs. Wings spread from its shoulders. The raveler leapt from its nest and flew, iridescent and terrible, gliding above the inferno. The abomination shrieked in fury and swooped down on Hobi. Amryn ran to cover him.

In the next second, the raveler stopped. Frozen in midair. Suspended above Hobi's head, it hung writhing in the grasp of an unseen hand. The hand of a sorcerer's son. The unbreakable will of one who was both N'si and raveler.

The mountain shuddered in unspent rage. Power channeled with singular intent. And they discovered the true potential of the beings they had become.

"Die, demon!"

With a defiant cry, they claimed this place for the Sorcerers of Maurya. And for all their kind to come. The spectral hand closed, and another Lahr ceased to be.

Only those trapped beneath the water remained.

"Back away! Let us finish this," said Ufa.

A spidery bolt burst from the walls and speared the water. Hundreds more bolts erupted from the rock itself. Fingers of star seed energy crisscrossed the lake and streaked into the depths. The Well soon glowed with a stark white light, silhouetting tentacles and wings writhing in the throes of death. Amryn shielded her eyes from the blinding light.

When the Well went silent, she looked out over the desolation. The lair was dark and dead, but for the scattered, flickering pools of oil still burning. She smelled the change in the mountain. Tasted the shift in its spirit at the passing of an ancient storm.

Lahr was no more.

"Threat eliminated," Ufa reported. "Water is an effective conduit."

Threat eliminated? Amryn and Hobi exchanged looks of amazement. He caught her in his arms and spun around, laughing. The gambit was over.

"How is my favorite conqueror?" he said.

"No worse for wear. And you?"

"Barely singed."

"Hold off on the celebration," said Tris. *"Look."*

A blood-red stain was rising from the lake's depths, billowing like smoke in the water. Scarlet wisps began creeping from the ribboned walls, and their ghostly tendrils curled over the smoldering lake, searching for the master to focus their hate. Rustling swept the shadows, no longer snickers but cries. Their sobs turned to heartrending wails, rising in a crescendo of despair.

Hobi held on to her as their swirling maelstrom of emotions enveloped the Well. Rage so raw it raked her bones. The anguish of the lost tore at her soul. The ghosts of those Lahr no longer held bound sought them out. Their scarlet tendrils circled around, weaving a ring around the only awareness that remained in the Well. Waiting to be claimed. Waiting to serve.

The power the unchained spirits offered was potent. It had served Lahr well. Yet it reeked of hate and jealousy and all the worst of humankind.

Power for the claiming.

Amryn felt the bile burning her throat and somehow knew it came from Tris' disgust as much as hers. This kind of power was not for them.

"We free you. Your duty is met," she told them.

"Go from this place," said Hobi. "Seek the mists. Claim the rest long denied you."

"Go in peace, Mauryans." Tris bid them, his voice gentle as a breeze. "The monsters are dead, and your families are safe in our care."

The ghosts closed in around them. Hobi held her closer as they circled. She sensed their confusion. Their weariness. Then one scarlet wisp parted from the others and sought her.

"Be still," said Tris.

The ghostly tendril curled up Amryn's leg, then slithered to Hobi's arm. It coiled around his neck. Amryn reached to brush it away.

"No, wait," said Tris. *"Give it time."*

Its scarlet tendril curled over his drakmu, as if reading his destiny in the patterns on his skin. Then, with a whispered sigh, it faded away.

One after another, the unchained spirits of Mauryans sacrificed throughout the centuries came to taste the truth of their intent. Amryn steadied her nerves as each ghost, in turn, judged her and departed.

Until there were none.

"Our promise is kept," said Tris.

Chapter 38

Alternative

Sweat rolled down his back as the last of the spirits departed. Hobi wasn't convinced, despite what the Chalyns claimed, of a world of mist parallel to this world of substance. But wherever Maurya's ghosts had gone, he hoped their torment was over.

Hobi realized he was still clenching his fists. He'd been holding onto Amryn so tightly his fingers had cramped. When he pulled back, she looked up at him with those beautiful brown eyes he had come to cherish.

Was he capable of love? So it seemed.

"We liberated Maurya," she said. "Hobi, we did it."

"You sound surprised."

"You aren't?"

"Not in the least," he said. "But we aren't done until those damned walls come down."

"We can offer them a bargain, I hope. Some incentive to give the metalminds a nudge."

"An opportunity to supervise the reclamation of Watcher technology from the other dens should prove a compelling incentive," said Ufa.

"Why do I suspect the negotiations already started?" Hobi smirked.

"Getting Maurya ready to be reintroduced to the world is the bigger challenge," said Amryn.

"I never underestimate your powers of persuasion," said Hobi.

"Quan is doubling back," said Tris. *"Heard the noise. Sensed the void."*

"Rajin Chandra and Commander Vishal are returning as well," said Ufa. "However, they are unable to keep pace with the raveler."

"We'll wait for them," said Amryn. "We have tasks to ask of them all."

# # #

Standing on the deck of the *Seeker*, Hobi watched an amber dawn melt away another night. The sun shone warmer, and the breeze blew cleaner, untainted by the stench of Lahr. Maurya was the homeland he had set out to find, and he had seen it freed and secured. It was time to bring his people home.

Goblin purred around his ankles, and he bent to pick up the cat before she resorted to clawing her way up his leg.

"What's that? You couldn't wake Amryn to feed you?" he said. "Yes, you're absolutely right. I'm to blame."

Their first night back on the ship had left them little time for sleeping. Understandable, of course. After too many nights apart and a more than few brushes with death along the way, they'd shared an exuberant reunion. He had especially enjoyed showing her how—

Soft footsteps cut short his musings, and he shifted the cat to his shoulder.

"Ah, Amryn. You're up early."

"You left off the best part."

"What's that?"

"When I climb out of bed earlier than any reasonable person would and seek you out after a night of passion, the recommended greeting ends in '*my love*.'" She leaned in and whispered. "You could add it at any time."

Before he met Amryn, his relationships had the endurance of dry kindling tossed on a fire. But this, he wanted to last. She had accepted him for what he was, but what would she do once the walls no longer held her here? He only knew wanted her to stay.

"Amryn, my love." He wrapped his arms around her. "Keep holding me to account. I'll pick up as many new habits as you wish."

"Only this one," she said. "Well, except for the asking instead of commanding. Let's keep that one, too."

"That's it? No more rough edges in need of polishing?"

"That's it."

"Sounds too easy."

"Get used to the idea," she said. "We suit each other well."

She rested her head on his shoulder. They watched the sun rise over the lagoon as bantee lowed in the grasses. Yes, they did suit. Quite accidentally and with no great cleverness on his part, he'd happened his way into an actual relationship. He'd met his match. Incredible.

"Since we're up and about, we should make plans," he said. "We have a few Mauryans to persuade before the next phase of our conquest."

"That's why I came looking for you," she said, stifling a yawn. "Already working on that. Sent a message. Received a response."

"The Assembly invites you to address them this afternoon." Ufa sailed up and bobbed above her head.

"Come back to the cabin, my love." Amryn took his hand. "We have a speech to craft."

# # #

Hobi and Amryn entered the Assembly Hall as they had on the first day, escorted by Vish. But this time, Quan walked in with them, having exchanged his plain white robe for sapphire blue satin draped in beaded silk, no doubt his companion Liya's handiwork and far more befitting an ancient sea god.

Watch guards, councilors, and senior leaders of every house crowded the chamber. Even the Silhad seats were filled, though the Silhad faces were younger and humbler than before Gagan's failed rebellion. As Hobi and Amryn passed by, Mauryans rose and offered nods of respect. Word had spread of their battle with Lahr, the bitters, and the antidote. The wariness they had encountered on their first visit to the chamber was gone. And in its place, a tentative acceptance.

But what was most noticeably missing, not only in the hall but throughout the city, was the oppressive paranoia that had suffocated the place. Maurya could breathe again.

Vish stepped aside when he reached the speaker's well. He rested his hand on Amryn's shoulder, making it clear to everyone watching, she had his support. When Amryn stepped into the well, Hobi paused and met Vish's steady gaze. They had not forged the same trust with one another as they each had with Amryn. But knowing she found them both worthy of hers was enough.

Hobi took his place beside her in the speaker's well, wearing the same N'si vanlors as the day they had masqueraded as emissaries of a Republic that no longer existed. But their masquerade was over. The vanlor was no longer a pretense, but an acknowledgment of his heritage—a heritage N'si and Maurya shared. He was Mauryan now, accepted as one of them. And he was determined to show them what they could become.

Chandra watched from her chair. The aura of power she had emanated before was dimmer, as if she were incomplete without Janak standing behind her. Tired lines etched her face as she stood, and the tinkling rings on the rajin's robe drew a grimace of irritation from her. She was tired of the pretense, too.

"The matter before us today is the raveler treaty," she said without preamble. "The prior treaty is forfeit. Before deciding whether to negotiate another, or with whom, I asked the Assembly to honor your request for this hearing. You bring a unique perspective to recent events and to the nature of our coexistence with ravelers."

"We are grateful for the opportunity to share what we know," said Amryn.

"As our own expert in the subject of raveler treaties, the Minister of History will lead the questioning," said Chandra. She sat and waved the old scholar forward. "Rekha, please."

Recusing herself was an unexpected move, but Hobi admired her cunning. If Chandra had any hope of keeping her secret from spilling during this bloodletting of truth, she would need to distance herself. He would do what he could.

The historian's apprentices set a stool in front of the rajin's chair, and Rekha perched atop it like a hardy old owl. She eyed them with open curiosity.

"Ambassador Nisari," she acknowledged Amryn. "Are you here as an emissary?"

"Yes, though not of the Republic."

"As I thought. Then we will continue to address you as such." Rekha shifted her attention. "Prince Hobizadi... what was it... Ravadaron? "

They both knew she would find no such house recorded in the archives, no matter how long her apprentices searched.

"I am Hobi," he said. "N'si by birth and Mauryan by blood. Sired by Yuji Tatsuo, last of his house. Orphaned and claimed by Gar. I refuse to bear the name of my father's murderer."

Rekha raised her brow. "Understandable. But if you are Mauryan, you recognize the significance of our names. Without such, every house could vie to adopt you into their own."

Amryn had anticipated being asked to declare their affiliation to one of the Mauryan houses. Most in attendance would assume they had joined House Ajagara. But they had agreed it would be shortsighted to shift the balance of power so drastically and permanently to only one of the seven houses.

"A wise observation," said Hobi. "Then let me make my allegiance clear. From this day on, I am Hobi Nisari."

House Nisari would become the eighth house of Maurya. And it would be the first, perhaps the only, house of the Sorcerers of Maurya. Rekha was shrewd enough to jump at the concession.

"Delegate Nisari, then," she said, summarily granting House Nisari speaking rights within the Assembly. It may be only a temporary accommodation, but he had expected it would come harder than it had. "Let us begin with the fundamental question. What are you?"

Rekha was blunt. Good. They would not waste time.

"The answer is one we are still discovering for ourselves," said Amryn. "But such a fundamental question must seek the fundamental source of truth. Only one among us can bear witness to the events that brought us before you today. House Nisari recognizes Quan, the first raveler, as the historian of record."

The few murmurs of surprise soon dissipated. Rumors had accomplished the intended dulling of the slap of reality. Enough of them had witnessed the old window washer transform into a beast and fling ice spears at Gagan the Elder to know he wasn't human. Frankly, they seemed relieved he was on their side.

Quan took to the speaker's well, seeming amused by the human compunction for protocol, even when staring into the face of the inconceivable.

"As it happens, I have indeed seen it all." Quan kept to the singular reference of himself, and his amiable tone invited a sense of familiarity. But, of course, Quan had been studying human nature since the first human stepped foot on this world. "Where shall I begin?"

Rekha's eyes lit with the eagerness of a hawk spying a hare. What a treasure trove for someone who relished history as she did.

"With your earliest recollection."

"We do only have the afternoon," said Quan.

"Do you agree to subsequent interviews on any omitted specifics?"

"Within reason."

"Then summarize," said Rekha.

Quan needed no prompting. He enjoyed telling the story again. And he shared the story of his kind eagerly. Just as he first had for Yuji, and then repeated for Hobi. Thus, the history of ravelers and humans was recorded for the archives, both joys and regrets, and the wish to coexist. The only omission of any significance was Chandra and Janak, and their role in protecting the outlander fate had washed up on their island.

"So, you walked among us as Quan," said Rekha. "Yet you told no one of Lahr and the bitters."

"Even living a few eons doesn't wear all the foolish out of a fool. I couldn't admit my failure with Lahr," said Quan. "I hoped to redeem the only other being of my kind. But there was no changing its nature."

"What are your intentions now?" said Rekha.

"Above all else, to protect my child."

"The raveler or its host?"

"Yes," Quan said simply.

For the first time, a frown deepened the lines on Rekha's face. Quan offered no clarification. Amryn stepped up to intervene.

"The topic is one on which Hobi and I can offer more expertise," she said. "If I may begin with an analogy, consider the Augmented. You are familiar with the bonding and attunement methods described in the archives, correct?"

"More so since your arrival," said Rekha. "I've read every reference I could find. Based on our observation, the devices are as uncommon in the outlander community as in ours. With no technicians trained to administer the activation, I wondered how yours was possible."

"Ufa can provide the details," said Amryn. "Plenty of details. And then he will offer details on top of details until you are tempted to toss him in a jar just to stop the details."

Laughter rippled through the hall. Amryn was exceptionally talented at winning a crowd.

"Ufa? The device has a name?" said Rekha.

"Ufa is his own person. His compassion and loyalty surpass many humans I know. And, thankfully, he has a sense of humor."

"You do not control its actions?"

"No more than you control guards who protect you or apprentices who assist in your research," said Amryn. "And Ufa has established a comradery with those of his kind here in Maurya."

"We have no augmentation devices," said Rekha.

"Madam, I am not a *device*." Ufa had withheld comment after the earlier slights, but he sounded ready to fling sparks. "Neither are the intelligences who have secured and sustained Maurya since long before you drew your first breath. They *chose* to intercept Lahr's destruction sequence. Acted in conscious defiance of its authority. I suggest you owe them a bit of respect for their long-suffering patience with *your* kind."

Every light flickered, and the air vents whistled in what Hobi was certain was metalmind laughter.

"To your original question, Minister," said Amryn. "Ufa is a symbiont, and I am his host. He takes sustenance through me, and I gain abilities I would otherwise lack." She waved her arm, and a flurry of dancing, jewel-colored sparks followed her hand. No weapon in Maurya could have penetrated the shield Ufa raised around her.

"But you are Augmented by choice," said Rekha.

"No, I am Augmented by a stroke of fate I couldn't dodge. Given what I know now, I wouldn't refuse the boon. But at the time, I might have. Had we arrived bearing a trunk full of Ufas, would you have chosen to host one?"

"Without hesitation," said Rekha.

"Then you have your answer," said Hobi. "Tris and I are no different, if you add flesh and bone back into the mix."

"And a few thousand years of mistrust," said Rekha. "Well and good for you, but we are justifiably leery after our last treaty with ravelers."

"Isn't that the key, though?" someone interrupted from the spellbound audience. "They made the last treaty without Sorcerers of Maurya at our end of the bargaining table."

Hobi suppressed a smile. The Sorcerers of Maurya. It was a name they'd given themselves during the heady bravado of victory. Yet, through the retellings and rumors, it had taken hold. He didn't mind. He could think of none that suited them better.

"Surely we can agree they add to our strength." Vish lent the support of House Ajagara his mother dared not voice. "Our ancestors came here as biologists and engineers. This station was tasked with nurturing the seeds our Republic had planted. What grander result of our labors than the evolution of a new lifeform?"

"A splendid new lifeform." A young Silhad sprang to her feet. "They stand before us now, culminating the Republic's dreams. Evolving ourselves into something greater. Reaching our potential. This was our purpose, our reason for being here, and we are witness to its birth."

Hobi sent the earnest young Silhad an appreciative nod. If she represented the future of her house, Silhad might yet survive Gagan's disgrace.

"One mutation does not constitute a new species," said Rekha.

"Species as a concept assumes procreation," said Amryn. "Ravelers replicate. If Maurya is to have more Sorcerers of Maurya, we will need more Mauryans as hosts."

The eagerness taking hold a moment before evaporated. Rekha shifted on the stool. Hosting a raveler didn't have quite the same appeal as being Augmented.

"Perhaps in time," she said. "You must understand, for generations, we have watched our loved ones turned into Elders. Hollowed out by the ravelers they *hosted*."

"Lahr was not a symbiont."

"Yet, our revulsion runs deep," said Rekha. "Until that begins to wane, we will study you. Because that is what scientists do. We will learn from the one mutant we are lucky didn't kill us all. If it had been more like Lahr than Quan, we might not be having this conversation."

"Respectfully, you are missing the point. The difference with Hobi and Tris, compared to the horror that was Lahr and the Elders, is the codependence of symbiont and host. The raveler detaches from the consciousness of the whole and exists as a unique being, attuned instead to the consciousness of its host. That attunement to its host forges a loyalty as irrevocable as in the Augmented."

"Then why not argue the Augmented were also a distinct lifeform?" said Rekha.

"Because Ufa would not be Ufa if he had been activated back then. At some point over the centuries he spent waiting for purpose, he gained self-awareness he would not otherwise have sought. Otherwise, he could not have sustained himself. And he could not have initiated the activation process."

"An interesting theory," said Rekha. "It merits study, as do any intelligences within our network that Ufa has identified as sentient. Those you call metalminds."

"Study and nurture? Is that all we make of such extraordinary opportunities?" Vish objected as he strode up to Rekha on her stool. By the startled gasps that followed, he must have just trampled several of their precious protocols. "When will we wake and dare to live again? Venture out to taste the freedom we have won?"

Hobi read the room. They simply were not ready. Not yet. Perhaps not for many years to come. He had expected as much, even counted on it.

"There is an alternative," he said. "Maurya can honor its heritage. Your ancestors were accomplished biologists and engineers. The weebul, bantee, and tarchu are testament to their skill. Their purpose, and your heritage, is nurturing seeds and evolving potential. You can continue this tradition, nurture and evolve sorcerers, without becoming hosts."

"You already ruled out procreation," said Rekha. "If hosts are required—"

"Maurya can acquire hosts from the N'si. Blood of your blood. Exiled by circumstance. Let us come home."

"N'si are our kin," said Vish. "Hobi and Amryn have proven they are more like us than not. And they will add their considerable strength to ours. N'si survived the very dangers we shut ourselves off from."

"N'si or Mauryan, you are unique among humans. You carry elements of the same design," said Quan. "Like tapestries woven on the same loom, your patterns and colors differ, but a common thread runs throughout each of you. It is to this thread the bitters attuned. No others we have encountered have it, and it is necessary for the bonding."

"Then let us combine our lineage once again," said Vish. "We hold the keys to unlock technology the rest of the world seeks. With our knowledge and expertise, the skill of our metalminds, and the fighting prowess of our sorcerers, no one will dare challenge Maurya. We can bring down the walls, welcome the N'si home, and rejoin the world, confident of our place in it."

# # #

Hobi paced outside the hall. Chandra had called for a vote.

"Perhaps you should have spoken," he told Tris. "I should have made it clearer when I was relaying your words instead of my own. The Assembly barely got a sense of who you are."

"Stop fretting," said Tris. *"We showed them our truth. We interact with others as suits our natures. If any other sorcerers had been in that hall, they would have heard me clearly."*

"As I did," said Quan.

"And I," said Amryn. "You were right not to portray us otherwise. They need to understand what we are, if we're going to make more of us."

"Which begs the procreation question," said Hobi. "If you and I were to have children, in the usual way, what would they be?"

"Extraordinary," said Tris.

Vish stuck his head out the door and waved them back into the hall. When they entered, the entire Assembly was standing. Chandra smiled.

"Bring them home," she said.

Chapter 39

The Call

Amryn read their words one last time before sending the message that would forever change the world she had known. Hobi looked over her shoulder as she tapped her fingers on Chandra's desk, fixated on the com tablet. Ufa readied the metalminds to send the first message to leave Maurya in thousands of years.

> *We, the people of the sovereign nation of Maurya, hereby declare our independence from all authority hitherto claimed by the Kishar Republic. We seek to establish diplomatic relations with our fellow Earth nations in the furtherance of trade, the sharing of expertise, and the advancement of science and technology.*
>
> *We have activated transceivers in other stations formerly in service to the Republic. Those receiving this message may respond to arrange a meeting with our emissaries at the coordinates to be provided.*
>
> *Sincerely,*
> *Ambassador Amryn Nisari*

Hobi was tempted to reach past her and press the blinking tile that would reintroduce Maurya to the world. But the words carried her name beneath them, so he refrained, though only barely. Eventually, she reached out and sent the message on its way.

"Message delivered," Ufa reported a second later. "Scheduled to broadcast in the facilities now known as the Watchers' Dens at hourly intervals until instructed otherwise."

Amryn blew out a sigh and sat back in the chair. "Now, we wait."

"How soon could the first emissaries arrive?" said Vish.

"Chalyns, within days," said Amryn. "For my father, it could take weeks under sail, even on Nefi's fastest ship. Others will follow on the dates we set. We don't want everyone arriving at once."

"And we insist each sends a single ship, agreed?"

"Yes, Vish. Relax. Hordes of outlanders won't overrun us."

Chandra stirred from her solitary stance at the window. She gathered her discarded rajin's robe off the jhula and tossed it to Vish.

"It's yours," she told him. "When you have it altered, pay the tailor extra to cut off those damned rings. I'm going to pack."

"Pack what?" Vish frowned.

"My bags," said Chandra. "The walls are coming down. You have no idea how long I have waited to say those words."

"Mother, you can't simply leave."

"Of course, I can. That's why I have you."

Chandra walked over to Hobi.

"I loved your father," she said. Sentiment misted her eyes, and she brushed Hobi's cheek. "Janak and I both loved Yuji, in our own way. We wanted to leave these islands with the outlander we had befriended. But we stayed for a duty we were born to bear, and we raised Yuji's son together."

Hobi shot a glance over her shoulder. Vish stared back at him. Something about his look...

"How could I have missed it?" said Tris. *"Yuji's scent..."*

"I didn't know," said Hobi. "I swear. I didn't know."

"Of course not. How could you? Yuji left before I knew I was carrying his child. If he had known..." Chandra paused. "He might have stayed. We might have died for our recklessness." She shook her head. "What's done is done. There was no reason to tell anyone until now."

"I can think of several reasons. Shall I list them for you?" said Vish.

"Why now?" said Hobi.

"Because within a span of days, I have mourned my first love and grieved my dearest friend. With Yuji and Janak both gone, I'm left to carry on as I think they would have wanted. That starts with telling you the truth. Then leaving Maurya in your capable hands. And going to explore the world Janak longed to see."

Hobi was still preoccupied with studying Vish when Chandra leaned in to take a parting kiss. It was a sentimental indulgence, perhaps, but unnerving given the circumstances. Chandra smiled to see she'd rattled him.

"You are so like Yuji," she said. "Bringing Maurya back into the world was his dream. Now both his sons can make it so. Build his legacy."

Chandra turned and left them staring at one another. The same thought jerked their attention to the swaying jhula. Quan opened his eyes and sat cross-legged on the swing. Hobi would have sworn the old raveler had fallen asleep. He'd heard every word.

"You knew," said Tris. *"You wily old fish."*

"You knew," said Vish. "Damn it, Quan. You should have told me."

"I was about to. Eventually." Quan yawned. "Chandra and I struck a bargain. I would keep her secret, and she would listen to my guidance regarding your upbringing. And you see? You turned out fine."

Vish stood dumbfounded. Hobi could understand him being a bit unsettled. He'd had enough of those moments himself lately. But, seriously, it wasn't as if he'd just learned he had a raveler living under his skin.

"Well, this is awkward," said Amryn. "Would it help if I mentioned I like you both?"

"No," they said in near unison.

"How can you be half N'si?" said Hobi. "Your stripes are barely—"

"Mind your tone," said Vish. "You realize this makes me your elder brother."

"Elder? Horrid choice of words. Your future as raj clearly hinges on me handling any aspects of the job requiring charisma."

"Raj? You came to conquer. And you expect me to govern?"

"Well, you helped with the conquering." Hobi shrugged. "So, I am giving the job back to you. Governing is tedious."

"No, thank you." Vish shoved the rajin's robes at him. "I don't want it. I have other plans."

"Exploring the world with your mother?"

"Quan offered me the next symbiont."

"Oh."

Well, that certainly shifted the balance. Hobi needed to set out the game board and play through a few moves.

"No, you need to trust your brother," said Tris. *"And I can't believe I'm saying this, but you need to trust Quan. He vetted Vish long ago. There's no taint in him."*

Of course, there wasn't. If there had been, Amryn would have found it. Like it or not, Hobi had a new player to factor into the plans. Such as they were. His plans had culminated with liberating Maurya and getting them to offer the N'si sanctuary. What was left to do but bring them here?

Hobi handed the rajin's robes to Amryn. "Here you go, Ari princess. You'll make a fine rajin."

"Oh, no." Amryn backed away. "Scientists do not—"

"Alert. Attention," Ufa shrilled an alarm. "Our message elicited a response."

Chapter 40

The Walls

Amryn should have learned by now never to underestimate the Gyakari. After receiving her message, her father called in all favors owed, and a Chalyn stormrider appeared in Naré. Lifted by the winds of his mindgift, an Ari ship was soon skimming the waves of the Endless Ocean, guided by the summoner's wind. They would reach the coordinates by midafternoon.

She wondered whether the stormrider manipulated the wind in the same manner as Hobi and Tris. There was science behind any magic, of course, but did the mindgifted draw energy from their surroundings, or did they assert their will on its substance? It would make a fascinating study. Apparently, she had several lifetimes ahead to figure it out.

"We'll navigate our way out this cage, barely," Hobi said as he climbed to the helm.

He was back from his swim. He'd gone to check the channel the ravelers were chewing through the mountainside to give the *Seeker* passage out of the lagoon. Quan said it would take a few weeks to widen and deepen the canal enough for the ring island to serve as a harbor for trade ships, but the *Seeker* should be able to squeak through, with Hobi conjuring a current to lift them.

"I hope the swim calmed your nerves," she said.

"Why would I be nervous?" said Hobi. "It's only the Emperor of Ari and the King of Rhynn. I'm sure plenty of captains have invited them to the Endless Ocean to negotiate with sorcerers. Happens all the time."

"Though seldom with my mother along."

"Not helpful, my love."

Amryn decided not to mention the rest. Not only were the Gyakari, Resa, and Nefi on their way, but several of the most powerful Chalyns were accompanying them. One of those Chalyns was their chief, King Sethlyan of Rhynn. But having so many of the others come for this first meeting, she had not anticipated. It seemed the Chalyns recognized the significance Maurya held. Making allies of the world's last gatekeepers of Watcher technology could unlock mysteries they would need generations to decipher without guidance.

In time, they would discover there was more to Maurya than science. The islands were an ancient wellspring of magic and home to the oldest sentient being on earth. And soon, Maurya would be a breeding ground for sorcerers whose elemental power would exceed that of the Chalyns' mindgifts.

Amryn had tactfully left that part out of her messages.

Cora whistled up to them. "She's free as a bird, Captain. Anchor's stowed, and she's eager to get out of this pond."

"Hoist the sails," Hobi said with a broad smile. "Let's catch a raveler wind."

"Coming around," said Tris. *"Brace yourselves."*

A feisty wind whipped up, and the *Seeker* surged ahead like a restless colt given free rein. The crew whooped and cheered as the ship got underway again. They'd been harbored here for too long. They were ready to feel the roll of the tides and taste the salt spray on their faces.

"Take us leeward, Tris."

"Calibrated. Ten seconds until we reach the cliffs."

Hobi gripped the wheel to the creak of wood and groan of the sailcloth. Sweat glistened on his skin. He drew a deep breath and closed his eyes, summoning the water to do his will. Amryn caught her balance as waves swelled beneath the ship, lifting it as it hurtled towards an impossibly narrow crevasse in the mountain ring.

"A swim might calm your nerves," Tris teased.

"All right, I deserved that one." Amryn clung to the rail. "Now, will you pay attention to what you're doing?"

"Five seconds," said Tris.

"Amryn, take the wheel. Hold her steady," said Hobi.

She grabbed the spindles, and he leapt to the deck below. All around the hull, the current rose to his command. They were almost on it now. The ragged gash in the cliffs gaped before them.

"We'll need another fathom to clear the rocks," said Tris.

"I'm trying." Hobi grimaced. "Quan, you might help, you know."

A sudden rush of surf smacked the stern with a petulant swat, and a curtain of water washed over the decks. Quan could be a jackass at times. But his pique at not being invited to the meeting was enough to save the hull from splintering against the rocks. Timbers squeaked in protest as the *Seeker* scraped through the channel.

"Bring her around," said Hobi. "Set sail for the walls."

Amryn wrestled the wheel around, and Rafael ran to trim a foresail. Sails snapped, and the ship surged for the sea as though waiting for this moment. Chattering gulls circled in a clear blue sky, and Amryn breathed in the salty tang she had missed. As the ship headed out past the breakwater and away from shore, she threw a glance over her shoulder at the shores of the island she had doubted they would ever leave.

They'd done it. They were at sea again. Amryn let out a cry. Not a mere cry, but a roar. For the sheer joy of being alive.

"Masterfully done," said Tris.

"The odds of success were infinitesimal." Ufa reappeared at her shoulder. "My algorithms need refactoring to account for the unaccountable."

"That's us," said Hobi. "The unaccountable. Come, Amryn. Look off the bow."

Amryn left the wheel to Rafael and ran down to Hobi. They balanced their way out the bowsprit together, as they had so many times. A sly smile curved his lips, and he nodded towards the hull beneath their feet.

Ravelers had transformed the ship. The *Seeker* shimmered in the jewels of the sea, like a dream crafted of its mystical beauty. Iridescent fish scales and sparkling abalone shells covered the timbers, and coral roses framed the portholes. Amryn stared in awe at one marvel after another.

"It's magnificent, Tris," she said. "Truly magnificent."

"A ship befitting the Sorcerers of Maurya. My gift to you."

Amryn was coming to understand the depths of their power. Ravelers could reshape their world time and time again. Carving a channel through the mountainside was merely a chore. Transforming the *Seeker* had been a joyous expression of artistry. The entire island chain was malleable to the ravelers who had always called it home. They could shape a new Maurya to suit their growing numbers. She could only imagine the wonders they would create.

There would be no place for fear in such a world.

"Approaching the coordinates," Ufa floated out to announce.

So entranced by the ship's transformation, she was slow to notice they were approaching the walls. Through the shimmering energy that had unwaveringly shielded these islands through the centuries, as if she were looking out from the far side of a mirror, she saw the Ari ship waiting for them on the other side. Yet, the ship beyond the veil saw only Endless Ocean, just as the *Seeker* had when it first ventured into this hidden realm.

Amryn smiled. She was ready to live the life she'd chosen. And Maurya was ready to meet the world.

"Lower the walls," she said. "Let them see what we have become."

About the Author

L.H. Leonard writes epic fantasy because she prefers imaginary worlds to dysfunctional real ones. She's been a technologist (computer geek and manager thereof) in the financial and media industries for most of her career and sidelines as micro-publisher Each Voice Publishing. When getting paid doesn't matter, she's an animal rescuer, artist, almost-master gardener, and a pretty good cook.

She and her husband live happily ever after in Georgia, where their forever home is a short trek from the Chattahoochee River through woods filled with deer, coyotes, owls, and the occasional bear.

Their progeny are creative individualists, the eldest of whom has given them a small tribe of grandchildren.

Please visit with her at lhleonard.com to chat.

Books in the Rootstock Series

Please visit RootstockSaga.com for character lists, gallery, historical timelines, chapter extras, and more.

Legend of the Storm Hawks

Path of the Spirit Runner

The Witch of Lurago

Heart of a Chalyn

www.ingramcontent.com/pod-product-compliance
Lightning Source LLC
Chambersburg PA
CBHW072131250626
47159CB00007B/2649

9 781732 874480